Ash Grove

A Novel

Wanda Fries

Ginkgo Leaf Press

Ash Grove

A Novel by Wanda Fries

This is a work of fiction and any resemblance to real persons alive or dead is purely co-incidental and not intended by the author.

Gingko Leaf Press

Copyright 2012

Cover photo by Mikial Damkier/Dreamstime

ISBN-13: 978-0615626192
ISBN-10: 061562619X

For Kevin & Robin Dalton, John Polk, Pearlie Jenkins,
Shanna Purcell, Cory White, Jon New, Kenny Burton,
Brian Morrow and all those who got lost in the wood
and the melody—

But most of all in memoryof my beautiful mother, Pauline,
and my wonderful daddy Henry—

The soul has many motions, body one.
An old wind-tattered butterfly flew down
And pulsed its wings upon the ground—
Such stretchings of the spirit make no sound.
By lust alone we keep the mind alive
and grieve into the certainty of love—

Theodore Rhoethke

Took a walk in the clouds
stole the thunder from the night
and there was no one around
to talk about wrong and right
there was no one around
to call it a crime
so I tucked the thunder up under my arm
and called it mine—

Pearlie Jenkins

She stood there in my doorway
Smoothing out her dress,
saying, "Life is a thump ripe melon,
so sweet and such a mess."

Greg Brown, "Rexroth's Daughter"

With sorrow, deep sorrow
My heart it is laden;
All day I go longing, in search of my love;
I lie here alone, beneath the green bower,
O ash grove, the ash grove,
Alone is my home—

Folk Song

# Anne

I suppose I should warn you right up front that this story belongs to a ghost. I don't imagine you believe in such things. As a citizen of the country of the living, you have that luxury. Most of the time, even I don't know if I'm real or not, or if I exist only in stray fragments of dreams left behind to trouble my son's sleep. You can try to kill off your mother, but she never truly leaves you, does she? She's a virus in your bloodstream, a fever in your brain.

I do know that my days are sharp with longing, and longing is real enough. What do I long for? For what you have. The smell of a baby's head in the hollow of my shoulder. Sex that's hot and sweet and salty. I could write a book about the nerve endings of one fingertip, the different colors of green in a field of grass. I could write a chapter about the tongue. O, let me tell you, the tongue is unappreciated by the living. You can't imagine how you will miss taste and texture, the cold of ice cream, the sweet-tart smoothness of the flesh and skin of the apple, the way ripe peach skin feels the same to the tongue as the back of a lover's neck.

How I envy you the days that wind ahead like the meander of the river, while you follow with your senses, ears tuned to the wind, hands trailing through the water in the dark. Being alive means you're too busy going on to the next experience to miss anything. You have to keep tasting, no matter what the warnings. And anyway, if God didn't want Eve to eat any of those apples, why did He point the tree out to her? Why did He give her a tongue? And then the other tree, the one that was always there, but only the serpent knew? She should be beatified, not condemned. Saint Eve, *who found out the terrible secret that death was in the garden. If there was an antidote, she was pushed out into the world before she could learn that secret, too.*

Death came as such a surprise to me. I still remember Sister Annunciata's face one Christmas Eve when I was nine. I had rushed into the church at the last minute, wearing my pipe-stem halo and coat hanger wings. "Baby Jesus is waiting," she hissed into my ear. "Someday you'll want Jesus, and he'll make you wait." Maybe I should have paid more attention.

Father, forgive me, I have sinned. It has been a lifetime since my last confession. I didn't light enough candles. I fingered the beads of my rosary, all the time imagining how outside the dark church the blessed grass was waiting under a robin's egg sky. But I was too busy being alive to waste time with my knees numb against an oak kneeler. Now the time has come for me to say I'm sorry, and I'm not.

Unfinished business. That's what they say keeps us here long past the time when we should have faded to a wisp of memory, a draft of cold air in a dark corner under the stairs. Do you see my son shivering on the front porch of Samuel Brothers Funeral Home, turning up the collar of his brown leather jacket, too thin for this late January wind? People say he looks just like me—the same dark hair, with a widow's peak; the same Irish blue eyes. He has come a long way for this funeral, but not just to mourn his father. He has come because of me. Among this company of strangers, he huddles just under the edge of the dripping eave, uncertain and alone.

I have watched him grow up. I suppose that's some consolation, though I have longed to touch him. Often, at night, I bend by his bed to blow him kisses; sometimes, he stirs in his sleep and brushes his cheek with his hand. He is so beautiful, almost too beautiful to be a man. Would you think less of me if I told you I was once very beautiful, too?

One

Standing on the front steps of the funeral home, Will Brinson watches the woman walk up the sidewalk that leads from the parking lot behind the building. He knows her at once, though she is thinner than he remembers, and her hair has turned a dull white, the color of shoe polish. She walks with the same small, apologetic steps, her shoulders rounded as if to hide her nearly six-foot height. Her head droops forward, her face turned toward her left shoulder, to hide the birthmark on her cheek. He flips his cigarette into a pile of wet snow at the curb and meets her at the bottom step.

She looks up when he reaches her. Then she lifts her hand to touch his face. "Will."

He puts his arms around her. She still smells like peppermint. He smiles. When he was little, maybe five or six, he used to follow her through the house begging for candy. She always kept peppermint sticks in the pocket of her housedress; every so often, she'd reach inside and break off a little piece of it for him.

He wants to hug her hard, but he's afraid to. When did she get so old and sharp-boned? He pulls away and looks into her face. "I can't believe you knew me right off. After all this time."

"Why, of course I knew you," she says, laughing. "You're like my own. How could I not know you? I've missed you."

"I've missed you, too, Aunt Betsy," he says. Until that moment, he has not realized how glad he would be to see her.

She takes his arm in hers and presses it against her side. "I was sorry to hear about your father. Stupid, stupid thing. It's hard for me to believe, as much as we all went through years ago, that such a thing could happen after all this time."

"I haven't had a chance to talk to Doc yet. I just got to town little bit ago, and I came straight on up here. What did happen?"

She shakes her head. "I don't know a thing. I don't know if anybody does."

He hears a guitar and a girl's voice from inside, singing a Baptist hymn, but it takes him a second to place it. "In the Sweet By and By," he thinks. He doesn't recognize many hymns. Though Cleave grew up nominally Catholic, or he would not have been allowed to marry Anne, he was not a church-goer; in Virginia, staying with his grandparents, Will had refused to go to mass on Sunday. They dragged him along sometimes. But most of the time, too old and tired to fight him over it and lost in their own grief, his grandparents had left him alone.

He looks at his watch. "I guess it's time," he says, gesturing toward the green-painted double door. "You are coming up to the house? After the funeral, I mean? You have to come. I can't face all these people by myself."

"Of course, I'm going to come."

Doc Beecham sticks his head through the open doorway and motions them inside. Will puts his hand under Betsy's elbow to help her up the steps, and they walk into the dark foyer and then down the red-carpeted center aisle. A white-haired man leads them to a row of chairs at the front. He has a dyed-blue carnation in his buttonhole and the solemn face of a professional undertaker. At the front of the chapel stands a dark gray casket banked by flowers; Will tries not to look directly at his father's body.

It's a good thing seats have been reserved for the family, he thinks. The little chapel—or do they call it a viewing room?—is almost full. Some of the old miners have come and sit formally, wearing their good suits if they have them, collared shirts and pressed dark pants if they don't. This doesn't mean, he thinks, that they had any use for Cleave Brinson. It means that in a small town, when somebody dies, people take the time to satisfy their curiosity and pay their respects.

White-haired and feeble, Will's grandfather, Judge Connelly from Virginia, sits at the outer edge of the aisle and Will and Betsy have to squeeze past him. Will is surprised to see him. When he sits down, he looks at Betsy with an eyebrow raised.

"I didn't want him to come," she whispers into Will's ear as he sits down beside her. "He's too feeble to be traveling so far. But when I got the car loaded, he was sitting inside with his black suit on. What was I supposed to do? Stubborn old goat."

Across the aisle from the family, sit the dignitaries. Will knows they have come as much to be seen as to see. Too bad, he thinks, that Cleave is not alive to see them in their black-suited splendor—the local druggist who closed up shop for the morning; the bank president who made a fortune when coal was high; the state representative Cleave used to send campaign donations to; the county judge executive who used to get a case of Jack Daniels and ten pounds of fresh Gulf shrimp flown in by Cleave's company pilot every year at Christmas. Closest to the aisle is an ex-governor Will recognizes from a picture that hung in Cleave's study. In the photograph, his father and the governor are on the steps in front of the Capitol, smiling broadly, shaking hands. Their showing up at the funeral is a testament, he thinks, both to the corruption of eastern Kentucky politics and the influence his father once had.

Most of these people came to his mother's funeral, too, and some to the inquest that followed, though Will was too young to go or even understand most of what went on then. Now, he feels stung once again with resentment. How much weight did that carry with the judge, he wonders, when behind Cleave Brinson sat an ex-governor, several of the region's most prominent businessmen, and the suspect's father-in-law, Judge Connelly of Virginia, Himself? "Well, they sure do stick together," he remembers somebody (Betsy?) saying afterward. "You have to give them that."

For a long time Will clung to his knowledge of Grandfather's presence at the inquest as irrefutable evidence of his father's innocence. How could Grandfather bring himself to be there if Cleave had killed Will's mother? She was his daughter, after all.

Later, when he lived with them in Virginia, Will realized that his grandparents were the kind of people who simply would not allow themselves to believe certain things. They had entrusted their daughter to Cleave Brinson, who moved in the same circles, lived by the same rules, as they did. They could believe it if he were accused of adultery; men, after all, were men, and there were certain compromises wives, especially the wives of important men, might be called on to make. They could have believed it if Anne had come home in tears, accusing Cleave of ignoring her, or of making her unhappy, maybe even of shoving her during an argument. Grandmother would have dried her daughter's tears, sitting beside her on the edge of the bed in Anne's pink-flowered childhood bedroom, and the next morning would have sent the girl home to her husband where she belonged. But certainly, they could not believe that he had killed her.

Sitting next to Grandfather, Doc Beecham shifts in his chair, crossing his legs first in one and then in the other direction. Of all those who are here, Doc is the only one Cleave could have claimed as a true friend. Doc has aged less than the rest of them, but he has always looked older than his age. He still has the same soft body and hollow, sagging cheeks, ruddy from years of too much bourbon.

The service is long, but simple. A high school girl in a black dress sings "Amazing Grace," accompanying herself on a honey-colored guitar. Each of the dignitaries is given his time to speak, to catalogue Cleave Brinson's contributions to the economy of the area, to charitable causes. He was at the forefront of mine owners who purchased safety technology long before Congress passed laws to make companies comply. He paid better than union wages. He gave so much money to help renovate the high school gymnasium that the school board named it after him. By the time they finish, surely, Will thinks, his sins will have been washed clean.

When the time comes to file past the coffin, Will stays in his seat. He has never been able to figure out exactly who his father was, but he knows for certain the man eulogized for the last forty-five minutes was even more a stranger than the body lying at the front of the little chapel, his face caked with mortuary make-up, a white satin pillow underneath his large head.

"Are you all right?" Betsy whispers when she sees him in the vestibule. He nods and she nods, too, squeezing his arm.

She rides beside him to the cemetery. They sit in the back seat of Doc Beecham's blue Cadillac Seville while Grandfather snores softly in the front. They follow the new four-lane road that has been cut straight through the mountain. The old road curls to the right like a ribbon beneath and above them. Then they cross the river, and there, in a flat area Brinson Mining Company stripped several years ago, is a little island of fast-food restaurants and shopping centers, the largest anchored by a bright new Wal-Mart.

"Can you believe this?" Doc Beecham asks from the front. "How much this has built up? You're too young to remember it, but years ago that sum-bitch Mo Udall passed a law to make coal companies put the mountain back just like they found it, but you have to admit this is an improvement. With the flood wall and all this construction, you might be anywhere in America right now."

"Except for the unemployed miners on the draw," Will says softly, but Doc doesn't hear him, and Will doesn't have the heart to start a fight.

After a mile or so, Doc flips on his signal light and turns underneath a white-painted wrought-iron arch. "New cemetery, too. When they built the floodwall, the Corps of Engineers relocated the graves out of the old one. Good there weren't any Injuns buried here. We'd have had to move the whole goddamned town instead."

A tobacco-colored tent stretches across the open grave where Cleave will lie. Doc pulls onto the edge of the grass, and they get out. Will goes around, helping his grandfather out of the car while the pallbearers carry the coffin from the back of the hearse to the grave. This time the service is mercifully short. After the pallbearers lower the coffin, Will takes his turn to toss in a handful of dirt, dusting his hands together when he is finished.

He thinks of his mother, buried years ago in a Catholic cemetery in Virginia, and glances sideways at Betsy, who stands motionless, her face turned, as it is habitually, toward her left shoulder, to hide the mark on her face. He and Betsy, the keepers of Anne's secrets, have never talked about that time, about all that went on in the white house on the hill. For years, Will tried to tell himself that he only imagined most of what happened, including the tall man he saw one afternoon in his mother's room, that he only dreamed he saw them together in his mother's bed. But Anne looked up at him. He did not imagine her face, her absorption as she rocked back and forth, straddling the man, as if she were not his mother at all, but a stranger with his mother's face. He will never forget that when he called out, softly, "Mommy?" she looked at him blankly for a second, as if she couldn't think who he was.

Then her eyes filled with panic. They stopped. He saw them stop. But he didn't see her get up from the bed and fumble for a shirt, a robe, a gown, something to cover her body, and follow him down the hall. She caught him at the door of his room and put her arms around him from behind, leaning her face across his shoulder, whispering against his ear.

"Will," she said. "Will, baby. That's a friend of mine. We were just playing a game. It's all right. Everything is all right."

But it wasn't all right. He had seen the look on her face, how her eyes had been empty of him, full of something else he didn't understand.

And a few weeks later, he was in Virginia. And she was dead.

# Two

After the funeral, Will finds Doc Beecham in Cleave's den, sitting at the bar and nursing a shot of whiskey. The house has not changed since Will's childhood. Most of the rooms are bright and airy, with honey-colored furniture and light-carpeted floors. French country, Anne called the style. She redecorated soon after her marriage. Had she lived, the house might have gone through a half dozen different styles. Redecorating was an acceptable occupation for bored housewives of her generation, particularly if they had money to spend.

Cleave was never stingy with his young wife as far as money was concerned. He didn't mind what she did with the house, either, as long as she left the den alone. This was his throne room and sanctuary. He was especially proud of its size, thirty feet by forty, larger than most of the houses around here, he used to brag, leaving him enough room on one end for a wet bar and a billiard table, and on the other, for a library and a home office. The bar was always well stocked, and the library's shelves were filled with fifty or sixty leather-bound volumes of the classics. Of these, Will guesses no more than one or two have actually been read. His mother was the reader in the family, and her taste was eclectic and restless. She ordered her books from a bookstore in New York and kept them stacked in two-foot piles in their bedroom.

Cleave did allow his wife to make a couple of minor refinements. The furniture, though worn, was expensive, and is still upholstered in the rich green and blue fabric Anne bought on a trip to Cincinnati; a plaid carpet in the same colors covers the floor. Will can remember lying awake at night, listening to the smack of billiard balls, the rumbling, half-drunken sound of male laughter. Though Cleave was always more comfortable working than he was at parties, in this room he was always the amiable host, for this was not a room, Will guesses, so much as a setting where Cleave could display himself as the wealthy squire he had always wanted to be.

Will gets himself a beer from the refrigerator and sits down beside the old man. "So," he asks, leaning his elbows on the bar. "Give me the details. What happened, Doc?"

Doc sighs. "You won't believe it when I tell you. I reckon Millard Messer's oldest boy—you remember Millard, don't you, that ran the tipple for years?"

Will nods.

"What happened is, Junior Messer hid in those trees across the road, out in front there, and then, when Cleave came out of the house Tuesday morning to get the paper, I reckon Junior just stood up, took aim, and—cold-blooded as you please—he shot Cleave twice in the chest."

Will leans back in the chair. "But why? Did Junior rob him? Take anything from the house?"

Doc shrugged. "No, at least not that anybody could tell. Cleave just had on a robe, and his billfold wasn't touched. They found it upstairs on the nightstand by his bed. Sheriff had me look around, too, since I was familiar with the house. If anything was missing, you couldn't prove it by me."

"How do they know it was Junior?"

"Oh, they *know* it was him. Boy's plumb stupid. He ran off after it happened, but the dumb son-of-a-bitch left shell casing and a walking stick whittled out of white oak. Oh, and an empty cigarette pack laying there in plain sight by the road that matched the butts that have his spit all over them. Left it all in plain sight, if you can believe it. Didn't even try to scuff dirt over the shells. They said his fingerprints were all over the place."

Will walks over to the window and looks out. A mimosa tree grows at the back of the house. In the summer, the tree is full of feathery pink blossoms, the ferny leaves drooping and exotic. His mother had hated that tree. "It's a weed," she said.

But Cleave said Grandma Brinson loved mimosa trees and he'd be damned if Anne was going to tell him what to do. Once, the summer after she died, Will took a saw from the tool shed and tried to cut the tree down, but he only cut himself on the sharp blade. He sat there, crying, holding up his bleeding finger, until Betsy came looking for him. He still had a scar on his finger.

When he was much older, the tree died, and Cleave himself cut it down, but when Will mowed the grass in the summer, he always mowed over a cluster of new sprouts. Cleave must have nursed one of them along until the tree grew back from the roots. Anne was right. Mimosas were weeds. As a landscaper, Will always suggested that homeowners who wanted flowerbeds cut mimosas down. If they didn't, they would pull hundreds, maybe thousands of seedlings, persistent as bad memories, out of their beds all summer long.

Will had always thought of Cleave as having that kind of resilience. He still can't wrap his brain around the idea that his father is gone. "I know Cleave made a lot of enemies when the UMWA tried to organize here," he says. "But what in God's name could Junior Messer have had against him? I always thought Millard was a scab."

Doc shrugs. "Shit, Will. That boy's crazy. He's shot up or huffed every drug, legal or illegal, he could get his hands on for years. He's already done time for cooking meth. Mean, too. Got in a knife fight a few years back over some girl. He hurt the other fellow pretty bad. It's a wonder he didn't kill him. I figured his family was glad when they broke ground to build a federal pen here. Have him close to home, case anybody wanted to go see him."

Will remembers Junior as a red-haired boy with a big mouth, always picking on somebody smaller. "He did like to fight. I tangled with him a few times myself."

"He's been worse since Millard died. The old man had emphysema. The family tried to file a wrongful death suit against Brinson Mining, on account of black lung, but the lawyer told them they didn't have any hope of winning. Millard smoked like a son of a bitch all his life. Lawyer said the family'd be better off suing R. J. Reynolds."

Will turns away from the window. "They got Junior locked up here?"

Doc shakes his head. "Haven't caught him yet. Sheriff figures he's up in Detroit, staying with one of his cousins. But they'll catch him. With all the computers they've got now, they could probably single out a cockroach in an International House of Pancakes. Hell, put his picture on that America's Most Wanted show and offer a reward. One of his cousins'd probably turn his sorry ass in for a case of beer."

Ash Grove

"I imagine they'll catch up with him sooner or later," Will says. He drains the last of his beer and crushes the can in his hand. "You've gotta have money and influence if you want to get away with murder."

Doc spins around on the barstool to look at Will. "Are you still beating that horse? Let me tell you something. I will swear to my dying day Cleave Brinson didn't have anything to do with what happened to your mama. He had his faults, but he loved her. He loved you, too."

"She belonged to him," Will says. "He didn't like to lose what was his, that's for sure." He walks back to the window, looking out at the mimosa tree. The limbs reach almost to the damp ground, casting the back of the house in shadow. "Doc?" he asks, his chest tight with longing, his voice almost a whisper. "How do you know he didn't kill her? Did you ever ask him?"

"No. I didn't need to ask him."

"Well, *I* did."

"What did he say?"

"He didn't say anything. He just turned around and walked away."

 # Three

When Will Brinson is seven, the year his mother will die, he tells her he remembers being born. At first, naturally, she doesn't believe him. But for once, he does get her attention, drawing her eyes away from the distance where the trees in the twilight lose their edges and mountains curve against the sky like flesh.

She stops pushing the porch swing in the gazebo. The chain stops screaking, and she looks right at him.

"Where on earth do you get these ideas?" she says, a laugh in her voice. "You don't remember any such thing."

But he does. And he holds his hands at his cheeks, remembering the warm dark of her body, and then the cold metal forceps the doctor used to pull him free. Voices. The smell of sweet pickles, and stronger, the gunmetal smell of blood. Finally, the doctor freed his head, then his shoulders, and the cold air of the hospital room fell like a blow against his red skin.

His mother puts her arm around him then and draws him close to her. She is warm. His bare arms feel how warm it is to be folded close to her. He smells lilacs. Do the flowers hang from the dark bush at the foot of the kitchen steps, or is this the smell of her warm skin? He doesn't wonder long. All he wants is to wrap himself up in the smell and the warmth.

"Who am I to argue with you, Will?" she asks. "I can't believe you remember. It's more likely you've just heard Betsy and me talk about it." She gives him a little tug toward her. "We almost lost you. But then, maybe you do remember. I've read how some people have died and been brought back. They say their souls float up above their bodies. I guess that could *happen to a baby, too."*

He turns the idea of dying around in his mind. He has never seen a dead person, but he thinks a dead body must look like one of the porcelain dolls his Grandmother Connelly keeps in her bedroom. They are always so cold and still, watching him from behind their blue eyes.

He doesn't want to imagine himself dead, even for an instant, so he takes comfort in the idea that someone can hear a story so often he believes it is his own. After all, the doctor who delivered him is a friend of his father's, and he likes to tell anyone who'll listen about how he and a miracle once saved Will's life.

Doc Beecham cared for Anne all through her pregnancy without any problems. But at term the baby fell silent, no kicks, no detectable heartbeat. He induced labor and delivered the baby hoping things would turn out all right. Sometimes a baby will get itself turned the wrong way, and it's hard to hear a heartbeat. But once he got a look at the baby, Doc says he was so sure Will was dead, he cut the cord and handed the baby to the nurse who assisted, already wondering how he was going to break the news to Cleave. The nurse who took one look at Will, and then, without bothering to wipe off the vernix and blood, laid him in an isolette lined with a pink and blue striped blanket. Then she turned away.

When Doc tells this story, and Will has heard him tell it often, he hesitates before estimating the number of minutes Will lay there, blue as the haze that falls every night over Jewel Mountain. "The boy was dead," he says, maybe to some friends at one of Cleave's billiard nights, or to his own son once when he and Cleave took the boys to Lexington to see the Wildcats play basketball. "The nurse knew it, too. In fact, I looked at the clock, so I would know the correct time to write down.

"I was sewing up his mother, and it must have been four minutes—no, it was at least five—and I just happened to look over. No reason why, except to think how sad a stillbirth is in cases like this, the baby full-term and well formed. Then I saw the cord flutter, real soft, it's a miracle I even saw. Before I had time to think about it one way or another, I put my mouth over the baby's face, my hand on its little chest and breathed. This is the gospel truth," he vows, whether or not anybody seems to doubt him. "Not some rumor. I was there."

"Not a thing wrong with him, either," Doc always adds, laughing, his hand squeezing Will's shoulder. "Except for his looks."

You should have let me die, Will will want to say, later, when he stands at the cemetery and understands that his mother is dead. Instead, when the doctor swings Will up into his arms, to comfort him, Will scratches Doc Beecham's cheek, leaving drops of blood like a string of beads.

"Here, now," Cleave says sternly, father and mother both now. His face is dry, but what does this prove? Men aren't supposed to cry.

But the doctor pushes Cleave's trembling hand away. Then he lets Will down gently, lets him slide down the long rope of his arms and holds him for a moment against his legs before the boy twists free.

"He's just a boy, Cleave," Doc says, just as Will pulls away. "He doesn't mean anything by it. He's hurting. Let him be."

 # Four

Every Wednesday, the year Will is six, he goes with his mother and her sister Betsy to the county seat. They leave right after breakfast, and Will sleeps in the back seat of Anne's white Lincoln. Later, at the beauty shop, while Betsy gets a manicure and Anne has her hair washed and set, he kneels on a green vinyl chair at the front of the shop, his chin resting on the chair back. Through the plate glass window, filmy with hair spray and grime, he watches the traffic on Main Street. He is a good boy, everybody says so, just like a little man, and he always sits quietly, waiting, not a bit of trouble.

Sometimes he listens to the women talking, to his mother Anne and Aunt Betsy, and to Angela, who owns the shop. But their words float over and around him, like a foreign language, musical and strange. After a while he finds himself daydreaming, transported into the gray world on the other side of the window, riding in one of the Mack trucks that groans and rattles by with its load of coal, or watching the pigeons that roost in the eaves of the dingy courthouse across the street.

Sometimes behind him, he hears Betsy resisting a manicure, then giving in and offering her long fingers to Angela's daughter who is in charge of nails. "I have such ugly hands," she always says, and Angela says, "You do not. Doris, you tell her. She has pretty hands. She's got long fingers just like a piano player. She just needs to take better care of herself instead of fussing over us all the time."

Betsy is the one who takes care of Will, mostly. She is even teaching him how to read. Anne says Betsy has a teaching certificate, and until he gets big enough to go off to school in Virginia, Betsy will be his teacher. The schools around here are all right, his mother says, but not for somebody who has to be ready for a real college, like Vanderbilt or Virginia.

Betsy is a big woman with long, dark hair that she winds into a bun at the back of her round head. She lays her hands flat on the surface of the Formica table. "Lord," she says. "It's not like I'm going somewhere to get all polished up for." But Will can tell she really wants to have her nails painted. She does this every Wednesday. For the next day or two, while the polish is still fresh, Will often catches her holding her hands out in front of her to admire them. Usually, she keeps her face tilted toward her left shoulder to hide a birthmark the color of burgundy. The mark covers her cheek from just below her temple to her chin. When she is home and her hands aren't busy with needlework or housekeeping, she covers her cheek with her left hand, her fingers kneading the discolored cheek as if she might rub the birthmark away.

Anne has made a game of this errand, for Will's benefit. She has told him that she works for the state department, and they send her special coded messages. He must never tell anyone—not anyone—but especially not his father. If he does, all their lives will be in danger. Will feels a little shiver of fear run down his spine when she says this, tilting his chin toward her and looking him very solemnly in the eye. But he isn't really afraid. He thinks his life is just like a movie.

Later, when Anne emerges with her dark hair shiny, the bottom edge curled into a flip, they all walk together to the post office so Anne can check her special box. There is always at least one envelope there, white and mysterious, and sometimes four or five. Other times they will go to the window to pick up a package that Anne asks for using her maiden name, Anne Connelly. Betsy always stands a little apart from them when they are in the post office, looking at the bulletin board by the plate glass window, her hand covering her ruined face.

"I won't, Mother," he promises her, his eyes solemn. He is a thin, serious child, more like a grown-up than a little boy. Anne says he has a face like one of Grandmother Connelly's Hummel figurines, with cheekbones that are high and delicate and long dark lashes that flutter when he is excited, like a black bird's wing.

From the post office, they head up the street to Farrell's Drugstore for lunch. They sit at the counter where Will can twirl around on the stool, kicking his legs in the air. Anne always orders him a cheeseburger plate, *and she buys him an ice cream sundae for dessert, even if he doesn't eat his sandwich. Sometimes, while they eat, Anne reads her letters. When she finishes each one, she folds it carefully, sliding it into its envelope, then later puts the stack into a zippered compartment in her big black purse.*

When their food comes, Betsy cuts Will's cheeseburger into bite-sized pieces and shakes ketchup into a thick pool beside his fries. "Now, eat," she says, handing him a salad fork. "You're skinny as a chicken. You, too," she says to Anne. "You can't live on love."

"You can't live without it," Anne replies, pouring cream into her coffee, swirling it around with her spoon. "When you love somebody, really love somebody, Betsy, you'll change your tune."

Betsy laughs, and waves her hand toward the tables behind them, empty except for a table full of old men talking politics. "Now just which of those handsome men do you think I should offer my hand to?" she whispers. Then her mouth twists. "I keep waiting for someone who thinks my face is a treasure map. You'd think it would happen sooner or later. And he'd better look at least as good as Clark Cable. 'Excuse me, ma'am,' he'll say, Rhett Butler to my Janet Leigh, 'but is that a map of South America?'"

"Oh, Betsy." Anne reaches over and squeezes Betsy's hand. For a second, Will is puzzled by the tears that spring to his mother's eyes. Didn't Betsy mean to be funny? "You hide behind that birthmark. You really do. You just don't want to go through the aggravation of fixing yourself up. Not that I blame you. One of these days women are going to find out that their minds are more important than their looks, and they'll run the world."

"Miracles do happen, I guess," Betsy says, digging her fork into a bowl of chef's salad. "Maybe I'll find somebody who'll love me for my mind, just the way I am."

Will leans his head against his aunt's arm. "I love you, Betsy."

She reaches over and rubs the top of his head. "See. I've got the handsomest beau of them all."

"He's smart," Anne says. "He knows how to pick somebody who'll stick by him." Will can smell her perfume. She smells sweet, like lavender and roses. "Look at all Betsy's put up with from me."

Five

Cleave and Annie had a fight;
He wired her car with dynamite.
She climbed into the car to run,
And blew herself to Kingdom Come.

Will sees the three boys in front of Felton's store before they see him. They stand near a shed with bags of cement and feed piled underneath. One corner of an olive-green tarpaulin nailed across the front has been secured with a block of coal the size of man's head, but the other corner flaps in the November wind. Rough-hewn scrap lumber is piled at the top of a concrete block retaining wall, and the boys stamp their feet in front of it, close to the edge of the store's front porch.

Two of the boys are Will's age. He knows them from Brinson Company picnics. But the tallest, a redheaded boy with white, freckled hands, is older, maybe twelve or thirteen. When he sees Will, the older boy elbows the fat kid next to him, and the boys look at each other. Then they move so that they face Will in a semi-circle. The redhead stands in the middle, his feet a little apart, his mouth slack, and a lit cigarette dangling from his left hand.

Will keeps walking toward them. He feels a little twitch in his stomach. These are rough boys, miner's boys, and he doesn't know what will happen. When Anne was alive, she never let him play with boys like this, but now Cleave never pays much attention to him one way or another. Betsy tries to take care of him, but she doesn't know how to tell him no. Since his mother died, Betsy can't stand to see him upset about anything. That, at least, has its advantages.

When Will gets closer, the fat kid pulls something red out of his pocket and hands it to the red-headed boy, who lights the end with his cigarette and throws it at Will's feet. Will jumps back as the firecrackers explode. The boys laugh, the fat kid slapping his leg with his hand. "Boom!" he says.

"We better watch it," the other boy, the one Will's age, says. He has white hair, clumped and oily as corn silks, and light blue eyes. "We don't want to make him mad. He might sneak up on us some night and blow us all to hell."

"Yeah," the fat kid says. "Your old man teach you how to make a car go boom?"

The boys laugh again. "Oh, he might do a girl that away," the redheaded boy says. "But I ain't scared of his pansy ass."

The boys edge a little closer, and Will looks around the yard for something, anything. Just as he sees them close in, he has his hands on a three-foot length of scrap lumber, and he starts swinging it.

He doesn't see the door to Felton's store open or the tall man with auburn hair come rushing out. He doesn't pull back even when the man comes up behind him, pinning his arms and picking him up. He keeps trying to wrench himself free, his legs flailing in the air. "Here now," the man says. "No call for you boys to be fighting. Make peace, not war. Ain't that what the hippies say?"

The man pulls the length of wood out of Will's hand and throws it back onto the kindling pile. The redheaded boy stands to the side of the other two, who are crying. The fat kid holds his hand over his left elbow, and the blonde boy has blood and snot running out of his nose. He wipes it on his coat sleeve.

"Ah, Daddy," the older boy says. "We was just messing with him a little. He don't know how to take a joke."

The man sets Will down. Will is crying, too, but as soon as his feet touch the ground, he lunges for the blonde boy. The man grabs Will up again. "Whoa, now, son. It's over."

"He hit me with that big old stick," the fat kid says, whining. "He don't fight fair."

The man laughs, still pinning Will's arms and holding him tight. "You got three on one, you really expect somebody to fight you fair? You boys go on home now. I reckon I can hold Rocky Marciano here long enough to give you a head start. And you," he says, as he twists with Will in the direction of the red-haired boy, "I'll give you a whipping myself, I ever catch you egging these little 'uns on again."

The boys stand for a minute, but then the skinny one takes off running and the fat kid follows. The redheaded boy looks at Will for a second, then very slowly flips his cigarette into the road before he turns to go back inside the store.

Will feels the man's arms loosen, and he stands there. When he hears the man's boots clunking on the porch steps, he turns around to see who had been holding him. The man stops before he goes inside, and then looks around to see if Will is still behind him. Will recognizes him. He works at the tipple, first shift. He must have just got off, because he still has his work clothes on, though his face is little moon of white. "You're Cleave Brinson's boy, ain't you?" he asks.

Will nods.

"What was that all about? I heard firecrackers. Is that what started it?"

Will shrugs.

"They say something about your daddy?"

Will still doesn't say anything. He stands there, red-faced, and looks down at the dirt.

The man shakes his head. "It ain't right. I tell mine, easiest way in the world to get your head knocked off is to throw off on somebody's family. Ain't nobody around here knows what happened to your mother. People just like to think they do."

Then he shakes his head and laughs. "Well, I don't reckon them three will bother you no more. You don't fight fair, boy, that's a fact. You got the right idea, though, same as them Japs when they bombed Pearl Harbor. Ain't no such thing as fighting fair. If you got to fight, you might as well fight mean."

When Will gets home, Betsy is in the kitchen, the newspaper open on the kitchen counter in front of her. Her cigarettes, lighter, and ashtray are arranged in a semi-circle beside her elbow. This is her before-supper ritual, the paper and a smoke.

From Cleave's den, he hears the television. He takes his wet boots off, leaving them on an old newspaper Betsy keeps by the door.

Ash Grove

Hearing him, Betsy looks up. "Where've you been? You look like you're half-frozen."

He shrugs. "I went down to the store and bought a candy bar. Here," he says, taking a Payday bar out of his pocket and laying it on the table beside her cigarettes. "I got you one. With nuts, the kind you like."

She folds the paper and picks up the candy. She starts to unwrap it, then stops. "I don't know what I'm thinking. I better save it till after supper. I've got a roast on. You hungry? It's about done."

"Smells good."

"Is something the matter, honey?"

He wants to say, What happened to my mother? But he can't. The words stick in his throat like a big glob of peanut butter, and he can't say a thing.

"I don't know if I like you going down to the store all by yourself."

"I'll be okay. I saw some boys my age down there today."

"Doing what?"

"I don't know. They were just there, I guess." He takes his coat off and hangs it on the back of one of the kitchen chairs. He wants to tell Betsy about the boys, about what they said. He would look good in the story. The man made it sound like he was protecting his family honor or something. But he's afraid to tell her. If she knew, she might tell him not to go to the store anymore by himself, and he likes it this way, he thinks, Betsy preoccupied, forgetting to watch over him every minute.

She gets up and walks to the counter. She takes a cellophane-wrapped plate of cookies out of the cabinet, then gets a glass and pours him a glass of milk. "You're growing. I don't guess a little snack will hurt you. It's gonna be a little while before we eat."

She motions for Will to sit down. Then she stands behind him and lays her hands on his shoulders. "It wouldn't hurt for you to have some friends. I don't know if Anne was right to keep you away from the children who live around here. People can't help being poor. Maybe Cleave was wrong to let her. Maybe we need to get you in school. I can teach you your school subjects, but there are other things you need to learn that I can't teach."

From the den, they hear Cleave's recliner creak, then his heavy footsteps across the floor. They turn to see him leaning against the doorframe, ice and whiskey in a monogrammed glass.

"I thought I heard you in here," he says. "I've got to go back down to *the mine office before supper. You want to go with me?"*

Betsy looks from Will to his father; she's smiling like somebody who just won a prize. "Of course, he wants to go," she says. "Don't you, Will?"

"I guess so," he says. When his mother was alive, she never allowed him to go near the mine, not even to the office with his father. The one time Cleave took him anyway, he climbed all afternoon on a pile of block coal next to the building and came home black as the miners at the end of their shift.

"Well, don't sit there like a knot on a log," Cleave says. "Put your coat back on."

Will leaves his cookies untouched on the table and grabs his coat from the back of the chair. Cleave goes to a closet in the hallway and comes back to the kitchen wearing a plaid jacket, holding his black wool Fedora in his left hand. In his right, he still carries the glass of whiskey, but he drains the rest and leaves the glass on the counter. "Ready?"

But without waiting for an answer, he heads toward the door.

Will follows him into the winter twilight and climbs into the passenger side of the pick-up truck. The gears whine as Cleave backs out of the long driveway lined with the black shapes of trees. The vinyl seats feel cold against the back of Will's thighs, and he raises his butt up to tug the bottom of his coat underneath him. He is as uncomfortable with his father as he would be with a stranger, but he doesn't know what to say to break the silence, doesn't know how to make himself feel at home.

Then, startled, he hears Cleave laugh. Cleave laughs from deep in his belly, stops to shake his head in disbelief or wonder, then laughs again.

Will turns his head toward his father, but he still doesn't say anything. Cleave glances sideways at his son. "I got a call from Millard Messer before you got home," he says. "He told me about that fight you got in down at Felton's." Whoo-whee,' Millard says, 'that boy of yours sure is a wildcat. Took on three boys, one of 'em mine, and bigger. Backed 'em all down.'"

Cleave reaches across the back of the seat to lay his big hand on Will's shoulder. His fingers dig into the muscle as he kneads it, and Will wants to squirm away. But he is afraid that if he father takes his hand away, he will withdraw not only the pain, but also this rare and wonderful praise.

A few days later, back in front of Felton's, Will sees the two younger boys again. They kick a tin can back and forth, and it clangs when it hits the frozen ground. The fat kid holds a bottle of Coca-Cola in his hand, and his pudgy fingers are red and chapped. When they see Will, the boys stop and back up to the shed, wary.

Will's stomach tightens, but he feels excited; he almost hopes they'll come at him. He will hurt them if he has to; it will feel good to hurt them. He has brought a bat with him this time, just in case, and he stops, holding it up for the boys to see. "Don't start anything," he says.

The white-haired boy puts one foot in front of him, scraping it across the dirt. "We ain't aiming to. We wadn't trying to make you mad the other day."

"I got a big old bruise still yet," the fat kid whines.

Will stands the bat on the ground between his feet, leaning on it, his palm resting on the end.

"Can you hit a ball with that?" the white-haired boy asks. "When it's warm enough, we play about every day over by the school. You can come sometime, if you want."

"We can always use some hitters," the fat boy adds. "My name's Cecil. He's Raymond."

Will studies the boys. "I might come and play. Sometime."

Later, he will wonder how he managed to survive that year and the four that came after, or what his mother would think to see him playing between the coal camp houses with the other boys, sometimes even girls as rough as the boys or rougher, his shirt tail hanging out, his shoes scuffed and black. Betsy fusses at him, of course, but she can't do anything with him. Worried like her, the miner's wives come out onto their front porches in faded dresses, their sweaters buttoned crookedly, their hands cupped over their eyes. But they can no more control these children than they can control the coal dust and road dust that coats everything, the clothes that hang on the lines behind the camp houses, the floors just swept.

But what do the children care, running beyond the reach of their mothers' voices? They go to the creek and swing out into the cool, green-gold dimness, on vines as thick as their father's thumbs. They sneak up to the tipple and play soldiers in the moonlight, climbing to dizzying heights and leaning out over the darkness below. Sometimes somebody gets hurt, just as their mothers have warned them. One boy, Henry Jenkins, pretending to be Superman, swung from near the top of the tipple, but he lost his footing and fell. For a long time, Will remembers the way Henry's arm was twisted under him, the way the blood looked black in the moonlight from a scratch on Henry's face.

For a while, Henry has a cast on his arm, and they try to stay out of trouble. But they are children, after all, and before long the cast is gone, Henry is healed, and they have forgotten. Will Brinson, mean enough to fight dirty, and wild enough to try anything, is the biggest daredevil of them all.

Six

Will stands at the sink, getting a glass of water. He looks out the window to see a woman, Payton Mounce's mother, coming to the back of the house. She has on an old pair of black shoes, the strings loose, and no stockings, her head bare in the wind. She comes up the back step, knocks, but doesn't wait for an answer. She opens the door and sticks her head in.

"Will?" she says, breathless, when she sees him at the sink. "I need to find your daddy. There's been a roof fall, down at Number Two."

She walks in, leaving the door gaping behind her. She lays her hand on the back of a chair. Will thinks she looks like a crow, standing there, her black hair uncombed and her skinny chest heaving. Her black eyes dart as she looks around the room. "I got to find him. They's men trapped down there. We don't yet know how many."

Betsy must have heard the commotion, because she comes into the room and heads straight to the closet to get out a blue wool coat and a flowered scarf to tie around her head. "Cleave's at the courthouse. He said he was going out to the job, soon as he was finished in town. I'll come on with you, Aleida. There'll be plenty to do. Will," she says, as she heads for the door, "you better stay here in case Cleave comes here first."

The door slams behind them, and he stands looking out the glass panes, watching the women head down the hill on foot.

He waits a few minutes and then puts on his own coat and heads toward the mine. The ground, soupy with black mud, is littered with trucks and people, like a church meeting. People mill about, their trucks parked haphazardly, one with the driver's door left open and the radio playing

Charlie Daniels. Women huddle together. Some of them have babies wrapped in quilts and slung over their shoulders. Their faces look worried, their mouths drawn into tight straight lines, but they rock back and forth, as if their bodies respond in some automatic way to the weight on their shoulders, even when their thoughts are far away. The older children play on the end loaders and dozers, silent and yellow by the tipple, but for once, when their mothers call, they don't hesitate before they come.

Will sees his father near a pile of rubble close to the mine face. A little cluster of men stands near him, their hands in motion, their faces animated, as if they are trying to decide what to do. But Cleave doesn't have any expression at all.

A girl with long, curly dark hair stands close to Will. She is slender, with turquoise earrings dangling from the lobes of her ears. A freckled hand, raw with cold, holds a thin blue jean jacket tight across her narrow chest.

"Do they know how it happened?" Will asks her.

She shrugs, not looking at him. "They was setting jacks, I reckon, and the top fell in." She stops and her mouth hangs open, the lower lip trembling. "This should never of happened. Jimmy—that's my husband— Jimmy knowed all along they had bad top, told the foreman, too. But did anybody listen?" She stops, and her face crumples into tears. "I tried to get Jimmy to go to Cleveland. Anything would be better than the mines."

Will doesn't say anything. He doesn't know what to say. An older woman wearing a black raincoat, a wisp of a blue headscarf tied under her chin, comes up behind the girl and lays her arm across the girl's shoulders. "You need to go sit down, Ginny Lou. You got a baby to think about."

The girl lifts her face from her hands and her mouth tightens. "Look at Cleave Brinson over there, strutting around like some big shot. Ain't nothing to him. He don't care who gets hurt, long as he gets his coal."

The other woman looks at Will, and then whispers something to Ginny Lou. The girl keeps her eyes ahead, without looking at Will. "I don't give a good goddamn if his daddy's Jimmy Carter," she says.

At noon, the clouds break and the sun comes out, pale and cold as fresh butter. The crowd quiets, and then a whisper runs through it like wind through the branches of the Virginia pines. "Hush," a man a few feet away from Will says to his wife. "They're bringing somebody out."

Ash Grove
35

Will sees Betsy standing near a little knot of women, and he goes to wait beside her. The rescue team has pulled one man free. They keep pulling rocks away and piling them into a little pyramid. Doc Beecham, his medical bag open, kneels beside the man's head, while the other men work to free his legs. From somewhere behind them Will hears a woman start singing, a high keening sound, the high notes sharp as the shift whistle. "What a friend we have in Jesus," she sings, "all our sins and grief to bear. What a privilege to carry everything to God in prayer."

Doc stands then and looks up at Cleave. He shakes his head. Then Cleave takes off his coat and lays it across the man on the ground, covering his face.

Will turns to look at Betsy. He starts to speak, but something in her face frightens him, and he turns back to watch while the bodies, one by one, are brought out of the mine and laid on the frozen ground.

"Will," Betsy says softly, without turning to look at him. "I want you to go home now. You mind me now. I want you to go home and lock the door, and I don't want you to open it for anybody but your daddy or me. Do you understand?"

He nods. Then he weaves his way through the crowd and runs up the hill toward home.

He falls asleep on the sofa in his father's den, a quilt across his shoulders and a Hardy Boys mystery open on his lap. When he hears Cleave and Betsy, he thinks at first he is dreaming. Their voices are rhythmic and shushing. He struggles to lift his eyelids.

"You know what can happen," Betsy says. "You wouldn't want him to get hurt."

Then Cleave says something, his voice lower and harder to hear. "Would you take him to Virginia?" he says finally, his voice deepening. "All hell's liable to break loose here."

"He's awake," Betsy says, as he opens his eyes wide and looks at her. "Will, honey. We're home. Get up and go on up to bed."

"Did you get them all out?"

"We got them all out," Cleave answers.

"Were the rest of them all right? Except the one, I mean."

"Three of the other men were hurt pretty bad, but we sent them on up to the U.K. hospital on a helicopter."

Will nods. He wants to ask, Who? But he is so tired now. Sleep is like a weight on his eyes, pulling their lids down. He thinks he could sleep for days.

Cleave pulls his son to his feet. "Help me, Will. You're too big to carry. Go on upstairs now. We'll talk tomorrow."

But they don't. Will and Betsy leave at eight o'clock the next morning, but Cleave has already gone down to the mine office, and there is nobody to say goodbye. Will helps Betsy load the suitcases into the trunk, and then climbs into the back seat of Cleave's Lincoln. He puts a pillow against the door to lean his back against, and he stretches his legs out across the cold leather seat. He rests his cheek against the seat back and closes his eyes.

He tries to see the faces of the boys and girls whose fathers were trapped in the roof fall. Some of them had to have been the fathers of his friends; he knows Henry's dad works that shift, and he thinks Stevie Robertson's father does, too. Will they think it was all Cleave's fault, like that girl, like Ginny Lou? Will they hate Cleave, and Will, too, for being his son?

He never even had the chance to tell them he was sorry, sorry for what happened, sorry that their fathers had to ride scoop buckets into a thirty-eight inch coal seam where they died. He tries to think what he can do. Maybe he can send cards from Virginia. But he doesn't even know where to send them. He doesn't even know who was lost.

And anyway, he is so tired. His body must weigh a thousand pounds. It is so hard to care anyway, when, every time something important happens, they send him away.

Seven

Betsy pours herself a cup of coffee and comes to sit at the kitchen table. She has put the food away, and what didn't need to be refrigerated sits on the kitchen table sealed in margarine tubs and plastic zipper bags. Will sits on the other side of the round oak table, his chair tilted so that the back rests against the wall. He has his feet propped up on the table's edge.

"Get your feet off the table, Will. Didn't I teach you anything?" Betsy asks. But her voice is light, teasing. Her words say one thing, but her eyes say another. You're still my little boy.

"It's my table now," he answers, grinning, playing the game with her. "As the only son and heir to the Brinson Mining fortune. Not that there's much left of it. At least I don't imagine that there is, the way mining around here's been the last few years."

Betsy frowns and purses her lips, then takes a sip of her black coffee. "Your daddy knew how to make money. Knew how to keep it, too. You might be surprised."

He likes sitting with Betsy like this, like old times. She could never stay mad at him. She always let him get by with things. All his life women have treated him this way, especially since his mother died. He has always been a bad boy, but not too bad, just bad enough to be interesting.

"You sure you don't want something to eat before you go to bed?" Betsy asks. "There's some of that Italian cream cake left that Ruby Siler sent over. All I have to do is get it out of the refrigerator and cut you a piece. It wouldn't hurt you a bit to fatten up."

"I'm not hungry, Betsy." He leans his head against the wall behind him, closing his eyes. The bright kitchen light makes his head hurt. He's tired, dead tired, but he doesn't want to go to bed yet. He has always been this way. The more exhausted he is, the harder it is for him to rest.

He takes his feet off the table and the front chair legs bang against the tile floor. He goes to refrigerator and gets a beer. Then he leans against the kitchen counter, cradling the can in his hands. "I didn't expect you to come back here," he says. "After everything that's gone on. I remember a lot about when I was a little boy. You don't owe the Brinsons the time of day. I wouldn't have blamed you if you hadn't wanted to come."

She shrugs and scoots her chair around to face him. "You're old enough to know now that people do all sorts of things they don't especially want to. Besides, if I hadn't come, I wouldn't have seen *you*."

Will studies her face for a moment, and then shakes his head. "I still can't believe it, that anybody could kill Cleave. He always seemed—I don't know, like somehow he would live forever." He hesitates. "Betsy, what do you think happened here? I don't just mean what happened to Cleave. I mean before, too? To my mother? Doc says there's no way Cleave had anything to do with it, but—"

She looks up at him, startled. He says, "It's just that being here—like this—well you know it has to bring back all the questions nobody's ever answered."

"Oh, Will. When are you ever going to let this go?"

To reassure her, he says, "I don't think about it all the time. Sometimes I go for years and I don't think about it at all. But how can I keep from wondering? First, she dies the way she did. And then, Cleave—Betsy, he had to have something to do with it. I've been over this and over this in my mind, and it's the only explanation that makes any sense."

She sighs and comes back to sit at the table, folding her arms across the worn oak surface. "I don't know what happened, Will. I really don't." She is silent for a moment. Then she looks at him and shakes her head. "No. I just can't see it. I never have been able to believe that he killed my sister."

"They arrested him, though. If he hadn't had—"

"No," she says. "You're wrong there. The sheriff came out and talked to Cleave, but he never arrested your father. Said at the inquest there wasn't enough evidence to arrest anybody. As far as I know, the case is still open, though what that means after all these years—"

Will pulls out a chair and sits next to her, his arm touching hers. He looks at her profile, thinking that she could have been pretty, almost as pretty as his mother, except for the birthmark on her face. He saw on the news not long ago that doctors were using lasers to make marks like hers practically disappear. They called them port wine stains. But he was glad, once upon a time, that she wasn't pretty. It makes him ashamed to admit that, even to himself, but it's true. It made her belong to him somehow, in a way that none of the women in his life, especially his mother, ever had.

Feeling a sudden tenderness for her, he lays his hand over hers. "You knew her better than anybody." Then he smiles at her. "Did you know I found her letters?" he says. "One summer when I was here, I found them in a box on the top shelf of her closet. I know you remember. The ones she used to get at her post office box, instead of here at the house?"

Betsy laughs. "The ones from the State Department?"

He nods, laughing, too. "For the longest time, I believed that was the truth. That she was some kind of government agent, and foreign spies blew up her car."

"Too bad you had to hear different. She did write some letters for a while for some environmentalist group, maybe the Sierra Club. I can't remember for sure which one. Cleave hit the ceiling when he found out. That's the maddest I ever did see him. He said the damned tree-huggers were trying to ruin coal mining, and here was his own wife, aiding and abetting. Now, don't look at me like that. All married people argue. There's a big difference between that and murdering somebody."

"Did you know she was going to leave with him? With the man she was writing to? The last letter, he talked about the plans they had made to go."

He offers this as another piece of evidence, but Betsy doesn't seem impressed by it. She shrugs and lifts her coffee cup. "He might have thought she was leaving with him. She might even have thought so. But I doubt she would have gone."

"But they loved each other, didn't they? And the letter said—"

"I don't care what the letter said. I knew your mother better than anybody did. When it came down to it, I'm telling you, she wouldn't have gone. How could somebody like him be acceptable to our family, to Judge

Connelly of Virginia?"

Will smiles. He used to think that title was part of Grandfather's name, because he heard it so often.

"Your mother might have been wild sometimes," Betsy goes on. "She had some pretty radical ideas, considering. But it was important to her, who she was, where she came from. She took pains to keep up the appearance of things, to be who she thought she ought to be. Not that she'd admit that in a million years, maybe not even to herself."

He starts to argue. But then he remembers the parties Anne hosted a couple of times a year for the miners' wives and daughters.

"You were about to shake your head," Betsy says. "And then?"

"I was thinking about those afternoon teas." His mother would invite fifteen or twenty women whose husbands worked at Brinson Mining, and ask them to bring their daughters along. The women wore their Sunday skirts and blouses; the little girls wore frilly pastel dresses that might have been stylish a decade earlier. Most of the dresses looked shabby, as if they had been made over and handed down. Will always stood off to the side of the room with his head down looking at the floor, hoping to avoid calling attention to himself. What he remembers most is a rustle of brightly colored skirts that made the girls look like a flock of tropical birds.

Even as a child, Will could see how strained these afternoons were. Anne hovered, a chilly smile on her lips, the mistress of the manor holding court. The women held themselves awkwardly, sipping Earl Grey tea out of Havilland teacups, not saying that they would have preferred coffee, trying not to show how afraid they were to move or speak.

One afternoon, a little girl of nine or ten dropped her cup. The porcelain hit the table on the way down and shattered, leaving the tea soaking into the cream-colored rug. Anne rushed toward the girl to tell her it was all right, just a cup—maybe it was a family heirloom—but after all just a cup, nothing worth causing a child to come to grief.

But before Anne could weave her way through the room, the mother stood and turned sharply to face her daughter. She said something and the girl burst into tears. Then the mother, a tired-looking woman with dark brown hair, slapped the girl across the face, hard, leaving a red handprint on the side of her face.

Will can never forget the look of shame and hatred on the woman's face when she said goodbye to Anne at the door. It was as if it had been Anne, and not the child's mother herself, who had struck the girl.

"I always wondered why those women put themselves through it, when they were obviously so miserable. You know all of them—even my mother—would rather have been doing anything else."

"Who knows why? Cleave was the boss. Maybe they thought they were helping their husbands. Maybe they wanted to see what the inside of this house was like. But I'm right, aren't I? Anne took it seriously, being Cleave Brinson's wife. She thought she ought to bring some culture into the community. Raise people's standards." She grins. "You didn't have to be a Republican to think you knew what people should value better than they knew themselves."

He laughs. "Surely you're not saying maybe some woman she snubbed at tea—?"

Betsy laughs, too. "But I bet more than one felt like wrestling her down on the front porch and pulling her bald-headed. She probably deserved it, too. I don't guess it ever occurred to her that she might be able to learn something from them."

"But you loved her. How could you love her if she was like you say, fickle and snotty and all the rest?"

"Why does anybody love anybody? In spite of, that's why. When you're young, you think you love people because of the goodness in them. When you get older, you see that love doesn't always make much sense. I've gotten to the point myself I'm not sure anything makes any sense. Listen, honey, are you sure you don't want some cake? I'm going to get me some."

He shakes his head. She gets up, opens the refrigerator door and takes out the cake; then she gets a plate out of the cabinet. "Besides," she says, opening the drawer and getting a fork before she walks back to the table and sits down. "Anne couldn't help being who she was raised to be. For all practical purposes, your grandfather picked out Cleave Brinson for my sister. He bestowed her on him the way, when he was in the state legislature, he might have bestowed project funding on someone who had sent some campaign money his way, and she stepped from the house of one man who had always told her what to do, straight into the house of another.

"But, oh, Will, she was so smart. She was always asking questions people didn't want to hear. Sometimes I think she should have gone to graduate school or gotten a job, instead of getting married so young. But then I remember how restless she was, too, how she flitted from one thing to another. She'd write poetry for a while and then the next thing you know, she'd spend all her time playing the piano. For a time, when we were young, she even thought about being a nun. Can you imagine?

"You asked me about those letters. Well, you're grown up now and you might as well hear it. Jim Tilson was not her first, and he would not have been her last. All those letters, all those lovers—that was a little game Annie played. It had as much to do with our father as it had to do with yours."

She takes a bite of her cake before she goes on. "I felt sorry for Anne, but I felt sorry for Cleave, too. He thought he was the luckiest man in the world. He was rich, he was important, and he got to marry a beautiful woman seventeen years younger than he was. Then look what he ended up with. A part of me wouldn't have blamed him for throwing her out on her tail. But you had to love Anne. I don't even know why. She would do the most outrageous things. She could hurt people so bad and not even know what she did. But she had a good heart. One time, I saw her take a pretty little beaded bracelet right off her wrist and hand it to a woman—at one of those awful tea parties, come to think of it—just because the woman said she liked it. She didn't do it to impress anybody. She just did it because she felt like it, and she never said another word about it.

"And she was good to me, Will. I never expected to have anything. And it wasn't just my face. I think I would have died living the life Daddy had planned for me, but I lacked whatever it took to do something about it. The spinster daughter! God, your poor Uncle Pat. The only thing worse would have been being the oldest son. Though, the way it turned out, Pat was the only one who ended up with what I guess you could call a normal life.

"But you know, Anne loved me just the way I was. You'll think I'm crazy, but I think sometimes she was the one who would have liked to trade places, because she thought I could do just as I pleased. She told me everything, shared everything. Even you. I took care of you, when you were little, same as if you were mine. She never resented it, the way some women might. Never worried you'd love me more. Never any nonsense like that."

Will gets up and walks to the sink, staring out the window into the dark. Maybe she didn't love me enough to resent you, he thinks, but then he remembers being curled like a puppy against his mother's side. She was warm, so warm, and she smelled clean like lavender and baby powder. In one hand, she'd hold a book open, and with the other, she'd caress his hair.

Other times, they'd play, and she'd be as rambunctious as he was. They'd chase each other through the house, hiding in all the nooks and crannies, slamming doors as they scuttled from one closet to the other to hide. It was almost as though they were both children, and Betsy mothered them both.

"Cleave must have known there were other men."

"Some people don't know anything they don't want to know."

He comes back to the table. He pulls a chair out, turns it to face him, and straddles it. He looks at her intently. "Tell me why you think somebody else killed her."

"Well, think about it. Cleave drove the Lincoln at least half the time. He was going to Frankfort for a Coal Association meeting that Thursday. People knew it. They wouldn't expect him to drive his pick-up truck, although that's what he did."

"That's Doc's theory, that whoever wired the car wanted to kill Cleave. But—"

"But what?"

"What I keep coming back to. There's only one person that we can say for sure knew Anne—and not Cleave—was going to be in that car."

Betsy picks up her dessert plate and sweeps imaginary crumbs from the table onto the plate. "You remember that big strike, the one the year before your mother died?"

"Bits and pieces. I was pretty young, then. I remember more about the one when I was thirteen, right before Cleave sent me to live with Grandmother and Grandfather in Virginia."

He does remember riding in the truck once with his father during that time. They passed a big fire built on the side of the road. Men had signs and were huddled around the fire. He was frightened. The men had shouted at him, waving the signs at them, but Turtle Miracle—mountain people pronounced his name Marricle—the company's land agent, rode on the passenger side. He had a rifle between his knees, and when they drove past, he held it up so that the barrel gleamed over the edge of the dashboard.

"People got hurt in that strike," Betsy says. "They got the union in, but the miners were out of work for a long time, and when they finally did get their contract, they didn't get near the raise they thought they should. Then—oh, I don't know, three or four months after that—a man got killed setting jacks." Jack-setters have one of the most dangerous jobs in the world, Will knows. They go in before the mine timbers are set, to make the roof safe for those who follow to work the coal.

Will folds his arms across the chair back, resting his chin over his hands. "Killing somebody is so—personal, somehow. I can see men like that blowing up a bulldozer to shut a job down, but blowing up Cleave Brinson in a car?"

"Junior Messer sure had something against him that was personal."

Will looks at his aunt. He is so stupid. He never thought the two events might be connected. Why has he not thought of that? Could they be?

Betsy gets up and carries her plate to the sink. "Anyway, I'm tired, Will. I'm going to bed. You haven't figured this out in thirty years. I doubt you will tonight."

She washes the dish, dries it, and sets it back inside the cabinet. She shuts the door softly before she turns back to him. "Do you ever hear from Deana Perry?"

He looks at her, startled. "Deana? What in the world made you think about Deana?"

"I don't know, really. But I always liked that girl. Or maybe it's just— it seemed to me she really cared about you. You know, I always felt sorry for her, too. That father of hers didn't treat those girls right."

"No, he didn't. I knew he bullied Deana and her sister, but I never went around there much. Deana didn't want me to. I think she was embarrassed about his drinking, about how they lived."

"I don't doubt it. Wayman Perry was a mean man. He was president of the local union here for a years and caused a lot of trouble, always drinking and stirring things up. I guess he finally got so far down in the bottle, he couldn't cause trouble for anybody but his own."

Will looks at her. "I didn't know that. That he was in the union. Or if I did, I must have forgotten it. Was he in the union around the time my mother died?"

Betsy tilts her head at him, thinking. "I'm not sure exactly. Oh, Will, all these questions! It all happened so long ago."

"Sometimes it seems that way to me, too. And other times— Do you know I still dream about my mother?"

"I would imagine you do."

Will doesn't tell her how many nights he wakes up in the middle of the night, completely panicked. He's always alone in the woods or in an airport, lost, and calling for her. Sometimes, he'll tug on a woman's skirt and feel a blessed relief, but when he looks up, he doesn't see his mother's face, but a stranger's. Other times, he can't remember what happened in the dream, but he wakes up feeling that he isn't dreaming at all, but that his mother is really there, in the room with him. He can feel her breath against his cheek and smell the lingering fragrance of baby powder and lavender perfume. He knows this is crazy, but often, still—and him a grown man— he will wake up with tears on his face. Is it any wonder, he thinks, that he can't stop asking questions, can't reconcile himself to losing her and never knowing why? It isn't so much that he can't let go of her. She won't let go of him.

"Betsy, somebody knows what happened. I just have to figure out who. If Wayman Perry was in the union, maybe he— Well, anyway, it's a place to start."

"I suppose if he's still around here and his liver hasn't killed him, you can ask him, but I have to say I don't think he'll be much use. His brain's probably so pickled by this time he'd be lucky to remember who he is, let alone anything that went on around him."

She is silent for a moment, thinking. Then her face lights up and she studies him for a moment. "I know," she says, smiling. "What if you call Deana and ask her if she remembers anything. I mean, sometimes people say things that don't seem important at the time—" She stops at his look and raises her hand toward him as if to keep him from answering. "It's just an idea. You probably don't even know where she is."

"You're right. I don't know where she is. You're being a little obvious, don't you think?"

She grins. "I'll bet her sister knows where she is." Then she tilts her head at him and shakes it, laughing at herself. "I'm sorry," she says. "Don't pay any attention to me. I'm just a silly old woman who needs to mind her own business."

She wipes her hands on the sides of her hips and yawns. "Well, if you won't let me run your life, I really am going to bed before I fall asleep on my feet. Don't you stay up all night. It's been a long day. You need to get some rest, too."

At the door, she doesn't turn around, but she turns her head so that he can see the unblemished part of her face in profile. "I will say one more thing, though."

He laughs. "I just knew you would. What?"

"Wayman Perry wasn't the only one who didn't treat that girl right. You didn't treat her right either."

"No, I don't guess I did."

The sheets are cold when Will slides into bed at 2:30. He has emptied a six-pack of beer and had a couple of shots from Cleave's stock of bourbon. The bed keeps spinning, and Will sets one foot on the floor beside the bed to steady it. It seems so strange to be in this house with his parents both dead, though he cannot remember ever living in this house when it did not feel empty.

He wonders if there was ever a time when his parents' lives might have turned out differently from the way they did. The years from thirteen to seventeen, under his grandfather's watchful eye, he stopped being Will Brinson, who ran wild with miner's children, and became William Connelly Brinson, supposed to amount to something. He learned then that happy families do exist. He still remembers Uncle Pat arriving at the Connellys' every year, the day after Christmas, his Suburban loaded down with children and his trunk full of presents. He remembers that the whole character of his grandparents' house changed with Pat's arrival, as if a drafty concert hall suddenly filled up with music from a brass band.

What had Pat discovered growing up, that his sisters had never figured out? Was Pat just lucky? Once when Will was a teenager he had asked his cousin Teresa why Uncle Pat was so happy, when he'd grown up in the same house as Betsy and Anne. She looked at him blankly for a moment before she said, "I don't know. That's just Daddy. That's how he looks at the world."

"But why?" Will persisted.

"It just is," Teresa said. "I guess he was just born that way."

But later Will thinks the answer is not so simple, not a nature-versus-nurture question that can be settled once and for all, though Will is sure that when he left Virginia and never went back, Grandfather blamed the disappointment on some throwback in the Brinson family history. What else could explain how a Connelly could go so wrong?

Sometimes he thinks he should have stayed in Virginia and not come back here at seventeen. At first, he hated being at his grandparents' house, but later, he learned to adapt. He remembers how much he loved Grandmother's garden. He loved Grandmother, too, loved teasing her, though he didn't know this at the time. Once, he remembers, he was fifteen, trimming the hedges at the edge of the backyard. When she called him, he stopped, waiting for her to come outside. He could see her through the screen, pulling on her gloves. She wore a shell-pink linen dress with a waist-length jacket, just fashionable enough to make her attractive, but not fashionable enough to make it look as though she thought she was still young. A little veil draped over her matching hat. Her fine skin sagged beneath the veil's lace edging, but clearly, she was once as beautiful as Will's mother; Grandmother looked the way he imagined Anne would have, had she lived long enough to be a grandmother. He remembers Grandmother always looking a little wilted, the way the roses—her backyard had masses of roses—looked right before petals fell.

"Are you going now?" he asked, holding the large-bladed shears in his right hand. The sweat ran down his back and his smooth chest.

"I'm going. But Will, don't you even think about going in the front to work until you put a shirt on. If I hired a colored boy to do that, I would expect him to put some clothes on."

He ignored her, as he supposes now she must have expected him to. "Where are you headed?" he asked her. "Church bazaar or garden club?"

"The garden club, if it's any of your business. But I won't be back until late. After the meeting, I'm going to the country club to have lunch with Bess Wilkinson." Pearl had liked Bess Wilkinson. He remembers she had a long nose and looked just like a dogtooth lily.

He waved the garden shears toward his grandmother. And then he grinned. "If you drink too much hooch and need a ride home," he said, "just give me a call."

"Oh, you!" she said and let the screen door slam with a little slap behind her.

Will grins, remembering how he and Grandmother studied each other as if each was a particularly exotic exhibit at the zoo. He must have turned back to the boxwoods, the shears making a thwacking sound and the branches rustling softly as they fell to the ground. He discovered that year in Virginia that he loved yard work, all of it, whether he was pruning hedges, mowing grass, or pulling weeds. He loved the feel of the dirt under his knees, the way the moisture from the ground seeped into the denim of his jeans.

But more than anything else, he loved growing flowers. He took over Grandmother's garden. While she was out sipping sherry and listening to some gardening expert's tips on winning the top prize at the rose show, Will was there in his own little Eden, taking pleasure in the rhythm of his hands. There, time disappeared, and, no matter how annoying the insects, how suffocating the heat, on his knees, bareheaded to the sun or wind, he turned the dirt twelve inches down, digging in compost and peat moss. In the spring and early summer, he planted and sprayed, fed and mulched, and then, in late May or early June, he was rewarded with his most beautiful flowers yet, pink peonies with blooms so heavy, that without staking the stems would bend all the way to the ground and roses with their sweet, heady scent.

He saw his grandparents nod to each other in relief and approval, but even this did not spoil the garden for him. He remembers working for hours and hours, saying the names of the plants under his breath—lavender, lilac, lily, hyacinth, hibiscus, hydrangea, crocus, bougainvillea, oleander, and narcissus. He named the flowers Grandmother had, and the ones, flipping through catalogs at night, he dreamed of having.

He and Grandmother agreed that there would be nothing common in this garden, nothing like the black-eyed Susans or goldenrods that grew alongside the road back in Ash Grove. In the autumn, the first year he took over the garden, he planted a bulb Grandmother brought home from a garden-club plant exchange. Even now, years later, he has yet to discover its scientific name, though he is certain it is some type of hardy amaryllis; the following spring, some strap-like leaves appeared, and then died, leaving the ground bare. Then, in late August, almost overnight it seemed, a flower rose. This was the verb he chose, the only word he could find that fit. A flower rose, like that picture of the goddess on a seashell. It had a single stalk with a rich pink bud that bloomed into three or four trumpets. Of all the flowers in his garden, this was—and is—his favorite, a flower that appears to die, but lies under the soil, dormant, waiting. Grandmother said Jane Nelson called it a resurrection lily, but Netta Sams said it was a naked lady. Will had promised to divide the bulbs that fall and give some to Netta, but he never got around to it. He kept all the bulbs himself and planted them in a bed at the back of the garden. A fourth of the bulbs he sells in his landscaping business had their start in Grandmother's Virginia garden.

He knows that the garden saved him. He was fourteen, almost fifteen, and he had done—what? Something. He was always doing something. Shoplifting, sneaking out at night, or smoking in the boy's bathroom at school. But the shit hit the fan when Cliff Sandifer stole two bottles of Very Old Barton from home, and four or five of the boys he and Will ran with skipped school and sneaked over to the granary to hide under the railroad bridge and drink it. Will and Cliff shot-gunned nearly a whole fifth, and Will ended up so drunk he passed out and pissed in his britches. The cops found Will and Cliff around midnight. One of the boys had gone on home, but when his parents put the pressure on, he ratted out Will and Cliff, and his parents finally called the police.

"Piss ant didn't even give *his* name," Cliff hissed to Will in the back seat of the squad car. "I'll kill him."

Just inside the front door of his grandparents' house, Will remembers the sickness breaking, like surf. He puked on the rug in the foyer until there was nothing left in his stomach. He puked until he thought he might die puking, and truth to tell, looking at Grandfather, he sort of hoped he would.

"It's ruined," he heard Grandmother saying. "It's just ruined." She was crying and she kept saying the same thing over and over again. The sentence kept rolling through his head. What the hell was she talking about?

It was dark the next day before he could blink his eyes without feeling that the top of his head would come off. All day he had lain upstairs, the heavy drapes pulled. He had no clue that he was in worse trouble this time,

Ash Grove

50

until he sneaked downstairs, hoping to make his escape before either of his grandparents saw him, and he had to explain, apologize, and listen to their crap.

But his grandfather came to the door of the dining room and motioned him inside. Grandfather wore his suit to dinner, always, and he had on a dark gray suit with a blue tie. Will had on a Virginia Cavaliers tee shirt and jeans with the right knee ripped out. He followed Grandfather into the large room, lit blindingly with a crystal chandelier that hung over the center of the mahogany table. Grandmother was already seated, but she didn't look at Will.

"I don't really feel like eating," Will said. "If it's all right with you, I thought I'd just—"

"Damn it, son!" his grandfather said, the words a little explosion in the quiet room. "It is not all right with us. You will sit with us through dinner, I don't care whether you feel like eating or not."

"You can't keep ruining everything," his grandmother said, and she turned her head to the left, away from them, lifting her chin. Her chin quivered as if she might cry, but she held her mouth in a thin, straight line. "I just thank God your mother doesn't see how you've turned out. I—"

"I'm sorry if I ruined something. I'll pay for whatever—"

"With what?" Grandfather said. "You ruined a rug that has been in your grandmother's family for over a hundred years. And just how would you go about paying for that?"

Will was silent. Judge Connelly of Virginia Himself had spoken. Will looked at the gold-rimmed plates; the edge of one caught the reflection of the firelight. Will remembered that when Cleave and Grandfather spoke, Cleave used the old man's title at the end of nearly every sentence. Why, yes, Judge Connelly, the company has been doing well this quarter. Could I get the door for you, Judge? Sitting there, dizzily watching the light spin around the rim of the plate, for the first time in his life, Will almost felt sorry for his father. He had not realized before that Grandfather had intimidated even Cleave Brinson.

"Go on," Grandfather continued. "Tell me how you plan to pay for the damage you've done."

Will shrugged, miserable. God, his head hurt. Every muscle in his body hurt.

Grandfather sat down at the table, and reached for a piece of bread, finally looking away and releasing Will from his accusing eyes. "You can't, of course," he said, buttering the roll. "But I guarantee you will be too busy to get into any more trouble. Mr. Randall has taken care of your grandmother's flowers, for—I don't know—it must be twenty years. Unfortunately, his wife has been sick and he will be unable to work here until she is better. This year, I want you to take care of the yard and garden work. And as soon as possible—I hope by this fall—you will go to boarding school."

"But why can't I go back—?" Will began.

"Why can't you go back to Ash Grove and live with your father? Is that what you were about to say?"

Will nodded.

"Because, son, you have been allowed to run wild too long. And don't think of crying to your father. He agrees that I know what is best for you. You need serious discipline. I know of a good Catholic boys' school in Richmond. It has a proven record of turning troubled boys around. An old friend mine, Father Drury, is the dean. There's a waiting list, but I've been a supporter of the school for years, and Father Drury has promised to find a place for you as soon as he can."

Will closed his eyes. He would die in a place like that. He wanted to throw something, but there was nothing in his hands to throw. He wanted to say, Do you always sound like you're making a speech, Grandfather? When you and Grandmother have a fuck, do you say, Well, Mary Margaret, this has been so delightful, we really must do it again? But for once he held his tongue. He had expected something to happen, that sooner or later they would get tired of him and send him back to Ash Grove. But not this.

"We are not without sympathy for you, Will," his grandfather went on, his voice a little softer. "You have lost a mother. But losses build character, if you view them the right way. You are not the only one here who has lost someone. Your grandmother and I have lost our daughter, your father has lost his wife. You are old enough, boy, to think of someone's sorrow besides your own. Now, sit down, and let's try to have a civilized dinner."

Will can still remember the weight of the heavy mahogany chair. He pulled it out and sat down, laying his hands formally on either side of his plate. The smell of the roast made his stomach heave, and his throat stung as he swallowed. He wanted to cry, but he would not give them the satisfaction.

But somehow, miraculously, the garden redeemed him. At first, he resented the work, resented not being allowed to see his friends. But later he found that his body was grateful for the work that left him too tired for anything, even resentment.

Once he began working in the garden, he was always the first one up. He deadheaded the spent blooms and watered before the mid-day heat. At twilight he came out on the back steps and sat with his back against the rough red bricks, looking at the flowers he had worked so hard to grow. If his grandparents were at home, he poured himself a cold beer they pretended not to see him drinking. If they were gone, he rolled a joint to go with his beer, and sat inhaling the smoke deep into his lungs and exhaling the smoke into the humid evening. He didn't read or sing or think. He was tired, bone-tired, too tired to be sad or to go out looking for trouble. And because of this garden, his grandfather had forgotten all about St. Benedict's School for Boys, and Will had earned the right to be left alone.

Would it have been better if he had stayed there, if he had gone to college and become a lawyer the way Grandfather wanted him to? He can't imagine it, getting into politics like Grandfather or into business like Cleave, but maybe it would have been better to follow the path that Grandfather had been so willing to clear. But then his Grandmother died, and he did not seem to have a choice. He could not bear it there any longer. The garden had been for him, but it had been for her, too. She had been the one person who had believed that he had a special gift, a green thumb, she called it, though these conversations were always private between the two of them, and never in front of Grandfather. No, he did not have the heart to stay there without her. And here in Ash Grove, waiting for him, were all those memories of his mother and Deana Perry, with her heart in her eyes.

Why had made Betsy think about Deana after all these years? Is it just being back in Ash Grove that brings back all these memories? When Will came back from Virginia, not to live with Cleave but to escape Grandfather, he remembers how Deana used to sit downstairs in the kitchen table, playing her guitar and singing. She was pretty good, with one of those high, light Appalachian voices that knows how to find its way through a ballad.

They had left Ash Grove at seventeen and eighteen, young and full of dreams. They planned to end up in Nashville. Will was going to start a landscaping business, and Deana was going to wait tables and camp outside the Bluebird Cafe until she got her big break.

He remembers a fragment of a song she wrote about him— *He takes the inside of the fast curves; there's nothing he ain't seen. But unraveling behind them is the ragged edge of her dream. He's nobody you'd even notice, but his skin smells just like rain, and his eyes burn like a fever in her brain. She'd swim the coldest river, climb the tallest peak; he's like the very air she needs to breathe.*

He used to get lonesome and look her up every so often, but he hasn't seen her for five or six years now. Where did she end up, he wonders, little dark-haired Deana? Last year, in between women, he thought about trying to get in touch with her, but for once he stopped himself. Even without Betsy there to tell him, he knew he wasn't being fair. After he left the last time, did Deana find some other motherless boy to love, the way she had tried to love him? But she was not his mother, and the more she had held him, rocking him awake from his dreams, the more he felt as if her eyes were a dark pool of water he was being pulled into, wearing lead weights.

Though Betsy's motives tonight were obvious—to find Will someone who might love him as much as Betsy does—it occurs to him that she could be right about one thing—Deana might be able to help him figure out what happened to his mother. If Wayman Perry was as involved in the union as Betsy remembers, maybe he did hear something, know something, about what happened to Anne Brinson? At least this might be a place to start.

Sometime—not now, but in the weeks to come—maybe he will call Lily and try to get back in touch with Deana. It might be too late to ask her for anything. He can't blame her if she never wants to speak to him again. But he hopes she knows, somehow, deep down, that he was no more in control of his feelings than she was, that he had not meant to hurt her. Surely, by now, even she knows that leaving was the best thing he could have done for her.

He thinks that his whole life, he has ridden the current of an invisible river, following a boat that carries the ghost of his mother. He used to think that if he could find out the truth, he would be free of both Anne and Cleave, free to live the way he thinks other people live, who do not dread to fall asleep and wrestle with their dreams. But he isn't so sure anymore that learning the truth is even possible. And if he learns the truth, what will it change, now that even Cleave is dead and so many years have passed? Well, he's too tired and too damned drunk to figure it out this minute. Finally, maybe he can go to sleep.

He closes his eyes, and the bed is still spinning, like a white paper boat blown toward the open sea. Most of the time, he feels exactly like this—weightless on the surface of the water, as he swirls from one eddy to the other of memory and grief.

 Eight

The preacher comes and sits by Wayman Perry's bed; Wayman's wife Jolene comes out of the bathroom, drying her hands on her jeans. Just like that old woman to sic the preacher on him when he's helpless and can't shake loose. Preacher likes to pray loud, this one does, with his voice like whiskey and honey. Sometimes he breaks open his guitar case in the hospital waiting room and has a prayer meeting complete with songs.

Jolene kneels beside the preacher, and he starts in. "Lord Jesus, we know that you hear us. You know what is in our brother Wayman's mind and heart. Even now, he might yet have time for repentance. The thief on the cross went that very day with Jesus to Paradise. No man knoweth the hour when the Son of Man cometh. He cometh like a thief in the night. But if this good woman's husband can hear us, Lord Jesus, Hallelujah, give us a sign, so that she might rest easy, knowing that she will see him again in thy kingdom. We pray this in Jesus' name. Amen."

He looks at Wayman, his little eyes black as a bill collector's, and he takes Wayman's hand in his. But Wayman can't feel the hand. Wayman isn't down there, trapped in his body the way they think he is. He's high up somewhere, close to the ceiling where it's freezing, watching everything that happens in this room. He sees the tube that runs down his throat, the IV that drips into his veins. He sees Brother Hardwick's bent head, his beauty-shop blonde hair brushed into a pompadour like Porter Waggoner's. It hangs over the edge of his collar in a little fringe. He's wearing a light blue sport coat. All he needs, Wayman thinks, is some sequins on the front of his jacket, to be dressed up for some Grand Ole Opry of the soul. Well, he ain't no goddamned brother of Wayman's.

Wayman has known this old boy half their lives. He knows George spent twenty years singing Hank Williams songs in honkytonks, before he got religion. Wayman hit a few licks with him a time or two himself. Before the first stroke, even when Wayman was blind drunk and tried to play the guitar left-handed, he could play rings around this preacher on the guitar. He could smoke George on any song he wanted to play, you name it, Carter family, bluegrass, gospel or Duane Eddy. Wayman thinks George is a Praise-the-Lord-Channel wannabe if he ever saw one, but no matter what he tells Jolene, he don't have no recording contract with God. Wayman knows George ain't nothing but an old broke-dick drunk, who traded in whiskey and loose women for gospel music and glory, for a different kind of hunger in a woman's eyes. Stupid woman. And now Wayman is going to die and leave her to her religion and an old reformed drunk not much better than himself. If Wayman could get up from this bed, he'd slap that freckled hand off Jolene's shoulder and kick George Hardwick's ass.

All of a sudden, thinking of it, his mouth opens and closes like a fish, and he's smack back in the middle of his own misery. He can't catch his breath, but his throat makes a gargling sound, and his hand flies up into the air, flopping around like it's got a mind of its own. He can hear himself shouting, but the sounds don't make any sense.

But George Hardwick has heard what he wanted to hear. "Hallelujah! Praise Almighty Lord Jesus!" the preacher says, half-rising and leaning over the bed. His face is flushed with triumph, as if Wayman, moved by the Holy Spirit and Brother George's prayer, has found a direct line to heaven like the saints of Pentecost, not calling down salvation in earthly words, but in tongues. He grabs Wayman's hand and wiggles it back and forth in joy. "Ask and ye shall receive," he says. "Seek and ye shall find. We asked God for a sign, Sister Jolene, and what does he send us? Signs and wonders. That's all I got to say."

Wayman doesn't know if he feels sorrier for himself and his own lost soul, or for his wife, soon to be his widow. Oh, honey, he wants to tell her, there ain't never going to be no end to what George Hardwick has to say.

Wayman knows his time is near and he is not ready. He's a miner on his knees in the dark. It was never death that scared him. Hell, he used to wish for it. He used to say, bring it on. Let me pass out piss drunk on the railroad tracks and get run over by a train. When I go into the mines tonight, let a rock fall on my head, take me quick and clean.

No, what scared him was going slow into death like a miner trapped in the black damp, that he would break into an old tunnel of memories and smother in the bad air. That he would drown in his own loneliness, the way he has heard the doctors tell Jolene he is drowning in the fluid around his heart.

Pigeons flutter around the bed; it's always a good sign when the pigeons can still breathe. Their breasts are all snowy except for their stethoscopes. Somebody shoves an oxygen mask over Wayman's face. Lord, Jesus, he prays—or is this George praying? Help me. I don't need no ticket to Paradise. Just give me air and air.

When they take the oxygen away, Jolene and Preacher Hardwick kneel again by the bed.

"Oh, Lord Jesus," the preacher says. "We thank you that you have come into this man's hard heart and softened it for your kingdom. Though we die, hallelujah, yet may we live. We thank you for Sister Jolene who has endured hardships, yea even to the boils of Job. But did she give up on Brother Wayman? No, Hallelujah, Praise God, she did not. Now, another soul is anointed with the precious blood of the Lamb, your own boy Jesus, our Savior and Lord, and will soon be on its way home."

Soon. Son, he thinks. You don't have a clue when I'm going or where. His sins are black as the coal in the stockpile, and his good points won't register as much as a thumb on the tonnage scale. The difference between him and the preacher is, Wayman Perry ain't asking for no special favors. He knows what he is.

Where is that girl? They have all been here but Deana. How can he let go of living when he still has so much left to say?

❧Nine

Deana Perry wakes trembling, pulling the quilt tight around her. A web of moonlight shines through the lace curtains at the window and leaves a speckled pattern on the floor. It's late January, but thanks to a strange warm front, last night was warm enough for Deana to sleep with the window open. But now the room is so cold, almost as cold as the mine in her dream. For a second, she half expects to see her daddy kneeling at the foot of the bed, his dark clothes smelling sharp like sulfur, like whiskey and coal dust, his mine light bobbing a yellow circle against the wall.

The phone jangles again. She reaches through the dark to the nightstand to turn on the lamp. She lifts the receiver, blinking in the sudden flood of light.

"Deana?" It's her sister Lily's voice on the other end of the line.

"Lily? For God's sake. What time is it?"

"I don't know. Five-thirty? Six, maybe? I don't have my watch on. I've been in this hospital so much lately, I've got my days and nights mixed up. I don't know if this is early or late."

Deana sits up against the pillows, pulling her knees up to her chest, the quilt across them. Down the road, she hears a car start and then idle, the engine running to clear the windshield of frost.

"What did you say? Slow down. And speak up. I can barely hear you."

"It's Daddy," Lily says. "He's here in the hospital. At first, they thought it was just a light stroke, you know, like the one he had the last time. But it's worse. Deana, he's real sick. It's not just the stroke. It's his heart, too. The doctor was just in here a while ago. He said if Daddy had any more family besides me and Mommy, I'd better give them a call."

"Don't you believe a word of it," Deana says. "Don't you worry. That old son-of-a-bitch has been at death's door before. He's like the bunny on that battery commercial. He just keeps on going."

The harshness of her voice, still heavy with sleep, startles even her. For a moment, the line is silent. "Well," her sister says, finally. "I thought you'd want to know. I'm just making the call."

"I didn't mean to sound so hateful."

As usual, she thinks, his timing's not worth shit. Sophie's in the middle of the school term. Deana's car is running hot, and she hasn't had the time or the money to get it fixed. Is she supposed to take off work and run back there every time he drinks himself into the hospital?

"It's just not a real good time for me to get down there," Deana says.

"It's not like he picked it to irritate you. Sometimes things happen to people that they don't plan."

"It's not that I don't want to come," Deana says. But she isn't fooling anybody. The truth is, going to Ash Grove right now is the last thing in the world she wants to do. "I'm sorry, Lily. I know everything's on your shoulders. But I've got to work, and if I don't get somebody to look at my car—"

She opens the drawer of the nightstand and roots around. There. Her glasses are on top of the book she was reading before she went to sleep, on the floor beside the bed.

"Let me think a minute," she says, trying to figure out what to do. "Look. If I can get one of the women in the office to cover for me, I can come up early in the morning. But I absolutely have to be back by the first of next week. Will you be at home when I get there, or do you want me to come straight to the hospital?"

"I don't know. How can I know? I mean, maybe if you could let me know what time you think you'll get here?" There is silence at the end of the line, and Deana knows her sister is trying not to lose patience with her. "Tell you what. Why don't you just come on out to house when you get to town? Even if I'm at the hospital, Wes'll be home with the kids. We can figure it out from there."

"That'll work. I've got your number. If anything happens to change my plans, I promise I'll call. It'll be good to see you all. It's been what? Almost a year?"

"Over a year. You and Sophie were here the Christmas right after Troy was born, but I don't think you've been here since. We really missed you this Christmas, especially Mommy. Missed Sophie, too."

Deana doesn't say anything. She can't think of a good reason why she didn't go home. She had told them she had to work then, too, but the truth is, Dr. Allman is always good to let Deana work a flexible schedule. Sometimes she even brings work home and fills out insurance claims late into the night after Sophie has gone to bed. She certainly could have arranged her schedule around Christmas, but for some reason, last year, Deana couldn't bear to spend Christmas in Ash Grove. She and Sophie had a wonderful Christmas right here, away from all that drama.

Besides, why does Deana always feel this need to defend herself with Lily? Deana and Sophie had picked out and mailed presents to each and every one of her family, and Deana told Mama she was sorry she couldn't make it for Christmas, but she would get down there as soon as she could. She had meant to go. Now she can hardly believe it's been over a year.

In the awkward silence that follows, Deana has a sudden impulse to ask Lily if anyone has called in the past few weeks, asking for Deana's address, but she stops herself in time. Her life and her choices are none of Lily's business, but that's never stopped Lily from poking her nose right in. No sense in giving her an excuse.

"Can you believe Troy's two years old now?" Lily asks, changing the subject from Deana's failure as a daughter to neutral ground. "I don't know what to do with myself, without a little baby."

Lily has four children. Deana always imagines Lily's children like one of those decals of stick families stuck on the back of mini-van windows, so that the small one is in the distance, their shapes getting get smaller and smaller the further from Ash Grove Deana gets. "Lord, "Deana says, laughing. "All you need, Lily, is another baby."

"That don't mean I don't want one." She hesitates a moment. "Deana?"

"What?"

"I'm glad you're coming home, even under these circumstances. The doctors don't know how much Daddy even knows about what's going on around him. He might not know whether you're there or not. Thing is, though, you'll know. You know what Mommy always said. That blood is thicker than water."

Deana laughs. "That is a proven scientific fact. Blood is thicker than water."

Deana hangs up the phone and pulls on the jeans and tee shirt she left crumpled last night on the floor in the bathroom. Then she goes barefoot into the kitchen to make a pot of coffee. She laughs again, scooping coffee into the filter, even though she can't figure out what is so damned funny. Whenever she hears that old expression, about blood being thicker than water, she thinks about the big oil spill that happened a few years ago up in Alaska. She remembers seeing some reporter standing on the shore and talking into the camera, while behind him flocks of bedraggled birds were mired in the pitch-black oil that coated the shoreline.

She sits down at the kitchen table. She looks out the sliding glass doors and to the east where the sky is just beginning to lighten. Lily didn't wake her much before her usual hour. Deana is usually up early anyway. Sometimes she sits right here, drinking coffee, to watch the sun come up. Other times, especially when the weather is pretty, she sits on the back stoop of her trailer. She sits out there a lot of times even when it's cold, an old quilt wrapped around her shoulders, her warm breath and her hot coffee sending steam into the moist air.

But this morning, she's shivering even in the kitchen. For some reason, she just can't get warm. Her guitar, an Ovation Legend she bought at a pawnshop, sits on a stand in the corner farthest from the window, to protect it from the heat and light. From habit, she picks it up and strums a few chords, but this morning she isn't in the mood, and she puts the guitar down and goes to pour another cup of coffee.

How can she expect Lily to understand how she feels? It's a bad time to make a trip, not just back home, but backwards, back to a place that she has tried so hard to leave behind her. It's not just Daddy, either. She doesn't hate her father, even though Lily and Mama think so. She doesn't even blame him anymore for her being so screwed up. She hates all that pop psychology crap, has no patience with all those whiney people who go through years of therapy and spend their whole lives describing themselves as Adult Children of Alcoholics—adult children is about right, she thinks.

She knows there's some truth to their complaints, but her attitude is, why not take a few months of Prozac and get on with it? Her father was just screwed up, too, had his own demons. What did he ever know but poverty and despair? If he's her excuse, what's his?

When she was a child, she used to think she could take care of her mother by taking care of Wayman. Sometimes she'd wait up with her mother until he came home. A few times, she followed him at night to the places where he liked to go drinking. Once or twice, she hid in the dark that pooled beneath the trees, standing sentry until he was ready to go home. It was as if, standing in the shadows, watching him play music with his friends under a yellow porch light, moths fluttering around his head, she might unravel the mystery at the heart of him that made him what he was. Later, she decided that maybe it wasn't mystery, but just weakness, that he had the same kind of mindless attachment to misery that makes a kid pick the scabs off sores just to watch them bleed.

Once, in freshman biology, the teacher showed the class a slide of the creatures living at the base of our eyelashes. Just imagine, the woman said, this whole microscopic world—no, these microscopic worlds—and we don't even realize they exist until we look at them through a special lens.

But she doesn't want to see her father with a special lens. She doesn't want to see him at all. Even thinking about him is oppressive, like those pitiful birds with oil coating their wings. It might be easier for her if she did hate him, but her feelings are more complicated than that. Oil and water don't mix, for sure, but blood and water do, making you all weak and woozy, pitching into the unknown, unable to keep steady on your feet.

Every time she thinks about Daddy, she wants to—what? Cry? Hit somebody? What good would either one do her? She might as well shake her fist at the moon. As Lily said, he probably wouldn't even know she was there. He never seemed to know she was there, anyway, unless he was pissed off at her.

One night, when she was eight or nine, she found him passed out on the side of the road and sat there for hours with no earthly idea how she was going to get him home. It must have been late fall or early winter, because she was freezing. She knelt beside him on the ground, huddled in an old blue pea coat, the arms slack at her sides like the sleeves of Marion Paluzzi, who used to sit all day in Felton's grocery store, telling anybody who'd listen the story of how he lost his arms. He had been going to check the big fan set up to pull the bad air out of the hole, but he himself was sucked right into the fan blades, as if fate had chosen just that moment to catch him by surprise. Fate, Deana thinks ruefully. How Appalachian. For years, the miners took Marion and made him a UMWA symbol. Every time they had a strike, they wheeled him out to the front of the picket line. Once, ashamed, Deana caught herself wondering what Marion would have done with himself if the accident hadn't maimed him. Misery-R-Us, she thinks. Who would we be without our misery to define us?

"Shit," she says aloud, and sets the coffee cup back on the counter with a sharp bang. Then she goes to the living room, opens the top drawer of the desk across from the couch, and takes out a white envelope postmarked the first of March, over two weeks ago. From the envelope, she lifts two small black and white photographs and then walks over by the front window where she can study them in the light. In the first, her mother and father, young and black-haired, laugh together on somebody's front porch, her daddy with his Gibson Hummingbird guitar on his lap. It's hard to believe they were ever that young, hard to imagine why they were laughing. On the steps, a little to the right, Deana, Lily and Robbie sit, their mouths ringed with Kool-Aid smiles.

Underneath, she finds the photograph of herself and Will, a place and a date scrawled on the back. Brinson Company Picnic. 1979. Other women and children sit in a half-circle in the picture. She doesn't remember any of them, but these babies, sixteen months apart, sit at the center of the picture on flowered laps. Deana's mother wears a shabby cotton dress and looks wilted, but Will's mother's linen chemise is smooth even in the August heat; a wide-brimmed hat shades her tanned shoulders.

The women's faces look strained, as if they don't have a clue about what to say to each other. One is a miner's wife; the other is married to the company's owner. At this feast of fried chicken and Jell-O salad, they are like diplomats from different continents.

The children look solemnly at the camera. At three, Will has already lost his baby fat, and there is something in his thin face already, as if he knows what was coming, as if he holds the future hidden in some dark place underneath his ribs. He sits tall and still, staring out, but Deana has her head bent, wispy curls a halo around her face, one hand raised as if, at the last minute, she isn't sure if she wants to wave or to disappear against the flowers of her mother's dress.

Behind the women, the men stand under a shade tree, talking politics, basketball, coal. Their faces are out of focus, their light shirts and dark pants a gray and white blur. Looking at the picture, Deana finds it impossible to believe that she cannot pick her father out. But there it is. Her father, Will's father, all those fathers, are unrecognizable, massed in the distance like a dark cloud, while their wives and children pose for photographs on metal folding chairs borrowed from the funeral home, like a field of flowers waiting for rain.

Deana's hands are trembling as she slides the photographs back into the envelope. She doesn't need to read the letter. By now, she knows the words by heart. But she looks at them anyway, at the black slope of his handwriting, familiar even after all these years.

Dear Deana,

I got your address from your sister Lily. I told her I was trying to find you for a high school reunion. I knew she wouldn't tell me anything if she knew it was me. I hope you are doing well. My father died in late January, and I was going through some boxes and found a couple of photos I thought you might like to have. The picture of your mother and dad belongs to you anyway. I don't know how it got mixed up with all my stuff. The other one is of us when we were babies. We really go back a long way, don't we? It makes you think.

I don't know if you keep up with any news from Ash Grove. You may know this already, but Cleave didn't just die. Somebody shot him, and his death made me start wondering again about that whole mess so many years ago about my mother. Doc Beecham always swore the union was involved in my mother's death in some way, and my aunt remembered that your father was in the union years ago, probably knew a lot of other people who were in the union, too. Did he ever say anything odd about my mother or father? I'd appreciate it if you'd think about it, see if there's anything you can remember. Maybe he said something and at the time and you didn't know what it meant, but now it makes sense?

That's about it, I guess. I've decided to stay in Ash Grove for now. If you do want to get in touch with me, my address is below. Phone number, too. I miss you, Deana. You may not believe me, but it's true. Call me when you get a chance to. I know we've got some history. That's why I'm scared shitless to call you.

Love, Will

Oh, Will, she thinks, and the world is fluid around her. All she has to do is see his name, remember his voice, and she has taken the bait, suddenly pulled like a fish through dark water. Now there's a song, she thinks. You've got me on a great big hook, but what's a girl to do, but keep hanging on for dear life, trailing in the wake of you?

She folds the letter and slides it back into the envelope. She wishes she could bring herself to tear it into pieces. She did try to throw it away, twice, once unread, and once after reading it. But she retrieved it from the wastebasket both times, in spite of herself, the second time, smoothing out the pages where she had crumpled the paper in her hand. Why is it now that Lily calls, wanting her to come home? All the Brinsons and Wayman Perry have ever done is hurt her.

What is it that Will wants from her, now that she has finally found some peace? He has always believed, since Deana was seventeen and left Ash Grove with him, that all he has to do is wander in and out of her life like a vagrant, taking whatever he wants from her and leaving nothing behind but this awful sadness. Sometimes over the years he has wanted sex; other times, comfort. Often she has suspected him of taking peculiar pleasure out of his power over her, his knowledge that no matter how much he hurts her, she will never turn him away. It occurs to her suddenly that she hasn't seen him in seven years. It can't be an accident that this is exactly the amount of time between biblical plagues.

She thinks of her mother, sitting by Wayman Perry's bedside, longing for Deana to come home and say goodbye. But how can Deana find it in herself to play the dutiful daughter, to pretend to feel anything for her father except pity and sorrow? If her mother knew Will Brinson was back in Ash Grove, she wouldn't even want her to come back. Jolene knows that Deana has Sophie to think of. The one promise Deana made to herself when she decided to keep Sophie was that she would keep her daughter as far away from the Brinsons as she could. Even with Cleave dead, and his secrets with him, all Will has to do is take one look at Sophie, and he can destroy the life Deana has finally carved out for them, without him.

No. She won't do it, she thinks, throwing the letter onto the desk. She won't go back there. Except for her mother, they can all go to hell for all she cares. She is not going to plow that old ground.

Ten

The summer and winter she is seven, Deana loves her father fiercely. He is handsome, and everybody knows it, with a dark complexion and black curly hair. Daddy is laid off and they have moved to Cleveland because one of Mama's cousins is here. And anyway, Daddy is tired of kneepads and low coal. He says he will find a fine job and make his fortune, but in their hearts, they know they will make do here until he gets sick of it and moves back home. He ends up working in a slaughterhouse. When he comes home, his skin is pale, not black with coal dust. When he walks into their apartment at night, the room smells like beer and blood.

They live in an apartment building with no grass around it and no place to play. Most of the time, Mama makes the girls stay inside, but when they do go outside to walk down to the corner grocery store or to school, Deana sees the city in fragments, all brick and wire and pavement. There's a liquor store down the street, and the men who hang around it frighten her. She twists her mother's dress tail into a knot and holds on. Mama has a list of warnings as long as the Ten Commandments. Don't talk to strangers. Don't take anything outside unless you can afford to lose it. Don't get near the street. When we are walking, never ever let go of my hand. She doesn't explain what might happen, but Deana never thinks of disobeying.

Her father is young, then, and mostly free of the weight of his terrible sadness. That year Mama and Daddy love each other just like John Wayne and Maureen O'Hara in those old movies Mama loves. Daddy grabs Mama when the girls are looking, giving them a big wink before he bends her back and leans over her for a kiss. Sometimes on Saturday nights, they get a teenage girl from downstairs to baby-sit, and they go out to the movies or dancing. Mama keeps her hair in rollers all that day and fixes it real pretty. Even on weekdays, Mama and Daddy fill the apartment up with talk. Deana loves waking early in the morning before Daddy goes to work. She lies in bed, warm under the covers, hearing Mama and Daddy's voices in the kitchen. Their words are indistinct and come to her in a soft whirring, incomprehensible as wings.

At supper, Daddy tips back his chair and rattles the pages of his newspaper. Mama stands with her back to him, dicing or peeling or slicing, and he reads interesting bits of news to entertain her. Then, while Mama, Deana and Lily talk quietly, he tells her about his day — about the boss who doesn't like him and makes his job hard, about his buddy Mario the Eye-talian who plays the concertina and wants to get together sometime with Wayman and his guitar. He's a man in love with the sound of his own voice, and he lays his thoughts open for Mama's inspection the way he takes the top off a box of rings he bought once for five dollars at an auction.

Her parents have friends, all of them musical, some of them hillbillies gone north the way they have. On weekends, their apartment is full of singing. Daddy works for a shop that doesn't have the union, and in between sets, he goes to the kitchen for a drink and tries to do a little organizing on the side. "Jolene hates it when I say this," he tells Mario one night, "but you know John L. Lewis is just like Jesus to me." But Mario shakes his dark head, grinning, and backs out of the kitchen, waving a can of beer in the air.

A woman from back home named Eloise comes to stay for a while. She's a distant relative, what Mama calls a grass widow; like them, she's come to Cleveland looking for work. At night, she sleeps on the couch, and during the day she's out looking for a job.

One night Deana wakes up and finds Daddy in the kitchen. He stands in front of the sink, the bare light bulb swinging above his head. For a second she is confused, because she is sure she heard people talking. But then her father turns toward her footsteps, and she sees Eloise behind him, her hand on his arm. Eloise's dark hair falls across the shoulder of her red kimono. It is the most beautiful thing Deana has ever seen, a dark bright red stitched with gold thread and tied with a gold sash. It's silk, she told Mama, a present from a rich boyfriend. Deana sees that the sash has come untied, showing Eloise's slip with its edge of white lace just above her breasts. Eloise is beautiful, too, and for a moment Deana aches with love for her, wanting to be all grown up like Eloise, to be her.

Eloise takes her hand away from Daddy's arm and reaches for the ends of her sash to tie it. Her hands look ugly, raw to the point of bleeding, the nails chewed into the quick, and when Deana sees Eloise's hands, the moment is gone. Deana feels cold, suddenly, and a little frightened, without knowing why.

"Daddy?" she says.

The two of them move away from each other, leaving a little space. "It's midnight, girl," Daddy says softly. Later, when his voice becomes hard and cruel, Deana tries to remember the softness. Sometimes she gets confused and it's almost like having two daddies, and she tries to guess which one of them has come home before she moves out of the shadows to greet him.

"Eloise and me, we've been singing. Did the music wake you up?"

"He's been teaching me a song he wrote. It's about the prettiest thing I ever heard. I swear, he oughta blow this pop stand and head on to Nashville."

"Lot of competition," he says, his voice level and matter-of-fact. But Deana can tell he's pleased. "It's hard to make a mark. What are you doing up, Sissy? You want a drink of water, or what?"

Of course. They were singing. Whatever it was that clenched itself like a fist in Deana's stomach relaxes, and she feels light as air. She moves toward them and steps between them, her arms around their waists, or maybe their legs, she is so little. The kitchen is cold, her little feet like ice cubes, but their bodies are warm. The touch of Eloise's kimono surprises her. Silk doesn't feel the way she always imagined, not like water or rose petals or slick like satin. It feels like skin.

Later, they all sit on the couch and sing "Sweet Dreams of You." Daddy plays the guitar, and Deana and Eloise rock back and forth together, like Loretta Lynn and Patsy Cline. Deana knows all the words. Lord, she's been singing since before she started talking, but Eloise, truth be told, knows about half the words and has to hum along.

In the morning, Deana wakes up on the green couch, a quilt dragged across her shoulders and hip, her cold feet sticking out at the bottom, her cheek stuck to the green vinyl arm because she has no pillow. She can hear Daddy pounding on the bathroom door, then Mama yelling at him to go away and leave her alone. She sounds like she's crying. Daddy pounds on the door until it rattles in the doorframe. Then he stomps away and stands a little distance from the bathroom for a moment before he walks back over and pounds again. "Leave me alone," Mama says again. "Why can't you just leave me the hell alone." Deana doesn't remember what Daddy says. She remembers the dark blue work shirt stretched taut across his back when he lifts his arm. She remembers his fist. Bang. Bang. Bang.

Then he spins around in a fury, grabs his coat from the closet, and goes out the door to work.

Mama comes out a few minutes later, dabbing at her eyes with a little piece of toilet paper. "Deana," she says. "You need to get up and get ready to go to school. I don't know what your daddy was thinking, letting you stay up so late."

"Mama? Mama, are you all right?"

"Of course, I'm all right. Get on up now. Get your clothes on."

"Where's Eloise?"

Mama doesn't answer. She gets a cup of coffee and sits down at the kitchen table. It has a yellow Formica top and chrome legs. One of Deana's friends from two buildings over, a country girl from Kentucky, not too far from Ash Grove where they used to live, says eating here is just like eating at Woolworth's back home, the chairs are so shiny. But when Deana told Mama what she said, Mama got mad and wouldn't let her come over anymore. She said what the Perrys had was just as good as what anybody else around here had, and at least she took care of her house, didn't let her children run wild and beat the furniture to death.

At school, Deana tries to concentrate. She's a good reader. The teacher says teaching her to read was just like feeding a baby with a spoon. But she can't get numbers in her head. Sometimes she still turns her fives and sevens backward, and even though the teacher thinks she's not trying, she is. Finally, at three, the bell rings, and she gets in line to go out the Springer Street door to walk home.

When she gets there, Lily is watching one of Mama's soaps on TV, but

Mama is in the bedroom with one of her sick headaches, the curtains drawn until her room is dark as a cave. She doesn't come out until seven. Daddy's still not home, but Deana has made herself and Lily peanut butter sandwiches. "Oh, baby," Mama says. "Thank you. I don't know how I ended up with such good kids."

They all curl up on the couch together. Deana reads another book in the Wizard of Oz series, Mama reads a romance novel, and Lily colors in a coloring book. At eight Mama gets up and paces around the apartment. She goes to the window and looks out, then to the kitchen to smoke a cigarette.

At ten, without saying a word, she goes to the bedroom. When she comes out, she has on a pair of slacks and a gray sweater. She gets her coat, then the girls', from the closet. Rough and urgent, she grabs first Deana and then Lily by the arms, stuffing them into the heavy wool coats. She ties the strings of their knit caps tight under their chins. Mama drags them out onto the cold, dark streets of Cleveland. Or is this Chicago? By now they all run together, all those cities they lived in, moving back and forth between the north and the hills of Kentucky.

For what seems like hours, they walk up and down the street where the bars are, looking for Daddy's car. Sometimes, catching a glimpse of a dark head, Mama stops and peers into a window. Near a doorway of one place, a man squats on his haunches, hunkered down with his collar up against the cold. Another man, thinner, and wearing a better coat, leans against the hard brick wall. Mama drags the girls past, and they keep on walking. They walk until Deana's heels burn with blisters, and her face is numb with cold.

Under a street light, a group of young men stand circled together, hands stuffed into the pockets of dark leather jackets, blowing smoke rings into the air. One of them whistles, and they laugh, but Mama doesn't turn around. She doesn't even notice they are there.

After a while, Mama drags them inside a doorway, and Deana feels the blast of heat against her cheek. She sees Daddy sitting at a booth close to the door with two men and a woman. He looks up when they walk toward him, his eyebrows lifted in surprise. Then he swings his legs around to sit sideways in the booth, his face white and set. Mama stands there, looking down at him.

"Well, Jolene," he says, his voice soft, that softness that frightens

Deana more than any shout.

"It's time to go home, Wayman," she says, just as softly. She still has Deana by the elbow, and Deana thinks that if her mother lets go of her, neither of them will be able to go on standing. They will have to sit right down in the middle of this dirty floor.

Daddy looks at her for a second. Then he laughs and turns to the man beside him, a heavy sour-faced man with beat-up hands. "You don't know my wife Jolene, do you? Ain't she purty?" He turns back to Mama, but he makes no move to get up. "Danny Parks come in here a little while ago and said he seen a woman looked just like you walking up and down the street, towing two kids. Course, I didn't believe that for a minute. Now I'll be damned if he wadn't right. They done turned you loose out of the looney bin and let you walk the street."

"You coming?" Mama asks. Her voice is level, but her face is pinched and red, and her mouth is trembling as if she might cry.

Daddy stands, lifting his dressy hat, a dark brown Fedora with a grosgrain band, off the table beside his shot glass. He puts the hat on his head, studying himself in the mirror above the table and sliding the hat to just the right angle to suit him before he tips back his head to empty the glass. He twirls his hand in the air. "Later, fellers," he says. Then he loops his arm around Mama's shoulders, reaching his hand around and squeezing her breast, cupping it just long enough to give everybody time to see. "Duty calls."

Daddy swings Lily up on his hip, grabs Deana's hand and heads for the door. Mama follows behind him, but now her mouth doesn't tremble at all, it's set and tight.

Mama and Deana follow Daddy to a parking lot behind the building, and he sets Lily down by the car. He fumbles in his pocket for the key, and unlocks the door. He pulls the door latch up on the back door, opens it, picks up Lily and sets her inside. When he slams the door, the car shakes. He turns and grabs Mama by the arm, shaking her. "Don't you ever shame me again like that."

Mama jerks her arm free and steps back. "Shame you? You had that woman in my own house—my own baby girl asleep there on the couch— In there just now you treated me like some tramp you picked up on the street. Now how in God's name am I supposed to—?"

But before she can finish, Daddy lifts his hand and slaps her hard across the face. She stops and looks at him, raising her fingers to her cheek. "One of these days, Jolene," he says, "I'm either gonna leave you or I'm gonna kill you. Right now, it don't matter to me which one."

When Deana is older, she will think about how she felt the next morning, waking up in her same bed, as if nothing has changed since the night before. Mama's face is a little bruised, and when she thinks the girls aren't looking, she tests its soreness with her hand. Daddy sits at the table, paper spread out in front of him, and when Mama walks past, he lays his hand ever so gently on her hip. When he gets ready to leave, he takes her hand away and holds it in his. He studies her cheek, shaking his head and looking as if he might cry. Then he kisses the bruise tenderly before he says goodbye.

He doesn't drink at all for a long time, not for at least five or six weeks. He comes home every night for supper; Deana thinks they're just like one of those families on TV, the Cleavers except with girls and hillbilly accents. Every so often, he brings Mama a little present, nothing much, maybe just a little box of candy or a bar of scented soap. But the way she hugs him, he might as well be bringing her diamonds.

The Saturday before Christmas, he goes out to find a Christmas tree. He doesn't come home at four. He doesn't come home at six. By ten, they're all worried, and Mama keeps watching out the window for his car. The girls lie down on the couch. Mama covers them with an old wool quilt, but Deana doesn't go to sleep. She lies there watching while Mama drags one of the dinette chairs out of the kitchen and sets it in front of the window. The chair is covered with torn yellow plastic that curls at the edges. Mama sits there by the window, her legs crossed, smoking one cigarette after another.

Deana finally nods off, but she wakes up as soon as she hears the car. She jumps up and looks out the window. Daddy drives an old green Desoto with swept-up back fenders. Late at night, it looks like a channel catfish swimming through the dark.

Mama gets up from the chair and heads out the door. Deana takes her place at the window. Her daddy has parked a good three feet from the curb, first try. He gets out of the car and starts toward the building. Then he turns around, as if he's forgotten something. When he sees how far out in the street the car is, he climbs back in. This time he gets the wheels on the passenger side all the way up on the sidewalk. He gets out of the car again and just stands there, as if he's trying to decide if it's worth the trouble to try to park the car one more time.

It's cold, on and off spitting snow, but Daddy doesn't have a coat on. He shoves his hands into his pockets and stands in the yellow circle of the streetlight. He looks up at the window of their apartment building the way Deana has seen him study a slow red light on an empty street, wondering if he should run it or wait.

Before he can decide, the snow picks up again, swirling around him. He is a statue in the snow, too drunk to know he's cold. Then he shakes himself and holds the keys up to the light. But instead of walking toward the building, he turns around and opens the passenger door to get something out, his coat, all balled up. He holds the bundle close to him and shuts the door. When he tries to step up onto the sidewalk, his toe catches, and he falls. The coat shoots out, a football fumbled, and pieces of paper whirl into the air, spinning in circles with the snow.

Mama is down the three flights of stairs by then. She doesn't have on anything but a flannel nightgown and she leaves bare footprints in the snow. Daddy sits up when he sees her, his knees stuck up in the air, blood from a gash in his forehead slipping down the side of his face.

Mama squats beside him and wipes his face with the hem of her gown. She puts her arm around him and tries to help him up, but he is too heavy, and he starts laughing. Or is he crying? He puts his head on her shoulder. He's just like a baby, and she starts rocking him, back and forth, laying her cheek against the top of his head.

They sit in the snow, rocking, and then her daddy lifts his head as if he's suddenly remembered something. He pulls the coat toward him and opens it like a bundle. The money spills out, and Mama laughs. Some of the bills twirl when the wind kicks up, lifting them into the air, and Mama cups her hands to catch them, as if they were lightning bugs on a summer night. Then Mama and Daddy get up and start picking up the money lying on the snow around them.

Not that she's in favor of drinking and playing poker, but even Mama remembers they have one of their best Christmases of all that year. Deana gets a new doll, a Charmin' Chatty, who says cute things like "People say

I'm precocious" when you pull on her string. Lily gets a tea set made out of plastic so it won't break.

When they head back to Kentucky, to Ash Grove and Cleave Brinson's coal mines, Daddy's girls all wear new dresses, even Mama, and they get a family portrait made at a photography studio before they go. They look so pretty, both sisters wearing red velvet dresses with white lace collars and Mama, a navy blue suit.

Later, when she gets religion, Mama will worry about that money, how they should have held on to it instead of wasting it on foolish things. Anyway, what good does it do, worrying about it now? They don't hang on to the money to see what all it will or will not do. For a while, their troubles will be miles away. They have themselves a merry little Christmas, a merry little Christmas, now.

Mama kneels on the couch, her face close to the window, the thin curtain pulled across her shoulder, the curtain white in the moonlight like a wedding veil. She keeps her hands folded in front her, fingers knit together. Except that her head is lifted, she might be saying prayer.

Deana lies curled up beside Mama. Deana's legs are hot and itchy under the wool quilt. "Mama?" she says. "Why don't you go on to bed?"

"I can't sleep till your Daddy gets home. He'll be tired, working so much overtime. I'll need to fix him something to eat. Second shift's about over. He might have had to work two shifts in a row, lots of the miners are out with the flu. He'll be along in a while. You go on, though. You're the one needs your sleep. You don't need to worry so much. You can't do nothing one way or the other."

But Deana doesn't go to bed. She knows Daddy isn't working a double shift, and Mama knows it, too. Deana pushes the quilt off and gets up to kneel beside her mother, her elbows on the back of the couch. Outside the moon hugs the rim of Jewel Mountain, turning the houses to silver. The houses look like they've sprung up like milkweed from seeds flung on both sides of the hollow at the mountain's base.

"It's a pretty moon tonight," she says to her mama, leaning her head against Mama's arm. "You remember the statues of angels in the graveyard close to where we used to live in Cincinnati? By that big church? When the moon shines on your face, it makes you look just like an

angel."

Mama laughs. "Go to bed, Deana," she says. "Lord, girl, what will you come up with next?"

"I'll wait with you awhile. Besides, if it was summer, it wouldn't even be late," Deana says. All summer long, the children along the Left Fork play past dark. Deana's favorite game is statue. She can stand so still, it's hard to tell if she's even breathing. She likes to pretend she's an angel, too, with the sword of justice at her side. The last time they played, she stood with her eyes closed and imagined herself walking down from heaven on a cloud carpet, her sword raised up high. Below her, all the children who didn't like the Perrys and said mean things about her daddy were lined up. Some of them hollered, "I'm sorry," but she could tell if they were sincere just by looking into their eyes. If they weren't, all she had to do was to tap their shoulders with her blade and they were cast immediately into a lake of fire.

She remembers that Will Brinson had to shake her shoulder twice, roughly, to get her to unfreeze. She looked at him in wonder, as if she really had been an angel out of Revelation and not a child. "I touched you, stupid," he said, glaring at her. "Now you aren't a statue anymore."

She pushed him away from her so hard he stumbled. When he got his balance back, he came at her, head lowered. Will had a reputation for fighting anybody, girl or boy, bigger or smaller, and for a moment she was frightened. But she stood her ground.

"I was doing fine here just being still," she said. "Who said I needed you?"

"I was trying to help you, stupid. The object of the game is to chase the other kids, not stand still like some moron."

Deana looked at him. She didn't know what to say. What could she say? He was right. She was a moron. He was so pretty, she thought. He was at least twelve or thirteen, but he was still skinny with a narrow heart-shaped face, the bones in it delicate as a bird's. His short-cropped hair was as black as the walnuts that fell from the trees behind her house, and she'd swear that his eyes were the exact color of rain.

"I'm silent and silver like the moon," she said. "I'm walking the night in my silver shoes." Stupid. Stupid. Stupid. She was too stupid to live.

Will looked at her a second before his fists uncurled and his arms dropped to his sides. Then he shook his head. "Lord. They're right. You don't have bat sense."

Then he ran lickety-split in the other direction and unfroze Loribelle Branscum, whose daddy was a mine inspector, while Deana stood there feeling even more like a fool.

In his own way, she knows, Will is crazy, too. He'll do anything. For one thing, he paid Loribelle's brother to steal a pair of her underpants, and he climbed to the very top of the tipple one night to hang them from a stick like a flag. He and Henry Mitchell took Will's daddy's truck all the way to Oneida, Tennessee, and talked an older boy hanging around outside into buying them a pint of cherry vodka, which they drank and then threw up in the floorboard of the truck.

Some people say because his daddy's rich he thinks he can do anything and get away with it. Some say he's just wild because of what happened to his mother. The people around here either hate him because of his daddy or feel sorry for him because of her. Deana knows, because of her own daddy, that Will feels better about the hate. Deana doesn't know exactly what she feels about Will. Though he would never understand it, she feels kin to him in some strange way, though they've never said more than a few words to each other. She knows his secret. He lives in the sorry hope that someday he will wake up from some bad nightmare and his mother will be alive again, just as she keeps hoping that her daddy will change.

She falls asleep, thinking of Will. In her dream, the two of them cross the old swinging bridge that hangs over Piney Creek and separates the houses from the school and the Free Will Baptist Church. The bridge swings back and forth and the water rushes just inches beneath them. Looking through the cracks between the planks, Deana can see the brown foam. They walk very slowly, and when they get to the middle, Will sits down and hangs his legs over the edge. The muddy water sucks at his feet. Deana takes hold of his shoulder and shakes it.

"You got to get up, Will," she says.

But no, somebody is shaking her shoulder instead. "Get on to bed, now," her mother says, whispering.

Deana rubs her eyes, and then opens them to look out the window. A pair of headlights sweeps its brightness against the window, blinding her, but she is wide awake now, watching Daddy stumble from the truck and *wave to his brother Al, twisting his hand in the air. When Deana waves, she always waves like the Queen of England does on TV, her hand cupped, waving back and forth in the air.*

Deana pulls at her mother's sleeve. Al kills the lights and her father stumbles from the truck.

"You come," Deana says, her mouth tight and set as if she really is a statue, her face carved out of stone.

Mama shakes herself free. "Go to bed, Deana," she says. She doesn't even sound angry. She sounds too tired to argue, as if she waited up because it is her habit to, as if she doesn't know any other way to be. "I know how to handle your daddy," she goes on. "Got years of practice on my side."

The truck backfires as Al backs down the road, echoing in the hollow like a Fourth of July firecracker. Now that he has remembered to turn his lights off, he keeps them off, with only the moon to see by. Deana's father walks toward the house like a man trying to keep his balance moving from one end to the other of a fishing boat. He puts one foot carefully in front of the other, his hands lifted as if he might grab any minute to a wire strung invisibly beside him in the dark. When he gets close enough, he reaches for the rail that runs beside the porch steps, but he misses and sags against it. They hear rotted wood give way, then the thud as he falls to the soft ground in front of the porch. Mama put out bulbs for Easter flowers there in the fall. Deana thinks that yesterday they were almost ready to bloom, but she wonders now how they can survive her father's weight. He curses softly, in what he probably takes to be a whisper. Maybe he'll just lie there in his own piss, Deana thinks, leave them the hell alone tonight. But already she can hear him getting up.

"Go," her mama says suddenly, the force of her breath hot against Deana's ear, and Deana unfreezes, the way she has heard hunters say animals sometimes do, realizing that they cannot make themselves invisible just by staying still. She runs on her tiptoes, not knowing then that the liquor makes him not only blind drunk, but half deaf, that he cannot hear anything over the clunk of his work boots against the porch's rotting planks.

In the back bedroom, Deana's sister Lily lifts her head from the pillows, resting on her elbows. Deana climbs into bed beside her and slides underneath the quilt, hugging her arms tightly about her chest.

"It'd be nice to get a good night's sleep every once in awhile," Lily says.

From the other room they hear the low sounds of arguing, then shouts like the bursts of gunfire that sometimes wake them in or out of season, though there aren't many deer left to shoot. Something shatters, maybe the coffee cup her mama left on the arm of the sofa. Her mama begins to cry, and Deana imagines her shoulders bunched together and shaking, hears the heavy sounds of her father's boots clunk, clunking across the linoleum floor. She thinks about the heaviness of those boots, the toes reinforced with steel.

One of these nights he's gonna come home all liquored up and kill her, and what if he does? He isn't rich, like Will Brinson's daddy, but he could say she fell; people would just take his word for it. People in the hollow don't like to interfere. Look what happened to Will's mother, her car had been wired with so much dynamite that she had to be buried in a closed casket, but when Deana went to the post office Saturday to buy some stamps, there was Will's daddy at the window to pick up his mail, big as life and free as anybody.

"It's her own fault," Lily says, pulling the quilt up around her ears. "She's the one that gets him started. Who says she has to stay up all hours of the night waiting for him? She knows how he is. He'd probably just go on to bed if she didn't wait on him mad as a hornet. Just gives him somebody to fight."

Deana sits up and swings her legs over the edge of the bed. The floor feels cold against her bare feet. "It's not her fault. It's not. I wish he was dead."

"You don't. He's our daddy. He's good to us. It's only this, and she starts it. He gets to drinking, you got to stay out of his way. What're you doing?"

"I'm tired of this shit," Deana says. "It's about time somebody put an end to it."

Deana feels at the foot of the bed for her socks, blouse, and pants. She tugs the nightgown over her head and pulls on her clothes before she digs in the darkness under the bed for her shoes. When she has slid them on, the pennies glinting up at her like copper eyes, she goes to the window and opens it, sliding it up carefully to keep it from screaking.

"Where you going? You go out that window, I'm telling. It's the middle of the night."

Deana drops to the ground at the side of the house and scrunches down, picking her path. She has forgotten a coat and she rubs her thin arms with her hands. The wind in the leaves makes a sizzling sound, like meat frying, and she holds her hands over her ears, which have already begun to ache in the cold. She works her way around the back of the house, rubbing her hand absently over the head of her father's coon dog, to hush its barking. As soon as she is on the other side of the house, past the windows, she runs toward the road, which cuts between the two rows of camp houses.

Mr. Felton's store sits at the end of the road, where the gravel ends. To discourage robbers, he keeps a light burning all night long. Deana slows to a walk, but the light seems to send her an invitation, and she feels the way she did when she got saved. She remembers the preacher, how he said, "You can't keep waiting forever. Sometimes you just have to decide." She feels that same calm, the same sense of not being in a hurry anymore. She knows where she is going. The important thing has already happened inside her. In a way, it was all done the moment she left the house.

She has to knock and knock at the door before Mr. Felton comes out of the back room where he sleeps. She can see him through the window as he stuffs his shirt down into his pants and zips them, holding the material tight at the crotch to make the zipper easier to pull. What hair he has sticks straight up in the air and his mouth hangs open, like a baby bird's.

"What?" he says, before the door is open, and his voice sounds thick with sleep. He stands looking at Deana for a moment before he reaches for her wrist and pulls her inside.

"Get in here, girl. What're you doing out this time of night? You ain't even got a coat on."

"I got to use the telephone. It's an emergency."

"Somebody sick at your house?" When she doesn't answer, he says, "You know where it is," he says, pointing to the end of the counter.

She nods, looking at the laminated sheet tacked to the wall with a list of numbers. The edge of the paper curls around the tape, and, at the very top, is the number she needs.

Mr. Felton watches to see what number she dials. "You want to stay here till they come?" he asks. She doesn't answer him, but after she's made the call, she goes to the window and peers out between the steel bars. She wonders if these are like bars they have at the jailhouse. She wonders how long they will keep her daddy there.

Suddenly, she isn't sure she wants to do this. If it was as easy as all this, somebody picking up the telephone and calling the police, why hasn't Mama thought to do it before? Her daddy gets on a tear when he's drinking, but it's not like he's a criminal or something, not like somebody all bad. Sometimes he is so good to her, when he isn't drinking, she almost feels like there are two daddies who live with them. She has no way to predict either his kindness or his anger. She tries to make herself fade into the shadows, waiting to see which version of her father has come home. It suddenly occurs to her that she can't send the bad part of her daddy away without sending the good one with him.

It takes the sheriff's department twenty minutes to get there. She watches them drive down the road toward her house, taking the car straight down the middle so that it seems to fill up the whole road. Then she waits.

"You need to go on home, now," Mr. Felton says, after a while. "Whoever it was bothering your mama, I imagine they got him under control now."

"It was a stranger," she says, looking over her shoulder as she stands near the door he has open for her. In the moonlight, patches of ice glisten on the stone steps. "I don't know who it was." She feels something heavy fall across her shoulders, an old black coat. The collar is scratchy where it bunches up around her neck.

"You can bring it back tomorrow," Mr. Felton says. Then he laughs. "Or today, I guess it is now," he adds, waving his arm in an arc to take in the whole of the sky, which has begun to lighten at the edges of the mountains to the color of a nickel that has lost its shine. "The days and nights all run together when you get old as me."

The sheriff's car pulls out as Deana walks back toward her house. She keeps her head down, pretending not to see it, but just as it passes, she catches a glimpse of the cage between the front and back. She wants to look in and see if her father is behind it, but she doesn't dare, she will have to say she doesn't mean it if she sees him, he will look small, and his smallness will make her pity him and be scared of him at the same time. She is so heavy with the weight of what she's done, it seems as if she has swallowed the darkness that lingers just at the tree line where the mountains stain the brightening sky like a purple bruise. The shadows press against her ribs, and she wants nothing more than to lie down in the dirt at the side of road, and, cold as it is, to sleep.

The house is silent. She slips around it anyway, thinking she can go in the same way she left. But the window is shut tight, and she can't raise it. She rattles it a little, trying to wake Lily, but though she can see her sister's hip curved like a heart under the blanket, she can't get Lily to hear.

At the front of the house, she walks as quietly as she can across the porch. She turns the doorknob in slow motion, but the door won't budge, either. She leans against it, wanting to knock, but she is afraid of what might happen, though she isn't sure what there is to be afraid of with her father gone.

She sits with her back against the door and watches the sky brighten. She doesn't know how long she's been there when the door opens and she falls backwards. Her mother looks down at her, and then walks away, leaving the door gaping. Deana hasn't realized how cold she is until she feels the heat from the cook stove. She closes the door to keep the warm air in and watches her mother take the coffee out of the white cabinet and set it on the table.   Mama doesn't look at Deana. "You'd better go on in the bedroom with Lily," she says. "It's time for me to wake your daddy." Her voice is as hard and flat as a stone.

"Is he still here?"

Her mother's eyes flare up for a moment, like the thin blue flames when she adds two sticks of kindling to the heat stove. "Why wouldn't he still be here?"

She sits down at the table and leans over, her head in her hands. She looks like the picture hung over the green chair in the living room, the old man with praying hands. Deana knows she should be scared now, but she doesn't feel anything except the way her skin aches as the cold leaves it.

She crosses the kitchen and stands behind her mother's chair. "I was afraid he was gonna hurt you," she says in a whisper. "Please don't be mad."

"I'm not mad," her mother says, but she still doesn't turn around.

Deana raises her hand toward her mother's shoulder and then lets it drop, feeling that something has flooded between them, impassable as the river when it crests in the spring time.

When Mama does raise her head, she looks toward the window, at some place Deana can't see. "You're too hard on people, Deana. He's never hurt me bad, not really. There's so much you just don't understand."

She sighs, getting up to fill the aluminum coffee pot. She sets it on the back burner of the stove. "And besides," she adds, her back to her daughter, "nobody asked you to do it. What made you think any of this was up to you?"

Deana has just fallen into a solid sleep when he wakes her, the flashlight shining into her eyes. She can tell from the smell that he's been drinking, but he's too calm to be drunk yet. His eyes, even in the shadows, have that soft, foggy look, and she knows it will be awhile yet before he gets angry. Even so, fear twists in her belly, sharp as hunger, and she tries to lie very still.

"Get up," he says, and then, when she doesn't move, a little more insistently, "Get up."

She swings her legs around to the side of the bed. He bends to pick up her shoes and hands them to her, watching her put them on. Then he grabs her arm and pulls her up. "I got to get my clothes, first," she says, resisting.

He takes her coat from the rail at the foot of the bed. "Ain't nobody going to see you."

They go out the front door into the moonlight. Her father still has hold of her arm, though she is resigned to going wherever he wants her to. He takes long strides and she has to walk in double-time to keep up. She wants to ask where they're going, but she's afraid to. He won't hurt me, she thinks, but she sees the glittery cap of the whiskey bottle sticking out of the pocket of his plaid work coat, and she doesn't know what he will do. She had tried to stay away from him after last night. He was so calm at supper that she thought maybe her mother had found some way to protect her, that maybe he didn't know why the deputies came.

They pass Felton's store, on fire with lights, and head for the footbridge. There she has to walk behind him because the planks are narrow, but he still has hold of her arm, half-dragging her behind him. The river is shrunk to the size of a creek this time of year, but the water catches the moonlight, turning it to diamonds. Her teacher at school has told her that if they leave the coal in the ground long enough, it will turn into diamonds, that both had started out as ferns that got buried and turned harder and harder with the passage of time.

Across the bridge, her father heads down the right fork of the river, not up the hill toward the church and the school. Farther up, surrounded by oak trees, stands the big white house Cleave Brinson built for his bride from Virginia and where Will and his father now live alone. On this side, the mountain has been carved out and the high wall looms over them. A little farther down, she sees the tipple and the coal stockpile, shining in the moonlight like a small black mountain.

They round a steep hill that has a few scrub pines studded in the side of it like pins in a pincushion. A sign next to the haul road says it leads to Black Jack No. 4, and trespassers will be prosecuted. Her father has started to breathe heavily, but he doesn't slow down. After they go another quarter of a mile, they come to a large clearing.

Their feet sink a little into the gray mud. A hole as long as a house, but only as tall as Deana's shoulder, gapes likes a black mouth in the high wall.

Her father stops. "See there? No. 4's been shut down while Brinson gets a new one faced up."

A yellow bulldozer sits to the left of the opening, its blade pointed at them. She wants to ask, Why are we here, but her voice and her thoughts do not seem to have any connection. She isn't even scared anymore. Her brain is as numb as her fingers. Everything here is strange to her. They might as well be on the moon.

The sound of the truck grinding its gears startles her and she jumps, but her father puts his hand on her shoulder.

"That'll be the night watchman on his rounds."

The truck swings around the hill and lights up the high wall faintly with its one good headlight. Deana sees the gleam of a shotgun barrel before the man hangs his head out the window, his face shadowy under the bill of his cap.

"Hells' bells, Nichols," her father says before the man in the truck has a chance to say anything. "Don't be apointing that thing at me."

"Is that you, Wayman Perry?"

Her father takes his cap off. His black hair is matted to his head, and his forehead is whiter than the rest of his face. "It's me."

"What in the name of sin are you doing out here this time of night? Who's that with you? Is that a girl?" Deana heard the laughter in his voice. "This ain't much of a place for no romantic rondayvouz."

Her father moves aside so that Deana is no longer hidden behind him. "This is my youngest girl, Nichols. You've seen her up at Felton's store."

Nichols peers at her through the darkness, and his mouth closes over the smile. "What are you doing up here?"

"You're not going to shoot me for taking a short cut through here?"

"I ain't supposed to let nobody around here at night."

"It ain't like I've not been in here before," her father says. "I don't intend to bother nothing." He pulls his pockets outside his coat. "I ain't got any dynamite." He laughs. "Anybody ever blow this place up, I'd start looking up yonder first." He nods in the direction of Brinson's house.

"I'm thinking," the man says. "I don't reckon there's anything up here you could steal. 'Less'n that girl can carry the bulldozer down on her back. Nichols moves the gun and hangs it on the rack in his back window. "Don't stay up here all night," he says. The gears grind as he puts the truck in reverse, and they watch his taillights disappear.

Deana's father takes her arm again, his hand so tight that it hurts. "Why'd you call the sheriff on me last night?"

"I thought you was gonna hurt Mama."

"You know'd I wouldn't hurt her. How many fights we been in? And she's never been bad hurt, has she? No, it's something else between you and me," he says. He has started walking again, and he pulls the bottle out of his pocket and takes a long drink. "You all got it easy, you know that? You got it easy because I come down here ever day that these mines are running coal. You think I got it easy?"

Deana's face aches in the cold, and she has started to be afraid again. "I never said you had it easy," she says, in a whisper.

"You're damn straight." They stand at the opening now. "You might as well get on your knees. This is low coal." He lifts his hand toward the darkness. "On in there's the face."

She tries to think what will turn him around. Her mouth crumples and

Ash Grove

starts to tremble a little, but she squeezes her lips together and clenches her fists, hidden in the pockets of her coat.

"I got something to show you," he says. "You know everything, don't you? Well, I'm gonna show you something you don't know. It's time you learned to think about somebody besides yourself."

The floor of the mine is wet and cold, though except for the dampness, the air is warmer here than outside in the wind. Under the coat, Deana still has on her nightgown and the rocks press into her knees. As she crawls forward into the dark, she grows lightheaded and feels herself spinning, but every time she stops, she feels her father filling up the space behind her, forcing her to go on.

She hears a rat-tat-tat sound, something scuttling, and stops again. "Most likely rats," her father says. "Well, we got rats in here, least we know the air's good."

She crawls a few feet further and stops to rest. She tries to get her breath, waiting for her father's hand to nudge the back of her thigh. When she realizes he isn't behind her anymore, she feels her lungs swell, as if she is swimming underwater and can't find her way to the top. She feels herself turning and turning in the dark, clawing at the sides of the rock as frantically as a blackbird they heard trapped inside the stove pipe last summer. In panic, the bird beat the thin metal with its wings. Lily heard the flapping before their mother got the fire started for breakfast, but it didn't matter that the pipe was cold. By the time Mama got the sections of it apart, the bird was dead.

"I won't do it again, Daddy," she tries to say, but she can't get the words out, now that she is ready to say them, and she is sorry, sorry that she told on him, sorry that she never lets him make her cry. She can look him straight in the eye, the thin switch stinging her legs, and not whimper.

You think you're too good to cry, he says. She stares at him, curled up at his feet like an animal, and watches the hand with the switch drop to his side, limp as the arm of a puppet in a show she saw one time at school.

She brings her hands out of the darkness and presses them against her face, forcing herself to lie still. They burn where she has scraped away the skin. She isn't crying now, either, but she hears sounds that must come from her, though they don't shape into any words or have any meaning that she knows. I'm sorry, I'm sorry, I'm sorry, she thinks, willing him to come back for her, thinking of the tears she will give him, now and forever, if he will only come back and take her out of this place. This is worse than anything, this darkness. She will do anything to leave it; she will do whatever he wants.

Eleven

Will wakes just as the sky above the mountains is brightening. It's nearly ten, but daylight comes late to the mountains, especially in winter. He goes barefoot down to the kitchen. Betsy is nowhere to be found, but she has left him a freshly brewed pot of coffee on the counter. He is so glad he convinced her to come back and stay with him for a while. He was so lost during the weeks following the funeral, but he knows he's selfish to have called to ask her. Without her, he doesn't know if he would have had the will to sort through the mountains of papers his father left behind.

He pours himself a cup of coffee and then wanders into Cleave's den to use the phone. He still feels thick headed from the beer last night, and his hand trembles a little as he lifts the receiver and dials. When she says hello, Katherine's voice is still heavy with sleep, and he frowns with irritation at his own weakness. He should never have called her so early. She never gets up until at least ten, and he knew she would still be sleeping. He is relieved that she is the one to answer the phone, and not Dan, her husband.

"Hello, love," he says, imagining how warm it would be in the bed beside her, her red hair loose and tumbled from sleep. It would be nice, he thinks, to be lying beside anyone, not barefoot and lonely in this cold house. "Miss me?"

"I'm sorry," she says. "Mitzi?" She sounds wide-awake now. "Mitzi's still asleep. Can you call back later?"

Now he knows that Dan must have been out on call last night, and is sleeping in this morning beside his wife. His wife, and not Will's, no matter how many times they have lain together in Dan and Katherine's bed.

"Call back at ten," she says. "I'm sure she'll be up by then."

He stands there for a second. Usually, in these circumstances, he will say something sexy to her, about the way the fragrance of her hair is an aphrodisiac, or the way the skin in the fold of her thigh feels like silk. Both of them like playing little games like that, the danger of it, and he has always known that she is just as likely to turn, aroused, into the arms of her husband as she is to lie there pining for Will. Katherine is not the pining type.

But this morning, the thought of Dan in the warm bed beside her stings him, and he can't think of what to say. He cradles the receiver without saying anything, and goes back to the kitchen to wait for Betsy. Where can she be? He knows she's awake, or there wouldn't have been any coffee.

He pours himself another cup and leans against the counter. He feels depressed, but surely, he thinks, not about Katherine. He doesn't know why he is upset. He has always found his relationship with Katherine to be a fine bargain, though he doesn't suppose he can call what they feel for each other love. He met her, as he has met a long line of women, when he was landscaping around her pool. She is six or seven years older than he is, though she won't tell him exactly how old. She's on her second marriage.

She is intelligent, but bored, though Will thinks that these days boredom is another name for laziness. Katherine has affairs the way some people watch television, out of lethargy. Will has never felt guilty about sleeping with married women, Katherine or anyone else. He figures he recharges their batteries, makes them feel exciting again, and by the time he's bored himself, they'll be just as ready as he is for both of them to move on.

Not that it always works out so smoothly. A few years back, a woman he slept with three or four times thought she was in love with Will and confessed everything to her husband. When her husband threw her out, she showed up at the door of Will's trailer, suitcase in hand. He let her stay there a day or two, but they were both miserable, and for the first time since Deana, he realized how much trouble a woman can be when she thinks she loves you.

"How can you be so cruel?" she asked him, the day she came back from a walk to find her suitcase packed and waiting by the door. "How could I ever think I was in love you?"

But he didn't feel cruel. He just didn't believe her tears. She called him once or twice afterward. She said she needed to see him to get "closure" and used some other bullshit pop psychology jargon. She came over one last time; they got stoned, and the sex was hot, quick, and angry. The last time he talked to her she said she was in counseling with her husband. Poor bastard.

In a few months, he will turn thirty-six. Katherine is not the first woman to tell him he has never really grown up. He doesn't have many arguments in his defense. He has a business, but it's seasonal, and he's never had medical insurance or saved a penny for retirement. He always knew he had money coming from his father, and sooner or later, from Grandfather Connelly, but he doesn't suppose a grown-up would count on that. He doesn't have a wife, or a child. He's never wanted to be tied down, to give anyone the power to hurt him. But sometimes he's wanted something he can't put a name to, somebody to tell him to be careful in the morning, maybe, or someone he can call without being afraid a jealous husband is listening on the other line.

He used to find himself dialing Katherine's number day or night, just to hear her voice on the other end of the line, but just as often he had trouble recalling what she looks like. It helps that he and Katherine are so much alike. "We're like nuts," she said once. "There's a tough old shell to break before you can get close to either one of us. Only thing is, I'm not sure there's enough meat at the center to make it worth the trouble."

The telephone rings again at a quarter of ten. When he reaches for the receiver, he thinks—hopes—at first that it's Katherine returning his call. But then he remembers that she was gone on a cruise with her husband when he heard the news about his father. You can't exactly call a woman who is married and leave a message on her answering machine. Why should she call him? Until this morning, she hadn't heard from him in three months, and besides, she couldn't call him if she wanted to. She has no earthly idea where he is. He knows it isn't Deana, either. Writing to her had been a long shot at best, and he isn't surprised she hasn't called or written him.

It isn't Deana or Katherine. It's Doc Beecham. "Will?" he says. His voice is excited, and he doesn't give Will time to respond before he goes on. "You will never believe what happened. Never."

My mother, Will thinks. He's found out something about my mother. But he doesn't say anything.

"Will? Are you still there?"

"I'm still here."

"Listen. I just got a phone call from the sheriff's office. I'm telling you. You're not gonna believe it."

Doc waits. Sometimes, Will thinks, Doc is just like a child. "What won't I believe?"

Doc stops to cough, but when he speaks, his voice is full of excitement. "They picked up Junior Messer. You'll never guess where."

Will feels his heart sink just a little. Of course, the news would be about Cleave. "I don't guess so. But I'll bet he was miles away from here."

Doc makes a little strangling sound in the phone. Is he coughing again or is he laughing? "No, no, no! Not even one mile. They caught him last night out in the woods behind your place. Had him a regular little campsite set up. Somebody saw his fire and called 911. When the deputies went out there, he didn't even try to run off."

"You're right. I couldn't have guessed this news in a million years. I always thought that was a big joke, that the criminal always comes back to the scene of the crime. Of course, I remember Junior being pretty dumb."

"Oh, it gets better. He's even dumber than that. He's been shooting his mouth off since they've had him in custody. Apparently, Junior doesn't even deny shooting Cleave. Says he'll tell the whole story, soon as they let him call a lawyer. And get this. He says you're the only one he'll talk to till the lawyer comes."

"Me," Will says, startled. "Why would he want to talk to me?" Will hears Betsy coming down the stairs. He turns, puts his hand over the receiver and says, "It's Doc."

"I don't know," Doc says. "But I figured you'd want to know what all's going on. You are going to go over there and talk to him?"

"No," Will says, startled. "Why would I?"

"Why would you? Listen, Will, if you're the only one he'll talk to—Well, that's something you have to decide. I'm not going to try to tell you what to do. Oh, there's something else, too. Something he said to the sheriff when they brought him in. Do you know anything about Cleave being sick before he died?"

Will shakes his head, considering. "No. But we didn't exactly stay in touch. I might go six months—more sometimes—without talking to him. Besides, you'd think if he had any kind of health problem, you'd know it if anybody did."

"That's what I thought, too. But if he was sick, I don't know a thing about it, and me a doctor and his friend. How can you stand not to go in and talk to Junior and hear what he has to say? It's got to be one hell of a story."

"That's probably all it is, too, some big story Junior made up to cover his ass."

"Well, I couldn't stand not to hear it, if it was me. If you do go over there and find out anything, you let me know."

"I will. Of course, I will. I'm glad you called to tell me."

Will hangs up the phone and turns toward his aunt. She has on a powder blue sweat suit and house shoes. In this light, she looks older, but maybe because she's tired. There are dark circles under her eyes and she has her hair pulled back into a tight ponytail.

"I wondered where you were," he says. "It kind of worried me. You never used to sleep late. I almost went up to check on you, but then I thought better of it. I thought maybe you made the coffee and just went on back to bed. I didn't want to take a chance on waking you up."

"That's just what I did. I got up early, but I had a headache. I thought maybe if I laid back down for a while it might go away. Did you say that was Doc on the phone?"

He nods. "He says he just got a phone call from the sheriff's office. Seems they caught Junior Messer. Right behind the house here, in the woods, Doc says."

"Behind the house? Lord have mercy, what was he doing out there?"

"I don't know. And get this. Doc says Junior admits to shooting Cleave, but he says he's not going to talk to anybody about it before he talks to me."

"To you? It seems to me you're the last person Junior would want to see. I don't know how he could look you in the face."

He shrugs. "That's what I think, too."

"Are you going over there?"

"I don't want to, but if I'm the only one he'll talk to— I have to admit,

I am kind of curious about what he's got to say."

"Well, I guess so. Do you want me to get you a cup of coffee while you think about what you're going to do?"

He shakes his head. "I don't guess I have to think about it, and if I'm going, I'd just as soon go on over there to the jail and get it over with. I will take a cup of coffee with me, though," he says, following her into the kitchen.

"Listen, Betsy," he says, watching her pour coffee into a stainless steel traveler's cup and put the top on. "Doc said something else. Do you know anything about Cleave being sick?"

"Sick?" She shakes her head. "No. But I didn't hear from your father much. Why? Did Doc say Cleave had been sick?"

"No. It's something Junior Messer said."

"Well, if Doc didn't know, I sure wouldn't have. I didn't think there was anything about Cleave Doc didn't know. They might as well have been joined at the hip with duct tape."

She hands him the coffee and pours herself a cup. "This has got to be hard for you, seeing Junior. Do you want me to go down there with you?"

"No. You don't feel like going. The funny thing is, now that I think about it, I guess I really am looking forward to seeing Junior. This thing—his murdering Cleave—it just doesn't make any sense. It hasn't from the very beginning."

Betsy looks at him quizzically, stirring cream into her dark blue mug. "Since when did murder ever make sense? We're not exactly talking MENSA material here."

"I know Junior's stupid. He likes to drink and grow a little dope, but he's not a killer. And you talk about somebody being stuck to my dad with duct tape, what about Millard Messer? Millard was always a scab. With Millard sick, the Messers might have been glad to get some money out of Brinson Mining, but Cleave treated Millard all right. There was no bad blood between the two of them, not that I ever knew of. No. I'm telling you, something's not right here."

"Maybe Junior's just mean, Will. Some people are. Anyhow, I didn't know you could tell by looking whether somebody was a killer or not."

"Well, obviously not, or I'd know what happened to my mother." Betsy lets that one pass. Then she puts her coffee down on the counter and stands thoughtfully, arms crossed. "You know Junior's always been a bully. No. You're wrong. I think that's just what he'd do, hide in the bushes and shoot a man in his bathrobe out to get the morning paper. As far as I'm concerned, I'm glad they caught him. Makes me feel eerie, though, knowing he was so close by. I didn't sleep a wink last night. I guess that's a good thing. If he'd come in the house here, I'd have heard him. Almost makes me glad to be headed back to Virginia. I just wish I wasn't leaving you behind."

Will is lifting his jacket from the chair where he hung it last night, but he stops for a second, startled, looking at her. "I guess I should have known you'd have to go back."

She takes a sip of her coffee and doesn't say anything.

Will folds his jacket, draping it across his arm, and picks up his coffee cup again. He looks at Betsy for a long moment. "Why do you have to go?" he asks. "Listen. I've been thinking. There's a lot here to take care of here. I don't know what all needs to be done. I'm probably going to have to stay here, for a while anyway. Frank can hire some extra help this spring to take up the slack. What I was thinking is, why don't you just stay here with me? It's not like I don't have room."

She looks at him, then. "Oh, honey, I'd love to stay here with you longer, but I can't. I have your grandfather to tend to. You saw how frail he was at the funeral. There's an LPN who helps me out—she's staying with him now, and a friend of mine from church checks in on him every now and then—but I can't be gone for too long at a time. I think it's a real good thing you're going to stay here, though. I used to think you ought to get as far away from here as you could, just forget about all that happened so long ago. This house—it's almost haunted somehow. But I've changed my mind. I don't know if you're ever going to be happy unless you finally figure out what happened here."

"This is a lot of house to be alone in. I'll feel like a ghost myself, knocking around in all these empty rooms."

"Oh, Will, quit being such a baby. I'll come back to see you in a few weeks. Now go find out what kind of big tales Junior Messer is telling."

The truck is cold, and Will sits for a few moments letting the engine idle before he puts it into gear. He wipes the condensation off the window and looks at the house, slightly shabby, with little of the grandeur it had when it was the most expensive house in town, but structurally sound. The place is his now. Cleave's money is his now, too, and from what the lawyer said, there's a lot of it. In Knoxville, he has a singlewide trailer where he lives, runs his business, and on rainy afternoons has sex with somebody else's wife. If he were to die this very morning, who but Betsy would even miss him?

He had planned to settle things and then go back to Knoxville, but here it is almost April, and even though Frank keeps calling, Will is still here in Ash Grove, with all his unfinished business.

Twelve

After work, Deana goes to pick up Sophie. She pulls into the line of traffic in front of the red brick school, turns the car off, and rolls down her window to let in the fresh air. Earlier in the day, it was raining, but now, though the sun isn't shining, the sky has lightened to a pale silvery blue. The grove of pear trees behind the playground is heavy with white blooms. When the wind blows, the petals loosen and flutter to the pavement, piled up against the curb like snow.

The children come out at 2:45, and Deana searches among them for Sophie. She comes bounding down the stairs in front of the school, her small dark head shiny, her little shoulders hunched over from the weight of her red Winnie the Pooh backpack. She smiles and waves when she sees her mother, running down the sidewalk to the car. She starts talking before she has the door opened.

"Wait till you get in, Tigger," Deana says. "I can't hear you."

"We had a GREAT day," Sophie says, taking her backpack off and sliding onto the vinyl seat. "We had a woman come and sing songs with a DULCIMER." It's the word she likes, Deana thinks. She loves the way the words sound in the air.

"Sounds like a great day," Deana says. "And it's going to get even better. We're going to go out in the country to see Suzanne."

Sophie unzips her backpack and digs through her papers. She pulls out a colored drawing and a tattered paperback book. "This is for you," she says, scooting the picture to the middle of the seat.

Deana glances down. "Is that me?"

"Yes. And me, too. See. You have blue hair because it's dark in your bedroom. Don't you think things look blue sometimes when it's dark?"

"I never noticed that. I'll check tonight and see. But you know I can't really study your picture the way I ought to and drive at the same time."

Sophie loves to draw. The last picture she drew of Deana, she drew her mother with a red crayon and her mouth a circle almost as large as the face. Mrs. Randall had saved that picture until a parent-teacher conference. "It's you," she had said, laughing. "I asked Sophie what was that a picture of, and she said, 'It's my mom, and she's yelling.' That child's a character."

Deana's feelings were hurt for a second. But then she had looked at the little drawing more carefully. Yes, she was yelling, but Sophie had drawn little hearts all around her, and then a picture of Sophie herself, small and floating high above it all, her mouth widened into a big red smile. "I make a big impression, don't I?" she said ruefully to Mrs. Randall, who replied, without a hint of irony in her voice, "Yes, I think probably you do."

Beside her, Sophie, chattering away, digs into her backpack again and takes out her lunch box. Deana always sends extra food so that Sophie will have something to eat after school. She's a bottomless pit. In her toddler birthday pictures, she always seems intent on the cake, smearing icing on her fingers, shoving them into her mouth.

What a joy she is, Deana thinks, for the twentieth time that day. Sophie takes such pleasure in everything, even going to bathroom. Deana remembers taking her into a rest area toilet one time, after they had waited and waited for an exit, remembers how Sophie's eyes rolled back in her head for the sheer joy of the release. Until she had Sophie, Deana would not have believed a child could grow up so open and trusting.

It is so scary having a child. Children make you vulnerable in a way you never were before. But it's wonderful, too, she thinks, with an emphasis on the word wonder. It's even harder to have a child by yourself, she thinks, and she can hardly believe how close she came to aborting Sophie or giving her up for adoption. She hadn't had sex in so long that when Will rolled into her life for two or three weeks the spring she got pregnant, she didn't even think about not being on the pill. She shakes her head, still ashamed of her own stupidity. Had she thought if she stopped taking the pill, she would be able to say no to him the next time he wandered into her life? Twelve weeks and two missed periods later, she had irrefutable evidence that she was wrong.

By that time, of course, Will had disappeared again. Deana finally got his number from a place where he used to tend bar in Nashville. Some nights she used to dial his number over and over again, until he answered, his voice thick from sleep. She had it all planned out in her mind what she wanted to say to him, but when she heard his voice, her nerve always failed her, and she'd have to hang up the phone. After a month or two, he either moved or had his number changed, and the tall Irishman who owned the bar claimed he didn't have an address or a new number. Maybe if she had told Jimmy why she needed to get in touch with Will, he might have told her how. But she couldn't bring herself to tell Jimmy about the baby. Will didn't love her. If he did, he wouldn't keep weaving in and out of her life. He would only hate her if she told him, and Mama would be the first and Will the second to tell her that if she was stupid enough to keep loving someone who treated her the way Will did, she had gotten just exactly what she deserved.

Suzanne was the reason she had kept Sophie. The owner of the restaurant where Deana waited tables felt sorry for her and told her about Sister Suzanne. Maybe, too, because he was Catholic, he was afraid she would have an abortion, and, of course, she did think about it. Even now, she isn't sure why she didn't just go to Louisville and get rid of the baby. It wasn't even that she was against abortion. Maybe being raised in Mama's Pentecostal church made her want to pay for her carelessness, and having an abortion meant she was getting off too easy.

Suzanne took her in for the entire pregnancy, and since then, Suzanne has been more like family than a friend. Even after Sophie was born, Suzanne helped Deana get into college, though Deana did not become a nurse the way Suzanne had wanted her to, or a teacher, as one of her English instructors had suggested. Instead, Deana had gone straight through, including summers, to get a two-year degree as a medical records clerk. She enjoys her work, though Suzanne says Deana could make more money and find more challenge doing something else. But as Deana sits day after day, typing in the numerical codes for disease and suffering onto the billing forms, she knows this is as close to other people's heartache as she can bear to come.

Deana remembers her time with Suzanne as though Deana's

pregnancy took place in some kind of parallel universe, or in a storybook, but not in her real life. She waited tables until the very last and stayed busy helping Suzanne in the clinic, to earn her keep. She learned to take blood pressures, fill out forms, and calm panicky parents on the telephone. But she watched her hands work as though they were foreign to her, and when she smoothed her hands across her swelling abdomen and felt the child flutter, it was as though the creature living and growing there had nothing to do with her and certainly nothing to do with Will.

She dreamed at night—disturbing dreams of babies born without limbs or of finding a baby floating underneath the green water of a pond, its dead eyes looking at her. And she daydreamed, though she knew it was stupid, of Will walking through the door, having somehow divined her condition in a dream. Why didn't you tell me? he would say. You don't have to go through this alone.

But the miracle was, she didn't go through her pregnancy alone. Suzanne was there with her at the end of every day, scooting the ottoman from the living room into the bedroom to sit in front of the bentwood rocker, making Deana put up her swollen feet. Later, she took Deana for her visits to the office of a doctor, a parishioner from Suzanne's church, Our Lady of the Mountains, who agreed to deliver the baby pro bono, as a favor to Sister Suzanne.

At five months, they looked at the baby's ultrasound. Suzanne traced the outline of the baby's hand as it fluttered against the screen, so excited that Deana felt compelled to warn her (Or maybe, she thinks, she is trying to warn herself?), "Just because I'm having this baby, doesn't mean I'm going to change my mind. You can't just take it home and keep it. It's not one of your stray kittens."

But Suzanne clapped her hands together in delight. "No, it's not a kitten. It's a baby girl. She's a miracle, that's what she is, and you're going to be glad you went on and brought her into the world. You wait and see."

Two weeks later, when Sophie was born, Suzanne was with Deana in the delivery room, wearing a blue tissue gown and a blue puffed hat on her red hair. Her hair curled around the elastic as though her head was on fire. When the baby came, it was Suzanne who took her from the doctor and brought her to Deana. Suzanne looked down at them, her eyes shining through tears. "Glory be and praise the Lord," she said, clapping her hands together. "Now why exactly," she went on, a little breathless. "Why exactly is it that you can't keep this baby?"

When the tears sprang to Deana's eyes and she turned her face away from the red, waxy, wondrous creature lying warm against her skin, Suzanne patted her hand. "Well. You don't have to decide this minute. I know you'll do what's best for her."

And Deana had tried, though she and Suzanne did not always agree on what was best. In the first few weeks of Sophie's life, when Deana was still staying at Suzanne's, Deana remembers the three of them sitting on the Suzanne's front porch. Deana pushed the swing back and forth, holding Sophie nestled against her left shoulder, over her heart. Framed by the porch posts, the night sky filled up slowly with lightning bugs and stars.

"You know you should tell him," Suzanne said.

Deana pulled the blanket up to cover the baby's head. "I can't. Besides, what makes you think he would even want to know?"

Deana knows now that the reason Suzanne kept insisting that Deana call Will is because of the loss of her own daughter. Over the dresser in the bedroom where Deana slept were five or six stern black-and-white photographs with white mats and narrow black frames. All of the photographs but one were of children, but even these were stark, the faces ethereal and severe. In Deana's favorite, a little black girl in a sleeveless white tee shirt, eight or ten, and thin to the point of being gaunt, stared out at the camera with a sardonic smile. She leaned back against a white cross, perhaps a marker in an old cemetery, her elbows looped around the crosspiece. In another, a young girl, photographed from the back, leaned out an apartment window, her head lifted as though she were looking for a little slice of sky between the tall brick buildings. She held a white feather in her hand, but on the wall beside her loomed a masculine shadow. Deana still shivers, when she visits Suzanne, looking at this one. In still another, a small white hand with a dark gash across the fingers held a black cross high in the air.

"They are wonderful, aren't they?" Suzanne said, watching Deana study the photographs a few nights after she came to stay with her. "They're my daughter's."

Suzanne laughed at the startled look on Deana's face. "It is surprising, isn't it, if you don't know. But some nuns—maybe a lot of nuns these days—take vows later in life, after they've had a husband and, yes, sometimes even a child."

"Where is she?"

"She lives in Seattle. I don't see her often. She doesn't like me much."

Deana shook her head. "How could anybody not like you? You ought to let me talk to her. Tell her everything you've done for me, how you—"

"She would say I should have done better by her, and that everything else I've done in my life is my way of trying to make it up. She might be right."

"What in the world would you need to make up for?"

Suzanne shrugged. "Like a lot of stories about women, it started with a man. Herbert was—how can I describe him? He was a man with a lot of bitterness hidden under great charm. I never was that pretty, but oh! Herbert was. He had sandy hair that curled tight, and the warmest light brown eyes. I was bashful and had already thought about some kind of religious life, but for some reason I still fail to understand, Herbert just had to have me. He'd come walking up my parents' front porch in the evening all dressed up, carrying a bouquet of flowers. He'd say the sweetest things, kiss my cheek in front of anybody and then smile to see me blush.

"Once we were married, things changed overnight. You hear people say this, that people can just change overnight, and I always had trouble believing it, but it can happen. It really can. Except— Well, the truth is, there were signs all along, I just didn't want to see them. When I was pregnant with Agnes, he was worse than usual. He'd talk about how fat I was getting. How I had always been so ugly. He didn't know why he had married me, I looked just like a cow."

"You should have divorced him."

"It's not so easy. One Saturday morning when Herbert slept late, probably hung over, and I went so far as to put a suitcase full of clothes and the baby's things in the back of the car. I sat behind the wheel for a long time, letting the engine run. Then I put the car in gear and pulled out of the parking space. I drove around for two hours, but finally, I just went home. Where was I going to go?

"I did try to get along with him, but the least thing would set him off. The only thing of worth in that marriage was my daughter. I guess that's why he took her. At heart it was the ultimate act of contempt."

"He took her?" Deana said. "Took her where?"

Suzanne shrugged, her eyes anguished, even after so many years. "Who knew? I didn't have a clue. Herbert was an oil rigger before I met him. He had literally worked all over the world, and I didn't know anything about his family. She was four years old when he took her, and I looked for them for years. Finally— Well, I didn't give up, exactly, but the day came when I realized that I was never going to find her."

"But you must have found her. You have the photographs."

"Actually, she found me. A few years ago I got a letter from Herbert's sister Teresa in Venezuela telling me that Herbert had gotten killed in an oil rig fire. She had been going through some of his things and found my address. Apparently, he had kept up with where I was, though why or how I was never able to figure out."

"Is that where he had taken her? To Venezuela?"

Suzanne nodded. "Herbert told both of them—Agnes and his sister— that I had died all those years ago. But of course, when she found my address, Teresa knew his story wasn't true."

"It's a miracle he was able to keep up with you at all. How old was— Did you say her name was Agnes?" she asked, and Suzanne nodded. "How old was she when you finally saw her again?"

Suzanne's mouth twisted, and she hesitated a second before she answered. "Certainly not a baby anymore. She was twenty-three."

"Good Lord. I don't mean to be hateful, but how could you believe in anything, even God, after all that?"

Suzanne shrugs. "I didn't."

"I'm confused again. You became a nun. How can you say that you didn't believe in anything?"

Suzanne arched her back a little, as if it felt stiff. They had talked so long that the sun had gone down, but neither of them got up to turn on the lamp. "Do you remember St. Peter's prayer?" Suzanne asked.

Deana shook her head. "No. I ought to, after all those Sundays when my mama dragged me to church, but I can't say that I do."

"'I believe. Lord, help my unbelief.' There were times when I thought my heart might stop because it was too heavy to keep beating. I went through the motions of the liturgy. I said the words of the prayers. Finally, I just realized what the Mother Superior at the convent said was true. Faith isn't a feeling, any more than love is. It's an action. Feelings can get you started on the right track, but some days you can't count on anything but — I don't know—putting one foot in front of the other and just going on."

Wednesday is Suzanne's early day, and when Deana and Sophie get to the clinic, they find her finishing up with her last patient. Suzanne is writing a prescription, but she glances up when the door opens, sees them, and waves them in with her free hand. Then she lays her arm across the woman's shoulders. The woman is soft and large, not just fat, but somehow swollen. She wears her yellowed gray hair pulled into a ponytail with a dingy shoestring. Deana remembers her from the days when she helped regularly at the clinic. She is a diabetic with high blood pressure and a drinking problem, and Suzanne has had limited success treating her. She's the sum of her bad habits, Deana thinks, somebody who is her own worst enemy.

Suzanne folds the prescription and hands it to the woman. From the counter, she takes a small white paper sack and gives this to her, too. "When you run out of these blood pressure pills, you call me if you can't buy anymore. Okay? Don't just do without. I might be able to get some more samples. I can always figure something out."

The woman nods. "I don't mean to run out. Sometimes, I just get so down I forget about everything. Hank, he ain't had no work for a month now. We got to eat before we can worry about medicine."

"I know you do. But you have the stamps. Don't let Hank sell them. And the medicine won't do you much good if you don't watch your diet, and that means drinking, too, Lena."

Lena looks away. She shrugs. "Well, you got somebody waiting. I need to get on out of here. You know I do appreciate it, Sister Suzanne, all what you do for us."

As the door shuts behind her, Deana walks behind the counter, tugging Sophie by the hand. "Poor Lena. She's always the same. By the way, who is the patron saint of lost causes? I've got a lost cause of a father myself. I might need a prayer."

"Jude," says Suzanne, putting packets of medicine into the yellowed cabinet behind her. "Probably a cousin of Jesus."

"You're kidding. You mean there really is one? I was going to nominate you."

"Oh, no," Suzanne laughs. "You've known me long enough to know I'm not eligible for any category of sainthood. But who knows? Maybe we're all lost causes. Except for you, sugar," she adds, reaching out a hand to Sophie. "I haven't seen you in a long time. Where have you and your mom been hiding?"

Sophie puts her arm around Suzanne's waist and leans her dark head against the older woman's hip. "Guess where we're going tomorrow? We're going to see my cousins," she says. "Did you know I have lots of cousins?"

Suzanne looks at Deana over Sophie's head, her hand smoothing the little girl's hair. "You're going to see your folks?"

"My father is in the hospital. My sister called last night and said he might not—" Deana glances toward Sophie and then trails off. She hasn't figured out exactly what, if anything, to tell Sophie about her grandfather. Sophie has never known him, really. Deana doesn't get back to Ash Grove very much—at the most once a year—and though Sophie knows Wayman is her grandfather, he's been sick most of the time since she's been born. Their visits to Deana's parents' house have been brief. They've stayed mostly at Lily's when they've gone. Sophie probably doesn't remember much except her grandmother's hugs and Deana's warnings to keep quiet to keep from disturbing her papaw.

Besides, death is such an alien concept to a child. What would Sophie understand if Deana did tell her? Would it scare her? Deana herself remembers going to the funeral of one of her uncles when she was a child and sleeping in a room with ten or twelve children. It was an old-fashioned funeral, one of the last ones she knows of before it became common in Eastern Kentucky to have the "viewing" at the funeral home, instead of letting the body lie in state in the front room of the deceased person's home. Deana was afraid to take a good look at the body, but she sneaked glances whenever she passed by, headed outside to play. She had not known this uncle, an older brother of her mother. It was the thrill of looking at a dead body that left her skin tingling with excitement.

Later, her father had sneaked out behind a smokehouse with a couple of the men who liked to drink. Deana's mother was lost in the murmur of women talk, leaving Deana free to play capture the flag and blind man's bluff with a whole band of wild cousins. It must have been June, she thinks, because the night had been lit up with stars and lightning bugs. She remembers the girls catching the lightning bugs and gouging their tails out to make jewels that glowed on their ears, foreheads and ring fingers until before they went out. Later, her grandmother Dorcas had come out on the porch to hush the children. Deana can still see her, a large-boned woman silhouetted by the light from the open door behind her. "You all hush, now," she had called to them. "Don't you know there's a corpse in the house?"

The children had all run deeper into the woods behind the house, still yelling and screaming, "There's a corpse in the house, a corpse in the house."

"Anyway," she says to Suzanne, "I had made my mind up that I wasn't going to go, but I've thought about it. We're going to head that way first thing in the morning."

Suzanne puts her arms around Deana. "I'm so sorry, Deana."

Deana pulls away with a shrug, and Suzanne adds, "I know how you feel about him. But it's going to be hard on you just the same, no matter how you think you feel. Listen, I'm through here for the day. Why don't we walk across the street to the house and talk awhile?"

Deana looks at her watch. "We can't really stay but a few minutes," Deana says. "I've got some packing to do. I just wanted to come out here to see you before we left."

Deana waits while Suzanne locks up the medicine cabinet and puts away some folders.

When Suzanne turns from the cabinet, she smiles at Deana. "Now I really am ready. Come on, and I'll make you some tea."

Deana and Sophie follow Suzanne out, standing in a bright patch of sunlight on the front stoop while Suzanne closes and locks the front door of the clinic behind her. Then they follow her across the street and up the porch steps of the tiny yellow house. Suzanne leaves her own door unlocked. Deana keeps warning her that this is dangerous, particularly with the kinds of patients she serves at the clinic. Suzanne pushes the door open and flips the switch to turn on the lamp as soon as they are inside. "You do have time for a cup of tea?"

"Do you have any hot chocolate?" Sophie asks.

"Of course. You know I always have hot chocolate. Come to think of it, I'll bet your mama would rather have coffee than tea?" She looks toward Deana, but Deana shakes her head, no, she doesn't really want anything. "Listen, sweetie," Suzanne says to Sophie. "You know where everything is. Why don't you put the kettle on for your chocolate while your mother and I talk?"

When Sophie disappears into the kitchen, Suzanne turns around to Deana. She motions to the chair, and then sits on the footstool close to the lamp, leaning toward Deana and folding her hands around her knees. She smiles and shakes her head. "I'll bet you're really looking forward to this trip. I take it your father is in bad shape this time?"

Deana nods. "But that isn't all, Suzanne. You'll never believe what else is going on. It's not just Daddy." Deana tilts her head toward the kitchen and listens to make certain her daughter is still occupied. When she hears the water running, she lowers her voice and goes on. "I didn't tell you the last time I was out here, but two weeks ago I got a letter from Sophie's father."

"My goodness. Didn't he show up out of the blue!"

"I haven't answered the letter yet, but— Well, he's come back. To Ash Grove. His father died a while back, and he's come home to—I don't know—settle things I guess. You remember me telling you about his mother? How she died and all?"

Suzanne nods.

"It's crazy. Somebody told him that because my father was in the union, he might know something about what happened. To his mother, I mean. I had made my peace with never seeing Will Brinson again. But now that my father's—"

Sophie comes skipping into the room. "I've got the water on," she announces.

"That's wonderful, sweetie," Suzanne says. "Could you get the cups off the hooks and get the rest of the things out, too? There are some cookies in a package on the counter. They're not homemade like the ones Mrs. Napier brings me, but they're good."

"Okay." She hesitates. She wants the cookies, but Deana can tell by the look on her daughter's face that she senses that there must be a conversation going on in here that the grownups don't want her to hear.

"Do I have to eat them in the kitchen?"

Suzanne grins. "Oh, you silly, you know I'm like a grandma, and I'd love to let you eat in here. But yes, you have to eat your cookies in the kitchen. Mac just cleaned this floor for me over the weekend, and he'd be so mad if I got it dirty." Mac is the church's volunteer janitor and helps Suzanne with heavy chores.

Sophie looks doubtful, but she heads back to the kitchen anyway.

"Sophie," Suzanne yells after her. "You can get the things out, but don't take the water off the stove. Call out when you're ready. Okay? I don't want you to burn yourself."

"I won't, Sister."

Suzanne turns back to Deana, then stops, and looks back over her shoulder toward the kitchen. "Won't what? Won't try to pour the water or won't burn yourself?"

"Won't try to pour the water," Sophie yells back, affectionate exasperation in her voice.

"That's good, honey," says Suzanne. "That's the answer I wanted to hear." She turns back toward Deana. "What are you going to do?" she asks, lowering her voice to keep Sophie from hearing.

"Suzanne, what can I do? If I did what I wanted to— But I don't know how much choice I really have. I'm afraid to take a chance, seeing him. It's like he's this huge magnetic field, and even when I know better, he pulls me right back in."

"Oh, Deana. All that happened so long ago. You've changed since then. I've seen it. Besides, you have Sophie to think about now."

"I am thinking about Sophie. I don't want him around her. I don't want him blowing hot and cold, wanting to be with her sometimes, and other times disappearing without a trace."

"But maybe he won't be that way. Just because he treated you like that doesn't mean that's the way he'll be with Sophie. Look at how having her has changed you. It's been a long time since you've seen him. You should try to figure out what you're afraid of, Deana. After all, maybe he's grown up, too?"

"I don't think I can stand to take that chance."

Suzanne leans backward and listens for Sophie. They hear the clatter of dishes in the kitchen. "I suppose you knew when you came here I'd tell you what I think. You know I don't think it's right not to tell Sophie's father about her."

"I can't tell him. I just can't, Suzanne. I won't let him hurt her."

"Oh, Deana. You can't keep her from being hurt sometimes. All you can do is wipe away the dirt and tears. All you can do is help her."

"Help her what?"

"I don't know. Help her understand, maybe. You've already done such a good job with her. There's not a day goes by that that child does not know how much she's loved."

Deana leans back in the rocking chair and looks toward the street without knowing what to say. Why couldn't men be like the Jesus Suzanne believes in, she wonders. Not that wimpy Jesus standing outside the door on those roadside paintings on velvet, or the one her mother's preacher used to preach about, who'd descend from the clouds on Judgment Day like Rambo with an AK-47 to put the sinners in their place. She wished all fathers could be like Suzanne's Jesus, who looked like a builder and a fisherman, who had been everywhere and seen it all, and could put his arm around your shoulders without complaint or judgment and make you feel you had it in you to keep going on. Maybe then she could believe in prayer, could believe that even a man like Will Brinson might have it in him to be a father.

Suzanne reaches across and pats Deana lightly on the knee. "But it's not my decision to make, is it? I'm just telling you that the longer you put it off, if he does find out about her—or if she finds out about him—there may be consequences you've never even imagined."

It is almost dark when Suzanne walks them to the car and puts Sophie in her seat belt. Then she walks around to the driver's side and leans in. "Be careful, Deana. Worrying and driving don't go together very well. You know you and Sophie are just like my own. You call me if you need me. Will you do that?"

"I will. You're the first one I'd call."

From the rearview mirror, Deana can see Suzanne standing on the front porch, watching them until the car is out of sight.

The next morning, Deana gets Sophie up at five o'clock and by six they've got the car packed and are on their way. At seven, she pulls into a truck stop to get gas a couple of hours from Ash Grove. It's one of those gas stations with a fast food restaurant built onto the side.

"I'm hungry, Mommy," Sophie says. "Can we get a sausage biscuit and eat it inside?"

Deana starts to say no, but they're making good time. What's the harm in a little break? And maybe, too, she thinks, she's stalling.

The restaurant is open twenty-four hours, but it startles her when Sophie points out that the people in the next booth are sound asleep. "Look, Mommy," Sophie says. Then she whispers, "They're sleeping."

At that moment, the woman struggles awake, tugging the brown and orange afghan tighter around her shoulders. She sees Deana and Sophie before they have time to look away, and blinks at them as if they are a part of a dream. She is a fat woman with frosted hair grown out long past its need for a touch-up, but her face is pretty and smooth. She has two children with her. The little boy, who looks about four, is leaning back against the plastic chair, his mouth open, snoring a little. The girl, maybe a year or so older, rests her head against her arm on the table. A ragged quilt lies in a heap under her dangling feet.

"Oh, my goodness," the woman says, blinking. "Did we all fall asleep?" She reaches up to smooth her hair. "We must be a scary looking sight."

Deana is midway into a shrug, embarrassed at being caught staring. Even in a public place, don't people expect a certain privacy when they sleep? But the woman goes on explaining. "We've been driving all night. From Houston. We're on our way to Lexington to see my husband's mother. She's in the hospital there."

Deana studies the woman, trying to figure out her age. She is one of those women who might be anywhere from her late twenties to her early forties, though, looking at the children, Deana guesses she is much younger than she looks.

"We were doing fine, then the hateful old car broke down," the woman says. "Hollis—he's my husband—he's over yonder across the road, working on it. That your little girl?" she asks, looking at Sophie, who leans her head into her mother's hip.

Deana nods. "Here," she says, taking a ten-dollar bill out of her pocket and giving it to Sophie. "You know what to order. Just remember to get your change."

"She's a real pretty little girl," the woman says. "She must be smart, too. Mine are wild as monkeys if I don't keep my eye on 'em all the time." By the tone of her voice and the affectionate gleam in her eyes, Deana sees that she means this as high praise. The woman tousles the little boy's hair, then reaches into a large bag by the table and pulls out a beat-up green thermos. "I hate to ask you, but do you care to watch them for a minute while I go to the bathroom and get this thermos jug filled up?"

Deana hesitates. Wild as monkeys? But the woman seems to have taken her agreement for granted. When his mother gets up, the little boy whimpers, waking, and Deana reaches across the seat back to pat him awkwardly. "Your mama's just going to the bathroom. She'll be back in a minute."

He looks at her blankly, but then he follows her eyes to see his mother and relaxes. He is a beautiful little boy, with longish black hair tangled from sleep and bright blue eyes. Irish eyes, her mother would have called them, and she would have predicted for the boy, because he is so beautiful, a bad end.

When the mother comes back, she sets the thermos on the table with a small package of powdered donuts. The boy reaches for them, but she pushes his hand away. "Give me a minute to get them open, Mr. Grabby. We have to save some for Daddy, too."

"Did you say you were going to Lexington?" Deana asks, making conversation.

The woman nodded. "We're not from there. Hollis's mother is real sick, so this time, they just sent her on up there. I hate to be on the roads when it's cold like this, especially with kids. Why is it things never happen at a good time? Anyhow, no need in worrying about it. You know how it is with family. Ain't one thing, it's something else."

"Oh, yes," Deana says, watching Sophie walk toward their table carefully balancing a cardboard tray with a large orange juice and coffee, the paper sack with the food dangling dangerously in her right hand. "I definitely know how it is with family." Deana stands, with her hands out. "You need some help, honey?"

"I got it." Sophie holds the tray at a slant over the table and lets the sack fall from her hand, while the cups teeter dangerously. Deana pulls the sack to the side, and Sophie sets the tray down with a little thud.

"See," Sophie says, in triumph. "I told you I could do it."

"How about you? Are you all from here, or are you traveling, too?" The woman doesn't seem to be listening for Deana's response. She is lightly trying to shake the girl awake. "Sissy? You want a donut?"

Just then a Ford Escort, so faded that it's hard to tell what color it once was, pulls up in the parking space in front of the window. "There's Hollis. Looks like he's got it running. Wake up, Sissy. Daddy's got the car fixed. We got to go."

"That's good. I hope his mother is all right," Deana says.

The woman shrugs, gathering her things and her children out of the booth. "She's old. She broke her hip last winter and it's been killing her ever since. It's just a matter of time. Anyway, what is it they say? Ain't nobody gets out of life alive."

While Sophie eats her sandwich, Deana watches the woman herd the children toward the door. From inside the dirty car window, Hollis peers out underneath the bill of his cap, a day's growth of beard roughening his chin. Looking at them, Deana can still remember all those road trips back and forth between Kentucky and Cincinnati or Detroit or Cleveland. She can still remember the cold feel of the window against her cheek, the smell of cigarette smoke and Kentucky Fried Chicken enveloping the interior of the car in a greasy blue-gray haze. She can still remember Cawood Ledford calling the plays for the U.K. ball game on the radio while her daddy alternately cussed the referees and cheered. She remembers watching her mother tearing open a little hole in the plastic so she could drink her scalding coffee without sloshing it over the side.

Impulsively, Deana feels in her jeans pocket for her money. She takes out eighty dollars, puts sixty back, and keeps the other twenty in her hand. If she gives herself time to think about this, she'll know it's stupid. It takes every penny she can scratch together to keep her little family of two fed, housed, and clothed. But before she has time to talk herself out of it, she gets up and heads for the bathroom. As she brushes past the woman, she shoves the twenty dollars in the pocket of the woman's old black coat, hurrying on so the woman won't know what's happened until she's looking for a Kleenex some place miles down the road. Talk about the patron saint of lost causes, she thinks. Throwing good money after bad.

In the restroom, she rinses her face and looks into the mirror. She doesn't look thirty-four yet, and for this she is ridiculously grateful. Even thirty can be old when people grow up hard and age fast the way her mother and daddy have. You could see it in sagging faces and bodies, the same as in the houses. When she left home—it seems so long ago, another lifetime, almost another person, really—she was running from more than just Cleave Brinson and his secrets, and Wayman Perry and his drinking. She was trying to get as far as she could from sagging porches and skinned paint, from bent shoulders and broken dreams.

She remembers when she and Will had left Ash Grove together in Cleave Brinson's new black Cadillac. "Did you just take it?" she had asked him incredulously, when she met him at midnight at the end of the dirt road a mile and a half from her house. But still, she had felt a little thrill at the back of her neck. This wasn't Cinderella's carriage, she thought, her eyes on Will as she slid into the seat beside him, but it would do.

"I borrowed it," Will had answered, absently, reaching across her to close the door, his eyes glancing to the left side mirror before he pulled onto the twisted highway that would finally take them far away. "What's he gonna do? Call the sheriff and have me put in jail?"

Four hours later, while Will was filling up the car, in a moment of weakness, Deana had called her mother. Listening to the phone ring, she tried to picture her mother, but already, she told herself, she felt so detached. How easy it was to go. Her mother had already begun to fade like the image of a mountain woman in a photograph on a sagging porch with Robert Kennedy Deana had seen in an old magazine once. The photo made her want to cry, without knowing why.

Her daddy answered the telephone, but he wouldn't even speak to her. "It's her," he said, and her mother came on the line.

"Where in the hell are you?" she said, and Deana was startled. Her mother almost never used swear words. "Just when I think you've got some sense, you go off and pull a stunt like this. Are you by yourself? You're not are you? You're with him."

"I just wanted you to know I was all right," Deana said. Now she wonders why she didn't just tell her mother Will was with her. Was it because she couldn't bear for her parents to think about her and Will together? They always made her feel so dirty. They could not understand how much she and Will loved each other. "I had to get away, Mama. I had to. I just wanted you to know I'm okay. I've got some money," she added. "I'll call you when I get—somewhere. You don't have to worry."

"Well, I am worried about you. When we got up and found you gone, we turned this coal camp upside down, looking. I thought you were drowned in the river. Listen to me. You think you're getting back at your daddy," Mama said, her voice low. "But you're not. You ain't hurting nobody but yourself. That boy's with you right now—don't tell me he's not—I've got enough sense to know better. You probably feel like you're Bonnie and Clyde or something. But, Deana, for once in your life, think. Where will he be a month from now? Where will you be when your knight in shining armor gets tired of his walk on the wild side with the coal miner's daughter, and leaves you stranded somewhere without a penny or a bus ticket home?"

"He won't. This is so like you. You always have to see the worst in people."

Her mother sighed in frustration. Deana could imagine her looking back at Wayman and rolling her eyes. "God," she said, "You don't have the sense to walk around in. Ask anybody in Ash Grove whether they'd want their daughter running off with Will Brinson. Don't you have sense enough to know he's trouble, Deana? You can make all the excuses for him you want."

"Maybe you've got it backwards. Maybe I'm the one who's trouble," Deana said. Why had she bothered to call them, to let them know she was all right? They didn't understand anything. They liked it back there in that little hellhole of a town. Most parents wanted better for their children than what they had, but not hers. Oh, no. They were miserable, and they wanted her to be miserable, too.

Through the window of the phone booth, she had watched Will pace back and forth in front of the pumps. Even in the early March wind, he wore a short-sleeved tee shirt, oblivious to the cold. He smoked his cigarette down to the filter and tossed the butt, still lit, onto the concrete near the hose. Even in the phone booth, the glass a greasy partition between them, Deana could see how the energy tensed the muscles of his shoulders and refused to let his legs stay still. She thinks now how, watching him, she had wanted to wrap herself around him and warm his cold arms with her hands.

Deana leans her face against the mirror and closes her eyes. And what will happen now, after all this time? If she sees him now, even with Sophie to think about, how can she be sure she will not follow him, the way the current of the river follows the pull of gravity toward the sea?

She rinses her hands and reaches for a paper towel to dry them. Things are different now. She's a different person, with a different set of values than she had then. There's more at stake. Then, she felt she had nothing to lose, but now she knows better. Surely she's past all that—what? What to call it? Desire? Love. Surely, she's too old to be entangled in those old feelings of longing and despair. For Christ's sake, look at the divorce rate. How can anyone with sense expect that kind of love to last?

But God help her, to this day, sometimes in her dreams she can still remember the way his skin smelled, that rain-washed smell of the air in late spring or early summer. She thinks again about how she stood in that phone booth, so many years ago, looking at him, knowing that no matter what he said or did or was, she would always love him. As she watched him walk across the pavement to the gas station office to pay, lean and loose-jointed and beautiful, she remembered how, at home once, the wind tore an electric cable loose and it blew wildly against the gray clotted sky, twirling fire into the air like a Fourth of July sparkler. The man from the electric company had to stay in his truck for what seemed like hours, waiting for the wind to die down, before he could get hold of the cable and reconnect it to the junction box at the top of the pole. How could Deana make her mother understand that Will made her feel that same sense of danger, the same heat?

But of course she couldn't; instead, she had lashed out. Now she wonders how many times can two people can say the same hateful things to each other. When do they get to the point where the words are blunt-edged and don't hurt? "Oh, get over it, Mama. What are you giving me advice for anyway?" she said to her mother, then. "You'd be the last person I'd ask for advice about men. I can't see you did all that well yourself."

"No. I didn't. But don't you think that means I might know something you don't? I had two kids and no education. You could still make something of yourself."

"You don't even know him, Mama. You don't know everything he's gone through. And I don't care what you say, he's not a bit like Daddy. He loves me. What I think is important to him. I can't just walk off and leave him just when he needs me most of all."

"Need? Love?" Her mother snorted, a sound halfway between a sob and a laugh, and Deana hated, hated, hated her. Maybe that was why she called, she thinks, now, so she could hate them all over again, hate them both, grinding the guilt away like the last spark of a cigarette under her heel. Then she could go on down the road a few more miles, maybe get all the way to the other side of the world.

But her mother hadn't given up the fight yet. "And just how long is all this love going to last? I can tell you from experience, girl. You can talk about love, but you might as well put a pistol to your head for all the good it'll do you, and one of these days, you're gonna remember who it was said so."

Deana takes a deep breath and one last look at herself in the mirror, her mouth twisting in a wry grin. Well, Mama, she thinks, you told me so, and yes, I do remember it was you. Did you think I would be grateful for it? Maybe if Will had stayed with her long enough, Deana would have left and by now she would have forgotten all about him, or maybe they would have just gotten old and tired like everybody else. The way it is now, she can never know.

Because when all is said and done, she wonders, could it be that Will is the true reason she's on her way back to Ash Grove? Not because she wants to do the right thing by her sister, or even to see her mother, and certainly not because she wants to be there to see her father die. That can't be it, she thinks. It can't be. And if she does see Will, what should she hope for? That if he finds out he has a daughter, he will want to be a father and be a part of Sophie's life? Oh, no, she thinks, this is something new to fear.

Deana imagines Will and Sophie tumbling on the floor like puppies, squealing with delight, Deana abandoned on the edge of their relationship, looking on. What if Will loves Sophie so much he visits them all the time, insinuating his way into their lives? He'll be charming and fun, the way he can be sometimes. He'll spend more money on Sophie than Deana makes in a month and treat her like a princess, until Sophie loves him more than she does Deana. Deana winces, finding yet again the petty little truth tangled like kudzu around her heart. No. It's best to hope that if Will ever finds out about Sophie, he'll stay as far away from them both as he can.

She walks out of the bathroom and sees Sophie on her knees in the booth, elbows folded across the seat back. When Sophie sees her mother, she smiles and clambers down, running across the tiled floor. Deana smiles. Sophie is the most beautiful child in the world, beautiful and complicated, like her father, but Deana can love her, at least, without complication.

Sophie leaps, and Deana catches her, nearly stumbling from the force and weight. She wraps her arms around her daughter, and her daughter wraps her arms around Deana's waist. "Oh, Tigger, Tigger, don't bounce your mommy," she says. She jiggles the child up and down, laughing. My heart is light, she thinks, and she knows how corny that sounds, but that's how she feels whenever she sees her daughter, feels the energy that is Sophie filling up her arms. She feels that her heart is light and filled with light. Somehow, no matter how stupid and heavy she is, she will figure out some way to make the world her daughter lives in come out all right.

Of all the questions she has about the decisions she's made, she thinks, there are no questions about whether she made the right decision when she had Sophie. It doesn't matter where she came from, whom she belongs to, or how hard it has been sometimes to take care of her. Deana isn't sure she believes in prayer—in fact, most of the time she's sure she doesn't—but when she looks at her daughter, her heart makes its own prayer—Make me worthy, Lord. Please, please, don't let me screw her up.

"Come on, little girl," she says, lowering Sophie to the floor. "Let's get this trip over with so we can see Granny and Aunt Lil."

"And cousins!" Sophie answers, tugging at her mother's hand.

✺Thirteen

The county jail is a new building of mushroom-colored brick, built to replace a stone building from the twenties that finally fell into such disrepair the state threatened the county with loss of state funds unless it built a new one. Will stands at the curb and looks at the revolving glass door. Did the architect really have that good a sense of humor? He wonders what Millard Messer, Jr., could possibly have to say to him.

The truth is, Will can't believe any of this, not that someone shot his father, and certainly not that Junior Messer did it. Oh, he knows Junior used to be wild. They were in a scrape or two together when they were young. Once, in a fight, Junior was nicked with somebody's broken beer bottle before a couple of men came along to break it up. Will himself once got the hell beat out of him in a bar in Lexington, over some girl whose face he couldn't pick out of a line-up, but he was drunk. If he'd had a knife or a gun—well, he didn't. But that kind of thing happened in the heat of the moment. What is so strange is the premeditation of it, the way Junior apparently stood in the thicket of trees, smoking and whittling, whittling and smoking, waiting for Cleave to come outside.

No, Will can't imagine that Junior really meant to kill Cleave, and that's the only reason Will can bring himself to go through with this visit. Crazy son of a bitch was probably mad about something, just meant to talk to Cleave, maybe scare him a little. Had Cleave threatened Junior in some way, made him feel cornered? Had Junior waved the gun around, and somehow it went off? Shit, Will thinks, even if Junior had meant to kill

Cleave Brinson, he'd have been as likely to miss as to hit. He sighs, trying to get it all straight in his mind. Well, he thinks, there's only one way to find out what Junior did and why.

Will steps onto the portico and makes the circle to the inside. Despite its newness, the jail still smells like piss. Will approaches a plump woman in a gray deputy's uniform who shuffles through some papers at a desk, a telephone receiver held between her shoulder and her ear. "Now where did he say he was?" A space. "You know he's lying through his teeth. You keep putting up with it, girl, he'll keep on."

The woman glances up at Will and motions toward a clipboard on the top of the counter that holds a pen tied to a string and a sign-in sheet. She lowers her voice, as if by whispering she can keep Will from hearing what she says. "Listen, Shawna, I've got to go. You let me know what happens when he gets home tonight. Don't take no crap, you hear me?"

She cradles the receiver and looks up at Will, all brisk efficiency. "Okay, honey," she says. "What did you need?"

"I'm here to see Millard Messer," he says. "Do I sign my name on this sheet of paper here?"

"Now wait a minute. It's not as simple as all that. What reason do you have to see him?" She looks at his flannel shirt and jeans doubtfully. "You his lawyer?"

"No. I'm Will Brinson. But I've heard he's asked to see me."

Her made-up face brightens and then darkens, almost at the same instant. "Oh, yeah. They said you might come to see him. That he'd been asking for you. I'm sorry about—well, you know."

Will nods, but he knows she's more excited than she is sorry about the drama unfolding. Can you imagine his coming to the county jail to see the very man—the very man! she'll say later, probably to the same friend whose phone call he interrupted—who murdered his father.

"You have a seat over there, honey. I'll call back there and have the deputy bring him right up."

When he lays eyes on Junior Messer for the first time in twenty years, for a second, Will almost feels sorry for him. Junior looks like some kind of red-furred exotic animal, peering at Will from behind the jailhouse glass. Don't get too carried away, Will reminds himself. There's obviously a darker side to Junior than Will remembers. And who knows what he was doing camped out behind the house?

Besides, it's crazy to waste too much pity on a piece of wasted DNA like Junior. Even when they were in grade school, every time they played a prank, Junior was always the one who got caught standing around, still trying to figure things out while the other boys scattered to safety. He was never a snitch, though. He always kept his mouth shut while the rest of his partners in crime went about their business. Of course, Junior, like the scapegoat he was, was suspended or expelled.

It never seemed to occur to Junior that there are consequences for being caught. Will is amazed, given the trouble Junior is in, at how comfortable Junior seems. He's looking at Will companionably, as though he expects Will to be here not as a grieving son or a vengeful relative, but an old friend. What on earth is wrong with you? he wants to ask Junior. Don't you have any idea what kind of a mess you're in?

Junior taps the bottom of the cigarette pack and slides one out. He looks forlorn in his prison denims. Will remembers Junior in his better days wearing blue jeans with the knees out, and a ratty Jimi Hendrix tee shirt. Back then he had a bushy red pony tail and sideburns, but now his hair is cut close to his head, the hair curved back in a horseshoe shape around his temples where it has begun to thin. He's still as skinny as he was when they were young, but now Will notices a sunburst of lines around Junior's eyes and a strand or two of gray in his bushy red mustache. The hair on his arms is springy, curling around the fabric of his work shirt where the sleeves are rolled up to his elbows. Junior glances at Will with his head tilted slightly down toward the table. He grins nervously, his own eyes darting past Will's, almost as if he's embarrassed to look Will in the eye.

"Long time, no see, Brother Brinson," Junior says into the phone. He slaps his midriff and then waves his free hand at Will. "I figured you'd be fat by now, like your dad. But hell, boy, you look almost like you have to work for a living, like me."

Will lets the words slide off him, answers as if this is what Junior really wants to know, as though Junior has called Will here so they can catch up on old times.

"I do work hard. I'm a landscaper. I'll bet I work harder than your sorry ass. Seems to me I don't remember you hitting it too hard when we were young. I just remember you making runs up the interstate for the bootleggers and hanging around Felton's shooting pool."

Junior lays his forearm at the lip of the counter and studies Will. He still has the ghost of a grin on his face, but behind it, like a ghostly image on a scrambled TV station, Will can see Junior thinking. "That's cold, Will," Junior says, lifting his hand to take a draw off the cigarette. "It ain't like I was always rolling in money, like you. I have to say, though, you always was good to share. We used to have us some wild times, though. You always had the finest weed in three counties."

Will laughs. This is the craziest conversation he's ever had. What were you supposed to talk about with the man who shot your father to death in his bathrobe? Where is Junior's remorse? Why has Junior asked him to come here? Of all the scenes he imagined after talking to Doc, the real event is even stranger. But he plays along. "We did have some wild times. But I believe, even if I'd have been as dumb as you, I'd of straightened up before now. Don't you ever watch the late show, Junior? Even the crooks in bad movies know not to return to the scene of the crime."

Will sees a flash of anger on Junior's face, but he grins again, covering. "Be the best place to be, I figured. I figured they'd be up north looking, thinking I was long gone from here. Come on. Tell the truth. I bet you never figured they'd catch me."

"No," he says, slowly. " I didn't. Anyway, I thought you'd be up north somewhere, staying with one of your cousins, not lighting signal fires behind my house. Damn, Junior, I thought even you were smarter than that. If you'd stayed up in Detroit—Well, I don't imagine anybody would look for you very hard up there. What made you come running back down here? Why'd you make it so easy?"

Junior grins again. "It didn't scare you, did it? Them finding me in them woods out behind your house?"

"Why would it scare me? I always could beat the shit out of you. But I have to say, it doesn't make any sense to me. Did you think you were invisible or something, out there waiting for the mother ship?"

Junior drops his right hand to the counter, drumming with his tobacco-stained fingers. Then he sits up straight in the chair, looking through the glass at Will, as if he cannot believe what Will is saying. "I didn't think they'd be anybody prowling around back there at night. I want to hide, I figure the last place they're gonna look is back of your house, and I figured I'd see you and be gone in twenty-four hours. And Jesus, you know why I come back. Fuck it. I come to get my money." Junior's voice has risen in intensity and his mouth trembles a little at the corner as if he is trying to hold back tears.

Will shakes his head. "You really are one crazy son of a bitch. What in the hell are you talking about? What money?"

Junior looks over his shoulder, then leans forward and lowers his voice to a whisper. "Don't try to put nothing over on me, son." He spits the low words into the receiver. "You know what money I'm talking about. The money your daddy owed me. He was supposed to put it in a bank account I set up in Detroit, but something got mixed up somehow. I come back down here to get my money."

Will looks at Junior blankly. "Money for what? What in God's name are you talking about?"

Junior stares at Will, then leans forward again, his left arm folded on the white laminated counter. He studies Will for a moment through the glass, then leans back again. He waves his hand into the air, sending puffs of smoke swirling toward the ceiling. His eyes narrow. "Don't you get smart with me," he says, still keeping his voice low. "I'm not somebody you want to mess with."

Will shakes his head. Three chairs down, a man and woman are leaned close to the glass, whispering into the telephone, as close as they can get to each other with a window in between. From where he sits, Will can see a black tear from the woman's mascara marking a little rivulet from her eye to her chin.

Will shakes his head again. "That just goes to show you how dumb you are, Junior. What in the hell can you do to me? You're in the county jail. You think the guards are going to let you out to whip me? And anyway, remember who always whipped who?"

Junior leans close again and winks at Will. "Listen. You don't have to play it tight to the vest with me. It's not like you didn't get plenty. I ain't aiming to take it all. All I'm asking for is what I got coming, what your dad said I would get. I'll be outa here soon enough, soon as I get me a good lawyer. They ain't got nothin' on me, except circumstantial evidence. And you'd best remember, rich boy, I ain't the only Messer in Ash Grove."

"Junior, I'm the last person in the world you should be worried about. What you need to worry about is keeping a needle out of your arm."

A brief look of dismay flashes in Junior's eyes before he tilts his head to the left and grins again. This time when he raises the cigarette to his lips, his hand is trembling. He has to cradle the receiver in the curve of his shoulder and hold the cigarette with both hands. He steadies himself, takes the receiver in his right hand again, and then takes three or four deep draws from the cigarette before he lays it down in the aluminum ashtray in front of him. He studies Will. "Damn," he says, after a moment, in a little burst of air, like a tire deflating. "Damn. You don't know, do you?"

"No, I must not," Will says. "And I don't have all day to waste in here, like you do. If you don't get your story straight, I'm going turn around and go home and leave your sorry ass to rot in here. Let's try it one more time. You hid in the pine thicket across the road from the house and you killed him. Now what exactly is it you think you have coming to you?"

Junior taps another cigarette out of the pack and lights it on the one he's just finished, and then grinds the butt of the old one into the ashtray. "Damn. Damn it to hell. I never thought he wouldn't have left something behind explaining the situation, that even a sumbitch like Brinson would just leave me hung out to dry." He takes a long puff on the cigarette before he goes on. "I'm telling you, now, this is some story. You better listen close."

Junior blows smoke into the air, and as he brings the filter back up to his mouth, his lips tremble. "Your dad, one day he calls me up, says he's got cancer. It's already gone to his liver and he's seen people go like that, and it ain't no way to die, he says. He don't want to wait on the cancer to kill him. 'Man,' I tell him, 'that's hard.' But as you can see, it don't hardly have nothing to do with me. It ain't like he's family or something. I think, I ain't no preacher. Why's he calling me?

"He says when he first found out it was terminal, he decided the easiest thing to do would be to just blow his damn brains out. One time, he says, he took the gun out of his desk drawer—that pretty gun he's got—you know the one? Pearl-handled .38. Sweet. He showed it to me one time when my daddy had to go over there to get some papers.

"Said he got out the gun, then he sets down in that big leather chair behind his desk. He loads the gun. Told me he set there a long time, cradling it, waiting to get his nerve up.

"But then, he tells me, he has a change of heart. He does things that way, he says, he leaves you a big mess to clean up. Now me, I figure it's easy to talk about putting a gun in your mouth and pulling the trigger, but you ever tasted gun metal, you know it ain't that easy to do, unless you're too drunk to know what you're doing. And hell, if you're drunk, you'd probably be having too good a time to remember what you was planning. Cancer's awful, but I can see he must have been wondering, sitting there, did the doctor make a mistake. But if he wants to say he's worried about you instead of his own sorry self, that's all right with me. Ain't my place to point out the truth. Like I told you, I wadn't even sure why I was in on this conversation in the first place.

"'Besides,' he says, 'I do it myself, all that insurance money I paid in over these years, what happens to it? Well, I'll tell you, Junior,' he says, like me and him is old friends. 'It's gone, that's what happens to it. What's the good of that?' he says, and I have to admit, I don't see the point in doing it that way, letting the insurance company off the hook and all that good money go to waste.

"So I tell him, 'I know what you're saying.' I tell him I seen movies like that. Double indemitty they call it. You die of natural causes, you get it all. You die in a accident, you get twice what you was supposed to. But you shoot your damn brains out, you don't get enough to hire a woman to come in and sop up the blood. I see right away that shootin's no good, and tell him so. I tell him what he needs to do is go over a mountain in his car. I can show him how to rig it up, so it'll look like he was just the victim of circumstance."

Junior waits for a moment before he goes on, basking in pleasure at how smart he was, smart enough to give Cleave Brinson advice. "Your dad, though, he don't want to do it that way. 'I can't do it in a car,' he says. Tells me it's too much like what happened to your mother."

Junior studies Will to see if he's taking all this in. When Will doesn't say anything, Junior raps the table once with his knuckles and says, "That was the very minute, I should have backed away. I see that now. I figured I could get me a little money out of it, helping him rig up the car. But if he didn't want to do it that way, I shoulda just washed my hands of it, son. But I don't. I just let him keep on talking. See, what he does is, he hires me to kill him. Says he's gonna die anyway, it'd be merciful, like shooting a crippled horse or a dog with the rabies. 'Only thing I ask,' he says, 'is don't let me see it coming. I might fight to save myself, or I might try to run from you. It's instinct.'

"We figured out the logistics, how it would work, how much, and where he was gonna send the money. Then, I showed up at his house one morning, and I put him out of his misery. Only, after it's done, I head up to Detroit and find out he didn't get my account set up, like we agreed to."

From the street in front of the county jail, Will hears brakes screech, and then a loud horn. From across the room he hears the woman laugh. For a moment, he has the urge to laugh, too. If this were a movie, he thinks, not real life, would it be a comedy? "Now I know what your defense will be. You are absolutely out of your mind," he says. "Of all the stupid stories I've ever heard, this has to be the craziest. You can't really expect anybody with walking around sense to believe this asinine story?"

Junior shrugs. "Your daddy had tests run. I don't know if Doc Beecham run 'em, or if your dad went up to Lexington to keep things secret. You don't believe me, check into it. They's bound to be a bill or something laying around. But I know one thing, you want that insurance money, you got to take care of me first. You don't want me telling all I know. You don't find out what happened, I guarantee some insurance investigator will, or the cops will. Insurance company ain't gonna write you no check, they find out your daddy committed suicide, only he had some help."

"It's not suicide, Junior, if you shot him."

"What about them old boys want to go out in a blaze of glory and shoot it out with the cops? Ain't you never heard of suicide by police? They don't charge the police with murder, do they? Me, now, I'm a poor boy watched my own daddy die of emphysema on account of the black lung. Died gasping for air, and didn't get a dime, not a goddamn dime, no insurance to worry about. You know where he got it, too, he got it working his ass off in your daddy's mine. But your dad, he wanted it quick and easy. You figure it out. You might be surprised how sympathetic people round here'll be. By the time I get done telling my side, I'll be a hero. You just wait."

Will turns around and looks out the window for a minute or two, trying to take all this in.

"You tell whatever it is you need to tell," he says finally to Junior. "You may not believe this, but I don't care about the insurance money. I never did care about Cleave's money. Anyway, even without his life insurance, I've got the house and Cleave's assets. There's more than enough money for me to get by on. To tell you the truth, I don't even know what there is. Don't much care."

Junior leans forward until his breath fogs the glass. "Oh, you care about it, all right—Ain't a man alive don't care about money."

Will shakes his head. "Don't you get it, Junior? They know you shot Cleave. They have the evidence. And this—this wild story of yours—it just makes it worse. You'd be better off just saying you were wild grieving over the death of your own father. You'd be better off pretending you didn't know Cleave was sick. It was bad enough you shot him, but if you'd shot him as a favor—as a mercy killing—you might have got some sympathy. But you didn't. You killed him for money, you poor stupid son of a bitch, and if you don't keep your mouth shut, they're gonna put you on death row."

"You got to get me a good lawyer. You owe me that. You know you owe me that."

Will sighs. "I don't owe you shit."

Will finds Doc in his office. A whole host of doctors—most of them foreign, from the Phillipines, India, or the Middle East—have taken up residence in the new office buildings clustered around the hospital. But Doc still has his old office downtown, near the old hospital—now a nursing home—and apparently comes in every day whether there is anything to do here or not. Will remembers once or twice—when Cleave actually had to have Will with him, for one reason or another—that Doc had allowed Will to sit on the top of the big mahogany desk and play with a stethoscope while Doc and Cleave had drunk bourbon and talked about politics and basketball.

What does Doc find to do here? Will wonders, but then Doc says he still sees a few patients from time to time, probably old friends of his who haven't gotten quite old enough or sick enough yet to move on to one of the new doctors closer to the hospital and the lab with its up-to-date procedures and equipment.

Will sits down in the chair in front of the desk and Doc sits behind it. Will scoots the chair back a foot or so, and, leaning back with his hands laced behind his head, puts his feet on the corner of the desk, his ankles crossed for comfort. He realizes suddenly that this is exactly the way Cleave had sat, all those years ago. He sits up a little straighter, then, and takes his feet off the desk, crossing his legs so that his left ankle rests on his right knee.

"He's a liar," Doc says. "Craziest damn story I ever heard."

"I think so, too. But would Junior be smart enough to make up a story like that? And then, when you think about it, doesn't it sound like just the thing Cleave would do? He wouldn't like being sick."

"No. But Junior's story is still a stretch. I'll tell you what I will do," Doc says. "I was your dad's primary physician. I can call up the hospital and get his records. If he did have any tests run, or any lab work done, I can find out. I can check in Lexington, too. I know one or two docs he might have gone to. If he was trying to hide something, he might have gone up there. He hated going to the doctor— Most of the time, with me, he'd just drop by for some penicillin if he felt too bad to work. Wouldn't hardly even let me look at his throat. He would have had to know—almost be sure— something was wrong before he'd even have had it checked. He had lost some weight, but cancer—? Jesus, that's some crazy story."

On his way back to the house, Will passes the jail again. He thinks of Junior's face when Will stood up to leave, the little bit of fear behind Junior's watery blue eyes, like the dark shadow of a fish that starts to surface but dives instead back into the dark water. Junior isn't as comfortable as he's trying to appear to be. He's scared. As crazy as this story is it sounds just like Cleave Brinson, just like Junior Messer. Cleave always had to be in control of everything, and Junior—? Well, Junior was always too stupid to come in out of the rain. If the story is true, does this mean that Will owes Junior at least the courtesy of trying to clean up Cleave's mess? But even if Will tries to help Junior—and he's a long way from deciding he should—Junior will have to realize that there's a limit to what even the best lawyer in the world can do.

Poor silly bastard, Will thinks. Poor silly bastard thinks because I have money I can get him out of this. Well, he thinks, welcome to the club of all the poor assholes that Cleave Brinson screwed.

❧Fourteen

Deana drives the last few miles to Lily's house in the deepening shadows of the early winter afternoon. Lily and Wes have built a new house since the last time she's been here, but the location is the same. They lived in a used single-wide trailer while they were building, and Deana knows Mama has moved out of the subsidized apartment complex where she and Daddy were living into the same trailer, now set a couple of hundred feet from Lily and Wes's back deck.

She looks over at Sophie, who has fallen asleep with the corner of her plaid blanket wrapped tightly around her hand. She snores softly, her mouth open and moist at the corners. Her right cheek rests precariously against the vinyl of the door, just at the bottom of the window. Deana used to tease Sophie a little about snoring, but Sophie was so offended that Deana finally stopped, though she still thinks it's funny. Everything about Sophie has been of interest to Deana since her little girl was born. She thinks of all the discoveries she's made—for instance, she now knows that for weeks, maybe months after birth, a baby's head smells just like Johnson's baby oil, that a baby's breath smells just like sweet milk for a long time, too.

Deana reaches across and tries to tug Sophie toward the center of the seat. She wishes she had long enough arms to adjust Sophie's head. She can't stand it when her head falls forward at an angle like that, pulling against the fragile neck. Suzanne laughs at her, saying that if Sophie were uncomfortable, she'd wake up and change her position herself. But still, unless they are in a car, Deana always scoots Sophie down until she looks more comfortable. "What's that old joke?" Suzanne asked Deana once. "Put another blanket on the baby. Grandma's cold."

This is a new highway with a center passing lane and wide shoulders. To the left and to the right, newly marked spurs lead off into pine thickets and the curvy precariousness of the old road she remembers from so long ago. Lily lives on the last spur before town, the turn-off marked not just by a sign but also by a pawnshop. Hard to miss, even for Deana.

When Deana turns, she counts six new houses that have been built since the last time she was here. In front of each, straw mulches the mud pregnant with newly sown grass seed. Two skeletons of houses stand across the street behind Lily's, banked by construction debris and churned red clay. She drives past them, into the old part of the subdivision not under the control of the new restrictions—no trucks parked on the street, no outbuildings that don't match the exterior of the houses, and, above all, no trailers.

Though most of the people in the county still live in poverty, she knows from Lily and the state newspaper that a new chicken processing plant has given a few people who want to stay here at least a few jobs, although Lily says Hispanics have taken most of them. The new Federal prison ought to offer some employment, too. The nice houses belong to people like Lily's husband Wes, who works for the utilities company, or the foreign doctors who've moved into town, willing to take jobs even in a godforsaken place like Ash Grove to get a start. The hardy souls still left in town not lucky enough to have a job or a check drive two hours and a half away to work at Toyota.

Lily's house is a two-story with yellow vinyl siding. Two skinny Bradford pear trees flank the concrete driveway, a dark circle of mulch at the base of each. The covered porch has a porch swing half-obscured by a copper trellis that Lily told her on the phone will soon bear the weight of a white-flowered clematis vine. A basketball net hangs above the white-painted garage door, and Deana sees a boy—surely that can't be Wesley, Lily's oldest son, grown that lanky and tall?—standing a little to the side. He dribbles the basketball once, twice, feints one way, then the other, and then drives straight toward the basket. As he jumps, he lets the ball roll off the tips of his fingers. It spins, then drops, and bounces to a stop at his feet. He shakes his head, frowns, then makes a shadow shot without the ball before he picks the ball up and repeats the process all over again. He seems oblivious to her presence.

Deana blows her horn, one short beat and then pulls into the driveway. The horn blast wakes Sophie, who stirs and sits up rubbing her eyes. "We're here, sweetie," Deana says. "Look at cousin Wesley. Hasn't he gotten big?"

The horn must also have announced their arrival to Lily, who comes out the front door and watches Deana pull into the driveway. She is wearing jeans and a Kentucky blue sweatshirt screen-printed with a wildcat on the front. She has two-year-old Troy on her hip.

"You got your hair cut," Deana says, as soon as she has stepped out of the car to meet her sister, who is already halfway down the walk.

Lily reaches up with her free hand to fluff up the back of her short auburn bob, and preens a little for effect. Lily always complained that Deana was the pretty one, but it didn't really matter what they looked like as far as Mama was concerned. Mama always knew how to put the girls in their places. No use being proud of the looks God gave you, she said, or complaining about them, either. If one of the girls came home bragging that somebody said she was pretty, she was really in for it. "Somebody nearsighted, it likely was," Mama would say. "Don't go getting the big head. Don't go thinking you're somebody." Lord, Mama, Deana thinks, slamming the care door behind her. How could any of the Perrys make the mistake of thinking they were somebody?

"I can't wait for you to see the house," Lily says, grabbing Deana's hand. She is curved like a question mark, the way Troy is slung on her hip. "We've still got a lot of work to do, but can you believe it's finally finished?"

"I want to see, too," Sophie says, running around the car and bouncing her slight weight into her aunt. Lily sets Troy down beside her, where he clings to her leg like a kudzu vine.

"Of course, honey," Lily says. "I'm so glad you're here. Look at you. You've grown like a weed."

"She's not the only one," Deana says, looking over her shoulder at Wesley, who has stopped playing basketball for the moment and stands watching them. "What have you been feeding that child?"

"Oh? Wesley? He's almost as tall as his daddy now. He wears size twelve shoes. Can you imagine? I don't know where he gets those long legs. Not from the Perrys. Come on, Mama's waiting inside the house where it's warm. She can't wait to see the two of you."

Inside, the house smells freshly painted and the hardwood floors are shiny and new. In the foyer, Lily has an ornate gold-framed mirror over a small cherry table. On the other side hang family pictures—Wesley in Little League wearing a batting helmet and holding a bat, Wesley in his orange and blue county middle school basketball uniform, Charley in soccer silks, posing with her foot on a black and white soccer ball. Anchoring the group of photographs is an 11x14 Olan Mills family portrait, all the Mounces in their church clothes smiling against a backdrop of shiny blue silk.

Deana follows Lily into the kitchen. "My goodness," she says, looking at the long granite counter-tops, the center island with a sink, the double oven. "This looks like something out of Southern Living."

"Their kitchen is bigger than our whole house," Sophie says.

Mama turns from the stove and wipes her hands on the sides of her jeans. None of the women in their family ever wore aprons. Deana's heart sinks. Mama's hair is almost completely gray now. She is thinner, too, than Deana remembers. When did she get so stooped? "Come here, baby," Mama says to Sophie, holding out her arms.

"Be careful, Tigger," Deana says, softly into Sophie's ear, holding on to Sophie's arm for a second. "You go hug her, but remember she's more fragile than I am. Don't bounce her or you'll knock Mamaw plumb off her feet."

But Sophie hugs her grandmother almost gingerly. It's Mama who pulls Sophie tight. "My goodness, Sophie Anne, look how big you are." She holds Sophie at arm's length by the shoulders. "See," she says. "You've grown and Mamaw's shrunk. This time next year, we'll be the same height."

"Hey, Mama," Deana says, and walks across the room to hug Mama, too. For a second the three generations of women enclose each other with their linked arms. "You smell like sugar cookies," Deana says, laughing.

"I'm baking sugar cookies. I thought Sophie might like some," Mama says.

"Sit down, Deana," Lily says behind them. When Deana turns, Lily motions to an oak table surrounded by ladder-back chairs. When she sees that Deana is comfortable, she sets the baby down, and he toddles off into the next room. Then Lily pours two cups of coffee and brings it over. "You still take it black?"

Deana nods. "I can't believe what you've done here. This is a beautiful house."

Lily glows with pride. "Did you know me and Wes did most of the work ourselves? We did almost all the finish work. I tell you, I thought we'd be ready for the old folks' home by the time we got it done, but we made it. Mama, you come over here, too, and sit down. Do you want me to get you some coffee?"

"I ain't helpless. I reckon I can get my own coffee." Mama pours herself a cup and comes over to join them, sitting between the two sisters. "But I'll have to go back over to my house before we go to the hospital and have me a cigarette."

"Now, Mama," Lily says, reaching up to brush her thumb against their mother's cheek. When Mama makes the slightest movement away, Lily's hand follows her. "Here. Be still. You got a little bit of flour on your cheek. Why don't I yell at Wesley to go get your cigarettes and bring them over here?"

"No. No need to bring them over here." Mama looks over at Deana. "I won't smoke in her new house. I don't want to stink it up. I want to smoke, I've got my own kitchen."

Lily looks at her sister, rolling her eyes. What can you do with her?

Deana wraps her hands around the coffee mug. The warm pottery feels good against Deana's palms.

"Did you have any trouble?" Mama asks.

"No," Deana answers. "We didn't have any trouble."

Mama hesitates, but then she goes ahead and says it. "People around here think you must live across the ocean somewhere, no more'n you get home."

Deana takes a sip of the coffee, burning her tongue, and then blows across the liquid in the cup. She sets the cup down on the oak table. She decides to let the remark pass. "Lily says Daddy's pretty bad."

Lily notices Sophie hanging around the counter, listening. "Sophie, your cousin Madonna is in the den watching TV. You want to go out there, too?"

Sophie nods, and Lily stands, goes to take the girl's hand, and whisks her out of the room.

Mama fumbles for something in the pocket of her blue sweater—the cigarettes she hasn't brought with her?—and shrugs. Then she folds her hands on the table. "It's awful, Deana, what old age and sickness do to a body. Only blessing is, the doctors don't give him long. I didn't want to call you, but Lily said we ought to let you know, so you could see him before he goes. You know how I feel about that. If you don't think enough of me to come when I'm living, don't come when I'm too far gone to know."

"I know how you feel about it," Deana says. "But Mama, even though Lily said he doesn't recognize anybody, let alone me, I came on. I can't help what I should have done a long time ago."

Now it's Mama's turn to let the words hang unanswered in the air. "I was at the hospital most of the morning. I just came out here to wait for you. If you don't care to drive"—Mama has never had a driver's license, and she means, in Kentucky speak, if you don't mind driving—"we can go out as soon as you get something to eat. Lily can watch your baby for you."

"I don't need anything to eat. We stopped to eat on the way." She knows this will bring a frown from Mama, too. Mama has no use for restaurant food or for people who think they're too good to eat whatever is put on the table. "I would like to go to the bathroom and wash my face. Can you show me where the bathroom is?"

"Lily Mae," Mama calls, turning her head toward the living room. Lily comes rushing back into the room, Troy toddling along behind her. "Will you get Wesley, Jr. to get her suitcase out of the car? You are going to stay a day or two, not try to turn around and drive back tonight?" Deana nods. "You all show her what room she's going to sleep in and let her put her stuff up there. She wants to clean up a little. Then I reckon we'll go on over to the hospital and see about your daddy."

Deana stands up, but she hesitates before following Lily. "I thought I'd stay over in the trailer with you tonight, Mama."

"Oh, it's a lot nicer here than my little place. You take one of the girl's rooms, and she'll stay over with me."

The bedroom at the top of the stairs is apparently Madonna's. It is a frilly girl's room—Deana knows Charley, true to her name, is a tomboy—with a frilly pink bedspread, white-painted furniture with gold trim, and a canopy over the bed tied at the corners with pink bows. Taped to the edge of the dresser mirror are nearly a dozen photographs, not of the family this time, but apparently of Madonna and her friends. Deana walks close to the pictures to study them more closely. From the largest photo of Madonna in a blue and gold cheerleading uniform, Deana sees that Madonna, too, has a connection to sports. We bleed blue in the mountains, Deana remembers. The only thing more important than Kentucky basketball is the school basketball played by the boys who long to grow up to be Wildcats and the cheerleaders with their perky ponytails and color-coordinated panties who leap and tumble and scream encouragement for their team.

She turns to find her suitcase already on the bed behind her. Wesley has apparently delivered it with that peculiar stealth that the most heavy-footed adolescent can adopt when confronted with an aunt he sees once a year.

Deana opens it, takes out a clean denim shirt, and then goes into the bathroom. The girls apparently have their own bathroom. Deana feels a little intimidated by all this gleaming porcelain. Does Lily clean this whole house by herself? How does she make all these children pick up after themselves? It's all Deana can do just to keep Sophie from looking like a bag lady's baby, and Lily has five who spend the whole day looking freshly combed and bathed.

Deana could make excuses. For one thing, she has a beat-up trailer and Lily has a brand-new house. But to be honest, she has to admit, at least to herself, that Lily has always been a wonderful cook and housekeeper. Even when she and Wes lived in a trailer even older than Deana's, Lily kept it immaculate and decorated with little whatnots she bought from a home decorating club. The children were immaculate, too. Lily made each of them keep one pair of sneakers in the closet that they weren't allowed to wear outside to play. If she even thought they might go somewhere, like a church picnic, and end up in the dirt, she put their old sneakers in the car and made them change before they set foot on open ground.

"I swear, Lily," Deana told her sister once. "Even your kids' tee shirts look ironed."

"They are," Lily answered, without a hint of irony. "It doesn't take but a minute to run a hot iron over their clothes, just to flatten the wrinkles out."

The bathroom is not quite so aggressively pink and frilly, but it, too, is painted pink. Pink and white towels wait, folded neatly and hung across nickel-finished rods. On the sink is a porcelain toothbrush holder decorated with roses and monogrammed with a gold M.

Deana turns on the hot water and lets it run. When the water is warm, she splashes water on her face, and then squirts liquid soap into her palms. When she has rinsed off the soap, she studies her face in the mirror for the second time today. Should she bother with the business of fresh make-up? she wonders, and then decides, no, no more pretending to be someone she isn't. It's not as if she's fooled anybody yet.

✿Fifteen

The hospital is one of those buildings cobbled together of old and new wings, the bricks unmatched as if the building were made of Legos. Deana heads for the front door, but she realizes that Mama has gone in the opposite direction, toward a side entrance. Apparently, Daddy has been here long enough for Mama to know the short cuts. She follows Mama to the elevators, then down a long tiled hallway. The nurses, busy behind their counters, don't even look up.

When Deana sees her father, her first thought is that this cannot possibly be Wayman Perry. Despite his ill health the last few times she has come home, she is unprepared for how much he has changed. Lying against the white sheets, he is all tubes and bones and copper-colored skin, weightless and dry as a hand of tobacco hung from barn rafters to cure. His face is gaunt, the skin beneath his cheek bones brown and hollow like the core of an apple. Is this it, then? she wonders. Is this what we all come to, at last?

"Oh, Mama," Deana whispers, and from behind, Mama slides her hand in the crook of Deana's elbow. "Oh, Mama, I had no idea he was this bad."

"It's hard to imagine, ain't it?" Mama says quietly. "He always was such a big ol' loud man." She moves her hand from Deana's arm and lays it on Deana's upper back, pushing her lightly into the room. "Go on in, over there, and we'll sit a while by the bed."

Crowded into the room are two yellow vinyl chairs, one a small recliner, a collection of racks for IV drip bags a heart monitor, and a small table with a plastic water pitcher and a florist's arrangement of wilted carnations. This is what hospitals call a semi-private room, but the only privacy is provided by a curtain that hangs between the two beds. Behind the curtain, Deana hears the old man in the next bed wheezing and mumbling in his sleep.

Deana sits in the upright chair and Mama perches on the edge of Daddy's bed, tucking the covers around his legs. "How long has he been like this?" Deana asks.

"Well, you know he's been bad, off and on, for a while. But when he had that first bad stroke six months ago, even when he got better, it was like something in him just didn't want to live anymore. Well, what can I tell you? It's like he just give up."

"It's hard to imagine Daddy giving up," Deana says, her voice lowered to barely above a whisper, as though Daddy might hear. "You'd think he'd hang on out of pure orneriness."

Mama looks toward Deana, and then away, not at Daddy, but at the little table beside the bed. "You're gonna think I'm awful for saying this. But sometimes I wish he'd just go on. What kind of life can it be, laying here, a feeding tube in his stomach? What's there to hold on to?"

Deana looks closely at her mother's face and is startled to see tears slipping down Mama's cheeks. Surely, she can't still love him after all these years? Could you call it love, all the arguments and fights? All that history—and misery?

"That doesn't make you awful, Mama," Deana says. "You're just thinking of what's best for him." Deana reaches awkwardly for Mama's shoulder, to comfort her, but Deana's hand falls short because of the distance between the chair and the bed. To cover the movement, Deana reaches up awkwardly, as if she meant only to tuck her hair behind her ear. "What's the use of him just lying here, suffering?"

Mama turns her gaze from Daddy's face and looks at Deana. "You don't think he is, do you? Suffering, I mean? The doctors say he don't even know where he is, but sometimes, his mouth opens— Oh, it's awful, Deana—the way he strains like he's trying to say something, only he just can't get it out. He tries to lift his head up, and when he finally gives up, his gown is wet with sweat, and he has little beads of sweat all over this face. What do you think he might be trying to say? I just feel awful, like he wants something, or something hurts him, but I don't know what it is."

Ash Grove

"He might not be trying to say anything. It might be some kind of—I don't know. Maybe it's some kind of muscle spasm or something, and he really doesn't feel any pain."

"I hope so. A body feels enough pain in life, he ought not to feel it when he's dying. I hope he goes peaceful, that's all I ask. But there's something else worrying me, but I don't reckon you're the person to ask. I don't—well, I don't know if you're a believer or not—but I'll tell you, I pray for you every night on my knees."

And I can't stand that kind of prayer, Deana thinks, that prays for the Jews and the Muslims—even the Mormons, the Lutherans, and especially the Catholics—to convert to that old time religion or else burn like a pine log soaked in diesel fuel at the center of hell. But she doesn't say this either. "I'm glad you pray for me, Mama. I can use all the prayers I can get."

"And you know how I pray for him," Mama says, nodding her head toward Wayman. "I always have prayed for him, even when I've seen his heart set hard against being saved."

"I know you pray for him, Mama. And as for his heart being set on anything—Well, I figure it's hard to tell much about a person's heart. Anyway, God probably hears you praying even if Daddy can't."

Jolene looks at Wayman's face before she goes on. When she begins speaking, her voice is as soft as if she's talking to herself. "There's something I want to tell you, though. See what you think. Brother Hardwick—he's the preacher at the Pentecostal church I been going to—you remember, don't you, that little white church house down by the creek, close by where the coal company office used to be before it shut down?"

"I remember."

Mama nods. "Brother Hardwick comes to pray with me sometimes. He's been such a blessing to me," Mama says. "I don't know how I could have got through all this—and not just Wayman's stroke either, I mean his drinking—if Brother George hadn't been here through it all to help me."

She looks at Deana intently, as if, instead of telling her something, she's really asking for an answer of some kind. "What, Mama? Go on."

"George—that's Brother Hardwick's first name. Well, I can't hardly believe it, after all these years, but Brother George says he thinks your Daddy got saved last week."

"Mama! Why didn't you tell me this before? You must be tickled to death. I know it's a relief to you. I know how you worried about him not being a believer. That must make you feel better about—him going on and all."

"But I'm not sure. For one thing, we don't know how much he hears or sees. Do you think if he got saved, he'd still be having these fits, like the ones I told you about it? It seems to me if he got saved, he'd be resting now, that he'd finally have made his peace with God. But he don't seem to have no peace. And what about being baptized? Do you think he could get saved, and him like that?"

Deana leans forward. Now she does reach across the space between them to take both Jolene's hands. "Mama, will you quit worrying about it? You know the Bible as well as any preacher does. If Jesus could save the thief on the cross, why couldn't he, at the last minute, hear your prayers and take care of Daddy? You said Daddy just gave up. Maybe he got scared and did his own praying. Maybe for Daddy, this is as peaceful as it gets. Will you not worry about this anymore?"

Mama pulls her hands free, embarrassed. "I knew you wouldn't understand. You try, but—you can't just say he's all right and he's going to heaven. There has to be true repentance. I reckon I—well, I just hope when the time comes he'll be all right."

Mama turns back to Daddy and fluffs the pillow behind his head. "Looks like them nurses would be checking in on him every now and then. What do you think folks do, if they don't have people to keep them doctors and nurses straight? You could die in here and wouldn't nobody know it till a janitor came in twelve hours later to scrub the floor."

"Mama, you're not changing the subject that easily. With everything else you've got to worry about, will you just let Jesus and the preachers see to Daddy's soul?"

Mama doesn't answer, but she does get up to straighten the things on the table. She throws the carnations into the wastebasket and takes the vase into the bathroom to rinse it. Then she puts it beside her purse so she'll remember to take it home.

They spend an hour talking about other things, mostly stories about Lily's children, and Sophie. "I wish I could see her all the time," Mama says, "the way I do Lily's. I don't mean to make a difference, talking about

Lily's children all the time. It's just that I see them more and know what all they're doing."

"I know, Mama," Deana says, but she knows she's guilty as charged, and it stings.

Finally, at 3:30, the shift changes, and the nurses come and go. They take Daddy's blood pressure and temperature. They replace the empty solution bag with a full one. The nurses seem interchangeable to Deana. Each speaks to Mama the way some elementary school teachers speak to people, as if she were five years old. But Mama doesn't seem to mind. The hospital staff Mama was so disgusted with earlier, accusing them of incompetence and neglect, seem to have no connection to these nurses she apparently loves. They rush in breathless and cheerful, draped in stethoscopes, delivering Daddy's medicines and Mama's hugs.

One of them does stand out, a heavyset woman with the elaborately wound bun and clean-washed face of a holiness housewife. Deana notices her because of her voice. She comes down the hall humming "What a Friend We Have in Jesus," and when she bursts through the door, she gives Mama the biggest hug of all.

"We just love your Mama," she says, giving Mama's shoulder a little extra squeeze before she turns to take care of Wayman. "We think she's just the sweetest thing."

And Mama, like a kindergartner praised by the teacher, beams.

Later, Lily calls, and the telephone in the quiet room is incongruously loud. Supper is nearly ready, she says, and it's Wednesday, church night. If they want to eat, they need to come on home.

"You go on," Mama says. "I'm going to stay here until they get out of church. Lily or Wes'll come to get me. I feel bad for not staying all night. I did try to sleep here in this recliner the first few nights, but then—well, I'm an old woman myself. I couldn't keep it up."

"Of course you couldn't. Do you want me to stay?"

Mama hesitates, and Deana hopes she will say no. "I don't reckon there's any need of it. They'll call us if there's any change. You won't be here that long, anyway. What difference would it make if you stayed one night?"

"Tell you what, Mama. Why don't you take a break now? Go on back with me? Daddy's resting. You need to rest, too. Anyway, don't you need something to eat?"

"You know how much I eat. I could about live on bean soup and bread crumbs. They got a cafeteria downstairs. I'll go get me a sandwich and a cup of coffee, if I get hungry. I'll just sit here in this recliner and look at a book. You go on, though. You've got a little girl to take care of."

But Deana sits with her a little while longer, until they run out of anything to say. Then she sits another fifteen minutes or so, while they read or pretend to read, each lost in her own thoughts.

When Deana does get ready to leave, her mother sits tilted back in the recliner with her feet up, peering through her reading glasses at the pages of a women's magazine. When Deana looks more closely, she sees that her mother has fallen asleep. In a moment, the magazine will fall from her limp hands. Deana stands, and then tiptoes over to slide the book gently from Mama's fingers. She lays it on the floor beside the chair.

At the door, Deana stops for a moment and looks back at her parents, her mama snoring softly, her daddy lying silent as a ghost in the bed. The dimness of the room makes a circle around them, and Deana stands at the edge of it, in the fluorescent light from the hall. She wishes, as she has a hundred times before, that she could wave a magic wand and change the world for them. She wishes she could do the impossible, whisk them away to some place warm, and buy Daddy a Hawaiian shirt and Mama a drink—a virgin piña colada—with a little umbrella tilted at the edge. She wishes she could take them into tacky stores where they could buy three of everything and not count a single penny. They really are just children, she thinks, even Daddy. They are children set down in the middle of the world that never had much use for them, no use for poor people in general.

She crosses back inside the room one more time before she leaves, inexplicably leaving the place she has made for herself outside the circle, outside the family. She has worked so hard to convince herself that if she stays away from here she can inhabit a still, green place at the center of her own imagination, untouched by the helplessness and despair she always feels when she comes home. But here they are, Mama asleep with her drugstore reading glasses sliding down her nose, her thin arms naked in the cold room, and Daddy lost somewhere on the boundary between this life and the next. Well, she prays, right along with Mama, that his soul will find its way home.

Ash Grove

Deana takes a blue waffle-weave blanket from the cabinet by Daddy's bed and tucks it over Mama's lap, sliding the sides of it gently so that it covers Mama's arms. When she has Mama tucked in, she stands by Daddy's bed long enough to look, really look at her father, just once before she leaves. Mama's right. It's almost obscene, she thinks, for people to lie so helpless, not knowing who might be looking at them. Daddy never could stand for anybody to feel sorry for him, and now he looks so vulnerable, lying there, strands of his thinning white hair clumped together like corn silks above his freckled forehead, his skin hanging loose from his neck, like chicken skin. A little washed-out gully runs down between his ribs where the muscles have gone slack. His cheekbones stand in sharp relief against the cavernous skin underneath them. The left side of his mouth is drawn up slightly. Is this from the stroke?

Lightly, Deana touches the left side of his face with the back of her hand. This skin is dry and smooth. His dark hand against the white sheet looks blue-veined and knotted, like the roots of a dead tree heaved out of the ground in the spring thaw. She moves her hand from his face, and touches the knobby bone at the side of his wrist. With all the mistakes she's made, who is she to judge anybody? She has loved him and she has tried, fiercely, not to love him. But she sees now. Despite her feelings one way or another, she is bound to Wayman Perry by ties of blood and history, and she always will be.

Suddenly, his hand turns palm up to grasp her wrist. He struggles to lift his head from the pillow and opens his eyes, looking at her. His mouth works open and shut, a thread of spit leaving a trail down his cheek from the corner of his mouth. His grip is surprisingly strong. She tugs hard, but she will have to tug even harder if she wants him to release her. She cannot pull her wrist away without being afraid she'll hurt him some way. Then, just as suddenly, he relaxes his hold. He falls back, exhausted to the bed, just as her mother described, his eyes closed, the eyelids twitching, his forehead and upper lip beaded with sweat.

Without thinking, Deana turns and runs from the room, like a child darting from porch light to porch light in the darkness of an empty street. She does not even look back to see if her mother has been awakened by the struggle, does not even stop to notice whether her running down the hall like a madwoman has drawn the attention of the nurses. Anyway, how many times a day on this death ward full of old, worn-out people do they see worse?

By the time she has made it to the elevator, her heartbeat has begun to slow and so has her breathing. She leans her face against the cold, celery-colored wall to steady her heart, and then pushes the down arrow. The smooth whirring of the cables reassures her that rescue is on the way.

As she steps inside the open door and pushes the button for the ground floor, the weight of their sorrow—her sorrow?—constricts like a hand grasping her lungs. At any given moment, she thinks, no matter how hard we try to protect ourselves, guilt and despair assault us like the flaming sword of some avenging angel, to shatter the fragile defenses we've built around ourselves, and break our hearts.

Sixteen

At Lily's Deana stands at the counter closest to the sink shredding a head of lettuce for a salad, while Lily stirs spaghetti noodles into a pot of boiling water. She finds a strange comfort in the chaos of the Brody's family life, especially after the eerie quiet of the hospital. From the family room, she can hear the television, the network news turned up loud. The commercials are even louder, of course, and occasionally, like a burst of gunfire on a still street, she hears a little scream from one of the children, as they fight for territory or plunder. Does Wes keep the TV turned up to drown them out?

Deana remembers how she used to daydream that she and not Lily would be the daughter Mama moved in with. She would be married to Will, of course, and they'd all live in the big house Cleave owned. She always pictured Mama sewing in one of those white Adirondack chairs, a basket of quilt pieces at her feet. Mama never sewed in real life, except when she had to. As long as Deana could remember, Mama detested repairing a rip or replacing a button. But this was a daydream, so never mind. Deana would lie on a blanket close by Mama, reading a book and occasionally looking up at the canopy of leaves with its border of bright blue sky. She would have children, too, maybe not so many as Lily, but enough to cause their own racket. They would chase each other, squealing, startling Mama when the screen door to the kitchen slammed behind them. "All right, now," Mama would remind them. "Play in or out." But she would not really be angry. In Deana's daydreams, anger was the furthest thing from anybody's mind.

The steam from the boiling water rises, carrying the fragrance of basil and garlic through the room. Until she came in from the crisp wind outside and smelled the simmering tomato sauce, Deana didn't realize how hungry she was. Beside her, Lily is cutting chunks of chocolate chip cookies from a roll she has just taken from the freezer. Deana watches the efficiency with which Lily wields the knife, making the slices and the spaces between them uniform on the cookie sheet. She concedes to herself that cooking is one more department in which her younger sister is superior; at home, most evenings, Sophie gets canned soup and grilled cheese sandwiches, and if Deana's really feeling ambitious, an omelet. Sometimes—more often than she'd like to admit—they make do with a raw fruits and veggies and a bowl of corn flakes for dessert.

"Sophie is going to want to move in with you," she says, only half-teasing, to Lily. "First, she gets to hang out with all these older girl cousins, and now she's going to get a home-cooked meal, complete with garlic bread."

But Lily is distracted, trying to get the family fed and out the door for church. She barely glances at Deana. "Charley, get in here and set the table," Lily yells, turning her head toward the living room. "I wish Mama would come home to eat. I swear, Deana, if we don't watch her, she's going to end up in worse shape than Daddy."

Deana cuts the tomato into small cubes, and then arranges them in the center of the lettuce. She feels embarrassingly pleased with the way the arrangement looks. Well, at least, she thinks ruefully, at least I'm still the artistic one. "She said she was going to get a sandwich from the cafeteria at the hospital. Maybe she'll eat later, when Wes brings her home. How does this look?"

Lily looks at the salad, then into Deana's eyes, smiling at her sister before she turns back toward the counter, pulling out the drawer with the silverware. "You've made it look so pretty," she says. "Not that my bunch will appreciate it. They're all on a see food diet—see food and eat it."

Lily grabs a handful of forks and butter knives, and, wrapping them in a stack of bargain paper napkins, lays them near the end of the counter to wait for Charley. Charley, fourteen and chunky, waiting for her last growth spurt before adulthood, takes a stack of plates from the cabinet and begins to set them on the table. Her lips bunch a little around her braces, and when she smiles, she displays a row of orange-rimmed teeth. Lily has explained that these are her school colors, and that colored braces are the latest rage in orthodonture. "You better hope Sophie's permanent teeth come in straight," she tells Deana. "You have no idea how expensive it is to put braces on their teeth."

Deana hasn't even thought about the future of Sophie's teeth. So far, she has been able to keep her daughter fed, and with a good eye for a bargain at yard sales and consignment shops, she's managed to keep her clothed as well. But in the future, how will she be able to afford all the things Sophie needs? Where will she find the money for the braces, the piano lessons, the clothes, the shoes, and the college tuition?

When the Brodys pile into the van to go to church for Wednesday night services, Deana begs off, but Sophie wants to go with them. Deana hesitates. She has always been so careful about churches. She makes excuses—doesn't Lily have enough to put up with, taking her own crew, without having an extra child to worry about? When Lily says the older girls would be thrilled to watch out for Sophie, Deana has to say what really bothers her. She explains that her daughter has never heard a hell-fire-and-damnation sermon in her life. What if she's scared?

But Lily waves these objections aside. "For goodness sakes, Deana. We don't go to one of them holy-roller churches like Mommy's," Lily says. "It's the second Baptist. There's not even any preaching on Wednesday. The kids all go down to the basement and do a craft, while the adults have Bible study upstairs. They do stuff like glue macaroni in the shape of a cross to a paper plate. Then they spray paint the whole thing gold. She'll have fun. It won't hurt her to go."

Sophie has already linked herself arm in arm on either side of her two oldest girl cousins. On the left is Charley. She has her dark red hair in a ponytail and is wearing a pair of jeans and a white sweat shirt with a black screen-printed outline of Jesus, drops of black blood oozing around the edges of his crown of thorns. Above the picture, in black print, are the words "Second Baptist Youth Fellowship" and below, "His Pain—Your Gain."

To the right of Sophie is Madonna, her short-cropped blonde hair flipped stylishly. She wears a fake leather skirt cropped halfway up her thighs, a white, long-sleeved tee shirt, and a pair of gold crosses dangling from her ear lobes. She has on clumped black mascara and Cover Girl make-up. Deana knows the brand because it still has the medicated fragrance she remembers from when she and Lily were young. The make-up is a shade too dark for her fair complexion and cakes heavily across her chin, to hide a fresh constellation of pimples.

Is this what happens when MTV and the Trinity Broadcasting Network come over cable into the mountains? Maybe, Deana thinks, I should just take Sophie to South America or Australia, somewhere far away from Ash Grove and all its troubles. But in the end, she relents, imagining Sophie growing up to found an organization of cheerleaders for Jesus, with appliqués of crosses sewn on their tight sweaters, their pompoms waving at a screaming, fainting, slain-in-the spirit crowd.

She has fallen asleep on the sofa when the phone rings. At first, she is startled, waking in a strange place. It takes her a second to figure out where she is, and even longer to find the phone. She finds it beside the remote control for the television, on the table beside Wes's recliner. Even when she picks it up, she holds it in her hand, feeling the vibration when it rings for the fourth time. Should she answer, or does her sister have a machine to pick up messages? She clicks the talk button—why can't phones be uniformly designed? Each new contraption has its own mysterious layout of buttons. By the time she has lifted the receiver to her ear, the answering machine has picked up, too. She hears the Brody girls giggling, and then chirping out a greeting in unison, and she has to yell over the message to keep the person on the line.

"I'm sorry," she says. "Can you hold on a minute? I couldn't find the phone. Don't hang up."

When the machine falls silent, she says again, "Hello?"

"Deana?" The voice is faint, as though the speaker is leaning away from the receiver, or is calling from some place far away.

"Hello. Who is this?" Who on earth could be calling her who would know she is here, let alone recognize Deana's voice answering the phone? "Hello," she says again.

But the caller doesn't answer. There is silence, and then a little click indicating that whoever was calling has hung up. She frowns, holding the phone in her hand for a moment before she turns off the talk button and lays it back on the table.

And then, of course, she knows exactly who was on the other end of the line.

Seventeen

Instead of going to the mine office by way of the road, past Felton's store, Deana heads for a thicket of trees that shades a low point in the creek. She follows the path she and Lily have used ever since they were children, dodging now and then to keep from scratching herself on blackberry briars or snagging her jeans.

She doesn't stop running until she has reached the water. The bank is cool and dark, lined with trees and a thick growth of underbrush. She takes her shoes off and holds them in one hand. With the other, she holds onto a pine scrub to lower herself down to the creek. The summer has been dry, and even here, at its deepest point, the water barely reaches her knees. She uses the rocks in the creek as stepping-stones, and the stones are cold against her bare feet.

When she reaches the other side of the creek, her feet are wet, making the sand, dark and soft, stick to her soles. She kicks her right leg to shake the sand off, but even then, when she puts her shoe on, she can feel the sand rubbing against her skin. She puts the other shoe on anyway and follows the haul road, which curves around a hill planted with a thick stand of new pines. Mary Alice No. 2, the only mine around that's running, is just around the curve, and half a mile on up the road is the squat, cinder-block building where Cleave Brinson has his office.

With the second shift laid off, the mine is deserted except for an old yellow dog pawing and sniffing at a paper sack somebody has dropped on the ground. The coal stockpiles, shimmering in the heat like two burned-out hills, stand a hundred yards to the left of the mine.

Deana heads right, staying on the far side of the haul road where the dirt is red instead of black, hoping to save her shoes. To get to the mine office, she has to cross the railroad tracks, but the track is empty. According to her daddy, the mines won't ship any coal now until the first frost. It seems to her it's always the same with the coalmines, either boom time with Brinson running three full shifts and over-time, or bust time with half the miners laid off. They dig ginseng or grow marijuana deep in the national forest or they starve on welfare. Nobody cares, Daddy says, with the unions busted all over Eastern Kentucky. Soon, Daddy says, there won't be any deep mines left. Ash Grove will dry up and blow away.

Deana hasn't told anybody, afraid the news will get back to her daddy, but she won't be there to see it. She has every intention of working long enough to save for a bus ticket to Nashville, and she won't stay in Ash Grove any longer, not one minute longer than it takes.

The door sticks at first, but when Deana pushes it, it gives with a little pop and she almost falls inside. Cleave Brinson stands with his back to her, bent over a brown vinyl card table, pouring a cup of coffee. Behind the table, a large fan fills the single window in the room, blowing the smell of coffee toward the door where Deana stands, waiting for Brinson to turn around. Through the grill that covers the blades of the fan, she sees the sun slip behind the mountains, leaving a narrow band of red which glows like a bed of coals.

When he turns around, he stares at her for a second. He has no idea why she is here.

"I'm Deana Perry," she says, her voice lower than she means for it to be. She clears her throat and tries again. "Wayman Perry's girl? Margie Lawson said she'd tell you I was coming to work part-time after school."

"Oh."

She stands there awkwardly, watching him take off his glasses and lay them on the card table. Then he scoops up a spoonful of sugar and dumps it into a cup.

The cup is bone china, white as a new set of false teeth, and it has a fancy band around the top in navy blue overlaid with a pattern of gold lace. It looks out of place in this dusty room with its concrete floor and block walls, and in Cleave Brinson's hand, which is big enough to belong to a man half-again his size.

"Margie had to leave early today. Did she tell you what she wants you to do?"

"She said I'd need to keep the place straight. Add up the tickets from the scale house. What all else needs doing."

He nods, although he has already turned away from her to set the cup down, and she wonders if he even listened to her answer. She watches the cup slide away from his hand, gracefully, to rest in the thick dust she now sees covering the table. Without another word to her, he walks toward the door and takes a straw hat off a nail beside the facing.

"Truck tickets are on the desk over there. I need you to keep up with who's hauling what for me, how much tonnage, what all we're paying out. You and Margie keep up with your hours. You get the truck tickets done, you can push the dust around some. Sweeping in here's like raking leaves in a windstorm. I know it don't seem worth the trouble, but it's got to be done."

He steps past her and out the door. She watches him put the hat on and head for the blue Ford pick-up parked beside the building. He's got a shotgun in a rack in the back window, like most men around here. She wants to call out before he gets the truck started, to ask him if he'll be back before she leaves, to check her work. Is she supposed to lock up, or what? But she doesn't have the nerve to say anything else to him.

Two weeks later, Deana leans the vacuum cleaner sideways to fit it into the space between the rusty filing cabinets. The black dust hangs in the air, as if waiting for her to stop so that it can settle again onto the same surfaces. She moves the vacuum cleaner back and forth across the floor and watches Cleave Brinson, pretending not to. He sits in the big leather chair behind a metal desk writing small black numbers onto the green pages of a ledger book.

She has to keep an eye on him because she never knows what he is going to do. Sometimes he will stand straight up without warning and stride toward the door, cursing and mumbling, the way a cat will leap out of sleep and go through the motions of stalking before it lies back down on the floor. Then, when his hand touches the crown of his hat, he stops, leaves the hat on its nail, and goes back to his desk to sit down. Half an hour after she got here, he ran right into Deana, who absentmindedly crossed his path while she was dusting. He didn't say a word in apology or anger, but stood frowning at her, as if he couldn't think who she was or why she was there. She tries to see Will in him, but Will has been gone for so long that sometimes Deana can barely remember what he looks like. Sometimes she thinks she made him up to keep the other boys away, the boys she might like if she didn't know they would keep her in Ash Grove and make her life as miserable as her mother's.

Cleave Brinson has been a surprise to her. She knows he has a fine home, a white house big as a hotel, that he hires people, including Deana's mother, to cook and clean. Her daddy says Cleave Brinson got rich without ever getting his hands dirty, that he lives off the miners' sweat. Before, when she thought of Cleave at all, she pictured him, handsome and polished, standing in the drawing room her mother once described, his back to the fireplace with its dark mahogany mantle, his feet sunk into carpet as cool and thick as moss. She certainly never imagined Cleave doing anything, could never have guessed how much time he spends here. Working here, watching him day after day, she doesn't find him scary anymore, can't see him as the husband scorned and so jealous he killed his wife rather than see her run off with another man. Sometimes, while he is working, Cleave looks up and smiles at her, as if he has just remembered she is in the room, and she blushes, noticing that he is a good-looking man for his age, though of course he is way too old for her.

When she finishes sweeping, her time is up. She puts the vacuum cleaner in a closet. Their coats, hers and Cleave's, hang on a pole overhead.

"I'm gone," she says, softly, taking her coat off the hanger. It's an old wool coat from Goodwill. The lining smells pungent and sweet, like burning coal.

Outside, Deana drapes the coat around her shoulders. She takes a deep breath and blows smoke into the cold air. This is the first cold snap of October, and she likes the way the cold feels against her face and arms. A thin rim of light the color of a new bucket still shows ahead of her, at the top of Blue Knob, but the dark has settled thick below where the mountains overlap, black as the coal dust that coats her father at the end of his shift, covering everything but his eyes.

She shivers now, not wanting to go home. The wind has picked up, standing the dry leaves on their stems. Leaves skate across the thin layer of gravel, the bare patches of ground. Deana pulls the coat tighter around her, but she still doesn't put it on. The door opens and closes and Cleave Brinson stands behind her, his arm nearly touching hers.

"I thought you'd be long gone," he says, and she turns her head to look at him, the bulk of his dark plaid jacket, his face pale under the shadow of his hat. He's barely taller than she is, and standing beside him, she suddenly feels easy. Why, he's just like anybody, she thinks. He turns to lock the door, the keys a flash of silver.

"It'll be dark soon. Why don't I give you a ride down the mountain? The haul road's pretty rough. You might fall, trying to walk down it at night." Why, he's sweet, she thinks. She never suspected that he could be worried about her this way.

"I don't go that way. I just cross a skinny place in the creek."

He laughs. "Bobcat's will get you down there. If you don't break your leg or drown first."

He takes her elbow and steers her toward the truck. His hand is warm against her arm. Two more pickups sit by the tipple, but the yard is empty, except for a giant pyramid of black, the coal stockpile, and an empty freight car silent on the tracks.

Brinson opens the door on the passenger side and closes it when she has climbed inside. The truck is dirty. The dust that covers everything within miles, everything in the world as she knows it, coats the dashboard and the vinyl seats. When he turns the headlights on, they point two circles at the cinder block building, dim through a crust of mud. He cups the knob at the top of the gearshift. "Whose girl did you say you were?"

"I'm a Perry. My daddy's Wayman."

He looks at her for a second before he backs up. "I know Wayman Perry," he says. "Not the easiest man in the world to get along with, is he?"

Deana feels the distance between them. When she answers, her voice is hard and small, her mother's voice, why, no, I don't need any help, I don't need anything, we'll get along just fine, don't think you know anything about us, you don't know us at all. "He's all right," she says, the sound of the words nearly swallowed by the noise of the truck.

Brinson smiles. "Don't get all prissy about it. There are worse things than being hard to get along with. You might even call that a compliment,

Ash Grove

153

depending on the circumstances."

They don't talk—he seems to have forgotten her, and she doesn't know what to say—the rest of the way down. Brinson stops at the gate to speak to the night watchman, who leans his head to the side, trying to get a good look at Deana, but she ducks her head and turns toward the window. She knows how people think here.

At the foot of the mountain, she says, "You'd better let me out here. I can walk the rest of the way." Then she adds, answering the un-asked question, "My daddy sees a man bringing me home, he might misunderstand."

Brinson laughs. "I just bet he might. Well, I'll take you a little closer, anyway. No use in walking any further than you have to."

He pulls off the road in the one wide sandy spot just beyond Felton's store. She can see the lights from here, but not the store itself. "You can make it in a couple of minutes from here."

"I sure can," she says, opening the door. "I thank you for the ride."

He smiles at her again, this time facing her so that she sees that his teeth are white, small, and fine, like baby teeth. "It's been a long time since I snuck a pretty girl home," he says. "Get on to your house, now. You don't want to be out here on the road by yourself."

Then he pulls away, leaving her standing in the dark, the small brightness of the store a few hundred yards away.

When she goes inside the house, she brushes her teeth and then climbs into bed beside a sleeping Lily. All her life she has wondered what lies on the other side of these mountains. Now, thinking about Cleave, she imagines herself traveling with him to some place far away, an island maybe, walking along the beach, her hand looped into the curve of his elbow. She sighs and closes her eyes, looking up at the man walking with her through her daydream, but it isn't Cleave Brinson's face she sees. She falls asleep, looking up at Will, his face as clear to her as if he had never gone away.

Two weeks before Christmas, on the metal table she finds a small white box with her name written across the top in dark, heavy ink. She opens the box to find a gray velvet case. In the case is a gold heart the size of a dime suspended by a thin gold chain. It's not real gold, of course, but it's pretty. She takes the necklace out, and it takes her a moment to undo the clasp. She holds the necklace against the front of her dress, and then fastens it around her neck. She keeps the gray case and throws the box away. From time to time, while she is rinsing the coffeepot or adding up the tickets from the scale house, she reaches up to touch the heart with the tip of her finger.

That night, just before she gets in sight of her house, she puts the necklace back in the case and slides it into the pocket of her coat.

The next day Cleave Brinson is back. The late afternoon sun filters through the trees, and as soon as she rounds the bend, Deana sees the last gold light sparkle against the right front fender of the truck. Her heart beats faster, and she walks toward the building with her hands sunk deep in her pockets, fingering the gray case. The necklace hangs around her neck, and her face flushes with embarrassment and confusion.

Cleave comes out the door as she goes in. He is whistling a Beatles tune. When he sees her, he stops in the middle of a note, the shrill sound flattening like the whistle of a kettle taken off the stove. He looks at her for a moment the way he always does, as if it takes him a minute to remember who she is and what she's doing here.

She reaches up to cover the necklace, but his eyes follow the motion of her hand. "I see you found your Christmas present."

Her hand drops and she slides it back into her pocket.

She smiles. "It's pretty. It was nice of you to do."

"It didn't cause you trouble with your boyfriend, did it?" he asks, laughing.

She shakes her head. "I don't have a boyfriend."

She tries to think of something else to say, but she just stands there, feeling stupid, and Cleave has already looked toward his truck, already has one foot a step toward it. "Well, I got to go to town before the hardware store closes."

Deana stays half an hour past her time, hoping he will come back, though she doesn't admit that's why, even to herself. She feels silly. At least a crush on Will made sense—he was the cutest boy she had ever laid eyes on—but not her interest in Cleave Brinson. What is wrong with her? He's old enough to be her father.

She turns off the lights inside, turns the outside lights on, and gets her coat. She is halfway across the gravel lot, her flashlight bobbing up and down, when his truck pulls to a stop just outside the building.

Cleave climbs out of the truck and walks to the back, lowering the tailgate. "You headed home?" he calls to her, without looking around. While he talks, he pulls a large square box toward him. "If you'll wait a minute, I'll give you a ride down."

Without answering, Deana shuts off the flashlight and puts it in her coat. She walks to the door, opens it, and stands propping it open with her body while Cleave carries the box in, setting it down on the concrete floor near the door. He shoves it up against the wall with his foot.

He stands there for a second, as if he's trying to make sure he's done everything he needs to. Then he turns around. He reaches above Deana's head to grab the edge of the door, and with his other hand, he takes her by the elbow, pulling her forward so that the door closes behind her.

"Do you have to go home right now?" he asks, whispering, though she wonders who he is afraid will hear him. With the door shut, she can barely see him. The yellow light above the doorway shines weakly through the dirty windows. She moves, without realizing she is moving, until her back presses against the door. Cleave pulls her forward a little to slide his arms around her shoulders, leaning his body into hers. They stand perfectly still for a moment. Deana's arms hang limp at her sides.

Cleave moves his hands up her arms, and then lays his palms against her face, nudging her chin up with his thumbs. Her eyes are closed, and she doesn't open them. The kiss is wet and soft, like Robbie's mouth when he was little and used to gnaw with his gums on her shoulder. She isn't sure she likes the kiss, but she isn't sure she doesn't. She feels strangely detached, as if she is watching this happen from some space high above them, or as if she is swimming underwater, weightless. She has imagined this happening so often before, but with Will. Maybe this is as close to Will as she is ever going to get.

His hands move back down across her shoulders and from there to her breasts. He makes slow circles against her nipples with his thumbs. "Please," he whispers against her hair.

He doesn't talk anymore, and Deana opens her eyes once, then closes them again, though she isn't sure why. Maybe with her eyes closed this really is like a dream, something happening to somebody else, not to

Deana. She lets him help her to the floor where he has dropped his jacket to lie beneath her, trying not to think that she is following him to a place she might never find her way back from, a place where he, and not Deana, is in control. When she finally comes to herself, the weight of him on top of her, she wants to cry out, to make him stop. Instead, she pushes her hand against her mouth. She had been waiting for him to come back to the office, and he knew it. Now she has no right to stop him, and she is too ashamed to speak.

Later, on the way home, she doesn't look at him in the truck. She is trembling, and she doesn't want to have to look into his eyes. If she doesn't, then maybe there is still one place inside her where he hasn't been.

He stops at the same place he had dropped her off before. She flings open the door, jumping out before he has a chance to say anything. But he cranks open his window and sticks out his head. "Deana?"

She turns, caught in his headlights like a deer, her body tense and wary, her eyes round.

"Are you all right?"

She nods without looking at him. Then she steps to the edge of the road, giving him room to go around. A few yards ahead, he stops as if he is waiting for her, but she walks slowly, so slowly that he goes ahead with a little burst of speed, his tail-lights disappearing in the dark.

At home she sits on the edge of the front porch, her legs hanging over, her feet tangled in the black stems of dead marigolds. It is cold on the porch, but there is no wind. A narrow bridge of stars spreads across the sky between the two dark ranges of mountains. She shivers, cold with shame at her sin and her stupidity. Cleave Brinson had given her a necklace just like he gives the miners turkeys and hams, but she had acted like it was a diamond ring. He probably gave Margie one just like it. The present hadn't meant anything and what they did tonight didn't mean anything either. It didn't, to men. Isn't that what her mama has pounded into Deana and Lily? The boys have the fun but the girls have the trouble. Now, the moment Mama opens her mouth and gets three words out, Deana and Lily start rolling their eyes. We know, Mama, we know. You don't have to tell us the same thing over and over.

But Mama was right, and now who knows what kind of trouble Deana has gotten herself into? What if somebody saw them and tells Wayman

Perry? What if Will comes home, and Cleave tells him what they did? She knows it's silly to think the way she felt about Will would ever amount to anything, but she doesn't want him to know this. Why did she let this happen? She always thought that when this happened, it would be with Will, or someone like him, whom she loved. She doesn't love Cleave. It's like she was in a daze. What if they made a baby? Is this how people, in an instant of forgetting, can trap themselves in the very place they long to leave?

She takes the necklace off and finds a stick at the bottom of the porch steps. She digs a hole in the wet dirt at the edge of the bottom step and puts the necklace in the hole, shoveling dirt and leaves to cover it up. Then she takes the velvet case out of her pocket and flings it as hard as she can into the dark trees on the other side of the road.

Deana goes back after the Christmas holiday to pick up her last check. She had told Margie she had to quit the job at Brinson Mining because was falling behind in her schoolwork. If Margie would just leave the check on the desk, Deana would come in after hours, pick up the check, and leave her key to the office. For days she agonizes over whether to go into the office or not, but finally, she knows she has to. What will Margie think if Deana doesn't even bother to pick her paycheck up?

She is going out the door, into blowing snow, when Cleave Brinson's truck pulls up next to the building. She hurries past the truck. She can't look him in the eye. "I just came to get this." She holds up the envelope, and he nods.

"You want me to give you a ride home?"

No, she doesn't want a ride home, but she doesn't know how to tell him no.

She stands, looking miserably past him, but Cleave opens the truck door, and she doesn't know a graceful way to keep from climbing in.

Cleave settles behind the wheel. He starts the engine without speaking. They sit silently, watching the windshield wipers push aside the heavy snow.

"You don't have to quit working up here," he says. "It was just that one time. I'm not in the office much. You wouldn't have to be embarrassed."

She shrugs, with her face tight. She doesn't know what he wants her to say.

"You should have told me you—I mean, I thought you wanted to. I wish I knew what to say to you," he says. "A pretty girl like you. You ought to go with one of the young boys, not an old man like me. You're a real sweet girl. But I've already got somebody. A woman who lives in Frankfort. She's young, but not so young as you. Jesus, you can't be more than eighteen or nineteen."

Deana keeps her hands folded on her lap. Sixteen. But she doesn't tell him that. She hears his voice as if it comes from a long way off, a radio signal that has run into a mountain and can't find its way in.

He presses the accelerator and puts the truck in gear. The windshield wipers keep up their rhythm. Slap-slide. Slap-slide. Deana turns her face to the window, presses her cheek against the cold glass. She wants to say, What if I have a baby? But she doesn't. She says, "Will you stop the truck?" She doesn't want to cry in front of him, but her throat hurts from trying not to.

"What?"

"The truck. Stop the truck. I want to get out."

He pulls to the side of the road. Deana opens the door and gets out. She heads down the hill on foot, but Cleave climbs out, too, and follows, leaving both doors of the pickup gaping open to the blowing snow. He grabs hold of her arm and tries to turn her around. "Come on. Get back in and let me take you home. It's a blizzard out here. Don't be like this."

"I can walk from here," she says softly, pulling away. "It's just snow. But you better watch yourself," she says. "My daddy might just kill you if he ever finds out."

In early February, the mines shut down, and Daddy, laid off, is always under Mama's feet. Lying in bed, Deana hears them talking in the kitchen. She pulls the quilt up around her ears to shut out their words, but she can hear them anyway, though Mama is talking low, hoping Daddy will follow her example. She imagines her mother standing by the stove, in her habitual place, the linoleum thin under her feet. Mama has moved so often from the stove to the table that she has worn herself a path of faded flowers, the vinyl completely gone in spots so that they can see the wood floor beneath. She has her back turned to Daddy while she talks to him, Deana knows, even though she cannot see them. Mama has learned, as they all have—the best way to keep him from getting angry is to avoid looking directly into his eyes.

"Tell her to get her lazy ass out of the bed. Tomorrow I want her back in school," he says, and now she listens for the signal, the chair scraping the floor. He will come in here, maybe, and rip the quilt off her, pull her to her feet, not caring how the parts of her body are attached to one another; she will feel the twist of his fingers closed around her wrist.

"She's sick," Mama says, her voice still low, matter-of-fact, not pleading. Pleading enrages him, too. This is a house, Deana knows, where feelings are dangerous. No matter which ones they start with, Daddy ends up angry, Mama ends up crying, and somebody somehow or another gets hurt.

He grunts. "What's wrong with her?"

"Stomach. Can't keep anything down. She ain't eat a bite for two days."

"No wonder she don't feel like getting up. She needs to eat. I don't have much use for a grown girl laying in the bed feeling sorry for herself."

"She ain't feeling sorry for herself. She's sick."

"Sick, shit."

The truth is, they're both wrong. Deana is really lying here because she is waiting for her period. Or waiting for her daddy to figure it out, hear a rumor, come in here with his fists or his shotgun, and end her misery. Or waiting to die, which suits her, too, though she doesn't know if it's possible to die from humiliation and shame. It doesn't matter to her anymore what will happen. She feels like a radio with a fuse blown. Just an hour ago, she had looked under the quilt for her legs and couldn't find them. They had withered into nothing. Maybe if she lies here long enough, the rest of her will disappear, too.

She dozes, finally, but later an icy pain low in her back wakes her, and she arches her back. She must have cried out, because suddenly, the light bulb over the bed blinds her, and Mama and Lily stand looking down at her, stripping the covers away.

"Dear Jesus," Mama says, and it's a prayer and not cussing. "Thank the good Lord, this is another night Wayman went off after supper and didn't bother to find his way back home."

"What's wrong with her, Mama?" Lily asks. "Is she dying? Look at all that blood."

But Mama doesn't answer. "Go get me a wet wash rag and some towels. We're going to have to strip the bed down, but first we're gonna have to clean her up."

"Swing your legs down," Mama says, dragging Deana upright. "Sit here on the edge of the bed for me. Do you think you can sit up?"

She does, her teeth chattering. Then she sees the blood, too, all over her white panties, covering her legs. When she sits up, the blood runs in rivulets to her feet. Lily comes back in with a pan of water and a washcloth. Mama spreads Deana's knees apart and stuffs one of towels underneath her, to catch the blood still flowing, and begins to wash Deana's legs. Every so often, she has to dip the cloth back in the water to rinse it, and then she wrings it out and starts again.

"Mama?" Lily says again. "Mama, I ain't never seen this much blood. She's gonna die."

"She ain't gonna die," Mama says. "Now go get me a clean wash cloth and some more towels."

"What's wrong with her?"

"Oh, Lily, grow up."

Mama helps Deana to her feet. "You're gonna have to sit on the floor while I get the bed changed. Can you do that for me?"

Deana doesn't say anything, but she lets Mama guide her down to the floor beside the bed. Mama tries to hold the towel in place between her legs. So she isn't dead and she isn't dying. This disappoints her. Now she will have to get up one of these mornings, think of something to do.

Mama strips the bed quickly, leaving a mountain of covers beside the bed. When Lily comes back with the water, she puts Lily to work washing the rest of the blood off Deana's legs. When she has dried them, Lily lifts the wet, sticky tee shirt over her sister's head. When Mama has the bed changed, she gets a clean towel, folds it, and lays it across the metal footboard. Together, the two of them help Deana back into bed.

Mama pulls out the bloody towel and inserts the other, efficient as a nurse. When she has pulled the covers up around Deana's shoulders, she looks down at Deana. Her mouth is drawn down at the corners, leaving little creases on either side. "For God's sakes, Deana," she says. "Didn't *you listen to a word I said? How did you let this happen?" Then her mouth twists. "I know how, I guess. The question is, who?"*

Deana lies there, looking at the ceiling, at the blinding overhead lights above the bed.

Mama lays her hand briefly on Deana's forehead. Her hands are cold. "Girl, do you have any idea how lucky you are?"

In March, Deana and Lily are walking to Felton's. Deana didn't want to go, but Mama insisted, going so far as to pull her up from the porch swing. "You've turned into a ghost. You can't sit staring at the road for the rest of your life, like you're waiting for Prince Charming to come riding by."

"Why not?" Deana wanted to say, but she doesn't argue, it takes too much energy, more energy than it takes to go on and get up, start heading down the porch steps behind her sister.

She has been so sad lately, and she doesn't know why, but she has begun to unfreeze at the same time the ground has. She notices for the first time how much everything wants to live, no matter where it finds itself, even this awful coal camp. The daffodils push up out of the ground next to the porch steps. The mountain laurels grow even by the coalmines, though with their flowers, they look foolish and lonely, like a pretty woman trying too hard to stand out in all the ugliness around her, wearing high-heeled boots and too much rouge on her cheeks.

"Come on," Lily calls, impatient, ahead of her. Lily has on blue jeans, but Deana is wearing one of Mama's old dresses, loose and comfortable as a nightgown.

"I know you didn't want to come," Lily says, when Deana catches up. "I didn't want you to, either. You know what people are saying, don't you? That you sit on the porch swing all day like some old crazy woman. You even look old."

Deana walks beside her sister, puffing a little. She hasn't gotten much exercise lately, and she does have a hard time keeping up. Lily isn't the only one who's lost patience with her. For a week or two, Daddy threatened to whip her with a belt, but maybe she looked so vacant, like a stove with the fire out, that he couldn't work up enough anger to carry out his threats. She didn't care, still doesn't, but here she is, one foot moving ahead of the other, aware that feeling is coming back to her, like an old toothache, whether she wants to feel anything or not.

At Felton's they go inside. Deana looks at the floor in front of her, the old game. If she can't see them, they can't see her. But she feels them looking—Marion Paluzzi, slack-sleeved, over in the corner by the stove, lit this morning to knock the chill off; Asa Slusher whittling beside him, dropping the shavings into an old wash pan between his feet. Head down, passing a swirl of blue skirts she can't identify, she follows Lily, who turns to hand her two tin cans of evaporated milk, then walks to the counter.

When they set the groceries on the counter, Lily looks up at Mr. Felton. "Mama wants to know can you charge it till Friday, when Daddy gets paid?"

Mr. Felton hesitates for a moment, and then he says, "Just tell her to try to get down here before Monday. That's when I pay my own bills. Them delivery men, they don't give me this stuff for free."

Lily nods, her face flushing just a little, but she's used to this, and, after all, sooner or later, Mama tells them, he always gets paid.

When they are back outside, the sun is up, and the air has started to get warmer. A motorcycle comes roaring up to the front of Felton's, stopping just at the bottom step. The boy riding it has on a denim jacket and bell-bottom jeans. His body is lean and narrow, and there is something familiar about the easy grace with which he climbs off the seat and kicks the stand to lean the bike down. Deana turns, in spite of herself, to watch him lope up the steps. He turns slightly when he opens the door, and she catches a glimpse of his face.

Back home, they find Mama in the kitchen. Lily sets down the sack with a little flourish. Though Deana's heart is pounding, it is Lily who just has to tell this news. "Well, Mama," she says, "you'll never guess who's back. Will Brinson. We seen him at Felton's, riding up on a big black motorcycle."

"So?" Mama says. She shakes the can of milk before she sets it in the cabinet.

Lily shrugs. "I just wondered why he's back, that's all. Usually means he's in some kind of trouble. Do you think his grandfolks sent him back?"

"I wouldn't know. And I don't really see where it's any of our business."

Summer comes on hot and sudden after a cold spring. Deana slips out as early as she can, before her daddy wakes up, when the hills are still draped in darkness. The June air is thick with humidity and the scent of honeysuckles, and her body feels damp as soon as she goes out the door. She is sixteen and on the brink of something, but she doesn't know what it is, only that she has lived through the time when she wished only to wither into nothing, and now she is going to have to go on with her life. Her daddy has started to notice her again, to nag and to threaten. I'm not gonna feed you for the rest of your life, he said, just last night at supper. You ain't gonna lay around here like a retard or a head case the rest of your life.

Sure-footed, she walks down the road toward the creek and slips between the pine trees, to the bank where it's mossy and cool. She will sit with her back against a sycamore trunk, waiting for daylight, dreaming and thinking, and what she has started to think about most is Will. She has seen him two or three times already, started to memorize the shape of his face. He has blue eyes and black lashes a girl would kill for, and when she thinks about his body, thin but roped with muscles, she can already feel the shape of his back beneath her hands.

What she doesn't know yet is how she will make him notice her, make him fall in love with her the way, she sees now, she has always been in love with him. Maybe, the next time he comes out of Felton's, she will be waiting, straddling his motorcycle, her feet flat to the ground and her hair soft and shining down her back. She will wear the pink lipstick that brings out the sparkle in her eyes and shorts that show off her good legs. Or maybe she will bake a cake and take it up to his house. I heard you were back, she will say. My mother sent you this cake. Welcome. Whatever he likes, that is what she will be, the modest girl who can cook and sew or the wild girl who can ride behind him on his motorcycle, her arms looped tight around him, his ribs warm under her hands.

But she has to be careful not to lose her nerve. Once, she saw his bike parked over by Ray Slusher's house, his denim jacket draped across the handlebars. She went right up to it, took the jacket and held it against her face. She slid her arms into the sleeves and for a moment it was as if Will himself were holding her, and she felt so full of everything—desire, hope, love—that she stood there for a long moment wrapped in his warmth, his smell. But then she heard voices, and she panicked. She ripped the coat off and flung it down, missing the handlebars, but running away just in time. She was only a house or two up the road when she heard him on the front porch, his voice—his wonderful throbbing voice, low-pitched and rhythmic as a heartbeat—calling goodbye to Raymond, and then the sound of the Harley starting up. If she had it to do over again, she thinks, she would keep the coat on, walk up the road wearing it, and make him come to her to get it back.

She is so full of her dreams that when the sun comes up, dappling the creek bank with patches of light, she is lying flat on her back, looking up at the light green undersides of the leaves. She almost senses him before she hears him, and when she sits up to see him sitting on a tree root, a blade of grass between his teeth, she thinks it's her own imagination, that maybe she's dreamed him right there.

She blinks, but he doesn't disappear. He sits there, watching her, idle and wary as a lizard, and she has to speak first.

"What are you doing there?" she says. Her voice is sharper than she intends it to be, because she isn't ready for him yet. She thought she had this scene all planned out, her lines all memorized, but here he is and now she's going to have to make them up as she goes.

"I was out walking, just poking around. I thought you might be dead, so I watched you for a little while to see if you were breathing."

"Well, at least while you were poking around, you didn't poke me," she says, decides that sounds stupid, and then laughs, but her laugh sounds stupid, too.

He tilts his head, looks her straight in the eye for a long time, long enough to make her face feel hot. Then he shakes his head and spits the blade of grass into the red dirt at his feet. "I know you, don't I? That's what I'm trying to figure out. You look familiar, but I just can't place you. You're—?"

"We knew each other when we were little kids. I'm Deana. Deana Perry?"

He gets up, walks over, and drops to the ground beside her. He puts his hands on her chin, twisting her face from side to side, and then looks into her eyes. "Oh, yeah," he says, finally. "The crazy girl."

"I am not crazy," she says, her head tilted, in a voice she hopes is *flirtatious, knowing, not desperate and defensive, which is how she feels. This is not working out the way she wanted it to. He's touching her, but his hand wiggling her face around makes her feel like he's a horse doctor checking her teeth. "Anyway, if I remember right, you're crazy, too."*

He laughs, showing the sharp edges of his teeth. In front, they overlap the littlest bit, but Deana finds this adorable—that's what she used to hear girls in school say about their boyfriends, as they giggled and shared secrets in the girl's bathroom. O, isn't he just adorable?

"You're damn straight about that."

"Damn straight," she says, "fucking straight," so that he will know she is not just some dumb hillbilly girl who doesn't know what's going on in the world.

"I do know who you are, though," he says, tweaking her nose and grinning. "You're that scrawny little girl who used to follow me around all the time."

This time she will be the one to stare him down. "I was not scrawny. Anyway, I was deeply in love with you," she says, looking him straight in the eye. She tries to stare him down, but when he doesn't look away, she finally has to drop her gaze, her hands folding and unfolding a yellow-green leaf that has fallen from the tree to her lap.

"Too bad I wasn't old enough to enjoy it," he says. "Except, of course, I don't believe in it. In love, I mean."

He sits so close to her that she can feel the heat from his body, wishes she could lean her head against his chest. He pushes her hair behind her ear. "I'm glad to know you again, Deana Perry. I'm Will Brinson. I'll bet you're not one bit crazier than I am. Why don't you hang out with me this afternoon? I'll bet you know what there is fun to do around here, if there's anything fun in this godforsaken place."

Oh, yes, she thinks. Oh, yes, I do.

Two weeks later, she goes with him across the county line and they get one of the winos hanging around outside to go in and buy them a pint of vodka in exchange for a pint of Mad Dog 20-20. When he comes out with the bottle, Deana has to turn her head sideways. He smells like piss and perspiration.

"Have you ever had vodka?" Will asks, and she nods, though the

truth is, she's so scared of her daddy's drinking, she's never taken more than a sip or two of beer. She takes a pull of the bottle he offers her, and strangles on it.

"Slow down," Will says, taking the bottle away. "I'll get you a Coke or something to mix it with, if you want. I know what I'm going to do this summer. I'm going to teach you how to drink."

Through the summer, they roar all over the county and into the next one with her on the back of his bike. She winds her arms around his waist as tight as a morning glory vine, her eyes as wide as the open blooms, and Will keeps his promise. He teaches Deana to drink and to do a few other things, too, though when they are parked down by the lake, and Will leans back the leather seat of Cleave's black Cadillac, moving his body to cover hers, she holds Will's face between her hands as long as he will let her, and looks into his eyes. This is the only way she can keep herself from remembering the other face, and this new fear that if Cleave finds out about them, he will tell Will what happened. She knows, no matter how wild Will thinks he is, what he would think of her then. She doesn't think she could survive it.

A month or so after, when they are both a little drunk, Deana talks Will into going into one of the mineshafts, late at night. He's told her that even though he knew every inch of the tipple when he was growing up, he has never actually been underground in a mine before.

"You're kidding me?" she says, incredulous. "You're daddy owns half the coal in this part of the country, and you've ever been inside. Well, come on, chicken shit, let's go. We'll see how brave you are with a mountain over your head. You think you're so tough."

They are drunk and giggly, but when they get to the opening, he looks at her, suddenly sober. "Why in the world would anybody want to go in there?" *he asks.* "It's bound to be like crawling up the asshole of the world."

"You don't know what it's like, Mr. Rich Kid from Virginia. You've never been. The coal dug out of that mine is what you've lived on all these years, and you don't even know the first thing about it."

"I've never eaten shit, either, but I don't have to eat it to know it tastes, well, you know," *he laughs,* "that it tastes like shit."

She moves a little away from him. This is important to her, but she isn't sure why. It's important to her to go inside the mine and for him to go with her. She's afraid, too, but it's like showing him something about herself she doesn't know how to tell him any other way. She looks at him, trying to decide whether to give up the idea. Then she knows how to make him do what she wants. She has to show him that she sees he has a weakness. She knows him well enough to know that he will never give anyone, especially a girl, a weapon as powerful as that.

"You really are afraid," she says, her eyes sparkling with challenge. "What do you think is in there? The ghost of some old dead miner? Rats?" She doesn't give him time to answer. She reaches her hand to him, and then ducks past him into the opening. "Come on," she says. "I'll go first, since you're such a chicken."

She crawls in ahead of him, feeling the dampness of the mine floor against the fabric of her jeans. She really is scared, despite her insistence that they do this, but she is excited, too, with Will behind her. It seems to her that in some weird way this is a kind of test. A test of what is less clear.

A few feet in she hears a thump and Will squalling. "Goddamn," he says. "I always thought I was short, but I'm too tall to be a miner."

"Keep your hand over your head," she says. She tells him she's heard that some miners trail their hands above them. It reminds them to keep their heads low, but it's also a superstition; they think the roof can never cave in on them as long as they can feel the top. She tells him how her uncle worked shaft mines out west once, but came home to the low coal of Kentucky, unable to get used to the echo of falling rock. It was spooky, he said, knowing the roof was high in darkness above him, but unable to test it with his own hand.

She tells him how sometimes miners break through the wall into a shaft long abandoned, and the trapped gases smother them. She tells him how they live in fear of the suffocation they call the black damp, not knowing who might have dug into the mountain years before them, that they are distrustful of promises and maps.

But she doesn't tell him how, at twelve, she stayed in one of these tunnels for hours, not knowing as she felt her way along in the dark whether she crawled deeper to the center of the mountain or inched her way toward home. Or how, when she saw her father's dark shape fill the space at the drift mouth, she was afraid to call out to him, but huddled close to the cut rock until he found her, his Wheat light drilling a yellow hole in the dark.

When they have gone far enough, she stops so that he can feel the weight of the dark. "It makes you invisible," she whispers, wondering suddenly if this is what makes her father drink, if he thinks the liquor will make it impossible for anyone to see him.

"You are so strange, Deana. Can we go now? I can think of a whole lot sweeter ways to prove my manliness to you than freezing my ass off in here."

🌿Eighteen

Will sits on the end of the dark blue sofa, one heel on the edge of the thick cushion, his hands clasped around his knee. Deana perches on the arm of a wing-backed chair a few feet away and sips beer from a pewter mug. She is nervous, and she doesn't understand why. It's not as if what is going to happen between Will and her hasn't already happened half a dozen times before. But it will be the first time they've been together in Cleave's house. Deana has never wanted to come here, but this time Will insisted. For the entire week, Cleave is in Frankfort attending a coal association meeting, and Will wants to take advantage of his father's absence to make love in a real bed. She calls it that—making love—though Will has never once said he loves her, and the phrase itself—making love— sounds odd to her, as if people who made anything, even love, ought to have something left over to show for all that spent energy besides the loneliness she always feels, even with Will. She never feels as if something has been given, but always as if, instead, something she can't quite bring into focus has been taken away.

Will stares at her, the light behind him gold where it filters through the blinds hung over the window that faces west. With light behind him, his eyes look dark, shuttered. He has eyes of an indeterminate color, sometimes a light brown, like coffee with a little cream. Other times, they look almost gray, impenetrable, like the sky on a snowy day. She looks closely at him, trying to figure out what he might be thinking, but he stares her down, and she looks away. She loves him in hope and despair, joy and misery, and she *is disappointed, but mostly relieved that she cannot quite see his eyes for a moment, certain that they are neither windows into his soul nor a mirror where she can see any reflection of herself.*

He keeps staring. She can feel it, and she blushes. Then he stands and walks toward her, holding out his hands. He takes hers and pulls her to her feet. She leans her face against his shoulder, looking down at the blue and green plaid floor of Cleave's den. He lifts her left hand against his chest, his other arm draped around her shoulders, as if they are about to dance. "Damn, girl," he says. "Your hands are like ice cubes. If I couldn't feel your heart beating, I'd think you were dead."

She moves her face against the soft cotton of his shirt. It smells fresh, like sheets just taken off the line, and she wonders if he's been outside all morning until she came.

"So," he says, his hand under her chin, nudging her face up so he can look into her eyes. This close, his eyes are warm and brown, with circles like those in the heartwood of trees, and she can see herself in them, bathed in light like a star. "You want to go upstairs and see if I can get you warm?"

She nods, and he heads toward the door of the room, pulling her behind him. The stairs, carpeted in gray wool and patterned with worn red roses, are taller than she could have imagined. The wallpaper above the walnut wainscoting is covered with roses, too, but the flowers in the paper are smaller. Even though Deana wants to love this house, to appreciate its grandeur as much as her father would despise it, she can't help feeling that it looks a little overwrought somehow, like an old lady's garden late in the blooming season, when she has grown bored with thinning and weeding and has let the flowers become tangled and wild, setting seed.

Upstairs the hall is lined with white-painted doors. Deana thinks later there were five or six of them, but how can she be expected to remember with Will behind her, his warm breath against her neck? What can people find to do with so many rooms? Will, holding her hands behind her back, and pushing her a little to keep her moving forward, leads her to a door at the far end of the hall. Next to the door sits a dark table, which holds a vase of drooping white lilies, their petals edged with brown. In the ornate mirror hanging above the table, Deana sees her own face, white and ghost-like, except for two red circles on her cheeks. She reaches up to smooth her hair. Then Will opens the door next to the table and pushes her inside.

Ash Grove

The room is large, carpeted in rich blue, the creamy wallpaper covered with tiny blue flowers. Forget-me-nots. This room is lighter than the rest of the house. A tall double window, hung with cream-colored lace, faces east and frames the headboard of the red cherry bed. The bed, queen-size, is covered with an ivory satin bedspread, and the tall posts are draped with a canopy made from the same lace as the curtains. In contrast with the den, she sees, this is obviously a woman's room.

Will leads Deana to the tall bed and they sit side by side at the edge. The bed is so tall that Deana's feet dangle above the floor the way they used to dangle from the church pew when she was a child. The satin feels cold against Deana's hands, and so slick she is afraid she might slide off the bed to the floor.

"This isn't your room is it?" she asks. "It's so—feminine." Besides, there is nothing here to remind her of Will—no dog-eared paperbacks stacked by the bed, no record player or piles of records, no faint odor of cigarettes and sweat.

"No, of course not. My room is right at the top of the stairs."

Then Deana remembers her mother talking about Will's mother's room, the room Mama cleaned three or four times when Deana was small, filling in for a woman at Mama's church. Mama says the woman cleans the room regularly, even though nobody ever uses it. Deana looks around, noticing the objects that Mama took such pleasure in describing—the fringed lamp-shades, the vanity with its triple mirror where a woman could see any side of her face she wanted to see, checking the intensity of her lipstick, straightening the curve of her hair. On the vanity sits a mirrored silver tray holding four or five ornate bottles of perfume, some nearly full of amber liquid, now nearly as dark as aged whiskey.

Once, when Deana was eleven or twelve, Mama had come home humming. Deana remembers Mama walking in the door of their house smelling musky and sweet, having touched her finger to the top of one of the bottles of perfume and dabbed a drop or two at her throat. "No harm done," she said, laughing, though Deana could tell Mama was embarrassed at such vanity, at succumbing to the temptation to take something, even a drop of perfume, that did not belong to her. "It's so much stronger than cologne," she said, leaning her head close to Deana's face. "It only takes a little and you smell so good."

But the last time Deana remembers Mama coming here—maybe because her feet hurt or maybe Wayman was off on a drunk and who knew or cared if he'd be back—Mama had come home mad at the world, slamming the coffee pot onto the stove, raving about the injustice of a dead woman's closet full of warm clothes and shoes somebody ought to be wearing, how awful it was to live in a world where poor people do without supper and rich people have more than they need and let it all fall to ruin and waste.

But Deana tries not to think about her mother, or Cleave Brinson, or Wayman Perry. She tries to think only of Will, who has scooted away from her, across the bed, to lie down on the opposite side. He rests against the satin-covered pillow, his elbows bent, hands clasped behind his head. He says, not looking at her, but at the ceiling, "Actually," he says, softly, as if there might be a ghost in here he's afraid of waking. "Actually, this was my mother's room."

Deana nods. Her back is to him, but she turns her head toward her left shoulder, though she still can't see Will from where she sits. The satin bedspread feels cool against her calves, and for a second she thinks her teeth might start chattering from the chill in the room.

"I thought it must be," she says. She doesn't tell him that her mother had been in this room, polishing the dressing table, smoothing down the bedspread. When she is with him, she tries to forget who she is, who they both are. "I mean—it's so pretty, I didn't think it could belong to a man. They don't—you know—usually like things so flowery."

She waits to see what he will say, but when he doesn't answer, awkwardly, uncertainly, she lies down, too. She feels strange, the way she does sometimes when she is swimming, floating face-down in the water, when she opens her eyes to see an alien world all dim and green. Before, even with Will in control of her, they have been more on her turf than his. She's been the hometown girl, and he's been the boy who came back after a long time gone. She really is trembling now, but she isn't sure whether it's the cold room or her nervousness at being here. In the sudden silence, she wonders if Will has forgotten about her. He makes no move toward her, and in this big bed, even though they are together, there is so much distance between.

Finally, Will turns, lifting himself onto one elbow. He reaches for *something on the table on his side of the bed, but she can't see because his back has hidden his hand from her view. When he lies back down, he scoots closer to her, and she sees that he is holding toward her a photograph in a silver frame. The woman in the picture is smiling at the camera, though it seems to Deana that her eyes are looking at something far away. The woman has on a sleeveless dress with a shawl collar, her neck narrow and white. Her right hand rests on the shoulder of the small boy who sits in her lap. The boy is tiny, but he sits up tall and straight.*

It's funny, but Deana remembers her mother having just the same posture when she used to sit waiting late into the night for Deana's father to come home. Half of her is attending to the business at hand, stirring the pot or kneading the biscuits, but the important part of her attention lies somewhere else. Deana doesn't know what the woman is listening for, but she knows without Will having to tell her—maybe he doesn't know himself—that the boy is waiting for the signal from his mother that it is time to get down. He's her shadow, and he's learned the best way to stay close to her is never to let her know he's there. He's such a lovely little boy in his dark Sunday school suit and paisley bow tie. His mouth is prim and solemn above his pointed chin.

"Oh, Will," Deana says, taking the picture from him, the frame cold in her hands. "How sweet. You are so cute. You look just like you do now, too, in a way. Only, of course," she laughs, "you're smaller. Is this your mother?"

He nods.

"She was beautiful, wasn't she?" Deana wonders again, looking at the photograph, what Will sees in her when there are so many pretty women in the world, polished and gleaming like his mother. Deana's father likes to remind her that she herself is not much to look at, certainly no pageant queen, and she is so graceless and stupid that when Will does take her somewhere, she sits back in the shadows, afraid she'll do something stupid and make him ashamed. She wants to press her cheek against his hand in gratitude that he has chosen her out of all the other girls he could have, to bring into this room with all its revelations about what is closest to his heart. But she doesn't. She will wait for him to make the first move, to make sure she is welcome. She has that much in common with the little boy he used to be.

He takes the picture from Deana and leans over to drop it to the floor by the bed. "She really was. Very beautiful. When I was little, I used to think she was like a princess in a story. I used to come in here and run my matchbook trucks around the swirls in the rug while she curled on the bed and read. You remind me of her, a lot, always with your nose in a book."

Deana feels her cheeks grow warm. She is amazed that, in any small way, she could remind him of a woman like his mother. She doesn't take her eyes off Will as he strips off his tee shirt and lies back against the pillows with his hands behind his head. She wants to lay her hand palm down against his chest, but instead, she tries to lie as still as she can. This is the most he's ever told her. Please, she thinks, don't stop talking.

"She was so smart, my mother was. Most people don't know that. She was well educated, too. She majored in English at Radford. Before she married my father—my aunt Betsy told me this—she wanted to go to New York and work for a magazine. She could have, too. It's a shame she was so beautiful, when she could never be happy."

"Why would you say that?" Deana asks, in the little silence at the end of his words. She wishes she could say, Look around you. In the grand scheme of things, how bad could this be? But she knows better. After all, he lives in this big house, too, but it hasn't made him happy, has it?

She moves closer to him, curling her body against his back, and keeps her thoughts to herself. She is grateful for this stream of talk, for the blessing of not having to say anything. She is just the hick daughter of a coalminer. What could she possibly have to say? She wants to wrap herself around his body and never have to talk again.

Will turns to face her. He slides his arm underneath her neck, cradling her head. "Anyway, why are we talking about this now? I can think of better ways to spend this time. Can't you?"

With his free hand, he strokes her cheek lightly, the tips of his fingers soft and cold as snow. "You have really pretty eyes. I don't know that I've ever really looked at them before. They're not just one color, are they? They're not dead brown, like old leaves. They have these gold lines that shoot out from the center—like sunbursts?—and there are little discs at the center of the iris that are almost black."

"Those are pupils," she says, teasing. She lays her hand lightly on his hip, his belt hard against her palm, her thumb on the warm skin of his waist. She likes this mood better, when he looks at her, touches her, instead of being lost in his anger at all those people from his past.

"I know they're pupils. Women. You complain that men aren't romantic. Then when we do get poetic, you talk about pupils. Listen. Did you know that when songwriters say lovers gaze into each other's eyes, they're wrong?"

"Okay. I'll play. Why are they wrong?"

"Because you can't gaze into someone else's eyes. You can look at both eyes from a distance, but close up, like this, you can really only gaze into one eye at a time."

"That's not true. I can see both your eyes right now."

"Come on. Just a little closer. Now try it."

She does. She tries to see both his eyes, equally, but instead, when she really focuses, her eyes dart from one eye to the other. What pretty eyes, she thinks. She wants to fall into them and never come out. "You're right," she says. "Only one eye at a time. How come I never noticed that before?"

He rises up on his elbow and threads his fingers through her hair, tugging her head toward him. She can feel his moist breath against her face, smelling like beer and honey. "It makes you wonder about a lot of things people don't see, doesn't it?" he says. "Do you think people can tell the truth with one eye and lie with the other?"

"I don't know how you could tell," she says. Somehow, his mood has shifted again, but it has happened so quickly that she is confused. What exactly is he looking for here? She goes on, hesitant. "I mean, can you really tell whether somebody is lying or not? Just by looking?"

He doesn't answer, but there is something about the way he's looking at her that tells her, yes, something here has changed just a little. His keeps his fingers twisted in her hair, and when he tightens his grip, pulling hard, she almost cries out. Does he know he's hurting her? Part of her wants to pull away, but that's silly. See. His fingers loosen just a little, and she relaxes her head against his palm.

"Can I show you something else?" he asks.

She doesn't answer, but he must take her silence for a yes, because he pulls her even closer to him until they lie with the length of their bodies together, his forehead touching hers. "This is an optical illusion," he says. "Let me show you how this works. When I was little, my mom and I used to *play this game."*

Then he presses his forehead harder against hers, grinding it back and forth, just so that it almost hurts, but not quite. His fingers pull her hair a little tighter. "Don't I look like I've got one big eye?"

"Yes, you do," she is about to say, has begun to say, but suddenly he jerks her head back, hard, and just as suddenly jerks it back toward him so that their foreheads slam together. "What are you doing, Will?" she says, tears welling in her eyes. She blinks them back. He knows, she thinks, in sudden terror. That's why he insisted on bringing her here, to punish her because she did not wait for him, to punish her for Cleave.

He pulls her head back again, his fingers tightening again in her hair. He studies her face, and she blinks again to clear her eyes. "Two lovely eyes," he says, "The color of tobacco, or is it topaz?"

"Why are you acting like this?" Her voice is rough, and she turns her face away from him. Why does he always do this? She will say anything he wants her to say, do anything he wants her to do, be whatever he wants her to be. Why does being with him always have to feel like some kind of test? If he knows about Cleave, if this is what makes him so cruel to her, why doesn't he just say? Her throat tightens. "I love you, Will, but I don't know what you want."

Suddenly, his eyes look away and he lets her go. He moves his hand around to muffle the last part of the sentence with the back of his hand. Then he kisses her lightly on her forehead, as though he is healing her with his touch. "Shhh. Hush. You don't have to say anything. I scared you, didn't I? Oh, Deana, you didn't think I would really hurt you? I was just playing a little game."

"What kind of game?"

"I told you. An optical illusion. Have you ever seen the picture that has an old woman and a young woman? What you see—whether you see an old hag, or a beautiful lady—depends on how you look at it. I was just trying to see you from different angles, trying to figure out who you really are. Who are you, Deana, inside that pretty face? Are you just a sweet little chick, all hot for me, looking at me with those gooey brown eyes? Or are you a one-eyed monster who's out to break my heart?"

"Maybe that's all it is to you, playing some kind of game. How am I supposed to—?"

"To know? Exactly. You can't. That's the very point I'm trying to make. Just because you say you love me, how do I know if I can believe you? How am I supposed to know?"

She rolls away from him. The blue flowers in his mother's wallpaper blur. She hates it when he gets in moods like this. She never knows what he's going to say, or what he's going to do. And if he gets up right now and walks away from her, how will she ever be able to stand it? Her father can whip her with a belt until the welts stand out scarlet against the pale flesh of her thighs, and she will never even whimper, will not give him the satisfaction of making her cry. But all Will has to do is look at her, with that strange dangerous nothingness in his eyes, and she falls to pieces, just like that old Patsy Cline song her daddy used to get drunk and sing.

But now he has moved to lie against her, and she rolls over to face him, wrapping her arms around his neck. He smoothes her hair and kisses her shoulder with quick, light kisses. His hand, gentle and warm now, strokes her hair, and then moves to follow the curve of her hip, finding its way under her tee shirt to caress her skin. "I'm sorry. Please. Just forget it. Don't talk anymore," he whispers. "Please."

She starts to say something, stops—what is there to say? Instead, she sighs. She catches hold of his hand guides his palm over her breast, feeling his face move, softly now, against her hair.

In the afternoon they drive forty miles away to the Corps of Engineers lake. Will parks his pickup near the edge of the water, and they sit on the tailgate, their legs swinging over, and drink beer. On the opposite bank, he tells her, where the shapes of trees have begun to blur in the twilight, Cleave and Doc Beecham used to bring their boys fishing. Below, hidden by the dark water, is where Cleave's parents' farm used to be before the dam opened and flooded the fields. Though he knows the house and outbuildings were torn down first, he tells her, he still imagines them there, underneath the water, like caves for fish.

He slides his arm around her and she leans her head against his shoulder. Love, she thinks, oh, love.

"I've never shown this to anybody," he says, and she believes him, wants desperately to believe him.

For the moment she forgets about being frightened of him back at the house—no not really frightened, she thinks, confused—sometimes he confuses her, because one minute he'll tell her she's his special girl, the only girl he's ever really cared about, then he'll hold her so tight she is afraid she'll stop breathing. He'll say crazy things. So you think you love me? he said, once. Don't you know who my father is, what he did? You don't know what I might do, either, do you? And she remembers feeling the constriction of those arms, wiry and strong, his tongue pushing insistently into her mouth, not soft and gentle the way she likes to be kissed.

But now she gets down from the tailgate, turns, and leans into the space between his legs, her arms around his neck. She touches his face with her nose, nuzzling him, and he kisses her, his mouth moist and soft. She opens her eyes for a moment and sees the stars whirling above her, and she feels herself whirling, too, her body as warm as if she sat too close to a heat stove, and she doesn't care if she dies right now, if he kills her, if living means living without him, letting go of his body, feeling the cold when he moves away.

He moves his head and buries it against her shoulder, leaving a trail of kisses against the side of her throat. She lays her mouth against his ear. The wind leaves his skin smelling like sheets just taken off a line, and she moves her face against the warmth and the smell. "Will," she says. "Will, Will, Will," pressing the words against his ear.

Later, when they pull into the yard in front of her house, her father is waiting. She can see just his shadow on the front porch, black and shapeless in the moonlight. She kisses Will goodnight, but this time, thinking not so much of Will as of her father. She puts her hands on each side of Will's head, pulling his face around. She kisses him long and hard, stopping once to lick the edge of his mouth, turning them slightly so that her father can see. When he gets back into the truck, she reaches in the window, lays her fingers against his lips. Then, while he starts the engine, she leans against the truck's gleaming fender for a moment, head tilted toward the night sky, before she runs up the steps.

Her father laughs as she sweeps by him. In spite of herself, she stops. He looks sober, and she did not expect that. She waits, but instead of turning toward her, he keeps his eyes on the dark houses across the road from their own.

"Ain't nobody gonna buy the cow," he says softly, his voice is even meaner when it's soft, "when he can get the milk for free. So you can quit

dreaming you'll wind up living in that fine house up yonder, lording it over me."

Later, she is trembling when she climbs under the covers next to Lily, trembling with desire, humiliation, and despair. She feels the hot tears sting her pillow, but she will not sob, will not let Lily wake up and see the depth of what she feels, how helpless she really is. "Oh, Will," she whispers. "Will, you have got to get me out of here."

Nineteen

Deana crosses the bridge over the Cumberland River, and then follows the old road beside the creek bed to the house where Will Brinson grew up. She pulls the car onto the side of the road, getting as far from the edge as she possibly can, intending to walk up the long driveway to the house. She can see, even from this distance, that the porch lights are on, and a couple of lights from inside shine through the windows on the side of the house facing the road. She doesn't know why she is being so secretive, only that she hasn't decided what she'll say when Will opens the door to find her on his porch, or what she'll do. But it seems to give her some kind of advantage to surprise him.

She gets out of the car and goes around to the passenger's side. She searches the glove compartment for a flashlight, but when she can't find it immediately, she decides to make her way up the steep, curving drive by the light of the three-quarter moon. Hands plunged into her the pockets of her coat, she starts walking, following the pavement that winds between the pine trees.

She's breathing hard by the time she makes it up the hill. She almost hopes to find the house deserted, because she hasn't had enough time to think about what she will do if Will is home. Here she is, practically on his doorstep, and she still doesn't know if she's got the nerve to tell him, or even if she wants him to know about Sophie. Besides, what good will it do to tell him now?

She has forgotten, or tried to forget, that awful time with Cleave. But even so, she knows that the feelings she has about Will are the same emotions of anger and betrayal she knew right after Cleave first told her about the woman from Frankfort. Three or four times before Will came back to Ash Grove, she walked up this hill, and slipped around the back of the house. Then, just as she does now, she stood in the cold outside this same window, trying to catch a glimpse of Cleave Brinson sitting at his desk. She waited for a long time in the dark, but she learned that if she stood at just the right angle, and turned her face just so, she could see him behind his big cherry desk.

He had his head bent, and she imagined him adding the columns of figures that represented all his money, all his power over the people here who spent their lives buying what they needed from the businesses he owned and working themselves to death in his mines. Watching him, she remembers a strange combination of rage and wonder. How odd that, despite what they had done—what he had done to her—he seemed like a stranger sitting there. This couldn't be the same man who had come inside her body, who had been so close to her that sometimes, even after she had washed her head in the sink and sat with a comb by the fire in the kitchen stove, she could still smell the odor of his tobacco in her hair. She had hated Cleave and felt detached from him at the same time. She had alternated between such rage that she thought her heart might break in two, it was pounding so hard against the walls of her chest, and indifference and exhaustion so profound that she wanted to lie down in the dirt, right here outside his window, and sleep unto death. That's what she prayed for every night. It sounded right. It sounded biblical, to sleep unto death.

She remembers wondering what Cleave would say if he knew she was pregnant. Then, against the rising panic, she would think, surely she couldn't be, could she? When they did it, she had been in a fog, in a daze. Surely, you couldn't get pregnant when half of you—your body—was doing it with somebody, but your mind had wandered off?

Deana stands without making a movement toward the house and looks at the window that faces the back yard. This time there is a lamp on in the den, but the light is muted, so that she cannot tell if anyone is in the room.

The last time she had come here alone, to stand in these shadows, the light over the pool table was blazing and there was a woman with Cleave. This must have been right before she had that awful miscarriage, though it was awful only because of the blood and the cramping. She was thankful, even now, that there had never been a baby. She didn't have Suzanne then and hadn't known a thing about abortions. What on earth would she have done?

That night she had also stood half hidden by the boxwood, watching the woman with Cleave. Was this the widow Cleave Brinson claimed was so much more suited to him than a sixteen-year-old hillbilly girl? The woman wasn't even pretty, she remembers thinking with some satisfaction. From Deana's perspective, she was too old to be pretty, but even Deana had to admit she looked well-kept, her short blonde hair freshly trimmed and styled, her white blouse and dark slacks neatly pressed. Cleave and the woman laughed as they moved around the edge of the billiard table. The woman's blonde hair glimmered with colored lights under the stained glass lamp that hung over the table. Deana stood watching them, watching the ease with which Cleave put his arms around the woman from behind to steady the cue stick, the familiar way she relaxed against him.

Deana tries to remember now how she felt, but she only knows that when she went down to her knees, her left fist pressed against her mouth to keep from crying out, she found, in the grass beside her, a rock just the right size and weight to wrap her fingers around. She doesn't remember thinking about it first, but suddenly, as if she had been planning to do this all along, she stood and aimed the rock. She threw it with all the power she had, then turned before she even heard the crash behind her, to run down the hill to the road. Then, realizing Cleave might be following her, she changed course after a few steps and stepped into the woods at the front of the house.

A couple of minutes later, she saw Cleave come out onto the front porch and peer into the dark. She heard him swear. Then, when Cleave had gone back inside and closed the door behind him, Deana headed back down the hill, this time picking her way carefully through the thicket of pines. Now she realizes that those must have been the same pine trees where Junior Messer hid two months ago with his shotgun. Had Deana ever been that angry? If she had found a gun beside her instead of a rock, could she have killed Cleave, too? She cannot remember the anger, the fear. What she remembers is the cold air stinging her face, the moisture from the ground against her knees, the rough stone round and heavy in her hand.

She sits down on a wrought iron bench at the edge of the lawn and studies the lighted window. For days, maybe weeks after she broke his window, she was so exhausted she only got out of bed to pee, or to eat when her mother made her, her body weighted like some dead thing to the bed. Once or twice, she woke up sweating, panicked. What if Cleave knew she threw the rock? What would he do? Could he have her arrested? If her father knew she threw the rock, he might have to know why. Nothing could be worse than that, not even dying.

Once, after Will came back to Ash Grove, she ran into Cleave at Felton's store. She tried to pretend she didn't see him, and turned around at the door. But he followed her outside and accused her of terrible things, saying, in front of anybody who wanted to hear, that the only reason she was interested in Will was because she thought he had money.

"It won't work," he said. "We've seen hillbilly trash before." She remembers suddenly, clearly, that Cleave's voice was angry, but his eyes were afraid.

Even now, she can't figure out what on earth he was afraid of. Even if he thought Wayman Perry might confront him, he should have known Deana would be too ashamed to let her father find out. Of course, she never told him. She never told anybody—not anybody—about what had happened with Cleave, not even Suzanne, and certainly not Will. And now, Cleave can never tell him either.

Is she supposed to care, now that Will has become the one who makes hang-up phone calls, who has discovered he needs something she has? What does he want from her, really? Does he secretly hope that all he'll have to do is leave the door slightly ajar and she'll come running through? Or is it as simple as what his letter said, that her father might have some information that will help him learn, at last, how his mother died? If so, she thinks, this time the joke really is on him. Even if her father knows—or ever knew anything about Will's mother and how she died—the information is locked away in her father's stroke-afflicted brain.

And what about me? Deana thinks. Had it ever mattered to Will, even for a second, how she feels or what she wants? How easy it was for him, she thinks, to write a few words of apology on paper, especially when he thinks she has something he wants.

Who can blame her for realizing she finds some satisfaction in knowing that, if she wanted to, she could set off her own little explosion in the middle of his world? Now that he's the last of the Brinsons, what will he think if she marches right in the house to tell him he has a daughter? Will he take one look at Sophie and know her for his own, or will he ask for blood tests, humiliating Deana one more time? Suzanne tries to blame Deana because Sophie doesn't have a father. Maybe Sophie doesn't need one. From where Deana stands, fathers are more trouble than they're worth.

The Brodys are back from church when Deana gets back to her sister's house. The girls are in their pajamas and over-sized tee shirts. They tumble down the stairs one by one to give Lily and Wes hugs.

"Now, listen," Lily says, after kissing each. "If I hear you talking after you turn those lights out, I'll blister your britches. You hear?"

At the back of the line of girls, Sophie turns one cartwheel and lands beside her mother. "Sophie!" Deana says. "Do not turn cartwheels in the house. This isn't even our house, for goodness sakes. Quit acting like a monkey."

Sophie looks up at her mother, wide-eyed, and Lily says, graciously, "O, don't fuss at her, Deana. If my girls wadn't so long-legged, they'd be doing cartwheels, too."

Sophie leans her head against her mother and looks up. Deana slides her arms around Sophie's shoulders, sorry to have been so hateful. "Here, baby, give your mama a hug and get on upstairs. Where is she sleeping?"

"I'm sleeping with Charley," Sophie interrupts. "In a sleeping bag on the floor."

"Goodness, that does sound like fun. It's a good thing she's not sleeping in the bed with her," she tells Lily. "By morning, she'll be one big bruise from head to toe."

Wes, who has disappeared briefly into the next room, comes back with the baby, Troy. He has on a pair of yellow flannel pajamas with a zipper up the front and plastic padded feet. Deana remembers having four or five pairs of these when Sophie was little, and she feels a twinge at how fast these babies grow. Troy wriggles, struggling against his dad's arms to get down. Deana remembers Sophie at two, just as impatient at being held, when she had just learned to go at full tilt. "Whoa, now, buddy," Wes says, holding Troy a little tighter. "You can't play now. Look at you, rubbing them eyes. It's time to go to bed. Come here. Let's give Mommy some sugar, so she can sleep sweet."

"I thought he was already asleep," Lily says, leaning her head over to nuzzle Troy's head with her nose. "What did you wake him up for?"

"I didn't mean to. He was laying in there on the couch by your mama, but he woke up when I picked him up."

"I swear, Wes, I'm so tired, I don't know but what I'd of let him just sleep down here."

"Without a gate to pen him in? You are tired, woman. You might as well let loose Al Capone. If he woke up during the night, you wouldn't have no house left."

Wes is laughing, and Lily shakes her head. She nuzzles Troy's head again, this time rubbing her cheek against his soft bright hair. "Are you that bad, baby? Yes, you are. Mommy thinks you are."

He reaches out his arms for her to take him, but Wes whisks him away. "Your mommy'll come up and tuck you in after while. You can lay in the bed with me till she comes upstairs. Mommy's gonna visit with your aunt Deana."

"Come on in here in the living room and sit down," Lily says, when Wes and Troy have disappeared up the stairs. "My feet are killing me."

The furniture in the living room, like everything else in the house looks new. Lily has already told Deana that some of it came from junk stores and she refinished it. "I could call that table over there an antique," she said, earlier, pointing out a lamp table she redid. "All I know is, before I got hold of it, it was a piece of junk I bought cheap, and now it looks good to me."

It looks good to Deana, too. So do the book cases with the glass doors, stacked one on top of the other. The Brodys have more books than she expected them to, a whole set of World Book Encyclopedias—Lily got those at a yard sale, she revealed earlier—and a few novels and all the Audubon Field Guides. At the top sit all the trophies the Brody children have won.

"Where's Mom?" she asks Lily.

When Lily says their mother has gone back to her place, Deana slides off her shoes and leans back into the soft cushions of the flowered sofa, curling her legs underneath her. "She seems like she's handling things all right."

"She seems to be. I worry about her, though. You never can tell about Mommy. I'm glad she's got that place out back, so we can watch after her, when—well, you know. When Daddy goes."

"I'm glad, too, Lily," Deana says. She has not realized until now what a relief it is to have Lily so close to their mother. "I know I haven't been much help. And what's even worse is, I don't know that I'm ever going to be much help, living as far away as I do."

"Oh, Deana. That's not what I'm worried about. Me and Wes can handle that end of things. It helps me, too, her living so close by. Sometimes when we're going in every direction, you know what she does? She makes the kids soup and grilled cheese sandwiches, and brings their supper over here. If I need to run over to the school and get one of the older kids, she watches the baby. She helps me more than I help her. She don't need money, either. Mommy's got social security and daddy's miner's pension, as far as that goes. That trailer's paid for. For the first time in her life, she can buy anything she needs, though it's not like she'll spend a penny on herself even now. I don't want you to feel like Wes and me need you to help us take care of her. It's not that. It's just—" Lily hesitates, then says, with a little burst of air, as if she wants to say what she's got to say before she loses her nerve, "I just think you and Mommy need to talk to each other. I mean really sit down and talk. I'm not trying to make you feel bad, Deana, but it bothers her that you don't come around anymore than you do. Sometimes she gets to thinking about you and daddy and she just cries and cries."

Deana looks away, studying her hands as if she's hoping she'll find a script in them, to give her an idea of what to say. Here we go, she thinks. If you're not trying to make me feel bad, what would you say if you were trying? "I can probably come back here more often, if you think that would make Mama feel better."

"It don't make much sense to go on hating Daddy, when you see him paying for his mistakes the way he is. And Deana, he's sorry. You know he is."

Deana shrugs. "Maybe you know it. He's never sent any apologies my way. Can I ask you something? How have you been able to stand it, living so close by all these years, listening to them fight and scratch? I'd have been crazy."

"Let me tell you, it's not always been easy. But after you left, she never did take as much off him as she did when we were little. There's been nights she's come over here to sleep, and I've found her in the morning on the couch wrapped up in a quilt. And I will tell you one thing that'll make you feel better. The last time he laid a hand on her was over five years ago. You want to know what made him quit?"

"I hope it's because she took a frying pan to his head."

"That's about the way it was. She caught him on the front porch sober and put a gun to the back of his head. Cocked it. She said the next time he so much as came near her and breathed hard, she was going to shoot him dead. He must've believed it because that's the last time I ever know of him hurting her, physically, I mean."

"Lord, Lily. How can you raise kids, with all that going on?"

"You know kids. If it was me and Wes fighting like that, it'd be one thing. Besides, it's not like it was an every night thing. Whenever I heard things getting stirred up over there, I'd get Wes to take the kids to Dairy Queen. Then I'd call him on his cell phone when I got things calmed down and tell him it was safe to come home. Maybe people finally get too old to fight. Mommy spends most of her time down at the Pentecostal church, and Daddy—you'll never believe this—Daddy's been playing music off and on with the preacher down there, even though he acts like he can't stand him. Wes says the last few years, Daddy's been all tail and no dog."

"I couldn't stand it, Lily. I couldn't stand to live like that."

"I always figured people stand what they have to. Anyway, that's the difference between you and me. I just take him the way he is and try to keep him from killing somebody. I don't take it personal and I don't try to change him. Daddy's a drunk. The only reason he quit drinking is the doctors scared him, and the only reason he ain't started back is he's spent the last six months in and out of a coma."

"So, what you're saying is, I never did learn to stay out of his way."

"No, you never did. And Mommy's always been like that, too. She thought she could change him. When she figured out she couldn't, I guess she was just too old and tired to leave. Besides, Deana, what do you do when you've spent your whole life with the same person?"

Ash Grove
188

"But she hates him. You know she does, the way he's treated her."

"I don't know that, and you don't know that, either. You haven't been around to see the way it is when Daddy's sober and they're not fighting. It's Jolene, come here and listen to this man on the TV. Jolene, come in here and listen to me play this song. And worry about him! You never seen a woman worry more about a man. Do you know she tried to sleep at the hospital right in that old beat-up recliner after he had he stroke?"

"She told me that. So, listen, sister. Why is it some women are smart like you and marry the good men, and the rest of us keep trying to fix the lost causes?"

Lily looks at Deana and Deana drops her eyes, studying the rough cuticle at the base of her thumb. "What lost cause in particular would we be talking about?"

Deana doesn't answer.

"You went to see Will, didn't you? You told him about her. I knew it the minute I pulled into the driveway and your car was gone. Oh, Deana. What happened? What did he say?"

"About Sophie? I didn't tell him anything. I did go up to the house, but I didn't even go in. After I thought about it, I turned around and came back to your place without him even knowing I was up there."

"Well, good for you. I didn't know you had it in you. I think—well, you know what I think, Deana, and if you had a lick of sense, you'd never have got messed up with him in the first place. But you did. Don't you think he ought to help you some with Sophie? It don't seem right for you to have to struggle while he has it easy."

"I don't need him. Look. I've raised Sophie for over six years without Will Brinson's help. Until he wrote me a letter out of the blue to tell me about Cleave, I didn't have a clue how to get in touch with him to give him good news or bad."

"But Deana, he's still her father, no matter what either one of us thinks of him."

"No, he's not. He's a stranger. And until I can make up my mind what's best for Sophie, I'm not telling Will Brinson anything."

Deana spends all day Thursday at the hospital. Mounted close to the ceiling, the television keeps up a steady drone from the time her mother turns it on until she gets ready to leave at six. "I don't watch television much," her mother says. "I just keep it on for the company."

By the time an hour has passed, Deana is ready to go back to Lily's, but she forces herself to stay. How long will her mother be able to keep this up, spending most of her waking hours in the company of a man who hovers at the border between life and death, unable to give her any companionship? Even fighting with Daddy, Deana thinks, must have been better than this endless waiting.

Since the incident the day before, Deana has been unable to bring herself to touch her father, though she watches him from time to time. She thinks of Will's letter. What could Wayman Perry possibly know that would be of any use to Will Brinson? Daddy used to rant and rave about the union, and when Deana was little, she remembers that Wayman was always the first to agree to a walkout, the first to get on the picket line, waving his sign. For a time, he was president of the local, but that was before he started drinking. She can't remember whether this was before or after Will's mother died. Will just made that up, she thinks, that the union might have had something to do with Anne Brinson's death and that Wayman Perry might have heard who or why. And if Anne's mysterious death was just a pretext for finding Deana after so many years, what did he really want from her? What if he found out about Sophie somehow, she thinks, and feels her stomach tighten with a little knot of fear.

At five, the preacher from her mother's church comes by. Deana has gone to walk around the building and see if she can get the circulation in her legs going again. When she comes back to the room, she finds her mother and the preacher kneeling beside Daddy's bed. The preacher has on brown polyester dress pants that have pilled on the rear end, and his reddish-blonde hair is short on the sides and long at the back, cut in what the kids call a mullet. His plaid jacket is folded across the arm of the recliner, and his black Bible with its tissue paper pages lies open on the bed. When they hear Deana, the preacher gets up and puts his arm under Jolene's elbow to help her up, too. Then he sits on the end of Daddy's bed to let Jolene have the chair.

Her mother seems thrilled to see him, and Deana realizes he must be the preacher who, in that great roll call up yonder, has consigned her daddy's soul to the ranks of the redeemed. Deana is grateful for her mother's sake, but she can tell already that she isn't going to like him. He's one of those preachers who never get all the way out of the pulpit. Every other phrase out of his mouth is, Praise Jesus. He just got his car washed—that's why he's a little late—and now the forecast is for rain. Still, he says, praise Jesus my car's clean, even if it won't stay that way for long. He's just a little too Waco for her.

But he does give Deana a break from her mother and her mother's endless afternoon of soap operas. Jolene mutes the volume, brightening up considerably. Apparently, though the church is small, there is enough low-grade misery to make the soap operas pale in comparison. Deana switches the channel to CNN and watches the headlines scroll on the bottom of the screen while she listens to the hum of their voices in the background.

When the preacher gets ready to leave, he pats Jolene on the shoulder and gives Deana a firm, brisk handshake before he holds her hand in both of his. His hands are large and freckled, covered with springy blonde hair. "Well, little lady," he says, looking at her intently. "You sure do look like your daddy. If you're here Sunday, I'd love to see you in church."

"Oh, I won't be here Sunday," Deana says, wondering if it would be rude to pull her hand out of his grasp. "Anyway," she adds. "I'm not Pentecostal."

"That's all right," he says, patting her hand and wiggling it up and down and around and around, as if he's forgotten the rest of her is attached to it. "Ain't nothing wrong with that. When it comes right down to it, we all worship the same God. We just do it in different buildings. What church do you go to?"

"Catholic," she says, not missing a beat. "I go to the Catholic Church. I'm a Catholic."

Now, I got you, you old goat, she thinks, gloating. I can see it in your eye.

Brother Hardwick drops her hand, and to her delight looks briefly confused. He looks at her mother, and Jolene rises to her feet and comes to stand beside him, offering her own hand in place of her daughter's. "Deana has to get back to her work, but I'll be there. You know I'll be there, unless—?" She glances over her shoulder to where Daddy lies in the bed. Brother Hardwick nods, and after a parting flurry of praises, is gone.

"You are not a Catholic," her mother says, after Brother Hardwick leaves. She stands by the window with her arms crossed, watching Deana gather her magazines and snacks and water bottle together and put them in a green canvas backpack to take back to Lily's.

"No," she says slowly. "No, I'm not. I just didn't want to go to a Pentecostal church, and I didn't want to hurt his feelings, so I just said the first thing that popped into my head. I didn't mean to embarrass you."

"You didn't embarrass me. I don't have nothing against Catholics."

"You mean you don't think they're all going to hell anymore?"

"Not the ones who've been born again. I don't think they're right about a lot of things. Like Purgatory. You know one of them Popes just made that up. But that woman you know? That nun? If she hadn't of been there to help you when you had that baby, I don't know what you would have done. I guess I'd try to understand, mostly on account of her, if you wanted to be a Catholic, even if they do have a bunch of hocus pocus that ain't necessary to be saved. I worry about you, Deana, same as I do Wayman."

At Lily's, after Sophie has gone to bed, Deana takes a flashlight and walks across the lawn to her mother's trailer. Ever since Deana can remember, it has always been Mama's habit to stay up late. Sometimes Deana would get up and find her mother sitting at the kitchen table in the quiet, drinking coffee and smoking. She pecks lightly on the door. She's almost sure Mama is up, but she doesn't want to take a chance on waking her mother if, in the years Deana has been gone, Mama has changed. Mama calls, "You don't have to knock, Deana. Don't stand out there on the porch freezing. Come on in."

Deana pushes the door open. She can see Mama's silhouette back lit by the porch light on the small wood deck on the back of the trailer, as she sits at the kitchen table in the dark.

"Hey, Mama. I figured you'd be up," Deana says, quietly, not because there is anybody in the house to wake up, but because the silence of the house makes a quiet voice loud enough to be heard. "It was so dark in here, though, I didn't know whether to knock or not. I thought maybe you'd gone on to bed early. You must get tired, spending all that time in the hospital the way you do."

"Sometimes I get so tired I can't sleep. You ever do that? Get so wore out you can't even rest?"

Deana doesn't answer. Mama takes a draw off her cigarette. It makes a soft hissing noise, as the tip burns red. "You want me to turn a light on?" Mama says, but she doesn't get up.

"Nah." Deana's eyes are adjusted to the dark, and she can see her mother's face tilted toward her, back lit from the porch light, and the shape of an empty chair next to Mama. She goes and pulls the chair out. It makes a long scraping sound. Then she sits down. "Sometimes it's nice to sit in the dark like this and talk. Or think. Come to think of it, I'm always up too late, too. Maybe I got it from you."

"You want some coffee? I got some hot water over there. It's instant, though, not fresh brewed."

"I can't believe you, Mama, drinking instant coffee. I thought I'd never see the day."

"It don't seem worth the trouble to make coffee for just your daddy and me. It gets old and tastes bitter before we can drink it up. Then when I do want a cup, what's in the pot ain't worth drinking. Now with him sick, well, how many cups of coffee can one old woman drink?"

"You're not that old, Mama. Thanks anyway, but I won't sleep a wink if I drink coffee this late."

"I guess I must be used to it. It don't never bother me." Except, Deana thinks, you stay up until two every morning and have ever since I've known you.

Mama lifts her hand for a moment as if she might reach across and touch Deana's hair. Deana instinctively pulls away, and she tries being still. Too late. Mama drops her hand and looks away. Deana starts to say something, but maybe it's better not to say anything. And anyway, what would she say? From the time Deana was thirteen, she and her mother have been awkward about touching each other. Mama hugs her, and that's okay, as long as Deana can see it coming. But if her mother tries to touch her spontaneously, Deana always pulls away, instinctively. She ducks or moves to the side, or pretends to be picking lint off her shirt. Funny thing is, for the life of her, Deana doesn't understand why. It's Daddy she was mad at most of the time when she was young, wasn't it, not her mother?

I'm sorry, she thinks. I don't want it to be like this. How will she feel, when Sophie Anne is all grown up, if Deana reaches over to hug her, and Sophie won't hug her back?

Ash Grove

193

Mama leans forward in her chair. Deana can feel Mama's eyes on her face, even though it is too dark to see their expression.

"What?" Deana says. "It's so quiet in here I can feel you thinking."

"I don't have to say nothing. You know how I feel. I'm glad you're home."

Deana shifts in her chair. "You know what? I'm glad, too."

Mama gets up to make herself a cup of coffee. She pours the hot water and then spoons the instant coffee grains into the cup. She finds her way back to the table through the dark, holding her coffee out in front of her, as if somehow this will keep her from spilling it. "Are you happy, Deana? I always worried you wouldn't ever be happy. Seems like you always had a chip on your shoulder, like you always wanted the one thing you couldn't have."

"Like Will, you mean? He's not dead, you know. You might as well say what you mean."

"I know what I mean. I don't just mean Will. Like a lot of things. We never had much to give any of you kids, not like people do these days. But what I wanted more than life was for you not have to worry yourself to death all the time, the way I done."

"That's funny," Deana says, and for a second, she does touch Mama, lightly, pressing her fingers briefly against Mama's hand. "That's exactly what I always wanted for you."

They sit for a while in the quiet of the kitchen, not talking. Mama draws smoke into her lungs and exhales it into the dark room. Deana watches the shadows from the tree behind the trailer move back and forth when the wind blows. The shadows of the pine boughs are like water against the thin white curtain.

"I think I will get me some coffee, if it's all right," Deana says finally.

"I'll make it," Mama says, and gets up before Deana has a chance to.

When she brings the cup and sets it in front of Deana, Deana folds her hands around the warm cup. "I could have gotten that, Mama. You don't have to wait on me."

"I know I don't have to. I raised you to be able to take care of yourself. But that don't mean I don't like to wait on you while you're here, home with me." She sits down and turns her head toward her daughter. "I always hoped both my girls would be able to take care of themselves whatever happened. And both of you can."

"You know I can. I've had to."

"O, don't you worry about your sister. She's raising them kids right now, but when Troy starts kindergarten, I imagine she'll go back to school like you did, maybe make a teacher or something. She loves kids, and she's plenty smart." Mama hesitates, looking way from Deana before she goes on. "There's something else I wanted to ask you about, Deana. Did you know he's come back here? Will, I mean. He's living up at the Brinson's old home place. One of the nurses at the hospital said he'd started him up a landscaping business. Said he's built a greenhouse out back of the main house, trying to grow starter tomatoes and houseplants, like that. I'd say he's got plenty of room. I don't know how many acres the Brinsons have up there on top of that mountain, and lot has been sold off, but I know it's still a lot. You ever hear anything from him, I mean after—?"

"No, not since I had Sophie. But I already knew he was back here. He wrote to me out of the blue and told me about Cleave. He said he got my address from Lily."

Her mother looks up swiftly. "Oh, no, he didn't get anything out of her," Mama says, surprised. "She can't stand him."

Deana doesn't argue. Will did say he had pretended to be someone else. But why do Lily and Mama think it's their business to run Deana's life?

"He just wanted some attention, that's all," her mother says. "Wanted to make sure you hadn't forgot all about him. Wanted you to feel sorry for him."

"I doubt that. Last time I saw him, the last thing in the world he was interested in was me."

"Some men's just like that. It ain't as though they want you, they just don't want to think somebody else has come along. Too bad somebody hasn't. Why didn't you find somebody nice to marry and settle down with? To be a daddy for Sophie? I remember you dated that teacher for a while, the one who tried to get you to keep going to school. Whatever happened to him?"

Deana shrugs. "It didn't work out. I'm not the most trusting person in the world, I guess. And anyway, I kept finding things wrong with him. Now that I have Sophie, it's hard to risk letting somebody into our lives. What was it that you saw in Daddy, that made you take a chance on him?"

Mama laughs. "The same thing you see in a man when you look at him, the same thing you seen in Will Brinson. Why are you asking me? You've seen pictures of your daddy when he was young. But they don't hold a candle to how good-looking a man he was. He could turn a girl's head just by walking down the road. But it wadn't really his looks. It wasn't even his music. It was just him, something about him. He had this way of looking at you out of his eyes. When he looked at you, it was like you was the only thing worth looking at in the whole world. You know what kind of look I mean."

"O, yes. Yes I do. And women like us, we keep falling for it. We fall for it every time."

Mama sips her coffee and smokes, tapping the ashes from her cigarette onto a little piece of tin foil she has folded up. "I think we can't help seeing the little boy inside that man-sized body. No matter how big a man gets, or how much he blusters around, there's something about men like your daddy, and maybe this is the way Will Brinson is, too. When you look behind their eyes, you see just the littlest boy, and it don't take much studying to see he's scared to death."

"Scared of what?"

"I don't know. I guess it would depend on the person. Some men, I guess, is scared of being alone. Some of getting old. With your daddy, he was always scared of being knocked down and spit on, of somebody taking his pride. He didn't want nobody shoving him in the dirt and walking off. He didn't want nobody to forget he was around."

"If that's what he wanted, I'd say he got his way. Nobody ever forgot Daddy was around."

"Oh, but they did, Deana. They always did. What was there about him, really, to remember? When he come out of the mines at night, his face was as black as everybody else's. His feet was just as wet and cold. That's why he had to keep picking that guitar and singing them lonesome songs. That's why he had to keep reminding you and me he was a man."

Deana stands and walks over to the sliding glass doors and looks out at the clouds curling in fine tendrils like Mama's cigarette smoke across the face of the moon. "You know that's the way it is with every bully in the world. He tries to make himself feel big by making everybody around him feel small."

"Ain't you never done that? Looked at somebody who was laying in a ditch and felt good to still be standing? Drinking sure didn't help him none. Your daddy might have been a different man without the bottle, but we won't never know. I tried to get him to stop, but it didn't do me no good. You remember how we used to fight. Me and him used to go after each other till I thought we'd blow the house off the foundation. He wore me out, Deana. He finally just wore me down."

"Well, I guess he won, then."

"Wadn't anything to win. He won't make you feel small no more, honey. Ain't nothing left of him but skin and bone. But ain't nothing left good of him either, and that makes me sad."

"I remember some good things about him, in spite of how we got along."

"I know you do. Ain't nobody all bad, just like they ain't nobody all good."

"I remember when we lived up in Cleveland and he worked in that factory nights. I don't remember what kind of factory it was."

"They made something to do with cars, not the whole car, but some little part that helped you steer it. Wayman said it was the boringest job he ever had, making the same thing day after day, over and over again. He'd say, no wonder I drink."

"He wasn't as bad then as he was later, though. Was he?" Deana waits until her mother shakes her head before she goes on. "I used to stand in the window and watch him under the street light, waiting for his ride. Our car must have been torn up for a while, because I remember it was winter, and he had to get a ride to work with one of his buddies every night."

"That's when we had that old DeSoto. He was driving me to the grocery store one night and the gearshift broke off in his hand. It took a while to get the money to get another car."

"I remember one night it was snowing. In the lamplight, the snow looked yellow, with big flakes like the buttered popcorn we used to get when we went to the movies. Daddy had on a coat, but it must have been too light to keep him warm. He kept pacing back and forth, his breath making steam in the air. He held his arms right to his side and had his hands shoved down in his pants pockets."

Deana turns and looks at her mother. She can see Mama's face more clearly now with the moon shining through the space between the curtains. "Do you want to know the real reason Will wrote me?" she asks.

"If you want to tell me. I've already give up on trying to find out your secrets. Anyway, what I know or don't know don't make no difference anymore. That's something else for me to feel bad about, now when I look back on it, but—. When I used to look in your things, honey, I wasn't trying to be nosy. I just wanted to know if you was getting in any trouble. I wish I'd of knowed then I wasn't doing a thing but driving you away from us. That's just one of the things I wish I'd done different."

Deana looks toward her mother. As her eyes adjust to the darkness, it seems she can see, more and more clearly, the shape of her mother's face. "Don't. You're right. It doesn't make any difference now. You did the best you could. There are things I would have done differently, too."

"You was fixing to tell me about Will Brinson. What did he want? He didn't find out about Sophie somehow?"

"No, and if I have my way, he never will. The truth is, it had nothing to do with me. It was all about his mother. His aunt—you know, that big woman with the birthmark? She told him Daddy was in the union. Anyway, Doc Beecham has always said the union had something to do with Will's mother's death. That's crazy, of course. That would have been the stupidest thing the union could have done."

Mama sits with her head tilted toward her left shoulder. The room is so quiet Deana can hear the ticking of her wristwatch and the roar of silence against the curled mussel-shape of her ear. She thinks for a moment that maybe Mama has dozed off, which only goes to prove how ridiculous this whole conversation is. Deana has seen her do this two or three times over the past few days, fall dead asleep in the middle of a television show or a conversation, then rouse herself without even being aware she has been sleeping.

But finally, Mama looks toward the window where Deana stands, and then she looks away. "Funny, ain't it?" she says, softly. "How long you can keep a secret? Sometimes you can keep a secret so long you forget you have it, especially when the people who knowed it, too, are mostly dead. I used to think about telling you all this a long time ago. I used to tell Wayman sooner or later you was gonna find out some way. Maybe now, with him— I don't know. Would it of made any difference, I used to think, if you'd knowed what happened between your Daddy and Cleave Brinson? Would you still have headed straight for the worst man in the world for you, as far as your daddy was concerned? Deana, you don't know what it was like for him, seeing you take up with a boy who would remind Wayman of what he done every time he seen the boy's face. It couldn't have been worse, and there you was, determined to have Will Brinson, no matter what. And Wayman? O, he knowed more than you might think, girl. He knowed everything about what happened to that woman there was to know."

Twenty

He always knew when his time came she would be the one to part the curtain between the land of the living and the dead. Off and on for years, he has woken sweating from some dream of her. In the dream that makes him most ashamed, she comes to his bed and lies down beside him on her back. He comes and kneels, looking at her nakedness for a long time before he touches her, slowly, stroking the hills and hollows of her body with his curved index finger, her skin is so cold and smooth.

In the dream, it is necessary to go slowly. He knows if he takes his time, he can make her turn her face toward him. She was always a beautiful woman, the kind of woman who would never look at him. He used to see her come into the roadhouse out on 52 and sit at a dark table by herself, waiting. On open-mike nights, he used to sing sweet for her, tear up the guitar on some pretty Patsy Cline love song, but she never even once looked in his direction. When the man she was to meet came, he'd sit at the bar and glance furtively back at her, their signal, and she'd get up and go outside in the cold to wait for him. Wayman thought the man wasn't much, to have a woman like that wait for him in the cold and the dark.

And though in his dream she is lying like a gift at his knees, she won't acknowledge him even now. Her open eyes stare past him at the ceiling, like the eyes of the dead.

When he loses patience, he pulls her legs apart roughly and mounts her, thrusting inside her. He twines her gold hair through his fingers, pulling her head to the side, but this does not make her look at him either;

her eyes stare at the wall instead. His hand tightens in her hair. He thrusts thrusts thrusts thrusts, panting against her hair. Water spurts out of her mouth and leaves a pool of moisture on the pillow beside her head. He doesn't know if he is fucking her or reviving her, only please please please please please either look at me or close them goddamn dead woman's eyes. He wakes from these dreams with his dick hard and his heart pounding, and he cannot smoke enough cigarettes to keep his hands from shaking in the dark.

Other nights he dreams she is dressed in white, not like a bride, but like a girl ready to be led into the river to be baptized. In profile, her face is white as a marble tombstone, but when she turns to face him, he can see that the other side of her face is blistered and black. When she looks at him, it is no good either. Her eyes are dark, accusing, and now he turns his own face away, unable to look at what he has spoiled.

Tonight when she comes, it is the first time he has dreamed about her since his stroke. She looks like an angel, the light purling against her gold hair and her white body bright as if lit from inside. For the first time in months, his body feels light, like a young man's. She stands at the foot of the bed, her arm outstretched. What is she offering from the shell of her hand? He reaches out to her, but she is too far away. She opens her hand, and the silver coins spill one by one onto the clean white blanket on his bed. The coins clink together as they fall, and she waits, silent and still, to see if he will pick them up.

He won't. Why should he? And if he doesn't, then it will change everything.

But of course he does, the silver cold and burning against the palm of his hand. He needs this money, he needs it all, all thirty pieces, but for the life of him, he cannot remember why or what he did with it or what it changed.

He starts to gather the coins into a little pile. O, his hands are shaking, shaking the way they shake sometimes until he has a shot of liquor, or if he cannot get a shot of something, until he wraps his arms tight around himself, trapping his trembling hands under his arm pits like terrified birds.

Hands shaking, he gathers the coins, and he understands even as he does, that he is destroying the only thing he ever really believed in, the only thing he ever loved besides the bottle, besides the broken nasty thing he knows to be himself. He is selling out the union that has stood by him and all the other miners against the company, Cleave Brinson's company, for Brinson's silver and gold. He is as big a sell-out as Tony Boyle, worse maybe, because he goes into the mines every day with men who would lay their hands on a Bible and swear it, no, he'd never sell out the union, not Wayman Perry, he's a union man.

But here is the evidence, falling like judgment from Anne Brinson's hands. No praying will save him, no water will save him, no call to the altar will save him, because he will never be able to testify to what he has done. How can he stand up in front of the people at the Pentecostal church or a union meeting and say, this is my sin, in Jesus name forgive me? If he speaks what is unspeakable, Who then will give him sanctuary? Who will sit with him at the mourner's bench, praying and rocking and burning away his sin with tongues of flame? Who will call him brother? He is Judas, and like Judas hanging from the twisted branches of the olive tree, he, Wayman Perry, will die without Jesus and fall into the pit that is deeper than any mine he ever rode a bucket into and blacker than his own sin.

He gathers the money together in a pile and shoves it toward her. What good are dreams, if we can meet the dead but cannot save them? If we meet the dead and cannot confess at the edge of the grave what the living can never understand?

Here, he tells her. Take it. I done it. I done it for the money. I done it so Brinson could blame the union and break the strike. Blow up the car, he said. It'll show bad intentions. Might injure that sumbitch Turley, but if anybody deserved maiming if not killing— Oh God help me, honey, I didn't mean to do nothing to hurt you.

As if through plugged ears, he hears the monitor beside the bed stop beeping and begin to whir, the red line that is his life no longer dashed and broken and arched and curved, but straight and true. He sees her turn toward the door, and he knows suddenly, this is what it will take to end it. This is what he has been looking for thirty years without knowing it. He has looked for her at the bottom of a bottle and drunk at the steering wheel of a car on a curvy road and drunk and half-crazy with lust and meanness in the wrong card game or the wrong bedroom.

All that time he has been trying to find a way to follow her and make her forgive him. He has known this in some dark, silent place, like the weight of a stone pressing against his breastbone. Now, finally, she has come, terrifying and cleansing as flame, to beckon him to take his place at last among the dead, where he belongs.

⚘ Twenty-One

Will Brinson lifts the hoe and swings it, the sharp edge aimed at the chickweed determined to take over, even in the winter. Since he's decided to stay in Ash Grove, Will has spent hours and hours working around this place, trying to get at least a few things done before the ground freezes hard and the weather gets too bad to work outside. The contractors have almost built the greenhouse. He'll buy a lot of his plants from wholesale suppliers, but he still wants to offer some vegetables and flowers that he grows himself from seed.

Besides, having something to do keeps him outside in the clean air, rather than inside brooding. He loves this work. He loves, and has loved since he first discovered it, the rhythm of gardening, the way his muscles ache at the end of the day, and his mind is quiet and at peace.

His partner Frank thinks he's crazy, trying to start a new business in one of the most depressed counties in the state of Kentucky, but maybe, Will told him, that's where the challenge lies.

"What challenge?" Frank asked him. "You're not a business man. You go into business without somebody like me to at least keep up what looks like accurate paperwork, the damned IRS will be on your ass the first time you send in a tax return."

"I've got money. I'll hire an accountant."

"You do that. Hire you an accountant. But I still say you'll get tired of living up there in the middle of nowhere soon enough. By next spring, you'll be right back here. I won't take your name off the sign yet."

Maybe Frank's right, he thinks, as he chops weeds with a hoe. He's only been here a few months, and until he and Frank started their landscaping business together, he's never been able to stick with anything very long. He likes working with Frank for that very reason. Frank is smart, but he lacks ambition. Except during the very busiest seasons, a half day's work is plenty to keep their little shoestring business going. The rest of the time, they drink beer, play pool, and chase women. No wonder Frank can't understand why Will has decided to live on this mountain like a monk.

He should be lonely, too, but he's not, even though he doesn't know anybody here. Most of the boys he knew when he was young have left Ash Grove, or they've married and had families, and he no longer has anything in common with them. He sees them occasionally down at the hardware store or Kroger, but half the time he doesn't recognize any of the men or women who throw up their hands to greet him. Sometimes, when they tell him who they are, he has a vague memory of a teenage ghost who looks out of a middle-aged face. Most of the time, he just lies. They always seem a lot more interested in him than he is in them. But maybe that's the way it always was, even when he used to run with them when they were all kids.

If he misses anything, he misses—not Katherine, exactly—but having somebody warm and willing to take the edge off his hunger every now and then. He did manage to let her know where he is, but even so, he has not heard from her. He supposes she's gone on to other things. At night, he thinks about her, tries to miss her, but it's as though the part of him that desired her is numb.

He takes a long-nosed track shovel and digs a dandelion by the roots. For plants that have their start from such tiny seeds, their roots go deep. He tosses it into a wheelbarrow, with dug-up chickweed. At least you won't cause any trouble come spring, he thinks. For a while he just goes after dandelions—dig, toss, dig, toss—though he knows he's barely making a dent. Hundreds, maybe thousands, of seeds wait for warm weather to germinate.

The last time he talked to Betsy on the phone, she confessed that, like Frank, she is worried about him. She's promised to come back soon.

"I hate for you to be by yourself in that big old house," she said. "You ought to just sell it and move back here."

"I'll come and spend some time soon."

"No, you won't. You'll stay in that empty house without a friend in the world but Doc Beecham and brood about things you can't change."

He starts to tell her he does have one friend besides Doc—well, not exactly a friend—but he thinks about it a second and changes his mind. How can he expect her to understand, any more than Doc does why he has adopted Junior Messer? There probably isn't a soul who's heard about it who doesn't think he's crazy. A couple of times a week Will goes to the county jail to see Junior. Will takes him treats—cigarettes or candy—and maybe a NASCAR or wrestling magazine so he can keep up with the news of the world, or at least the only part of it beyond these mountains of interest to him.

Will is also the lone contributor to the Junior Messer legal defense fund. "Son of a bitch," Doc said, when he found out Will was paying the lawyer. "You beat all, son. The boy stands in the weeds and shoots your daddy like a dog, and you take him to raise."

"I know it's crazy," Will said. "But you know yourself why he did it. Cleave didn't think once about what would happen to Junior when he cooked up this big scheme."

Doc looked at Will skeptically, but he didn't have an answer.

"He used Junior," Will said. "Like he used everybody. You looked at the lab reports from the doctor in Lexington. You know Junior is telling the truth."

"He still ain't worth a shit."

"Maybe so. I don't have any use for Junior. That's not what it is. Junior killed Cleave, even he admits it. I don't want to get him off, and I couldn't find a lawyer who could get him aquitted if I did. But I don't know that he deserves to go to the chair. I feel the same way about him I'd feel about a coyote chewing its foot off to get out of a metal trap."

Will also knows that Junior thinks he's outsmarting him. Crazy son of a bitch. "I'm grateful on account of all you done for me," Junior said the last time Will went to see him. "But it's not like you don't owe me some consideration. You got that money on account of me. How does it feel to go to sleep on satin sheets, and me in here?"

But he doesn't tell Doc the real reason he feels responsible for Junior Messer, because Cleave has done enough damage, and if Doc wants to go on believing in the innocence of his friend, well, Doc has been good to Will at least, and there's no point in hurting Doc now. The night after his first visit to Junior Messer, Will woke up thinking of his father with such intense hatred that for a moment, he had trouble catching his breath. If Cleave could hire Junior without one consideration for what might happen to Junior after his death, then what else was Cleave capable of? Finally, despite Doc and Betsy's efforts to convince him he is wrong, Will is certain he knows what happened to his mother. Will owes Junior, because God help him, he is glad Cleave Brinson is dead.

When he finishes weeding, Will wheels the load over to a trash pile and dumps it. Then he decides to work on an area he has been terracing, using railroad ties to hold the dirt. He plans to display small shrubs here, burying their burlap-wrapped roots in shredded pine bark. He whistles. He's in a good mood, not those black moods that used to come at night when he tossed and turned, hearing the old house creak, but being more frightened of the ghosts inside his head. Let the dead rest—his mother, his father, even Wayman Perry. Doc Brinson called first thing to tell Will that Wayman Perry, too, is dead. He died early this morning in his sleep.

Will still finds it strange to be back here in Ash Grove when he spent so much of his life away or trying to get away from here. Even Cleave's money was an irritation; even though Cleave had always given Will plenty to spend—was that guilt, trying to buy Will's love? But Will didn't want his father's money. For Will, it has always been best to be unencumbered, not tied down by all those things people think they want, but that give other people the power to control your life. But he never considered until now that money without strings grants its own kind of freedom.

Now, because of his inheritance, he can do all the things he never used to think he'd ever do. For one thing, now he can build his own greenhouse. He can get a new truck that runs without constantly having to be worked on. He plans to buy a new mulching machine to make his own mulch and sell the excess. He imagines the whiskey barrel smell of the ground wood fibers, as the sun heats them and the moisture rises like steam. He can see in his mind the path he will make from the greenhouse to the main house, with purple-flowering thyme growing between the sandstones.

He will build a trellis over by the back door and grow red Blaze roses intertwined with the saucer-sized blooms of white clematis. He will tear up the old cement patio and build a deck with a small goldfish pond, set at different levels, maybe even with a waterfall, on one end. Next year, after he has worked all day, he will come out here in the cool twilight of evening, open a beer, and toast the lightning bugs whose phosphorescent tails bloom gold against the falling darkness. By the time next summer comes, he will have transformed this place from dwelling place of the dead to a garden of the living, where seeds open underground and thread their way toward warmth and sunlight, unfurling their tender leaves toward the sky. He will put flowers on Anne's grave.

By eleven o'clock, clouds roll across the sun and a spring drizzle begins. Will puts up his tools and goes inside to clean up. He hates to quit so early, but he doesn't have to be in a hurry. He has all spring to get ready for summer. He puts on a pair of clean blue jeans and a flannel shirt. When he has laced and tied his work boots on the back stoop, he gets into his old pick-up truck and heads to the jail to see Junior.

On the way, he stops to fill up at the cheapest gas station in town, the one that sits at the four-way stop just at the edge of town. He fills the truck up, pays the attendant who shivers behind the glassed-in booth, and climbs back inside the truck.

Just as Will is pulling out, a dented blue Honda Civic pulls in on the other side. Will looks at the woman—he always looks at the women—but she is leaned over, and he can see just the top of her head. She is dark-haired. Probably she's digging in the floorboard for her purse.

He waits for the woman to lift her head, noticing in passing that she has a little girl with her. That means she may be married, though that has never mattered much to Will. Sometimes the married ones are the quickest to tumble. But it isn't the mother but the little girl who is looking out the window at Will. Her heart-shaped face is a pink petal, like a peony, against the glass. He looks closer, idly bringing her face into focus. Her dark hair frames her face with a widow's peak, and she gazes at him with dark-lashed storm-gray eyes. The little girl looks vaguely familiar, and Will eases the car past the gas pumps, hoping to get a glimpse of the woman who has such a pretty little girl. When the girl's mother sits up right and turns to her left to open the car door, Will sees that she's pretty, too. Then suddenly, seeing her clearly, his heart races. Before she can see him, he guns the accelerator of the truck, too, and flies past her, pulling onto the highway without even checking to see if the road is clear. Deana. The woman was Deana.

"Are you listening, man?" Junior asks him, at the jail. "I'm trying to tell you about my case. Lawyer, he says it's a real benefit to me, having you on my side. Makes me look good. Says he might could get me out, if you'll go my bond."

"I'm sorry, Junior. What were you saying now?"

Junior's eyes fill with tears. "You got to get me out of here. At least till my trial. You owe me."

But Will's mind is a million miles away from Junior. He cuts his visit short, promising to get in touch with the lawyer as soon as he gets back home.

Will huddles, shivering, inside his coat as he walks across the pavement to the far end of the parking lot where he left his truck. He turns the key in the ignition and pumps the gas pedal. The inside of the truck is freezing cold, and a little fog has formed on the windows.

Back at the house, he takes an old photograph album from the bookcase in the den. He thumbs through the pages of photographs, starting with childhood pictures of his mother and Betsy, then on to his mother's wedding. She looked so beautiful, with a face bright with promise, without a single cloud. Was this because she loved Cleave, at the beginning, or because she was a young girl who felt like a princess in her white silk dress, wearing a wreath of pale pink rosebuds in her swept-up dark hair?

He looks at the photograph closely, and then snaps on the lamp beside the sofa to see more clearly. He flips the page, back to a picture of his mother when she was six or seven. She is sitting on Grandfather Connelly's front porch, on a white-painted wicker swing. She is wearing a little one-piece flowered playsuit with a gathered neck. Her small face is tilted. She holds her hand just above her forehead, in a little salute, to keep the sunlight from blinding her gray eyes. Once Will showed Deana this picture and told her that she reminded him of his mother, with her dark hair. But Deana's eyes are brown.

He traces the heart-shaped face of his mother in the faded black and white photograph. With his throat tight, he watches the two faces—a child's face behind a car window and this face—come together, shift apart, and come together again like an eclipse seen through a welder's glass.

❧ Twenty-Two

Deana pulls into her driveway at four o'clock in the afternoon. She has driven all the way from Ash Grove in a steady drizzle of rain that kept fogging up the windows, but now in patches of pale turquoise, the skies have started to clear. Most of the way, Sophie kept up a constant chatter about her cousins. The girls had curled Sophie's hair and taught her cheers and hand jives. Charley had even taught Sophie a couple of stinky ones, to tease her sister.

At first, the cheers had made Deana smile when Sophie chanted them, making stiff capital letters with her small arms. In a perfect mock cheerleader voice, she'd say, Totally! For sure! I just got a manicure! The sun, I swear, is bleaching out my hair! Twenty-six, thirty-four? I don't even know the score! So Go! Go! Fight! Fight! Gee, I hope I look all right! or the other cheer, Don't hate me cause I'm beautiful, cause I don't like you either. I'm a cheerleader! I'm a cheerleader!

Of course, by the time they passed the Corbin exit, Deana, irritated by both cheers, had begun to wish Charley had kept them to herself. Deana was so happy when Sophie stopped chanting that she allowed her climb over the seat into the back to take a nap without her seat belt. Curled up in a fog of delight left over from the attention of her older girl cousins, Sophie had finally—finally!—fallen asleep, about twenty miles from home. Now she lies curled up, unbuckled, in the back seat, because Deana couldn't stand, for another blessed minute, to listen to Sophie complain the seat belt dug into the side of her waist whenever Deana tried to get her to lie down.

"Okay," Deana told her. "But make sure you're lying all the way down. If you sit up, even for one instant, even if you just raise your head up, if I look back and see you don't have your seat belt on, you're in big trouble, girl. Big trouble."

Deana knows this is a mistake, to let Sophie ride in the car without her seat belt, even once. It occurs to her that this is another small sign of her inadequacy as a mother. It might be different, too, if she didn't know better, but she can recite both the safety statistics for seats belts and the odds that Sophie is going to argue about this every time they go anywhere. Deana has already begun to dread the small battle of wills that will take place the next time they get into the car.

Deana pulls the key out of the ignition, and looks back to check on Sophie. Well, at least this time they didn't crash into a tree, and Sophie is safe. Besides, even Sophie can't very well argue while she's asleep. The problem Deana has is that Sophie is already well on her way to being a skilled negotiator. Her favorite comeback when Deana tells her not to jump on a trampoline and not to swim in the deep end of the pool or go outside in the yard without her shoes is, "Well, Mommy, I did it before and nothing bad happened."

"Oh, boy," Suzanne said once, when she heard Sophie make this particular point. They were at the park and Sophie wanted to play over on the big playground on the other end of the parking lot where they couldn't see her. "I can see already, you're going to have your hands full with her."

Just tell me how to do this right, then, Deana wanted to say. And anyway, right now, curled in the back seat, Sophie doesn't look a thing like a budding spoiled brat or a future juvenile delinquent. She looks like an angel, lying with her dark hair fanned out around her face and the ratty corner of her green and blue plaid blanket twisted in one hand. The blanket covers only the upper part of her body, and her legs stick out of the bottom. Somehow, she has managed to kick off a shoe. She sleeps with her mouth slightly open and Deana can detect the slightest flutter of her lips as she breathes.

Deana grins wryly. The truth is, in most ways, Sophie is a lot like Deana when Deana was little. Except for this, she thinks with gratitude— despite all the mistakes Deana has made, unlike Deana when she was a kid, Sophie is happy.

Deana starts to reach over the seat to shake Sophie awake, but then she thinks, what's the point? She's only going to be inside for a couple of minutes to call Dr. Allman's office and pick us some clothes before they head back to Ash Grove for her father's viewing and funeral.

The wind gathers the clouds into a thick clot, covering the feeble sunlight. It starts to rain again, not hard, just a slow dismal drizzle. A wet brown maple leaf is airborne, and then plastered thickly against the windshield of Deana's car. She is so tired, that she half wishes she could sit here in the quiet forever, that the wind would gather all the leaves the winter has stripped from the stand of trees behind the trailer, until the leaves cover the car, leaving Deana and Sophie in a twilight world. Then maybe Deana won't have to make so many decisions all at once. It isn't enough that she has to go back and go to her father's funeral. After all these years, what possessed Mama to give Deana yet another secret to tell or to keep?

Well, Will, she thinks, I have found out everything, and trust me, there's guilt enough for Wayman Perry and Cleave Brinson, too.

She leans her forehead against the steering wheel, imagining herself making the call, telling Will to pick her up after the funeral, but not until after Deana's mother has gone back to her little trailer. Until then, Lily will be busy in the kitchen, Wes at the door, and Deana will have to be her mother's shadow, helping her to navigate her way through the comforting throngs of people with their covered dishes and murmurs of sympathy, until Mama is finally tired enough to sleep.

With Wayman gone, Deana is free, except for Sophie, to see Will anywhere and tell him whatever she wants him to know. Her mother had told Deana everything last night, even as Wayman was dying. How Cleave Brinson had hired Wayman Perry to help him finish breaking the union. How Cleave's driver was supposed to open the door of the car and detonate the explosives, making it look as though Cleave had been the intended target and had barely escaped death. But that same sunny morning—and who knows for what reason?—Anne Brinson had decided to drive down to the grocery store or to the post office, while her husband was in the house somewhere getting ready for his trip.

She must have asked Boyd Turley, Cleave's driver and bodyguard, to hand her the keys and sit on the porch drinking coffee until she came back with the car. Who knows why Anne didn't tell Cleave where she was going? Maybe she was angry with him. Maybe he was upstairs in the shower or shaving, and she was only going to be gone a minute, no reason to bother Cleave. Did Anne smile at Boyd, flirt a little? Deana thinks of Boyd sitting on the porch, looking over the edge of his newspaper at the pretty woman walking toward the car. He would have watched her until she opened the door and put the keys into the ignition. Maybe he worried whether or not she had room to get around his truck, parked behind and to the side. He might have offered to move the car for her, to let her get her Corvette out of the garage, but Anne would have waved him away. She wasn't helpless, and anyway, she could just take the Lincoln.

Jolene said someone reported that when the car exploded and burst into flames, Boyd had rushed over to try and fling the door open. He had burned his hands, and then Cleave had rushed out of the house, pulling Boyd away. Cleave was burned, too. Cleave would use that in his defense when the sheriff came to question him, holding up his bandaged hands and forearms, to prove that he had tried to save her. But the questions were a formality. No one in the eastern part of the state could touch Cleave without airtight proof, and the only proof was Millard Messer, who had approached Wayman Perry with Cleave's offer, and Wayman, who had known how to wire the car. They could not implicate Cleave without implicating themselves.

But Deana can give Will this much, this small comfort, if she decides to tell him anything. According to Jolene Perry, Cleave hadn't known Will's mother would be in the car.

What had gone through Cleave Brinson's mind when he heard the explosion? Wayman Perry had always claimed that Boyd Turley was a son of a bitch who carried a gun and fought the miners dirty, but Cleave had no reason to dislike him. Had Cleave felt sorry when he heard the car explode? Deana thinks of Cleave's coldness with her. She had been sixteen, and he had not given her a second thought, until Will came back to Ash Grove. Now she knows why Cleave had never told Will about her. He had not wanted to risk stirring up a hornet's nest of secrets. Wayman had his own reasons to keep silent about Anne Brinson's death, but Cleave must have wondered just what Wayman Perry might do, with that temper, if had found out that Cleave had not even had the decency to stay away from Wayman's sixteen-year-old daughter.

But at least, she thinks, her father had known that he was in the wrong, that he had betrayed himself and his principles. First, he had sold out the union, for whose cause his belly had growled and he had stood in the rain and the heat and the cold, sometimes defending his beliefs with his fists. And even more awful, even if he could console himself that Boyd was a scab who needed killing, how could he face, for the rest of his life, having killed an innocent woman by mistake? For one reason, and one reason only, she thinks, he must have sighed with relief. Cleave Brinson might have been able to use the death of his wife politically against the union, but because of his own complicity, he would never, ever have been able to implicate Wayman Perry, though her father must have trembled every time he saw the sheriff's car coming down the road. No wonder he had been so angry at her when she had called the sheriff that night so long ago. Deana cannot help but feel a small twinge of satisfaction. She had had more power over Wayman Dean Perry than she knew.

Wayman had been able to hide his guilt all these years, though Deana knows enough about keeping secrets to recognize a mixed blessing when she sees one. Keeping this one had killed her father, one bottle at a time. And for what? Money? Whatever money Wayman had always ran through his fingers like water. How much money could Cleave have given him, to be worth the price Wayman had paid? At least Wayman had felt enough guilt to suffer for what he had done. True evil springs, root, trunk, and branch, from men like Cleave Brinson who don't care who the hell they blow to kingdom come as long as they get their way.

When her mother had told her, Jolene had made Deana swear not to say anything until Wayman died, and Deana had sworn. But now, there is no longer any reason to keep this from Will, except maybe to protect him. At least now, not knowing, he can believe, if he chooses to, that Cleave had nothing to do with Anne's death. If she tells him, he will know his father is guilty, even if indirectly. What makes Will think he even wants to know the truth? Most of the time, we don't, she thinks, no matter how much we think we do. Besides, to tell him, she has to see him. This isn't the kind of story that can be told in a letter or over the telephone. He will have questions. He will turn to her, as he always has, and what will she do?

Deana imagines riding in the passenger seat of Will father's car, headed out to the dam where they used to go. He will pull the car—or would it be a truck, now, she wonders, with magnetic signs for his landscaping business on the doors?—into the same space behind an old concrete building where they used to hide in the dark and make love. She remembers how they used to sit in the car in the rain on days just like this one, their hands and mouths hungry in the blinding heat of his desire and her desperation.

She thinks again about parking with him by the river, her white blouse silver as a fish surfacing in the moonlight, her legs naked and white, wrapping around his waist, while above them arches a net of stars. She tries to remember the rough feel of his hand caressing first her calf and then her thigh, while his breath stirred the hair at the nape of her neck. She tests the memory, the way she's seen people put weight on a sprained ankle, testing to see if there is any pain.

She tries another memory, like the next slide in one of those old carousel projectors, sees him looking at her through dark sunglasses, a little smile at the corner of his lips. Has she ever really loved him? she wonders, or has he always been some sorrow-dark nightingale of a lover, a James Dean she made up to spite her father? And now, if she can finally learn to see him in the flesh, as he is, someone she has touched but never really known, will he lose the power to make her so afraid?

No, because now there is Sophie to consider. Sophie has made tender places where Deana can be wounded that she couldn't even have imagined when she left Ash Grove with Will so many years ago. How can she tell Will about his mother and not about Sophie?

Deana lifts her head, turns, and looks over the back seat at her daughter. It's easy to see Will in Sophie's heart-shaped face. Her eyes are dark-lashed like his. Once in the beauty shop getting her hair cut, Deana heard some stupid woman say that if she could only get pregnant with her married boyfriend's baby, she would at least have something to remember him by. The woman's head was helmeted with perm rollers, and Deana wanted to get up and ask her if the rollers were so tight they cut off circulation to her brain. As if a child were like a dead memento, a corsage pressed between the pages of a book.

She reaches for the blanket and tugs it, tucking it around Sophie's shoulders, then takes her own coat from the front seat and lays it across the Sophie's legs for good measure. She rests her chin on the seat back and watches her daughter. Sophie's chest rises and falls with her sweet breath going in and out, in and out. Oh, Sophie, she thinks, touching Sophie's face softly with the back of her hand. What a fucked-up family you have.

❧ Twenty-Three

Deana doesn't miss the irony that her wayward father's last stop before the grave is The Divine Love of Jesus Pentecostal Church. The church is in an old building that used to be a restaurant until the chains went in on the four-lane strip of road built next to the flood wall and killed what little was left of the town.

Since then, church members using scavenged materials have repaired it until it looks like the last outpost after Armageddon. Half of the clapboard building is covered with paint of an indeterminate color that has blistered and peeled to show the weathered wood beneath. The other half has been freshly painted a steel-colored gray that is nearly indistinguishable from the dismal February sky. Windows have been replaced with whatever was available, so that no window is the same size or shape as its neighbors, and some windows have been boarded up with plywood.

The pallbearers, all members of Mama's church, roll Wayman's casket from the back of the hearse and carry it inside. The interior of the church is as much of a cobbled mess as the outside. Mismatched pews are lined up on the left and right of sundry squares of linoleum, laid end to end to form a center aisle. Over the pulpit at the front hangs a single bare light bulb swinging from a cord.

The pallbearers are a motley group as well. Two older men are dressed in worn black suits, white shirts and skinny black ties. Another man has on overalls. Two of the younger men are dressed in collared sport shirts and khaki slacks. The last pallbearer is wearing his dark gray uniform from work at a garage or a gas station. It has a name patch over the left pocket, though from where she sits Deana can't read the name.

Deana is in a folding chair on the front row reserved for the family. She had been against bringing Daddy here, and had put up at least a token argument that a man who had never set foot in a church more than a handful of times while he was living ought not to be forced into church when he died. But Brother Hardwick had convinced Mama that at last Daddy had found Jesus, and what better way to mark his passing over into eternal life than to have his funeral at Divine Love?

Besides, Deana had used whatever influence she had as the returning prodigal daughter by arguing that at least the younger children—including Sophie—might be spared the ordeal of the funeral. Deana knows from experience that the funeral promises to be long and emotional. The preaching and singing will not be focused on the deceased, who has already made his bed, so to speak, but on saving the sinners in his family who might never set foot in church again until someone else dies.

I hate this, Deana thinks, as Brother Hardwick straps on his guitar and motions for the rest of the Divine Love Quartet to stand behind the pulpit with him. She has already spotted a rapture bumper sticker in the parking lot. On the back bumper of a sport utility vehicle, in red letters, was written "Warning! In case of rapture, this car will be unmanned." Deana's own favorite, irreverent reply, is the sticker she saw on the road when she went home day before yesterday—"In case of rapture, can I have your car?" Daddy used to tell Mama that maybe the rapture had already happened, and here she was, still with Wayman Perry, rejected by the Lord.

It's not, she thinks, that she doubts the faith of these people or their sincerity. She just resents that she spent so many nights of her youth tossing and turning and worrying about her immortal soul. But she never found that certainty that all the rest of these people seemed to take for granted. Even now, she thinks, after the preaching, I'll probably want to go right up there, bawling my eyes out, when they give the altar call.

And when the quartet starts, she is drawn into the music in spite of herself. For one thing, Brother Hardwick is a pretty good musician, though not as good as Wayman Perry had been. Brother Hardwick has one of those whiskey voices that make sobered up drunks sing really good gospel music. The tall, skinny man next to him—one of the pallbearers—sings a passable bass. The two women are both heavy-set and wearing black knit dresses, more suitable for summer. One is young with shoulder-length permed blonde hair; her skin is as pink as a white rabbit's nose. The older woman—her mother?—wears her gray hair wound up on top of her head like a bee skep. They sing soprano and alto, respectively. And oh, yes, they can sing.

The quartet begins with "The Great Speckled Bird" and "Poor Wayfaring Stranger." They sing, "O, Death Where is Thy Sting?" and "Were You There When They Crucified My Lord?" Then they stand to the side with their heads bowed reverently while Brother Hardwick prays for the Holy Spirit to move in this church the way it moved through the crowd at Pentecost, so that all should know Jesus as Savior and Lord.

After prayer, the funeral director moves to the front and opens the casket to reveal the body of Wayman Perry in repose. The rest of the Divine Love Quartet goes to sit on folding chairs at the front. Deana sees that she was right not to bring Sophie. What would Daddy think if he knew Brother Hardwick was literally going to preach to the sinners over Wayman Perry's dead body? Oh, Lord, she thinks, if he weren't already dead, this would kill him.

Deana refuses to look toward her father's casket. While Brother Hardwick warms up by reading a series of scriptures, she studies her hands. One thing is different from the times when she used to go to churches like this with her mother. Now Deana no longer feels that the preacher is speaking directly to her, and has been sent by God specifically to do so. Oh, how she used to pray and pray to be saved, only to wonder why Jesus wanted to torment her so. Why would he draw her over and over to the altar to own up to her sinful nature, only to leave her hands empty when they reached out, as the preacher right now was asking the congregation to do, and feel the nail marks in His precious hands?

Deana feels Mama take her hand, and glances across Mama's lap to see that Mama has Deana clasped by one hand, and Lily, who sits on the other side of Mama, by the other. Brother Hardwick looks down at Mama from the pulpit, and she beams up at him through tear-stained eyes. Daddy, if you can hear me, Deana thinks, pay attention. This is one time I'm on your side.

"Sister Jolene, you're sad now. You're sad and you're tired and you're bruised. But tonight, praise God, in Wayman Perry's home there will be no weeping and wailing and gnashing of teeth, there will be no tear-dimmed eyes. All will be peace and joy and love, for the soul of man never dies. Praise Jesus, Sister, Brother Wayman died in Christ.

"Brother Wayman died in Christ, brothers and sisters, and now he sits at the right hand of Jesus, in a better place, Hallelujah, a place beyond this vale of tears, a place where there is none that go hungry, none lame and halt, where no sickness will ever touch him, praise Jesus, ever again."

Brother Hardwick pauses to wipe his brow with a clean white handkerchief. "But I know—and you know, too, don't you, Sister Jolene?—that in this very room there are those who have not let Jesus into their hearts, who do not know him as their personal savior. He is knocking, brothers and sisters, knocking, knocking." Brother Hardwick raps his knuckles against the pulpit for emphasis.

"He stands on the threshold, but some are so caught up in the pleasures of the world that they cannot hear Him. I've been down that road, brothers and sisters. I've played in bars and sung the devil's music. I've played poker and chased women and been so drunk I didn't know which end of the bottle to crawl out of. But nothing of the world has ever fed my soul like the sweet blood of the lamb. What Jesus done for me, He'll do for you. But you have to give Him an answer. How long will ye harden your hearts, oh, ye sinners?

"He knocks now, but there may come a time when He will knock no longer. You will open the door and He will not be there. Brother Wayman waits on the other side. Sister Jolene can rest easy tonight, knowing she will meet him in heaven some glad day. Who among you loves sin so much that you will be cast into the pit and never see again your father, brother, friend? Will Jesus run his finger down the list of the redeemed and say, sorry, I never knew you?"

He lowers his voice at the end, and the woman with the beehive hair comes to stand beside him at the podium. The younger woman has strapped on Brother Hardwick's guitar and strums softly, still in her seat. The other woman begins to sing, softly too, her voice high and light, keening— "Sorry, I never knew you. I find no record of your birth. Sorry, I never knew you. Go and serve the one that you served down on earth."

Deana hears someone fidgeting behind her. She glances back, almost involuntarily, then turns to see a man somewhere between thirty and forty with red hair so bright that in the strange light of the church it looks momentarily as though his head is on fire. At least she needn't be embarrassed about being caught looking at him. Freckled and grinning, he is oblivious to her interest. He is staring over her head at the ceiling, his eyes wild, while his hands nervously clasp and unclasp his knees. He looks as though he doesn't know whether he is going to giggle uncontrollably or weep.

Suddenly he comes to his feet and shuffles down to the front. He stands with his head bowed, his shoulders trembling, tears dripping off the end of his nose. Who is he? she wants to ask her mother. Do we know him?

Brother Hardwick looks down at him gratefully. "Bless you, brother. Bless you."

Brother Hardwick extends the altar call through two more verses of "Sorry, I Never Knew You," and all four verses of "Just as I Am." But in the end, all that is drawn to his light is this one battered soul. With his hands clasped in front of him, his thin, rangy arms drawn to his sides like folded wings, the man stands with his side pressed tight against the end of her father's casket, like a moth in flames, clinging to the sleeve of God.

The crowd lingers for a few moments after the service, filing past Wayman's casket one more time, pausing as they pay their last respects to the dead to shake hands with the dazed red-haired man who stands beside Brother Hardwick, his face beaming and washed with tears.

Deana has already eased past her mother and sister and walked to the back of the church. She softly opens the door and goes outside to stand in the cold air. In a few moments, the mourners will climb into their cars and make the long procession to the cemetery. Standing with her back leaned against the aluminum conduit that passes for a railing, Deana notices a gray pick-up truck across the street. The driver is parked, his engine idling. He is looking toward her, and she looks away so he won't think she is staring. But he gets out of the truck anyway and slams the door behind him. Then he stands outlined against the gray paint of the truck. From this distance, and in this light, he looks the same as he when he had left her, and she pushes her hand against her mouth to keep from crying out, her eyes stinging with surprise and love, with fear and rage.

She is about to turn and run back inside, as if the church might offer her the same sanctuary it always offers lunatics and fools. But it's too late. He sees her and knows that she sees him. He waves, then walks toward her, his pace quickening as he crosses the street, his work boots splashing through the puddles at his feet. Now she will have to talk to him whether she wants to or not.

When he comes closer, she sees that he has changed some, too, just as she has. His face is harder, more chiseled than when he was young, but if anything, this has made him more handsome. He looks so much like Sophie that when Deana breathes in the sharp, cold air it feels like a splinter in her heart. But she is pleased to see that Will doesn't look as cocksure as he used to. He looks at her face, but his eyes glance off hers like a stone skipping across the surface of water. He can't quite look her in the eye.

Standing at the foot of the steps, he has to look up to talk to her. He moves a gravel to the side of the walk with the toe of his shoe. "Hey, Deana."

"Hey, yourself. What are you doing here?"

"I heard about your father. I wanted to come by to—well, you know—I thought I should pay my respects, see how you're holding up."

"I'm holding up fine." She looks him straight in the eye, and is gratified to see that for the second time during this encounter, Will is the one who has to look away. She lowers her voice until it is only a little louder than a whisper. "That's not why you came."

He looks at her for a long moment, and for a second—or has she just imagined it?—his lower lip trembles as if he is about to cry. "Okay. That's not why I came." His eyes scan the edge of the building, gaze off at the line of stores on the other side of the street. When he turns back to her, he says, softly, "Why didn't you tell me about her? Didn't you think I had a right to know?"

"About who?" She isn't going to help him. Besides, how does she even know he means Sophie? How could he mean Sophie?

He turns to face her. "You know about who. She's mine, isn't she, Deana? I mean, look at her. I knew almost as soon as I saw."

"You saw her?" she says sharply. "Where?"

"At the gas station. Sunday. I was on my way—I was on my way somewhere, and I looked over and saw your car. She was looking out the window at me. Don't lie to me, Deana. I know she's mine."

She looks at him steadily and shakes her head. "No, she isn't. She isn't yours. Maybe you lent me some sperm a few years ago. I had a daughter. But I'm telling you here and now, she isn't anything to you. You weren't anywhere around."

His eyes plead with her and accuse her at the same time. God, how that look used to make her weak. But she cannot afford to be weak now.

"That's not fair," he says. "I didn't know I needed to be around because you didn't bother to tell me."

She leans close to him and spits the words. "I couldn't find you."

He raises his hand, gesturing toward her, and then drops it to his side. "You didn't try to find me. All you had to do—well, you knew all the same people I knew. All you had to do was look."

"I called Jimmy Rourke. You apparently told him not to let me know where you were."

"Well, there you go. He would have found me if you'd told him you were pregnant."

She takes a step toward him. "Told him I was pregnant? I wasn't going to tell Jimmy Rourke you knocked me up and then left me hanging."

Behind Deana, people have started to file out of the church. She knows her mother and Lily will be at the end of the line. She walks down the steps and motions Will to walk with her a couple of feet away from the crowd. "Listen," she says. "We can't talk about this now. This isn't the place or the time. And it's not just Sophie. There's something else I need to tell you, whether I owe you anything or not."

He looks at her, puzzled. Then his eyes brighten with comprehension. He takes a step toward her, but she puts her hand out, instinctively, to keep him away.

"Not now. I'm not getting into it here. You can come to Lily and Wes's place around eleven-thirty or twelve, after Sophie is in bed asleep. We'll talk about it then. About everything."

He waits for a second to see if she will say anything else. When she doesn't speak, he turns and starts to cross the street, then pauses before he wheels back around to face her. His face is so nakedly hopeful that she is disconcerted. If I had a rock, she thinks, I'd knock that look off your face. "Is that her name? Sophie?"

Deana doesn't answer, but when he turns toward the street again, this time she is the one who stops him, clutching his shirtsleeve. "Will? If I had found you, what would you have done?"

He backs away and stands, looking at her. Then he shrugs, his face crumpling, and his palms turned up to be filled with the sprinkles of rain.

"That's exactly what I thought," she says, as Will turns away for a final time and sprints across the street.

Behind Deana, Lily slides her hand in the crook of Deana's elbow. "Come on, Sis," she says, softly. "We've got to go."

Deana climbs into the back seat of Brother Hardwick's blue Buick with Lily, and Mama sits in the front. Wes follows directly behind them in the Brody van with Lily's three oldest children. As Brother Hardwick eases the car behind the hearse to enter the flow of traffic, Deana looks across the street, watching Will climb back into his truck. She could tell him anything, she thinks, and he'd believe her. What she ought to do is make up the most hurtful story she can think of and leave him with that for all the trouble he's caused her. She could make up a story so awful it would kill him. She might just do it, too.

"Are you okay?" Lily asks her.

Deana looks at her sister, and it must show on her face, all those mixed feelings of dread and relief, because Lily asks her softly, "You told him."

Deana nods her head toward Mama in the front seat. She doesn't want to get into it now, not in front of Mama and certainly not in front of Brother Hardwick.

She watches Will pull the truck into the street. As his truck passes close by Brother Hardwick's car, she keeps her eyes right on it. She wants him to see she isn't afraid to see him. He doesn't have any power over her, not anymore. But he doesn't even bother to look in her direction. Instead, he is turned in the direction away from her, talking to someone in the passenger seat.

Looking closely—maybe she's curious to see whether he has a woman with him, but that doesn't mean she cares—she is startled to see that Will's passenger is the last person in the world she would expect to see. Kicked back in the seat as if he is accustomed to being there is the strange red-haired man who had answered Brother Hardwick's altar call.

"Was that Will Brinson?" Mama says. "I thought I saw you talking to him when we came out, but he bolted across the street so fast, I wasn't sure. Oh, Lord, Deana, what in the world did he want?"

Deana decides to give her mother the same explanation Will tried to give her. "He heard about Daddy. He just wanted to pay his respects. Listen. Do you know who that man is he had with him? The one who came in during the service and went up during the altar call? He looks familiar to me, but I can't place him."

Mama turns cater-corner in the seat and looks back at Deana. Mama has a tissue balled up in her hand, and her eyes are red from crying. "You do know him. He's older than you, but he failed a couple of grades, so you would have gone to school with him. That's Millard Messer's boy, the man who used to run the tipple. Now that's a story you'll never believe. Junior Messer is the one who killed Will's father."

"Now wait a minute. Let me get this straight? If he killed Will's father, what's he doing out of jail, let alone riding around with Will?"

"Will is the one that got him out," Lily says. "Will put up Junior's bond and I reckon Junior's out at least until he goes before the grand jury to be bound over for trial."

"Will got him out?"

"Oh, that's not even half of what Brinson's done for Junior Messer," Brother Hardwick adds. This is obviously the best story to hit town in a while. "Brinson is paying for the lawyer, and Junior's staying up at the Brinson house while he's out on bond. Brinson had to promise the judge he'd keep an eye on Junior and make sure he didn't take off."

"That doesn't make any sense," Deana says. "Why would Will do that?"

"Oh, let me tell you," Brother Hardwick says. "I got a buddy that's a deputy down to the sheriff's office. He said they couldn't understand it either. What they thought right from the first is maybe Will Brinson had something to do with the crime. Brinson showing such interest in Messer, they figured something shady was going on."

"And?"

"Come to find out, it wasn't Will Brinson hired Messer to shoot him. The old man hired him. He had cancer and when it went to his liver, he wanted Messer to put him out of his misery. Too big a coward, I guess, just to do it himself. He always did think he could control everything. When you think about it, crazy it as it sounds, if you knew anything about Cleave Brinson—"

"But why—?" Lily begins, but Brother Hardwick cuts her off.

"Brinson never paid him. Promised to wire some money to him, but never followed through. At least that's the story Messer's telling. He's either the dumbest man in the world, or the smartest, to make up such a yarn."

"I thought it was odd, Junior just showing up at Wayman's funeral like that," Mama says. "Wayman couldn't stand Millard Messer, and I don't imagine Millard had much use for Wayman either. Wayman always said Millard was a scab. Said he'd as soon turn his back on a rattlesnake."

"Now that's something I can explain," Brother Hardwick says immediately, as he turns on his signal light, following the hearse into the cemetery where Wayman Perry is to be laid to rest. "You know how the Lord works, Jolene. You seen the same thing happen with Brother Wayman. It wasn't no accident that boy was there for the Holy Spirit to move on him. Before the service, I seen him out there hanging around the door, and I said, Boy, don't stand out here in the rain. Come on in.

"I tell you, Will Brinson might have drove that boy to the church house, but Junior Messer come in because it was the will of God. Sure as the world, Junior Messer is gonna end up on trial for capital murder. Ain't no good gonna come out of it, even if he does have Will Brinson taking his side. Boy'll either spend the rest of his natural life in jail, or he could get the chair. I'll tell you exactly why he was at Brother Wayman's funeral. He come so God could give him one more chance to repent and be saved."

Gravel crunches underneath the tires as the car comes to a stop. Brother Hardwick gets out of the car and walks around to the passenger side and to help Jolene out. Twenty feet from the road is a bedraggled tobacco-colored tent with a few folding chairs set in front of the grave. The hearse sits with the trunk open and the pallbearers take the casket and set it on slats set over the opening.

The people from the funeral home have laid two-by-six boards from the graveled road to the gravesite for the mourners to walk across, else they would all sink into the mud. A group from the church has come as well, at least eight or ten, Deana estimates, without counting. Deana is grateful that these people have come to stand with Mama, that she hasn't been left to face this with only Lily and Deana by her side. Mama has been crying off and on since Deana got back to Ash Grove, but Deana can't help but feel that Mama's tears, like her own, are mostly tears of relief, and that thought makes her saddest of all.

Brother Hardwick has Mama by one arm and helps her navigate her way across the plank. He is so solicitous of her that once or twice Deana glances at Lily to see if she notices. When Mama is looking at him, Brother Hardwick is full of the Lord's business, with Praise Jesus this and Praise Jesus that. But when he looks down at Mama from across the coffin—thank goodness, they haven't opened it here—he looks like a little boy with his heart in his eyes. Deana has seen that look often enough to know what it means. He loves her. Imagine that.

Deana does have a sinking spell when she sees Brother Hardwick open his worn black Bible. Here we go again, she thinks. How long can one funeral last? But the conversion of a man about to face the death chamber must have been enough sowing and reaping for one day. He keeps the graveside service mercifully short, saying only a brief prayer and reciting, beautifully and from memory, the twenty-third Psalm.

At last, weeping, Mama, Lily and Deana each throw a clod of dirt into the grave of their husband and father. Then they turn and walk single file from the grave to the car in the rain.

"So what's this thing with Brother Hardwick and Mama?" Deana asks Lily, later, when the visitors have taken their Tupperware and clean baking pans and gone home. Lily and Deana are in the kitchen taking the dishes out of the dishwasher and putting them away. Deana is so tired she feels as though her legs are about to give way beneath her, but she knows there is one thing left tonight she still has to do.

Lily takes the basket of tableware out of the dishwasher and sorts it into the drawer. She grins. "Oh, you noticed that? Brother George has had a big crush on Mommy since she started going to his church."

"He doesn't do a very good job hiding it. Is he married?"

"No. Divorced. His wife left him a few years back when he was still laid up drunk. Cleaned out the bank account—not that there was much to clean out—and took the car and the kids and went back to Chattanooga, Tennessee, where her people live."

Deana puts the glasses into the cabinet. "Lord, that's all Mama needs. Another drunk. I don't care if he has sobered up."

Lily shakes her head, rolling her eyes. "Oh, there's no need to worry about Mommy. It's all on his side. But I'll tell you, Daddy was so jealous of that man it liked to have drove him into church, just to make sure Mommy wasn't fooling around." Lily looks over her shoulder to make sure they are alone. Then she lowers her voice, laughing. "Daddy told her if he ever caught the preacher laying a hand on her, he was going to go down there right in the middle of church and kick Brother George's ass."

Well, that sounds right, Deana thinks, grinning and shaking her head. That sounds exactly like something Daddy might do.

Lily leans closer to her sister. "So when are you going to tell me what Will Brinson wanted?" she asks, keeping her voice low.

Deana sighs. She has been trying not to think about Will and what he said, but it's already eight-thirty, and sooner or later, he'll show up at the door, and she'll have to face him. "He saw us. Sophie and me, I mean. Sunday when we were leaving town."

Lily's lips tighten in sympathy. "And I guess when he looked at her, he knew. Lord, that baby looks just like him. He'd have to be blind not to know. What are you going to do?"

Deana leans against the counter and folds her arms. "I don't know. I don't even know how much of it will be up to me. I wish things could just go on the way they are. Just me and Sophie."

"It'll work out," Lily says. "I don't know how yet, but it will. Maybe it's meant to work out this way. Maybe it's a sign."

Deana laughs. "You mean Will seeing me and Sophie in a gas station? I'll tell you what it's a sign of. It's a sign I picked the wrong time to be buying gas at the Minute Market."

"There are some good things that could come out of this."

"Like what? Like maybe I'll have to share custody? Or I'll have to let Sophie spend the summers with a father she hardly knows?"

"I don't know." Lily looks at Deana, her eyes wide with concern. "No judge is going to give him that much. Surely not."

Deana shrugs, her shoulders aching with dread and despair. "I hope not."

"But what would be wrong with her spending some time with him? I know I've said some awful things about Will Brinson. But he's surprised me lately."

"How has he surprised you?"

"Well, for one thing, he's stayed here a lot longer than I thought he would have. And another thing is the way he's been about Junior Messer. Rumor has it Cleave Brinson had cancer and hired Junior to put him out of his misery. Junior's dumb, but you'd have thought Cleave would have known what would happen. He just didn't care what would happen to Junior. It's like Will's trying to clean up one of Cleave Brinson's messes. You think?"

Deana considers this. "I can see him doing that. He always wanted to be different from his father, somehow." The way I wanted to be different from mine, she adds silently, to herself. "And anyway, I guess you're right. People can change."

Lily looks at her steadily. "You have. I don't think we have to hate him anymore, Deana. I saw you with him this afternoon and it was like— well, it was like whatever power he had over you, all these years, is gone."

"But not his power over Sophie."

"No," Lily says slowly. "But think about it. You have more power over the situation than he does. You really do. You can make the rules. Only be careful that—well, you know it's awful easy for two people to use a child to fight with and just tear a kid apart."

"I hope it's okay," Deana says, "but I told him to come here at eleven or twelve, after everybody else is in bed. It felt like—oh, I don't know. I guess I thought it would be easier if I met him on neutral ground."

"It's fine. I'll drag Wes out of the living room and make him watch the news upstairs in the bedroom so you'll have some privacy. Once the kids are in their rooms at night, they won't come down unless there's an earthquake or the end of time. Does that sound like a good plan?"

Deana nods.

"Well, I think I'll tell Wes what's going on. Then I'm going to go upstairs and go to bed. I'm wore out. You know where to find anything you need."

Deana gets a glass of water and turns the light off. She goes over to the table, pulls out a chair, and sits down, leaning her elbows on the kitchen table. Lily's back door has panes of glass and no curtains, and from where she sits in the dark, Deana can see that Mama's living room light is still on. Deana thinks about walking over there to check on her mother, but she is so tired, she can't face the thought of putting one foot in front of the other to go over there. What possessed her to tell Will to come over so late? She can't imagine how she'll find the energy to talk to Will about anything, let alone what happened to his mother and what they're going to do about Sophie.

She turns the old thoughts over in her head—what if she had told him, years ago—? Oh, Deana, let it go. Let it go. It is too late.

Lily said they didn't have to hate Will anymore. Did I ever really hate him? Deana thinks, or did I make that up because I wanted to hate him? For years, she thought she loved him. She doesn't know how to feel about him. But when she thinks about it now, she realizes that what she's felt about him, underneath it all, has been fear. First, there was the fear that he wouldn't love her, then that he would stop loving her. Then she was afraid that he would leave her, and he did. Now, staring across Lily's yard at her mother's softly lighted window, she is afraid that he will try to take Sophie away.

But how can Will take Sophie away from Deana, even if he tries? For all those years, Sophie has not known of his existence. Does Will think all he has to do is show up on Deana's doorstep and turn on the charm? That Sophie will go flying out the door, eager to be swept up like a princess into his arms? Sometime down the road, Will may be able to be a part of Sophie's life, but the best he can hope for at this point is the opportunity to exist like a distant planet in her orbit. Sophie may come to accept him, in time may even come to love him, but he will never get back all the years he has lost with her. If she weren't so worried for her daughter, Deana thinks, she could take some pleasure in anticipating his reaction to his daughter's rejection. But why would she? If she has really moved past the longing and the misery, what would be the point in taking pleasure at his sorrow now?

Besides, Lily isn't the only one Will has surprised. He has surprised Deana, too. This afternoon, she did not expect to see eyes look so wistful, or hear the trembling hope in his voice when he asked Deana to tell him his daughter's name. Should she have tried harder to find him? Should she have given him the choice about whether or not he wanted to be a part of Sophie's life? Even now, she doesn't want to hurt him; she only wants to protect herself.

And then Deana knows. She isn't the one who needs to be afraid. Will is. She thinks about Suzanne, whose daughter is still angry that her mother did not work harder to find her when her father took her so far away. She thinks of the letter and the picture Will sent her, of the two of them as children; the same wistful longing she saw this afternoon was already there years ago, in his eyes. And suddenly, her face crumples in dismay and sorrow at what the years of silence—Jolene's and Millard's, Wayman's and Cleave's—have stolen from him. No matter what she tells him tonight, it is too late to give any of it back.

❧Twenty-Four

Will Brinson parks his truck by the bridge over the Cumberland River and gets out. He walks to the chipped blue railing and sits on it with his legs dangling toward the water. It's ten-thirty, at least an hour before he is supposed to show up at Deana's sister's, but he didn't want to wait alone at his house until it was time to go. For one thing, Junior Messer is driving him crazy, talking and talking, and what Will needs right now is silence and time to sort this out. Junior reminds Will of all the things about his father he wishes he could forget.

Will turns his coat collar up to protect him from the wind and hunkers down for warmth. He didn't expect to have a chance to talk to Deana this afternoon. He just thought he would wait outside the church building until the funeral was over and maybe catch a glimpse of his daughter when she and Deana came out. But then Millard wanted to go in, and Deana came out early, and everything got all messed up, the way, with him, it usually does.

Behind Will, a car goes by and he hears the sound of the wheels singing past. Below him, the water is black with dim patches of light where the streetlights reflect on its surface. He doesn't know what he had expected from Deana when they did get the opportunity to talk, but for some strange reason it had never occurred to him that she would be so angry. Oh, he knows that he wrote her a letter explaining that he would understand if she didn't want to help him find out about his mother, that he would understand if she never wanted to see him again. But the truth is, down deep he didn't believe that for a minute. Why shouldn't he be able to crook his finger and have her right where he wanted her? It always worked before.

It was disconcerting when he didn't hear from her, but it didn't really matter to him, not until he saw her daughter Sophie, the child who is his daughter, too. The disappointment is as raw in his heart as the wind is raw against his face, aching and cold. Now he knows why Deana did not call him when she came to Ash Grove, why he had to find out she was here by accident. She does not want him to know his own child.

And why is that? He knows exactly why it is. It is because he is Cleave Brinson's son. She doesn't trust him. He can wear blue jeans and work with his hands. He can stay in Ash Grove or he can leave it. But no matter where he tries to go, when he looks in the mirror he will keep seeing Cleave Brinson's face.

Deana knows this, too. The truth is, if she had told him years ago that she was pregnant, he might have sent her some money for an abortion, but he would not have had one bit of interest in having a baby with her. Babies were red, wrinkly creatures who demanded all and gave back nothing. Babies were what girls used to trap men with, or like dolls that they crooned to and cuddled. They were of no interest whatsoever to him.

Why is it different now? He didn't ask for it, but Sunday he looked up and saw a part of his mother still alive, gazing out at him from beneath the dark lashes of Deana's little girl's gray eyes. He was a child when his mother died, but he has always been sorry he could not protect her. Was this his chance, finally, to recover something of his mother he could nurture and love?

Will shivers in the cold and slides his hands into his sleeves for what warmth he can find there. He has come here to be alone and think, but no matter how much he turns this problem over in his mind, he can't see any way things are ever going to work out. It is like finding his mother and losing her all over again, and he feels as helpless as he had when he was six years old and Doc Beecham had found him upstairs hiding in a makeshift playhouse and told him she was gone. Gone? What did that mean, that she was gone? When had he stopped looking for her to come back?

A blue Buick drives past, and then whispers to a stop halfway across the bridge. A man opens the passenger door and leans out. Will twists his head around and looks to see who has stopped.

"Hey, buddy," the man yells. "You okay?"

Will looks at the man, not saying anything. Will sees a shock of white hair, but he doesn't recognize the man. Maybe he wouldn't anyway, even if this is someone he knows or who knows him—the bridge is so dark. The man's white hair looks yellow from the streetlight, but from this distance, Will cannot tell anything about his face.

"That's not a good place to rest. You better be careful or you're gonna fall. They dropped the lake so far ain't hardly enough water left in the river to dive in. If you fall you'll shore as the world bust your head open on the rocks."

Will doesn't reply, and the man, apparently unwilling to drive on until he gets an answer, says again, "Are you okay? You look like you're in some kind of trouble."

The man gets out of the car and stands beside it with the door open. He has a dark suit on, and Will thinks he is probably a preacher. In a minute, Will thinks, he'll ask me if I know Jesus loves me.

The man holds out his hand. "You want me to call somebody? Or you could come with me to get a cup of coffee and we'll talk? Son, ain't no trouble so deep there ain't some way out of it. You just need a little help."

Will lifts his hand in a salute, waving the man away. "Whatever you got, preacher," he says, "I don't need it. I appreciate you stopping, but now you need to mind your own business, old man."

The man hesitates, but Will turns away from him and stares down into the thick, dark water. A moment passes. Then Will hears the door slam shut and the little sizzle of water underneath the tires as the car drives away.

It hadn't occurred to Will until the man said it that he might be startled and slide off the bridge railing into the dark water below, let alone that he might jump. He turns the idea over in his mind, to see if it frightens him, but he finds it strangely comforting. He has always loved water. In the summer, he used to dive and dive into the water from the bank a few feet from this bridge, swimming with his eyes open in the green-gold dimness of the water. Now he thinks of swimming through the darkness below him as a kind of peace.

He stretches one leg out in front of him, scooting all the way to the edge, to see what it might feel like to lose his balance. He circles his foot as if he is signaling someone. But who? He is alone. If he does plunge into the river, who would care? His mother loved him, but she is gone. Betsy would grieve him, but his death might be a relief to her, too, not to have to worry about him anymore. Certainly Deana has no reason to care what happens to him. She made that clear this afternoon. Even if he hired a lawyer and won the right to see his child, there is no hope he can ever win the little girl's love, not when Deana hates him. Well, he's given her good reason, and why wouldn't Sophie hate him, too? What did he have to offer a child anyway, except a child support check? He wouldn't even know how to start to be a father. As for Deana's information about his mother, it occurs to him at last that Betsy's right. What's the point of knowing now? It isn't as if he can go back and change anything. She is dead, and Cleave is dead. Maybe it would be better for everybody concerned if Will were dead, too, and the world was finished with the Brinsons.

He looks down into the black water. It would be so easy to dive into the darkness and never surface, never have to face Deana's accusing eyes, never have to let her daughter break his heart.

And so he does, slowly, so that it feels natural, like losing his balance, like falling into space.

But he has made an awful mistake. He doesn't want to die. He doesn't. He reaches out in panic to catch the railing, but he cannot reach it in time. He feels the rush of his senses as he falls, hears the wind flapping the legs of his trousers. When he hits the water, he hears the splash and feels the stunning pain against his limbs and chest, but despite the preacher's warning about the shallowness of the water, Will is thankful to feel himself plunging under the surface. No matter how far he goes into the water, as long as he doesn't hit his head, he will be all right. He is a good swimmer, but instinctively, he opens his mouth to breathe and strangles, flailing about. He is heavy, cold, so cold, and he knows that if he can't find his way to the surface, in these heavy blue jeans and work boots, he won't make it. His body might not wash up on the bank for weeks.

But then someone is in the water with him. His body is being pulled along. His head surfaces, and he gasps at the air. He opens his eyes, but he can't see anything but the dark water around him and, above, a net of stars. He hears someone say, "You're all right, buddy. That's right. Stay calm. Don't fight me or you'll drown us both."

No. He won't fight. Just help me, he thinks. He closes his eyes again and feels his body pulled through the water and then thrust upon the hard ground. He feels a mouth over his, and then hands working his chest and arms. "What did you think you was, boy? A fish?" he hears a man's voice say.

Will struggles to speak. He wants to say, thank you. But when he looks up, he looks straight into the gray eyes of his mother. Or are these Sophie's eyes? They are the last thing he sees before he closes his own.

Later he has a fever, burning up with heat that replaces the river's awful cold. He is floating; he thinks he must still be in the river, but it's daylight now, and he floats on the surface of the water. The white sun on his face is warm. Maybe he is dead. Maybe heaven is a part of the river. Sometimes his mother comes and sits by his bed. She smells like lavender when she bends across him with her dark hair falling like a curtain to hide the fluorescent light that hurts his eyes. He feels her hands brush against his face when she lays cool cloths across his forehead.

Then his mother is not his mother any more, but a little girl, the little girl she was a long time before Will was born. She sings and skips along the bank of the river ahead of him. He calls to her to wait and struggles to the bank, falling to his knees because he is too tired to stand. She stops at the edge of the swinging bridge that crosses the river between the woods on the left and a sunlit meadow on the other side. "Go back," she calls, her voice light and laughing. "You can't come with me. I'm too fast."

He calls after her, but she crosses the bridge, her little white legs flying, and then even the bridge itself is gone.

When the fever breaks, Will opens his eyes half-expecting to find her, but instead he sees Deana. Someone has closed the blinds, and she sits sideways in the chair, holding the book in her hand so the page slants toward the window to catch the morning light. She squeezes her shoulders together and rubs the back of her neck with her free hand, reaching underneath her dark, tousled hair.

She doesn't look up to notice that Will is awake, but suddenly, seeing her, he isn't frightened anymore. She loves him. She must love him. He wants to say something, but his eyes are so heavy, and anyway, what right does he have to ask for anything more? It is enough that in spite of all the history between them, all the ways he has found to disappoint her, when he was alone and his heart was broken, she came.

He sinks down into the softness of the pillow and goes back to sleep.

❧ Twenty-Five

Deana has set up four card tables in Suzanne's back yard and covered each with a white tablecloth, in honor of Sophie's first communion. In the center of each, Deana has placed blue bottles. Each holds a white peony, its huge sweet-fragranced bowl freckled at the ruffled edges of the petals with flecks of red.

Sophie skips from table to table, putting napkins in place, and laying silverware on top to keep them from blowing away in the sweet May wind.

"Everybody I know is coming," Sophie says gleefully. She still has on her white lacy dress and her white Mary Jane shoes. Her dark hair is curled and tied at the back with a pink satin bow.

And she's probably right. Deana has asked all the people who love Sophie and Sophie loves, even Jolene, though Deana knew when she called her that Jolene would never go to the service itself. "I wouldn't know what to do in that church, Deana," she said when Deana called to invite her family to come down. "All that getting up and getting down, singing all them songs I never heard of."

Deana has also invited Will. She has told Sophie that Will is her father, but she isn't sure how much of this Sophie understands. Deana has tried to avoid criticizing or praising him. She doesn't know whether or not, when it comes right down to it, he will come, or whether she wants him to. That was Deana's stipulation, and he agreed to it—if he wants to see Sophie, it is important that he make the effort to come and see her where Sophie is comfortable, at least at first.

That's about the only advantage, she thinks, of raising children in this day and time. So many families are screwed up right out in the open where anybody can see. Children know all about absent fathers and blended families. It's not as though fate singles any of them out for special misery. One of Sophie's teachers told Deana that sometimes it seems the children who have two parents in a traditional marriage are the ones who feel left out. The other girls don't want to talk to them. How could they be expected to know what it's like to have all these adults to adapt to, to keep a little suitcase packed by the bed to facilitate the child's movement from house to house, or even town to town?

Deana wonders if there will ever come a time when she can stop worrying about whether or not she did the right thing, not telling Will a long time ago, or not staying away from Ash Grove so she wouldn't have to tell him at all. She was so angry when Will didn't show up at Lily's house the night he nearly drowned, and so ashamed and relieved to learn that he was all right. But she still isn't sure how much she can trust him, even though he came to Lily's house the weekend after he got out of the hospital, scrubbed and awkward as a new in-law, willing to do whatever Deana wanted, as long as she didn't keep him completely away from Sophie.

Lily called three or four days ago to say that Will's Grandfather Connelly had died. From what Will told Lily, his aunt Betsy planned to sell the house in Virginia and move in with Will. At least if Sophie ends up visiting Will at some time in the future, Deana will feel better knowing Betsy is there, too.

She glances around to see that everything is ready, except for the food still in the kitchen. She sits in one of the folding chairs sipping a glass of soda and watches Suzanne at the far end of the yard. She stands under the canopy of new green leaves that dance above her from the branches of the maple tree, checking the grill. She is so organized. Deana can imagine her going down the list—charcoal, lighter, foil.

Deana is the absolute opposite. It amazes her how much she is like her Wayman, always restless, always asking questions. Maybe that's what he was always trying to tamp down in Deana, the part of her that was so much like himself. She dreams about him so often, now that he's gone, she thinks she knows him better dead than she ever did when he was alive. In the dream she had curled up in a recliner in the hospital, the night after Will fell from the bridge and almost died, Daddy came for her in the mine. He was wearing a hardhat with a Wheat light attached and a satin-trimmed black tuxedo, the white ruffles on the shirt streaked with coal dust.

"I'm sorry, girl," he said, holding out a blackened hand. But when she reached out to take it, he turned into a raven and flew away from her. She rose to her knees and put her fingers against the rough surface of the tunnel, looking through the darkness of the mine to the opening, where she could see the faintest glimmer of the cold, star-lit sky. "Come back," she called. "Come back. I can't find my way."

Because Deana is the only one of Wayman Perry's three survivors who plays, Mama gave her Daddy's Gibson. Daddy's guitar is larger than her Ovation and much harder for her to play, but playing it is, for some reason, important to her, as if the best part of Daddy, maybe the only part worth loving, is in the polished curves of the guitar that he cared more about than any living thing. Her friends certainly ooh and ahh whenever she gets it out of the plush case—maybe the scarlet fake fur is what they ought to have used for Daddy's coffin, she said to Mama once, before she thought, but Mama just laughed. "Maybe," Mama said, emphasizing the last syllable of the word until it sounded like it may be. "He'd of probably liked it better than what we did do."

And Deana plays and plays it. For the last few months she has been getting together with a group of women to play music a couple of nights a week. Deana loves these women. Lena Osborne, the bass player, is at least six feet tall with long straight blonde hair and no make-up. Redheaded Ida Long plays the fiddle, and Jeannie Thompson, who has short white hair and is old enough to be their mother, alternates between banjo and mandolin. They play mostly traditional ballads, sweet, sad songs of lost love and ghostly hauntings. But sometimes they play songs that one or the other of the women has written.

Ida is what Daddy would have called a brassiere-burning, man-hating radical feminist, though what that really means is that Ida never remarried after she divorced her husband twenty years ago, and she has the nerve to have a mind of her own. As a nurse, Ida has worked extensively with drug babies, and seen most of them suffer and some of them die. Ida has a fiddle tune about the babies, written in a minor key and called "Bitter Fruit." Ida herself might have turned off Daddy, but he'd never have been able to resist her music, even if he tried.

At three-thirty Deana's family arrives, spilling out of Wes's white van like a bunch of actors in a commercial on TV. Deana sees at once that Sophie is going to be disappointed. Madonna has stayed back in Ash Grove to go to the movies with her boyfriend. But all of the others have come. Charley and Wesley stand awkwardly next to the van until Sophie runs over and tugs them by the hand toward one of the tables. Then Sophie goes and gets her cousins something to eat.

Mama stands awkwardly, too. She has on a pair of washed-out blue jeans and a green knit top that has pilled badly. She steps behind the van and lights a cigarette. She takes a draw. Deana starts to get up, but Mama motions her back down. "I'll come over there in a minute," she yells. Deana knows that when Mama does come over to hug her, Mama will smell of the mixed-together fragrances—a generous dousing of a flea market knock-off of White Shoulders and menthol cigarettes.

What will they all find to talk about? When she sees Brother Hardwick climb out of the van, she has something new to worry her. Will he try to convert Father Michael from the errors of the Catholic Church? When she told Suzanne how nervous putting all of these people together made her, Suzanne just laughed. "You invited them, but that doesn't mean you're responsible for how they act. Stop worrying. Though I know that's like telling a leaky faucet not to drip."

Later in the afternoon, Suzanne's daughter comes. She is a dark, willowy girl with a diamond stud in her nose. She has brought along her new companion, and while Deana secretly hoped her family would think the two women were just friends, in spite of herself, Deana loves the offhand way city-girl Agnes introduces her to Lily and Brother Hardwick. "I'm Agnes. The nun's daughter? And this," as she wraps her arm around the blond woman's waist, "is my lover, Beatrice."

Deana has to give her Pentecostal family credit. No matter what anybody is storing up to say during the long ride home, even Brother Hardwick looks as though he doesn't think a thing.

When the girls from the band finish eating and get out their instruments, Brother Hardwick goes to the back of the van and gets out his. Deana was surprised to see him, but she caught Lily in the kitchen by herself and got the scoop. Apparently, he's still chasing, but Mama's still determined to remain the Widow Perry. Seeing the look on his face whenever Mama gets anywhere near him, Deana almost wishes Mama would just let him catch her, though—also according to Lily—Mama says in no uncertain terms that the last thing on earth she wants is to waste what few years are left to her putting up with another man.

The girls know most of the same songs as Brother Hardwick, but he plays much better rhythm guitar than Deana—almost as good as Daddy— so they get into some pretty fast tunes like "I'll Fly Away." They play until the sun begins to sink behind the line of trees at the edge of the road, and a few faint stars begin to glimmer high in the purple-colored sky above. Deana borrows Brother Hardwick's guitar—a really nice black Takamene—to play "Bonny Patmore," a song Ida learned from an Irish band that played at a fiddle and folk music festival she went to last summer and taught to Deana, saying it suited Deana's voice.

Deana lowers the tuning to open D, and Jeannie stands behind Deana's lawn chair to sing the harmony. Deana loves singing with Jeannie, whose voice reminds of her of good garden dirt and a still bend in the river. Against Jeannie's low tones Deana's soprano notes can dance until she feels her spirit take flight.

When they finish, Brother Hardwick reaches over to reclaim his guitar. "That's pretty," he says. "You need to show me sometime how you got that guitar tuned."

Mama slips behind Deana for a second and bends to whisper in her ear. "I wish your Daddy could be here. Wouldn't he just love all this music?" Do you, Mama? Deana wishes she had the nerve to ask. Do you really wish he was here?

But instead, she nods and keeps her questions to herself. How fragile all this is, she thinks. How fragile we are. She glances from face to face, seeing the shapes of them soften to gold in the late afternoon light the way images in old photographs fade. She thinks of the gospel teaching, that two will be standing in a field, and one will be taken, the other left. It's not fair, she thinks, that we only get one chance to do this, to live, and we make so many mistakes.

They are in the middle of "I Am a Pilgrim and a Stranger" when Will's truck turns onto the gravel drive. Deana watches the truck lurching across a pothole in the road as he makes his way to the edge of the yard and comes to park next to the Brody's van. Lily looks up startled from her chocolate cake to see if Deana knew he was coming. Deana nods to reassure Lily that he is an invited guest.

Will gets out of the truck and hesitates, standing behind the open door. Then he reaches inside to get out a gift bag stuffed with tissue and tied with bright ribbon. Deana looks across the yard for Sophie, but Sophie has already seen him. She watches him for a second with her head tilted. When she recognizes him, she looks swiftly toward her mother, a question fluttering briefly like a trapped bird behind her eyes. Deana can feel her own heart pounding inside her ribs, but she nods to Sophie and tries to smile. It's all right, honey. That's what she wants her face to say. Please, let it be all right.

Sophie still waits, uncertainly. Troy is sitting close to her feet. His chubby legs are dusty as he draws circles in the dirt with a stick. He doesn't even notice when Sophie moves a step or two away from him. Everyone noticed right away that Sophie has grown so much taller since Christmas, but from this distance, to Deana, she still looks so small. It is only in comparison to her young cousin that she has any size at all.

Will shuts the truck door with a thud, and then stands awkwardly, as if he is waiting for an invitation to join the company of strangers waiting in the shaded yard. Deana still wants to wrap her arm around Sophie's waist and walk with her to the truck.

The wind picks up, rustling through the tree branches. A thick cloud covers the sun, and Deana shivers. She knows then, suddenly, that Lily was wrong. Will still has some power over her. In spite of everything, or maybe because of Sophie, Deana will always feel for Will a tangled knot of love and responsibility, of hope and despair. But if he breaks Sophie's heart, Deana cannot bear it. Well, she can stand between them if she has to, can drive Will away with words or fists or incantations. Deana moves close enough to Sophie to take her hand, but before Deana can touch her, Sophie, without looking at Deana, raises her small pale hand in the air and motions her mother away. She is watching Will as if she's making up her own mind.

Suddenly, Sophie straightens her small shoulders. How did she get so strong, Deana wonders suddenly, with relief. No matter what accident of sperm and egg or collision of hunger and circumstance created her, Sophie is not Will's to take or Deana's to give away. Deana has loved her daughter fiercely, and that will have to be enough to make up for every blessed mistake she has made.

❧Twenty-Six

Will has driven the hour and a half from Ash Grove to Deana's with Betsy's warning echoing in his mind. "Be careful," she had said, when he went to Virginia for Grandfather Connelly's funeral. He had wanted to tell Betsy about his child in person. They had sat facing each other in two white wicker chairs on the screened-in porch that let in the sweet fragrance of the flowering crabapple trees planted on the south side of the house.

At first, Betsy's eyes were bright with joy, but almost immediately, the look faded. Will had simply looked at her, stunned, uncomprehending. Why should Betsy's reaction be so guarded? Back in late January, after Cleave died, wasn't this what she had hoped for? That he would find Deana and then there would be someone to love him, someone for him to love? And now he had discovered, not a lover or a wife or a girlfriend, who might leave him, but a daughter bound to him by ties of blood.

He shook his head at her, though, of course, she is only voicing the fear he himself feels. "Be careful? Why? She's mine, if that's what you're worried about. I could tell that the minute I laid eyes on her. She looks just like my mother."

She leaned forward, reaching her hands toward him. "I know she's yours," she said, glancing down to the white wicker side table, to the photograph of Sophie Deana had given Will. "I've got eyes, too, Will. That's not what I mean. I'm happy for you, I really am. And proud of you, too, for wanting to do the right thing. You should take responsibility for her, be part of her life. But you need to understand that she might not be as eager to get to know you, as you are to get to know her. She's almost seven years old. You have to give her time to understand what's happened, time to accept you. Baby, I just don't want you to expect too much."

At some level, he supposes he has heard and understood what Betsy had been trying to say. Perhaps this is why he had agreed when Deana asked him to wait to come and see Sophie until the celebration of her first communion. This would give Deana a chance to tell Sophie about him in her own way. Deana had also thought that if Will were mixed in with Sophie's grandmother, aunt, and cousins, Sophie would not feel the same sort of pressure she would feel if he came down to see them the first time by himself. Deana had reminded Will that he was a stranger to Sophie, after all.

Will had agreed to wait, but he did not tell Deana he had already begun stripping Anne's room, to get it ready for Sophie. Except for a few things he wanted to keep out for Sophie—some photographs and jewelry— he had boxed up all of his mother's belongings for storage. It had taken him the better part of a weekend to move the furniture and boxes to the garage behind the house, but when he had finished, he had sat down in the middle of the empty floor, suddenly exhausted, and as lonely as he had ever been in his life. He had laid his head on his forearms. With no one to see, he had sobbed long and hard for the first time since the bright afternoon, only days after his mother's funeral, when he had run into the house looking for her, his heart having forgotten for a moment that she was dead. He had been expecting to find her reading. Instead, he had found only the empty, echoing house.

He had not been able to save his mother, and in addition to the other crimes he could lay at Cleave Brinson's door, finally, without hope or doubt, he could lay her death, too. Deana had thought that knowing of Wayman Perry's involvement would make it easier for Will, but it had not. No matter what Cleave's intentions were, Cleave had killed her just the same. In the end, didn't that mean that no one mattered to Cleave but Cleave? Not even his wife, or his son.

Knowing for certain about Cleave's guilt has made Will feel an even greater obligation to Junior Messer, and to Ash Grove, too, where Will has decided, finally, to make his home. He has found Junior a lawyer from

Louisville who will probably get Junior a life sentence instead of death row. Will still tries to make time to visit Junior most Sunday afternoons, and he has offered to testify on Junior's behalf, to tell the whole truth at Junior's trial about the kind of man Cleave Brinson had been. By such acts, Will hopes at last to set himself free of Cleave Brinson's shadow. Perhaps then he can be the kind of father he wants to be for Sophie, so that Deana will allow him to be a part of his daughter's life.

Later in the day, after he had finished in Anne's room, Will had gone to the hardware store to buy paint so that he could begin preparing the room for the living girl he hoped would become part of his life. But he had been overwhelmed by all the choices. He had not known there would be so many colors. How could he know what a little girl would like? Instead of buying paint, he had taken a whole handful of the samples home so that Sophie, when she came this summer—of course, she would want to come this summer—could choose for herself.

Now, as he stands next to his truck watching Deana and Sophie, he has a sudden urge to climb back inside the cab, to put the truck in gear and drive as far away from here as he can. What craziness had made him think for one second that Sophie will even want to know him, let alone spend any part of her summer in his big, empty house? Deana is right. He is a stranger to Sophie, more profoundly a stranger than even Will's own father had been to him. Sophie can break his heart, he thinks, without even trying. She doesn't even have to hate him. All she has to do is look as if she would rather be anywhere else but with him.

To cover his apprehension, he takes the present he has brought for her from the truck and holds the gift bag looped over his hand. He and Betsy had spent the better part of an afternoon picking out the gift, a small gold cross in honor of the occasion, and Betsy had chosen the bag, gilded with bright magenta foil, stuffing it with tissue and curling bright metallic streamers from the handle. Will had been absurdly pleased with the way the gift looked. Now, feeling awkward and foolish with the bag dangling from his hand, he sets the bag back on the seat behind him. He turns back around, anxious to get this first meeting over with. He starts to walk across the grass toward Sophie, but something in Deana's eyes stops him, and he hesitates, understanding. He must wait for Sophie to come to him.

He sees Sophie lift her chin, straighten her shoulders, and wave away

Deana's hand. When she is directly in front of Will, she tilts her dark head up, shyly, at an angle, to look at him. He was wrong about her eyes. They aren't gray at all, but the same color as Deana's, with brown irises like sunbursts, and dark brows. But the heart shape of her face looks just like his mother's, and for a second, Will catches his breath, as though in some strange way, he has them both, his mother and Sophie, standing there within the reach of his hand. He looks across the yard toward Deana, his heart in his eyes, grateful that she has trusted him enough, forgiven him enough, to allow him this. But she has moved back under the shade of a maple tree beside the house, and he is too far away from her to read any reaction in her face.

The sun reappears from behind a bank of clouds, and Will looks down at Sophie, her face turned up toward the sun's brightness. He wants to say something, but he can't seem to find the words. Standing this close to Sophie, his heart lit from the bright, reflecting beam of her lovely face, his heart aches for his mother. If only she could have lived to see this child, her grandchild—

But she had not lived, and when Will searches Sophie's face again for some ghost of his mother, he cannot find her, and he understands that from the first moment he saw this child looking out of Deana's car window, he has been wrong. How could he have thought, for one instant, that the little girl in front of him was the ghost of anybody, even his mother, when she is so clearly Sophie, herself?

He smiles down at her, and wonder of wonders, she smiles right back.

"I'm Will," he says, his dread of her rejection easing for the first time since he climbed out of his truck. "Your mother said she'd tell you about me."

"She did." Sophie glances away from him, and then back, looking at him while she lifts her chin, motioning back over her shoulder toward the yard. "We're having a party. Do you want some cake?"

Yes. Yes, he does. He wants whatever she has to offer him. She reaches out, with the impulsive generosity of childhood, and he takes her hand, holding it gently, fearful of startling her away. "That's why I came," he says. "For your party. I would love some cake."

He smiles again, and she tugs his hand, pulling him forward. Across her dark hair, he sees Deana step out from under the shade of the maple tree and come across the yard to meet them halfway. Then, hand-in-hand, with Sophie in the middle, the three of them walk together toward the food, the music, and the laughter, to join the company of the friends and family his Sophie loves.

Coda

The three of us have been waiting for a long time, but I see him first. He sits with his back to us at a concrete picnic table underneath the twisted branches of a gigantic apple tree. He has his fingers laced behind his head, but I recognize him by the enormous wristwatch. Without turning around, he moves his right hand to tap the watch face with his index finger.

I pivot one last time, taking it all in—the yard with its flowering dogwood, the laughter and the music, the sigh of the wind in the leaves. Will sits at a table with a white cloth, a slice of cake in front of him. His daughter leans toward him, her eyes bright with curiosity, her elbows on the table, resting her chin on her hands.

I look at Deana in gratitude for giving him this chance. I call out in farewell to the granddaughter I never knew and the son I loved, leaving behind me the only wisdom I can claim—

> Look   listen   taste   smell   touch   love
> this day is bright with its blessings

But they can neither see me nor hear me. There, in the circle of the present, the trees hang heavy with late spring blossoms, but where I am going, the ripe apples have fallen from the tree, and all of the leaves are gone. I have become the wedge of light on a letter lost in the post, and my voice spills from my mouth like water.

Still, for one second only, the whirring wings of their voices beat *softly against my ears, and I ache to return to the burdens and joys of the living, to the past and the heart's desire. Sensing my hesitation, he stands and puts his hand on my shoulder. I turn, drawn by his touch. He tilts my face up, holding my chin in his hand, and I grow light, become light. Looking into the universe of his eyes, to the peace that passes understanding, I can finally see, as through an open window, the world where I am going, the place where I belong.*

There the planets whirl and the stars are born, but the restless heart falls still.

The Story Behind

Ash Grove

My family left Harlan County, Kentucky, when I was very young. Both my grandfathers were miners, and my father had no intention of following them into the drudgery of 36-to-48-inch seams of coal. Instead, as part of what I now realize was a massive out-migration of families from the region in the fifties, my father moved us north. He went from one factory job to another, struggling to make a living, while the hills and hollows of his childhood both repelled and beckoned him.

When I was in the third grade, he moved us back to Kentucky for good. In the foothills of the Appalachian mountains, he supported a wife and six children with construction and factory work, and, part-time, as a Baptist minister. One of my first writing experiences was in high school, as typist and editor for my father's book about the last days that he self-published and gave away as a radio evangelist.

My father was not able to go to high school, but it was his influence, most of all, that made me a writer. He loved to read, and though we could not afford to buy books, he flagged the bookmobile down, and later, took me regularly to the public library. He was also a gifted orator, whose preaching filled my childhood with the rich cadences of the King James Bible. My father taught me that language had rhythms just as beautiful as the music he played on his Gibson guitar. When he spoke of the sufferings of Jesus, it was in the voice of someone who had seen suffering himself. The preacher in my novel has my father's talents, but not his restless questioning or his eventual crisis of faith.

While none of my grandparents had much of a formal education, my father's mother, though she only went to the third grade, had the makings of a memoirist; she kept a journal in wide-lined, newsprint tablets like the ones children used to use in the first grade when they were learning to write. When I was little, she told me ghost stories for the truth. Years later she scolded me when I suggested she had only made them up; she considered this tantamount to an accusation of lying.

My mother's parents lived in a dark hollow in Harlan, in what was left of a string of coal camp houses stitched precariously into the hillside. I remember trips to visit them as depressing and claustrophobic. My grandmother walked with crutches—she had lost a leg in a logging accident before my mother was even born. My grandfather, a still, shadowy figure, was tall and dark like his Cherokee mother. He was fiercely loyal to the union. Once I remember a man coming by their home during supper with campaign literature, urging my grandfather to vote to re-elect Tony Boyle as president of the United Mine Workers of America. My grandfather never had the chance; in January of 1970, when I was fifteen, Boyle's challenger Joseph Jablonski was murdered, along with his wife and daughter. Five years later, Tony Boyle was convicted of ordering Jablonski's death.

I knew my grandfather had been an alcoholic, but had stopped drinking because of diabetes (he called it "bad sugar"). He had not been a gentle drunk. Once, when my mother was a child and my grandfather's temper flared into physical violence, my grandmother had him arrested. Over the years, when my mother told this story, usually through tears, it was clear her allegiance lay firmly with her father, who, she said, had gone to work in the mines at the age of ten and couldn't help drinking. She resented my grandmother for calling the sheriff, for the betrayal, not only of my grandfather, but an unspoken family code.

I suppose I began *Ash Grove* as a way of puzzling out the mystery of what I considered my mother's misplaced compassion and loyalty. It was from a photograph of my mother as a child, her face turned slightly aside, as though she is afraid of what the camera might see if she looks directly into the lens, that I discovered the character of Deana, another dark-haired girl with brown eyes full of heartbreak and hope.

But I was also interested in other issues—miners preyed upon by corrupt union officials in bed with the companies, the gulf between the wealthy and the poor, the difficulty of maintaining faith in a ruthless world, the ways that other people disappoint us, and the ways we disappoint ourselves.

As a writer, I have found that I am not so much a memoirist as a scavenger of stories. When I found a husband, as fate would have it, I married a geologist who moved me straight back to Eastern Kentucky, where he did prospecting and reclamation for a coal company. Most of what I know about men like Cleave comes from bits and pieces of stories my husband brought home, especially the graft and corruption between mine owners, union officials, and politicians. Ironically, after being released from prison, the union accountant convicted of complicity in the

Jablonski murders moved into a house across the road from our first home. I still remember the white glare of his tee shirt as he sat on his front porch in the moonlight, blowing cigarette smoke into the dark.

It was also from my husband that I heard the story of a coal operator who, to avoid divorce and possible bankruptcy, had supposedly blown up his wife in car. Like Cleave in *Ash Grove*, he was never formally charged, and, for all I know, was an innocent victim of circumstance and rumors fed by jealousy and boredom. Cleave, on the other hand, was created in the fictional world of my imagination.

Later, from my students—first as a high school teacher in Eastern Kentucky and then at a community college—I heard other heart-breaking stories of family violence and despair.

Ash Grove is not autobiographical, though it is based on my own experiences and the experiences I have been able to piece together from the stories I have observed and heard. My mother's unwavering resolve to defend and love a father who damaged her in ways she has never admitted or understood may have led me to write *Ash Grove*. But in trying to weave together a story about the filaments of fear and resentment, mercy and love that bind us one to another, I chose fiction, not biography or history, because, for me, the literal truth is never as interesting as the bewildering truth of the heart.

Acknowledgements

This novel would not be in its present form without the input and support of a number of people who read the manuscript along the way and offered encouragement and suggestions. I would like to thank Denny Fries and my children, Jesse & Megan, first of all, for their infinite patience. Megan, my adult daughter, still calls me by my first name because it was the only way she could pull me out of a fog of writing, the imaginary characters who took me far away, causing me to drive past our house or the school or the grocery store until she brought me back to earth. Denny has been the ground on which I stand, my husband and my best friend and strongest supporter.

I would also like to thank the Kentucky Arts Council and the Cornelia Dozier Cooper Foundation for financial support of my work. Belinda Gadd, Betty Peterson, Jeanne McDonald, Dana Carpenter, Phyllis Lawson, Sheryl Polk, and Terry Phillips-Weddle read the novel at various stages, offering advice and encouragement. Sharon Whitehead generously helped edit the manuscript, though any errors should be understood to be mine alone. Marly Rusoff believed in my novel and my writing and her insights and suggestions were fundamental to crafting and shaping the final manuscript.

Mostly I am grateful for all the people I've met through the years who have shared their stories, the patchwork from which I have tried to create a quilted whole.